Judith Lennox grew up in rural Hampshire and studied at the University of Lancaster, where she met her husband, Iain; they have three adult sons and two grandsons. She began writing in the mid-eighties, and her powerful historical novels have been widely acclaimed. Her novels *The Winter House*, *A Step in the Dark* and *Before the Storm* were all shortlisted for the RNA Romantic Novel of the Year Award.

THE HEART OF THE NIGHT

Judith Lennox

headline
review

First published in 2009 by Headline Review
An imprint of HEADLINE PUBLISHING GROUP

First published in paperback in 2010 by Headline Review
An imprint of HEADLINE PUBLISHING GROUP

3

ISBN 978 0 7553 5747 5 (A-format)
ISBN 978 0 7553 4486 4 (B-format)

Typeset in Joanna MT by Palimpsest Book Production Limited,
Grangemouth, Stirlingshire

Printed in the UK by
CPI Mackays, Chatham ME5 8TD

Headline's policy is to use papers that are natural, renewable and recyclable
products and made from wood grown in sustainable forests. The logging
and manufacturing processes are expected to conform to the
environmental regulations of the country of origin.

HEADLINE PUBLISHING GROUP
An Hachette UK Company
338 Euston Road
London NW1 3BH

www.headline.co.uk
www.hachette.co.uk

To Alexis, with love

Acknowledgements

Thanks and appreciation to Monika at GoPoland and to Marta, Hanna, Marcin and Katie for making my stay in Poland so informative and fascinating. Grateful thanks also to Marion at Headline, Bettina at Piper, and to my agent, Margaret Hanbury. And to Iain, as always, love and gratitude for having travelled so much of the journey with me.

Part One

The Confidante

April 1936–August 1939

Chapter One

Kay Garland met Miranda Denisov for the first time at a house in Charles Street in Mayfair. In appearance Miranda was strikingly lovely, with a broad forehead, high cheekbones and a full mouth. Her glossy, wavy black hair was parted to one side and tumbled over her shoulders, and her brilliant dark eyes contrasted with magnolia-pale skin. She looked older than her sixteen years. Though Kay, whose clothes were mostly home-made, and whose few items of jewellery had been inherited from her mother, knew little about such things, she recognized that Miranda's dress was simple, exquisite, expensive and taste-fully assembled. In manner, Miranda was pleasant and polite, if a little distant.

It was the second time Kay had been to the Charles Street house. She had applied for the post of companion to Miss Denisov after reading an advertisement in the 'Situations Vacant' column of The Times. Her friend, Brian, who worked in a second-hand bookshop in Charing Cross Road, had showed her the advertisement. 'Gentleman seeks refined and well-educated English lady 18–20 years as companion to his daughter. Must be prepared to travel.' Kay had never travelled further than the Isle of Wight. She longed to travel. She *ached* to travel.

The first interview had been conducted by the Denisovs' housekeeper, Mrs Ingram, a pleasant Yorkshirewoman. Her questions had been searching and direct. Miss Garland was eighteen years old, was she not? To what standard was she educated – which school had she attended? Was she in good health? Was there any history of tuberculosis in her family? Miss Denisov's mother, who had been English, Mrs Ingram explained, had died of tuberculosis.

Mrs Ingram had described to Kay her duties, should she be offered the post of Miss Denisov's companion. She would be expected to accompany Miss Denisov to her various lessons and appointments, as well as being a travelling companion for her. She would not be required to go to evening functions, dances and formal dinners – Miss Denisov's aunt, Madame Lambert, acted as chaperone on such occasions. Mr Denisov also required that the successful candidate improve his daughter's English – an hour or two's lesson each morning should suffice.

Now, a week later, Kay had been summoned back to the house to meet Miranda Denisov for the first time. The applicants had been whittled down to three, Mrs Ingram had told Kay as she showed her into the drawing room.

The room in which Miranda Denisov was sitting was splendidly furnished. The sofas and chairs had curled red-brown backs and arms, polished to a soft, burnished gleam. Blue and gold damask curtains hung in swags at the long casement windows. There were oil paintings on the walls and a beautiful Persian rug on the floor. A middle-aged lady in lilac chiffon was sitting on a sofa; she was introduced to Kay as Madame Lambert.

Introductions over, a few pleasantries were made. Then Madame Lambert peered at Kay.

'You look very young, if I may say so, Mademoiselle Garland.'

'Of course she's young, Tante Sonya,' said Miranda, a little impatiently. 'If I'd wanted the company of some tiresome old stick, I would have let Papa hire me another governess.' Miranda turned to Kay, and for the first time smiled. 'Tell me about yourself, Miss Garland. Where do you live?'

'In Pimlico, with my aunt.'

'You have a job, don't you? Mrs Ingram told me. Don't you like your job?'

Kay was currently employed as governess to the four children of a Mrs Harrison. Mrs Harrison did not believe in the compulsory education of children: children should only learn what they wanted to learn. Kay's efforts to encourage Storme, Syrie, Lionel and Orlando Harrison to want to learn about the Wars of the Roses or compound fractions often left her ragged with exhaustion.

'Not very much,' she admitted. 'I'd love to do something different.'

'What do you like to do? What sort of things?'

'Dearest Miranda . . .'

Miranda ignored Madame Lambert's interruption. 'Tell me, Miss Garland.'

'Well, I like playing tennis and cycling—'

'Cycling! Oh, I'd love to ride a bicycle! Papa won't let me – he says it isn't ladylike.'

Impossible, Kay thought, to imagine Miranda Denisov, with her perfectly styled hair and her cream pleated woollen dress, whizzing through puddles on a bicycle, as Kay herself loved to do.

5

Kay went on, 'And I love going to the cinema and the theatre – and reading, of course. I can browse for hours in a second-hand bookshop, can't you? And, oh, I think what I like doing most of all is just *talking* – you know, those conversations that go on for hours and hours, late into the evening. There's nothing nicer, is there?'

There was a silence. Kay began to feel a little anxious. 'Answer their questions briefly and pleasantly,' Aunt Dot had advised when they had discussed the interview the previous evening. Perhaps, not for the first time, she had let her tongue run away with her.

Then Miranda said, 'I think we shall get on very well, don't you, Miss Garland?'

Kay felt a thrill of excitement. 'Do you mean I've got the job?'

'Naturally you have.'

Tante Sonya frowned. 'Miranda, *chérie*, your father—'

'Papa will like Miss Garland, I'm sure of it, Tante Sonya.' Miranda dismissed her aunt's concerns with a flick of the fingers. 'And the others were so *dull*.' There was something conspiratorial in her smile as she glanced back at Kay. 'Yes, I think we shall get on very well.'

It was still raining when, shortly afterwards, Kay left the Denisovs' house. Excitement bubbled up inside her as she hurried home to tell Aunt Dot her news.

Kay's Aunt Dot worked for a women's magazine, answering readers' letters under the pseudonym of 'Cousin Freda'. Many of her correspondents were women who had lost fiancés and husbands in the Great War. Some were poor and lonely. When Kay was younger, Aunt Dot had sometimes read out their letters to her. No matter what the problem, Kay had always recommended they get a dog. She had wanted a dog so much, but couldn't have one because it would have been left alone in the house all day. Aunt Dot used to write back to her correspondents, telling them that work was a great balm to a troubled soul, and that affection and companionship could be found in friendship. Then she would take off her glasses and polish them, and sigh and say, 'The poor soul. Loneliness is a terrible thing, Kay.'

Though Aunt Dot had never married, she had taken her own advice and had a great many friends. Suppers at the Pimlico house were lively affairs, with up to a dozen people sitting round the small dining table. Aunt Dot's friends were all ages, and of varying nationalities. There were her colleagues at the magazine as well as friends from the various societies promoting pacifism, socialism and the League of Nations that she supported. There were artists and novelists and poets, many of them poverty-stricken. There was the Austrian therapist and the proprietor of the Italian delicatessen and the French family Dot had met while nursing at Étaples during the war, who had moved to London in the early twenties and set up a little school where the pupils were required to speak only French on Mondays, Wednesdays and Fridays. By the time Kay had left the school at the age of twelve, her French had been excellent. As well as old friends, there might be a woman Aunt Dot had got talking to in a shop or a girl Kay had met on the top deck of a bus: they all came to Aunt Dot's suppers.

Over the days that followed Kay's interview there was a rush of washing, mending and packing. Miranda and the rest of the household were to leave for Paris next week, Mrs Ingram had told Kay. Mr Denisov was already in Paris; he expected his household to join him as soon as the business of Miranda's companion had been settled. It was unlikely,

Mrs Ingram had added, that they would return to London in the near future.

It was April, cold and blustery in London, but it would be spring, perhaps, on the Continent. Kay dug out cotton frocks, a light mackintosh, shorts, a bathing costume and rubber swim hat. Aunt Dot ran her up an evening dress on her sewing machine. A smart hat must be found in case the Denisovs expected Kay to go to church with them, and stockings and gloves must be darned.

When Kay gave in her notice to her employer, she had to work hard to suppress the gleeful smile that threatened to leap to her face. A few days later, leaving home for the first time to take up her position with the Denisovs, she felt a sudden pang, and hugged Aunt Dot tightly.

When she arrived at the splendid Mayfair house, she had to remind herself that she was now part of the household. Mrs Ingram showed her to her bedroom on the second floor. The room was papered with sprigged wallpaper and furnished with a bed, wardrobe, a chest of drawers and washstand. Kay unpacked. Her clothes seemed to rattle around rather in the large wardrobe.

There was a tap on the door; Miranda came in. 'There you are!' she cried. She kissed Kay on both cheeks, then looked round. 'Such a poky little room. Our Paris house is much nicer, you'll see.'

'I think it's lovely.'

'You can see the garden, I suppose.' Miranda peered out of the window, down to a courtyard garden of clipped box and paving stone. She looked back at Kay. 'I'm so pleased you're here! Papa wanted to engage another governess for me, but I wouldn't let him. I'm far too old for governesses. My last one always had a cold. Whenever she spoke, she sniffed.'

Kay laughed. 'I must be an improvement on her. At least I don't sniff.'

'And the one before, Mademoiselle Fournier, used to rap my knuckles with a ruler whenever I got my lesson wrong. Sometimes she made them bleed.'

'I promise I'll never rap your knuckles. I don't believe in corporal punishment. Neither does my Aunt Dot.'

'Dot. What a funny name.'

'It's short for Dorothy. Aunt Dot was my mother's younger sister. She brought me up after my mother died. My father was killed in the war, you see, before I was born.'

'When did your mother die?'

'When I was three,' said Kay.

'So I had my mother for six years more than you did. Do you remember yours?'

'Only a little. She had fair hair like me. We lived in Hampshire. There were apple trees in our garden – I remember lying on the grass and looking up at the blossom and thinking it looked like snow. What was your mother like?'

'She was very beautiful. Would you like to see a photograph of her, Miss Garland?'

'Kay – do please call me Kay. And I'd love to see a photo.'

Miranda led the way to her bedroom. In the large, high-ceilinged room there were two long sash windows framed with rose-coloured curtains. The walls were papered a deep bluish-violet and the room was scattered with chairs upholstered in rose-coloured velvet. Arranged on top of the chest of drawers were a great many dolls. More dolls sat on the end of the bed. They were the expensive, old-fashioned kind of doll, wax- or porcelain-faced, dressed in velvet and lace.

'They belonged to my mother,' explained Miranda. 'She

collected them when she was a little girl. Some of them are very old. Do you like them? Sometimes I like them and sometimes I hate them.' She picked up a doll wearing a red cloak and hood. 'Guess who she is.'

'She's Little Red Riding Hood, isn't she?'

'Sometimes.' Miranda smiled. 'But sometimes . . .'

With a quick twist of her fingers, she swivelled the doll's head and the young girl's face was replaced by the wrinkled features of an old woman. Another twist, and a third face appeared, a wolf, red-eyed, teeth bared.

'When I was a little girl,' said Miranda, 'I used to be frightened of this doll. I was afraid that, at night, the wolf might come alive and swallow me up. So silly.' She put the doll back on the chest of drawers and handed a framed photograph to Kay. 'This is my mother. Wasn't she lovely?'

'Very.' Kay studied the dark-eyed, wistful, haunted face. 'You must miss her dreadfully.'

'I didn't see her all that often. Maman was always ill. Most of the time she was away, visiting a spa or staying at a sanatorium.'

'And your father? He's in Paris, isn't he?'

'Yes, you'll meet him very soon.'

'Do you travel everywhere with him?'

'We all do. Papa likes everything to be just so.' Miranda put the photograph back on the dressing table. 'I've been longing to have someone to talk to. Tante Sonya just complains all the time. We'll be great friends, won't we, Kay?' There was, Kay noticed, just a touch of anxiety in Miranda's dark eyes.

'I'm sure we will,' said Kay.

*　　*　　*

A few days later, they left for Paris. They were to travel to France on the Golden Arrow, which left Victoria Station at eleven o'clock in the morning.

Kay and Miranda shared a first-class compartment with Miranda's Tante Sonya. Tante Sonya was wearing a fur coat and a pink velvet hat trimmed with feathers. She shivered and complained of the cold.

Sitting in the carriage, Kay found it hard not to run her palm over the deep pile that covered the seats, and to refrain from picking up the sugar bowl and touching with her fingertip the crest surrounded by the words 'Pullman Car Company Limited'. As the engine drew out of Victoria Station, she saw first the sooty warehouses and sidings and then the backs of the houses, with all that was usually hidden – dustbins, lines of washing and small brick-built lavatories – exposed to the view of the passengers on the train. Then London slipped away and was replaced by the rise and fold of the green Kent countryside.

The engine slowed as the train made its way into the port of Dover. And then there was the intoxicating excitement of boarding the ferry and feeling the bob and swell of the sea beneath the deck. A steward showed the Denisovs to their private cabin. With a moan, Tante Sonya lay down on a bunk. 'We're going on deck, Tante Sonya,' said Miranda quickly and, taking Kay's arm, whirled her out of the cabin.

They stood at the rail, watching the coastline of England shrink away. The sea glittered and the gulls soared. There was a stiff breeze and Kay was glad of her scarf and duffel coat. Miranda, at her side, was wearing a coat of soft blond fur. She had put up the collar round her face.

During the crossing they explored the ferry. They drank coffee in the dining room and discussed the other passengers, making up names and occupations for them. Towards the end of the voyage they went back on deck. Kay's first glimpse of France was little more than a grey blur on the horizon. Then, slowly, coast, town and harbour formed from the mist. As she stepped off the boat, there was a moment of disorientation when the harbour itself seemed to sway, like the sea. With delight and disbelief, she thought, this is me, Kay Garland, in a foreign land, at last. During the railway journey through the flatlands of the Pas de Calais, everything enchanted her, from the red-tiled roofs of the houses in the villages to the shop signs – boulangerie, tabac, épicier – so much more exciting, she was convinced, than baker, tobacconist and grocer.

Cars met them at the Gare du Nord and drove them to the Denisovs' house in the Eighth Arrondissement. The house was tall and grand, with wrought-iron balconies. Inside, it was furnished in a similarly dark and luxurious manner to the house in Charles Street. Kay's bedroom on the third floor of the house was decorated in pale green and white. Looking out of the window, down to the road, she heard the hooting of car horns and watched the people hurry by. She felt a yearning that was almost painful in its intensity: she longed to explore the streets of this unknown and magical city.

But first, she must write to Aunt Dot and tell her of her safe arrival. She took out a piece of notepaper and wrote the date, 10 April 1936, and then the Denisovs' address, with the word 'Paris' triumphantly underlined three times.

That evening, at dinner, Kay met Miranda's father for the first time. Konstantin Denisov was physically imposing, a tall, well-built man with a broad chest, powerful shoulders and thick neck. His voice was deep and strong, and he addressed Kay in good but heavily accented French. Miss Garland must dine with the family when they did not have a social engagement, he said; it would be a privilege to have a native English speaker with whom to converse. Mr Denisov admired the English, who were an adventurous and practical people. It was important to him that his daughter have good English – the language had, after all, been the native tongue of his wife, Miranda's mother. He loved England, would have liked to have lived in a little house in the English countryside and grow apples and keep pigs. Sadly, business kept him most of the year on the Continent.

Dinner with the Denisovs was not at all, Kay discovered, like suppers at home. There were no friendly dolings-out of stews or pies, and no noisy but good-tempered arguments about politics or the latest books. The discreet service of the food and the array of china, glass and silver made Kay unsure, suddenly, that her table manners were quite up to scratch, uncertain that the brown velvet, puff-sleeved evening dress that Aunt Dot had made for her was smart enough. She was thankful that her feet, which she disliked because they were rather long and thin, like the rest of her, were hidden beneath the dining table.

Konstantin Denisov directed the course of the conversation. They all fell silent when he spoke. Once or twice, Kay became aware of his hard, intelligent, calculating eyes on her. During dessert, Konstantin's secretary, Luca, came into the room to tell his employer that a telephone call had come through, and Konstantin left the table. In his absence, Tante Sonya and Miranda seemed to relax.

Over the next few days, Kay became more familiar with the Denisovs' routine. Konstantin Denisov's servants and employees were a cosmopolitan collection – an English housekeeper, a French chef, a German chauffeur, an Italian secretary. Though

Konstantin Denisov himself was Russian, the household generally spoke French.

In the morning, Konstantin had usually left for his offices by the time Kay and Miranda rose at eight. Tante Sonya, who breakfasted in bed, came downstairs at ten o'clock, yawning and still somewhat *déshabillée*. Then there was an hour in which Kay taught Miranda English while Tante Sonya arranged the flowers and spoke to Mrs Ingram about menus. Miranda's English was already almost unaccented, so they passed the time reading Shakespeare together. As well as French and English, Miranda spoke fluent German and had a reasonable command of Italian and Russian.

At one o'clock they lunched with Tante Sonya, either in a restaurant or at the Denisovs' house. Afternoons were taken up by paying calls, shopping, tennis, and ballet lessons. Miranda adored her ballet lessons. If her father was displeased with her he refused to allow her to go to them, which made her miserable.

At four o'clock they had tea with Tante Sonya. Once a fortnight a hamper from Fortnum and Mason in London, containing Dundee cake, Cooper's Oxford marmalade and Tate and Lyle golden syrup, arrived at the Denisov house. After tea, Miranda rested for an hour and then they changed for dinner. At half past eight, Kay dined with the family. If Konstantin, Miranda and Tante Sonya were going out for the evening to a champagne dinner or a ball, one of the maids brought Kay a tray of supper in her room.

Tante Sonya owned a lapdog called Frou-Frou, who peeked out from the flurry of silk and chiffon his mistress wore during the day. In the evenings, Sonya became dramatic in black or crimson satin. In front of Konstantin, Tante Sonya was always respectful and anxious to please. Any lapse in the household she tried to cover up. But when Konstantin Denisov was not in the house, Sonya lounged on her favourite sofa, Frou-Frou and a box of chocolates to hand, occasionally licking her forefinger to turn a page of a magazine. Miranda's requests for a walk or a visit to the shops were turned down with a weary, 'But I'm so tired, chérie,' or, 'My poor head aches so badly.' From the beginning, it was obvious to Kay that Miranda had little affection for Tante Sonya. And though Tante Sonya called Miranda 'dear' and 'darling' and pressed little kisses on her, she quickly became irritated if Miranda dawdled or answered back.

A week after Kay arrived in Paris, she had just returned to the house after slipping out to post a letter when from the drawing room she heard Konstantin shouting. His voice was interspersed by Tante Sonya bleating timorously, 'But Kostya, my love!' Then there was a crash and a shriek.

Looking up, Kay saw that Miranda was leaning over the balustrade, listening. Kay ran upstairs. Miranda put a finger to her mouth, hushing her. Below them, the drawing-room door was flung open. Miranda grabbed Kay's hand, whispering, 'Quick, they mustn't see us,' and hurried Kay up the next flight of stairs.

'What's happened?' asked Kay.

'The Coreils – une famille très snob – have turned down an invitation to dinner. Papa blames Tante Sonya.' Miranda sounded pleased. 'He's furious with her. I hope he throws her out on the street.'

'But Miranda,' said Kay, shocked, 'she's your aunt.'

Miranda opened the door to her bedroom; they went inside. 'No, she isn't,' she said. 'She's not a proper aunt. She was my father's mistress once, a long time ago, that's all.'

Kay stared at Miranda. 'His *mistress*?'

'Yes, she was his lover.' Miranda sat down on a little gilt sofa. 'Hard to believe, isn't it? She's so fat and ugly and foolish. But yes, she was his mistress. She was married when my father first met her, to the unfortunate Monsieur Lambert. The poor man died a few years later – you can't blame him, can you, married to *her*. Death must have come as a relief. Of course, she doesn't share Papa's bed any more. He has another mistress now. Conrad tells me she's very pretty.' Conrad was the chauffeur. Miranda laughed. 'Don't look so shocked, Kay. Hadn't you guessed?'

Kay shook her head.

'I expect you think I'm hateful, the way I talk about Sonya, but she only pretends to like me. She knows that if my father were to guess how much she detests me, he would send her away and then she'd have nowhere to go. We only put up with each other because we have to. When I leave home to be married we'll never speak to each other again.' Miranda frowned. 'I hate her because she's always spying on me. She pokes her nose into my business. She listens when I talk on the telephone, sometimes she opens my letters. Once, I caught her reading my diary.'

'Perhaps that's just her way,' suggested Kay. 'Perhaps she only wants to make sure you're safe.'

'No, I don't think so. She hopes she'll find out something bad about me, then she'll tell my father. She thinks then he'll like her better than me. I told you she was a fool. Sometimes she takes money from my purse.'

Kay was appalled. 'Are you sure?'

'I can never remember how much money I have so it's hard to be certain. But she's always complaining that she never has enough money, and sometimes my purse is empty. I don't suppose my father gives her very much. Why should he? She doesn't do anything useful. And she's so mean. Whenever my father's away she wears dreadful old stockings, full of darns. Once, when her horrid little dog broke a vase, Sonya told my father that one of the servants had done it. My father dismissed him. Wasn't that wicked of her? And I get so sick of being stuck inside the house. "But I'm so tired, chérie . . . I have a headache, my love."' Miranda's imitation of Tante Sonya's whining complaint was uncannily accurate.

Kneeling up on the sofa, Miranda gazed out of the window. She gave a discontented sigh. 'Oh, I'm so tired of this house! Shall we do something exciting tomorrow, Kay?'

'What were you thinking of?'

Miranda smiled. 'Tomorrow I'll take you to meet my friends.'

Miranda's friends lived in the Rue Daru. Miranda had first met them at the Cathedral of St Alexander Nevsky, where she and Tante Sonya sometimes worshipped. The cathedral's ornate towers were topped with golden spheres; the representation of the saint on the frontage was made of gold and coloured tesserae. Many Russian émigrés had made their home in this district of Paris, after their world had come to an end in 1917 with the overthrow of the Tsar.

Her father despised his fellow exiles, Miranda explained to Kay as they made their way from Miranda's dressmaker to the Rue Daru. He thought them backward-looking and pitiful, stuck in the past. If Tante Sonya were to find out about her visits to the Rue Daru, she would put a stop to them immediately. But Miranda had learned, over the years, to steal an hour or two's freedom each day. Tante Sonya was very idle, and could sometimes be persuaded to allow Miranda to remain unaccompanied at the dressmaker's or ballet lesson. Tante Sonya might be strict about the time she would meet Miranda when the lesson or fitting was over, but was too stupid to realize that the dressmaker's might be rushed through in half an hour, or that Miranda might tell her a ballet lesson was to last two hours when in fact it only took one. Miranda had used those stolen hours to get to know the people from the Rue Daru. 'Madame Baranova gives a party every Wednesday afternoon,' she told Kay. 'They're such fun. People sing and play music and tell stories, and the food is delicious.' Miranda tucked her hand into Kay's arm. 'It will all be so much easier now that you're here, Kay.'

Alexandra Baranova was the wife of a general who had fought in the armies of the Tsar. The drawing room of Madame Baranova's flat was not at all large, yet Kay counted more than thirty guests, sitting on the sofas, chairs, floors and window sills. Heavy crimson velvet curtains, worn bare at the folds, hung at the tall windows. On side tables and mantelpieces were cobalt-blue ceramics and lacquered boxes bearing pictures of smiling girls in colourful folk dress and photographs of little boys in sailor suits and doe-eyed girls in pie-crust collars and long white skirts. The room had a faded elegance, an alien charm.

Kay was introduced to soldiers, poets and musicians. A prince spoke to her of his childhood in Russia: the crunch of snow beneath his boots in winter and the butterflies dancing above fields of waving golden corn in the countryside around the family's dacha in the summer. Once, he had been on a wolf hunt: his father had lifted him on to the front of his saddle and had ridden with him through forests where every branch was heavy with snow and the sun showed only as a white diffused disc set low in a pearly grey sky. He and his wife had once lived in St Petersburg, in a house surrounded by a garden of lime´ trees and lilacs. They had escaped Russia after the Revolution, during the turmoil of the civil war. Along with many other Russian exiles, they had settled first in Berlin, paying their bills by the sale of the princess's jewellery, which they had smuggled into Germany, sewn into the lining of her coat. In those days you could, the prince told Kay, live well in Berlin if you had gold or foreign currency. The city, always free-spirited, had been full of lively – if impoverished – theatres, art galleries, concert halls and cabarets. They had been surrounded by friends, so they had not felt alone. In Berlin, one had been able to buy Russian newspapers as well as Russian books. Not any more, the prince added sadly; Berlin had changed.

In the mid-twenties, when Germany's economy had begun to recover and Berlin had become too expensive, they had moved to Paris. Not long after they had arrived in France, the princess had died. 'I think,' the prince explained to Kay, 'that when we were living in Berlin, my wife was able to believe that one day we would go home. After we moved to Paris, she gave up hope. The doctor told me she died of influenza, but I have always believed she died of a broken heart.'

He asked Kay whether she missed London.

'A little,' she said, 'but I always wanted to travel.'

The prince smiled sadly. 'So did I, when I was young. Travel is a great pleasure when you know that at the end of it you can go home.'

At three o'clock, they ate cheese pastries and cherry tarts and drank tea, which was served in the Russian way, in a glass, with a spoonful of jam. Then there was a hush while a man with a black beard played the piano and afterwards a young woman recited a poem. Then Madame Baranova begged Miranda to sing. In a light, tuneful voice, Miranda sang a French song while the bearded man accompanied her. They were all so charming and interesting and so very kind to her, but Kay thought that a layer of sadness ran through them like a streak of black basalt through granite.

It was Alexandra Baranova – Shura to her intimates – who told Kay more of Konstantin Denisov's history. Konstantin had been cleverer than most, said Madame Baranova. He had seen in time which way the wind was blowing and he had invested in foreign businesses, so that, come the Revolution, he had not been, like so many of his compatriots, left destitute. Along with other Russian émigrés, Konstantin had moved to Berlin after the end of the Great War. During the Inflation, when pretty young Berliners were prostituting themselves for the price of a hot dinner, Konstantin Denisov had bought up an entire street of houses. A few years later, he had sold them for ten times what he had paid for them, and in doing so had made himself a very rich man.

It quickly became clear to Kay that Miranda, though indulged from birth with every conceivable luxury, had been very lonely. Miranda was waited on hand and foot but was rarely allowed a moment to herself. Everything must be done under someone else's watchful gaze. In some ways, Miranda was young for her age – those dolls, and her ignorance of how to buy a train ticket or toast a slice of bread or sew on a button. In contrast, Kay had been trained to be independent from the earliest age, had walked home from school and let herself into an empty house and made her own tea since she was nine years old. She knew her way around London, had worked for her living since she had left school. Yet Miranda was far more worldly-wise. At sixteen years old, Miranda had known what a mistress did and how she came to do what she did. With her father's business acquaintances – men two or three times her own age – Miranda was charming, confident, and a little flirtatious. Miranda's duplicitous, sophisticated world startled Kay, and sometimes shocked her.

The Denisov household was ruled by Konstantin Denisov. It was Kay's first exposure to absolute authority. Konstantin kept a close eye on his businesses and an equally close watch on his household. He was powerful, quick-witted and changeable. An ill-chosen phrase, a badly timed frown or smile, could alter his mood in a moment: charm and magnanimity turned to the wolf's snarl. There was a coldness at the centre of Konstantin Denisov that made Kay wary of him. It did not hurt him to hurt other people. Ruining a competitor or forbidding Miranda a treat was all the same to him, a necessary step to gain advantage or draw someone back into line. Most people would have balked at giving an old employee the sack or reducing a member of their family to tears. Not Konstantin. Kay never detected a scrap of regret or pity in Konstantin.

He was given to violent outbursts of anger. Once, Kay saw him hurl a porcelain figurine at a mirror, breaking both. Another time he struck his secretary with such ferocity that Luca ricocheted against the wall and slid to the floor, stunned. When Tante Sonya tried to calm him, fluttering and apologizing, Konstantin was insulting and cruel. Miranda, white-faced and silent, would try to hide during her father's rages, but when, on occasion, Konstantin caught sight of his daughter tiptoeing out of the room, he directed the full force of his temper at her.

After his fury subsided, Konstantin appeared relaxed and satiated, as if he had found release. He used his unpredictable temper to exert his control over his household, to keep them nervous, on edge, anxious to please, jealous of whoever was the current favourite. The Denisov household was one of conspiracies and deceptions, of men made jobless and homeless after a sudden fall from favour.

Towards her father, Miranda was invariably polite and respectful. She tried to entertain, to distract, to amuse. Sometimes Konstantin responded to her, calling her his little dove. His gifts to his daughter were indulgent, sometimes unpredictable – a bracelet from Asprey, a watch from Cartier, a companion with whom to spend her days. At other times, when Miranda misjudged her father's mood, he rebuffed her spitefully. 'What do you want, what are you trying to get from me?' he would snarl. 'I know your tricks. You're like all women, you must think I'm a fool, not to see through your games.' When her father jeered at her, Miranda wept. When he complimented her, she became cheerful and light-hearted. How odd, thought Kay, to be afraid of someone and yet to love them too. Once, she would not have thought that possible.

Miranda was at her best in company, where her father liked to show off his beautiful daughter. At the dinner table, she exerted herself to amuse the financiers and industrialists her father invited to the Denisov house. She had to judge it finely. Flirt, but never too much or her father might tell her she had behaved like a whore. Fail to bewitch and he would accuse her of sulking. No wonder she longed for a friend. No wonder that often, at the end of a long evening, she would creep upstairs to lie on Kay's bed, careless of how she crushed her expensive Vionnet frock, tearful and exhausted. *Tell me about your school, Kay.*

Tell me about Aunt Dot. Tell me about Brian's bookshop in Charing Cross Road. Kay's voice, speaking of the tranquil and the ordinary, seemed to soothe her.

Miranda's adventures – confided to Kay, and then, as they came to know and trust each other, carried through in Kay's company and with her connivance – were an attempt to carve out a life for herself away from her father's watchful eye. They were also a reckless gesture of defiance. Miranda took after her father in some ways. Both could be ruthless, both were strong-willed.

Kay's position in the household was anomalous, in some hinterland between servant and family friend. She sometimes wondered whether Konstantin Denisov had expected, when he had bought his daughter a friend, that they would become attached to each other. And because it seemed to her that Konstantin was interested only in what concerned him – the making and keeping of money – she thought he hadn't noticed.

Silly of her: Konstantin Denisov noticed everything.

Two months after the household's arrival in Paris, they left for Prague. A month in Prague, and then on to the Côte d'Azur for a fortnight's holiday. Then back to Paris. Travelling, always travelling. Their length of stay in each town or city was unpredictable. Sometimes they had a week's notice of their departure, but at other times Kay and Miranda would return from an afternoon's shopping to find the house in uproar, maids running up and down stairs with towers of folded clothing while the manservants carried out trunks to the waiting cars. Their removals were dictated by Konstantin's affairs. His various investments – property, coal, grain, banking – spread their tentacles across the Continent. A rumour of problems or opportunities in London or Berlin would send them packing their bags. A hint of financial instability in an Austrian bank and they would be on the train to Vienna.

They were never alone for long as they walked in the park or sat at a table beneath the awning of a café. Miranda would study them from a distance, the boys, her eyes covered by dark glasses, her head tilted to one side. '*Pas mal*,' she might say, with an air of approval. Or, 'No, no, he won't do,' and then her gaze would drift away, searching. The boys were handsome and charming, shy or exuberant. They were students from the university or soldiers on leave or clerks from government offices, banks and businesses. They gave compliments, offered cigarettes and cups of coffee, as they smiled their winning smiles and flashed their beautiful eyes. A procession of them, in city after city as the Denisovs roamed around Europe, the fleeting encounters punctuated by laughter, just for fun, never serious. All forgotten by Miranda as soon as the household packed its bags and moved on.

Until Olivier.

Chapter Two

In April 1937, a year after Miranda had first met Kay, the Denisov household went back to Paris. Though every town and city had become more pleasurable since Kay's arrival, Paris had always been Miranda's particular favourite. Miranda had often reflected on how miraculous it was that it had been Kay who had answered her father's advertisement. They suited each other so well. They found the same things funny, the same things ridiculous. They never ran out of things to say to each other, and when Miranda felt miserable, Kay always cheered her up. Her insistence, at the age of sixteen, that she be permitted to have a companion rather than a governess had been the first time she had stood up to her father. She had felt sick with fear. There had been a moment in their conversation that had teetered on an all too familiar knife edge. Would he shout at her, insult her, slap her face? But then, to her immense relief, her father had laughed, had told her that she took after him, and that he was glad to see she had spirit.

The Parc Monceau was only a short distance from the Denisovs' Paris house. That April midday, there was the scent of lilacs in the air. Turning the corner of the path, Miranda noticed the young man sitting on the bench. He had been there, on that same bench, the previous day, and something confident and easy about the way he sat, turning the pages of *Le Temps*, had attracted her attention as she and Kay had passed him.

Now, out of the corner of her eye, she saw him rise, fold his newspaper and put it in his jacket pocket. He was young, tall, broad-shouldered and slim-hipped, and his curling hair was the dark, shiny chestnut-brown of conkers.

'Company,' Miranda murmured to Kay. 'Who shall we be today? I'm Mademoiselle Dupont, I think, and my father has a shop, which sells, let me see, gloves. And you, Kay, are Miss Smith. My English, um . . .'

'Penfriend,' said Kay.

'*Bonjour, mesdemoiselles*,' said the dark-haired young man. 'Could I trouble you to tell me the time?'

Miranda glanced at her little gold watch. 'It's half past twelve, m'sieur.'

'Thank you. It's a beautiful day, isn't it?' He offered his hand. 'May I introduce myself? My name's Olivier Roussel.'

Miranda gave their fictional names and told the story about the glove shop. Monsieur Roussel smiled and murmured, 'A glove shop, how interesting.' Then he told them that he himself made films.

'How exciting,' said Miranda. 'And now you must excuse us, m'sieur, or we'll be late for our appointment.'

'Of course.' A smile, a nod of the head and an *au revoir* and then, when they thought they were out of earshot, they both let out a breath and fell against each other, giggling.

He was there again the next day, sitting on the same bench.

The newspaper was stuffed into his jacket pocket as he fell into step beside them.

'Mademoiselle Dupont, Miss Smith, what a great pleasure to see you again. I was hoping you'd come this way.'

'Were you, Monsieur Roussel? Why was that?'

'Perhaps you may remember that I told you yesterday that I make films. I have a little difficulty, I'm afraid.'

'Oh dear. I'm sorry to hear that.'

'My leading lady has let me down. She's unwell and I need to find someone to replace her. And I thought that you, Mademoiselle Dupont, would be perfect for the role I have in mind.'

Miranda paused in the dappled shade of a maple. Monsieur Roussel added, 'If that sort of work would interest you.'

'It depends.'

'Of course. On what, may I ask?'

'When you say *that sort of work*, exactly what do you mean?'

'Ah,' he said. 'You're right to be cautious. A strange man leaps out of a bush in the park and asks you to star in his film. Sounds, well, *dubious*, to say the least, doesn't it?' He took a card from the inside pocket of his jacket and offered it to Miranda. Then he said, 'When I say a film, that's perhaps an exaggeration. It's actually an advertisement promoting the virtues of the telephone.' He shrugged. 'One has to take what work one can. Most of the films I make are brief and informative – advertisements for private companies, short documentaries for the government extolling the industry of our fishermen or our wine producers. Or perhaps an instructive piece on the making of cement or the manufacture of ribbons, that sort of thing. Oh, and weddings, too – the blushing bride arrives at the church, and afterwards the wedding

27

guests breakfast in the splendid family home.' He spread out his hands in a gesture of regret. 'Money, you see. One day – soon, I hope – I'll make feature films. So you need not be concerned. Everything I have told you is true.'

An emphasis on the I and the you. Miranda blushed a little.

'This glovemaker,' Olivier Roussel continued smoothly, 'must be doing remarkably well to buy his daughter a costume from Chanel.'

Miranda's brows rose. 'You're very knowledgeable.'

'In my line of work you need to know a little about everything.' His smile broadened. 'Perhaps I might buy you lunch and then we can start again.'

'I'm afraid we have an engagement.' Such lovely brown eyes, Miranda thought with a pang, and so much laughter in them. So she said, 'But we have time for coffee. Tante Sonya won't mind if we're a little late. It'll give her the chance to drink another apéritif.'

They went to a café Olivier Roussel knew, a safe distance from the Champs-Elysées and Fouquet's, where Tante Sonya was waiting for them. Over coffee, Olivier told them about film-making. Not so glamorous as people tended to assume, he said. Most of his time was spent coaxing money out of financiers or trying to persuade somebody to lend him their Louis XIV chair for a prop. In this little film for the telephone company, all she would have to do would be to pick up the receiver and pretend to chat to a friend. Easy. A few minutes' work, though he should warn her that in his line of business a few minutes' recording tended to take hours.

'And this film – this advertisement – would be shown in the cinema?' Miranda asked.

'Yes, that's the plan,' he said. 'Would that be a problem?'

28

'No, not at all, no problem.'

Kay said, 'But Miranda—'

'No problem,' she repeated. Then, curious, she asked, 'But why do you want me?'

He said seriously, 'Because when you're on the screen, people will watch you. They won't be able to look anywhere else.'

Afterwards, when they were hurrying to Fouquet's, Kay said, 'Miranda, a film. Your father.'

'Naturally, I won't tell him.'

'You won't have to tell him. Everyone will see you.'

'Yes.' Imagining it, she sighed. 'How glorious.'

'If he were to find out—'

'He won't. Papa never goes to the cinema.'

'But someone he knows might.'

Miranda could see that Kay was troubled. Linking her arm through Kay's, she said, 'This film – this advertisement – no doubt it'll be shown in two or three fleapits in the poorest districts of Paris. And I'll wear lots of make-up and do my hair in a new way, and I've heard that people in films never look the same as they look in real life. And even if someone who knew my father were to recognize me, they'd never dare tell him, would they? So there's no risk, chérie, I'm sure of it. A film, Kay. Wouldn't it be wonderful?'

Olivier Roussel's film was made in a warehouse in Belleville, a working-class area of Paris. The warehouse was vast and dark with a miscellany of objects – a rusty car, pieces of furniture, items of machinery – to one side of it. Miranda had to do her own make-up, peering into the mirror of her compact, in Olivier's office. The office was a section partitioned off from the rest of the warehouse, very small, rather dusty, with one tiny window, high up. There was the smell of petrol from the garage opposite and a tabby cat lapping milk out of a saucer. 'Keeps the rats away,' Olivier explained to Kay as she stooped to stroke the cat. 'They're a damn nuisance. They store sugar next door and it attracts them.' So not much glamour there, then.

The brief drama was divided up into short scenes, like sentences. Every movement, every gesture mattered. And the time it took! A shot of Miranda smiling as she picked up the phone took half an hour to complete to Olivier's satisfaction. The inflexion of her 'Hello?' was rehearsed over and over again.

A lanky young man called Benoît wandered around the room adjusting lights and fiddling with the sound-recording apparatus. A small, slight girl called Agnès, very chic in black coat and beret, sat on a stool beside Olivier, shivering because of the cold, and writing in a notebook. Every now and then the telephone in the adjacent office rang and Agnès slid off her stool and tripped across the concrete floor in her high heels to answer it, sometimes calling out questions to Olivier and once holding out the receiver to him and saying, 'Olivier, it's Sylvie about her payment and she insists on speaking to you.'

A postman delivered letters, and a van slowed in front of the open doors of the warehouse and the driver leaned his head out of the cab and called out, 'Hey, Olivier, Jacques says he can do the eighteenth,' and Olivier waved to him in reply. And throughout all the chaos Olivier was calm and efficient and in control, checking through the camera lens, giving orders to Agnès and Benoît, and standing beside Miranda, his hand first touching her shoulder and then sketching out the movements he wanted her to make. And when at last the filming began and the doors were closed and everything inside the

30

warehouse was silent, Miranda's pale face rose like the moon out of the darkness and it seemed to Kay a moment of magic.

When it was over, Olivier offered to take them out to lunch. Kay phoned Tante Sonya and told her they had been delayed at the milliner's and would grab a sandwich. The lies slid out of her mouth easily as she stood in Olivier's office, surrounded by stacks of scripts and correspondence and telephone books. *What skill has been most useful to you in your career as a companion, Miss Garland? The ability to lie through my teeth.*

Kay sensed, on the other end of the phone, Sonya's natural indolence warring with her equally ingrained capacity for suspicion. Finally, she said, 'Very well. Three o'clock, mind, Miss Garland. Konstantin mentioned he may be back early today.'

The five of them ate in a café that was squeezed between a garage to one side and a factory that made paper to the other. But the steak and salad were good and so was the red wine. Miranda was effervescent, entertaining them with imitations of the Denisov household and film stars, and then Donald Duck, making them roar with laughter. Olivier filled their glasses and threw an open box of cigarettes on to the centre of the table and Benoît and Agnès helped themselves. Neither Kay nor Miranda smoked; Miranda always said that you could get away with a lot with Tante Sonya, if you were clever, but she had a nose like a truffle hound and would smell the smoke on their clothes.

Like most men, Olivier was too sure of himself, and so, because she thought of him then as just another charming friend, Miranda made sure to blow hot and cold a little.

Sometimes, when they met, she and Kay agreed to go for a coffee with him. At other times Miranda shook her head, glanced

31

at her watch, gave a little sigh and said, '*Désolée*, not today . . .'
He always took it well, gave a smile and a wave of the hand
before he walked away. He never objected that Kay was always
with her, never tried to prise her away from Kay, treated them
both with attentiveness and courtesy, as if he liked them equally.
Though Miranda could tell, she was certain, that he was attracted
to her. That look in his eyes, and the way that, at the least
opportunity, he let his hand brush against her arm to guide
her through a doorway or help her into a chair. Men had been
in love with her before, since she was fifteen years old, and
she was not foolish, she recognized the signs.

She liked Olivier because he was handsome and funny and
clever, and not at all pompous or full of self-importance like
so many of the other men of her acquaintance. She liked the
way the corners of his mouth curled up in small, cheerful cres-
cents. She liked the way he moved, the barely suppressed energy
in his stride. He was different from the men who dined at her
father's table, the men she dined and danced with, men her
father regarded as, if not equals, then at least worthy acolytes
or useful associates. They pursued her for their own reasons,
because they desired her or because they saw the advantage
of an association with the daughter of Konstantin Denisov.
Their barbed wit and their softly disparaging comments about
their fellow guests bored her. Miranda would have thought
Olivier easy-going and happy-go-lucky had she not witnessed
him at work. Working, he was intense, concentrated, serious,
a perfectionist.

There was about him, Miranda realized, a sense of belonging.
She felt no particular attachment to the various Denisov houses
and apartments that had come and gone over the years. *Home*
was defined by the whereabouts of the people she travelled

32

with. It might be a railway carriage, a suite in a hotel, even the interior of a car. Olivier was different. Olivier – she had recognized this early on in their acquaintance – belonged utterly to Paris. It was hard to imagine him anywhere else.

Sometimes, when they were able to escape from Tante Sonya, they all three went to the cinema. Miranda sat in the middle, between Kay and Olivier. The cinema was to Miranda a place of transformation. You came from the bright day into a darkness smelling of cigarette smoke and the musty, dusty odour of upholstery that had not been cleaned often enough. You were surrounded by courting couples and by jobless men taking advantage of a comfortable place to shelter. But when the curtains parted and the music sang out, you were taken to another world. And when it was over and you went outside, the daylight and the sight of people hurrying about their ordinary business was a shock because you were still half in that other world.

In the cinema, Olivier could not always restrain himself from murmuring, 'Clumsy, that. He should have made more of that,' or, when impressed, 'It's the lighting, don't you see, that makes the scene so dramatic. Those black shadows – that searchlight travelling across the wall.' Miranda would glance across at him and see the rapture in his eyes.

Olivier didn't have much family, only an elder brother in South America he hadn't seen for years. His father had been a professor of literature, his mother had had a pottery studio at their weekend house in the Île de France. After his parents had died, Olivier had sold the weekend house. He had sent half the money to Marc, in Brazil, and had used his share of the inheritance to finance the film company. 'There have been plenty of times,' he told Miranda, 'when I've wondered whether I might

33

as well have torn up the notes and thrown them in the Seine. But you have to take your chances, don't you?'

Miranda, too, was taking her chances. During that magical morning in the warehouse, Olivier had taught her a great deal. How to project herself for the camera, how to convey emotion to the round glass eye of the lens, how to make every word matter, whether it was for an advertisement for telephones or for the greatest film ever made. In turn, Miranda took it upon herself to entertain and amuse him. This was what she was good at: she knew how to please men. Smile at their jokes, tell a mild little joke of her own. Tell a funny story or mimic a mutual acquaintance. Flirt a little. That sort of thing.

Olivier told her she had talent. At first, she did not believe him. They were in his office. There were stacks of film scripts and box files on shelves and piled on the floor. On the desk was an Olivetti typewriter and a tray brimming with opened letters and notes about telephone calls. Pinned to the walls were film posters, torn a little at the edges: *Zéro de Conduite*, *L'Atalante*.

'You're not good yet,' he said, 'but you might be with training, with practice. You have *something*. A quality. It's uncommon and you shouldn't waste it.'

She made an unconcerned shrug. 'My father would never let me become an actress. This talent you say I have – it's not worth considering.'

'You won't live under your father's roof for ever, surely?'

'I shall until I marry.'

He studied her. 'How old are you really, Miranda?'

She had told him she was twenty-one. She had felt it gave her an advantage. Eighteen sounded so young, not much more than a child. She was twenty-one and so was Kay, her friend from England.

He guessed, 'Twenty?'

She shook her head, feeling a little dismayed.

'Tell me you're at least eighteen.'

'At my last birthday, in April.'

'That's a relief. For a moment I thought I might have to send you home to the nursery. And Kay?'

'She's twenty. Honestly and truly, Olivier. Cross my heart.' Miranda sketched a cross over her breast.

Olivier longed to make a proper film, a feature film, instead of advertisements and documentaries. He had a script that a friend had written. He let Miranda read it; she smuggled it home beneath the folds of her fur coat and leafed through it in bed at night.

'The script makes all the difference,' he told her. 'You won't make a good film out of a bad script. You can make a bad film out of a good script, though.'

'But you'll make a wonderful film, won't you, Olivier?'

'If I get the chance, yes.'

'What do you need to make your film?'

'Oh,' he said with a wry smile. 'Money. Always money.'

Olivier spent a great deal of his time trying to find money to make his films – films, he explained, were very expensive to make. Once, when they were in a café and he was telling them about his interview that morning with a prospective backer, and he was a little – well, thought Miranda, a little less cheerful than usual – she took off her emerald bangle and slid it across the table to him.

'There, you can have that,' she said. 'I expect it's worth quite a lot of money. No one will notice I haven't got it any more. Sell it, then you can make your film.'

And Olivier, who was never normally at a loss for words,

35

was silent for a long moment, and then said gently, 'It's very, very generous of you and I'm very, very touched but, you see, I couldn't possibly.' And he took her hand and carefully threaded the bangle back on to her wrist.

The longest day of the year, and all the girls were wearing floral frocks and sandals and were tanning their legs in the parks. Tante Sonya was in bed with a headache, curtains drawn, her room smelling of lavender oil.

In a restaurant in Montparnasse, Olivier was celebrating having found a backer for his film, a cheerful, red-faced Belgian called Vincent Charlier, who bounded to his feet when Miranda and Kay arrived and kissed their hands. The table was set up in the courtyard garden, beneath an awning of green and white stripes. Deep pink roses climbed up the walls enclosing the garden, and the tablecloth became scattered with broken bread and empty wine glasses as Benoît, Kay and Agnès argued about politics and Olivier discussed with Monsieur Charlier where he would set his film and who would star in it.

'Your heroine,' said Monsieur Charlier. 'The beautiful and elusive Camille. You must tell me who you have in mind, Olivier.'

'I haven't asked her yet. I'm hoping to persuade her.'

Monsieur Charlier followed the direction of Olivier's gaze. He gave a wide smile, and cried, 'My apologies, I didn't know you were an actress, Mademoiselle Denisov.'

Miranda murmured, 'Not an *actress* . . . only a little advertisement for telephones . . .'

'Tell you what, Vincent,' suggested Olivier, 'why don't we go back to my office and then I'll show you what Mademoiselle Denisov can do?' He signalled to the waiter, flung some notes on to the table, and they all left the restaurant.

Monsieur Charlier owned a car, a large Peugeot. They squeezed inside it, Kay in the front passenger seat, next to Monsieur Charlier, and in the rear, Agnès, Benoît, Olivier and Miranda. During the drive, as Monsieur Charlier hurled the Peugeot around corners, Miranda was aware of Olivier, sitting next to her, of his arm slung along the back of the seat, resting against her shoulders, and the warmth of his body as he leaned against her when Monsieur Charlier took a tight corner at speed. Sometimes, at balls and parties, she let her dancing partners kiss her, just to see what it was like, but so far, she had found it uninteresting, even repellent. She thought that if Olivier were to kiss her, it would be much nicer.

In the warehouse, Olivier pulled the wide front doors closed, unrolled the screen and showed Monsieur Charlier the telephone advert. He ran it through three times and, at the end, Monsieur Charlier applauded and cried, 'A star is born!' He was a little drunk, Miranda thought.

Then there was a great deal of handshaking and kissing and Monsieur Charlier left. While Kay was talking to Agnès and Benoît, Miranda went into Olivier's office, closing the door behind her.

She perched on his desk, swinging her legs. 'You know my father won't let me do this, don't you?'

She had told Olivier only a little about her father. She suspected he thought of Konstantin Denisov as a stern paterfamilias, who could be won round in time.

'If you'd like me to speak to him, to reassure him—'

'No, that wouldn't help.'

He looked at her consideringly. 'What do you want to do with your life, Miranda?'

'I don't know. I've always assumed I'd marry someone.'

'And until then? It's possible to make a living as an actress. Not easy, but possible, if you're good enough.'

'Am I good enough, Olivier?'

'Not yet.'

Miranda pouted. 'If you don't think I am, then why do you want me to act in your film? I don't know anything about acting. I can't think why you told Monsieur Charlier such a thing.'

'You won't cost me much. Newcomers are always less expensive.'

She knew that he was teasing her. And there was a heat in his eyes that excited her, that made her feel that anything might happen, that something glorious might happen. She said, 'Actresses have to be beautiful, don't they?'

'Oh, you'd scrape by.'

'Is this the only reason you like seeing me?' She made her mouth into a round red *moue*. 'Because you want me to act in your film?'

'Flirt,' he said calmly. He put his palms on the desk to either side of her, a glint in his eye. 'You're such a flirt, Miranda.'

'Does that offend you, darling?'

He smiled. 'No,' he said. Leaning forward, he let his lips brush against hers. 'Not in the least.'

You couldn't, by that summer of 1937, convince yourself that the Continent was all boat rides on the Seine and sunbathing on the Côte d'Azur. France existed in a state of fear and in-decision, Olivier told Kay one afternoon, when they were sitting in the Jardin du Luxembourg. France's population had yet to recover from the trauma of the war. She hadn't dared retaliate when, the previous year, German troops had marched into the supposedly demilitarized zone of the Rhineland. To one side of France was Germany, and to the other, Italy. Two dictators, Hitler and Benito Mussolini. Oh, and then there was Spain, of course, which for the past year had been in the throes of civil war. It doesn't, Olivier had said grimly as he smoked a cigarette, his eyes narrowed against the sun's glare, look promising.

'And England?' Kay asked.

'England doesn't want to know. England can't decide who are worse, the Fascists or the Bolsheviks. England doesn't want to be dragged into another continental bloodbath, as she was in nineteen fourteen.'

Kay's father had died in that particular continental bloodbath. Kay was a pacifist.

They saw it on the newsreels at the cinema, Hitler's glassy-eyed shrieking and Mussolini's puffed-up strutting and the explosion of violence, courage and blood in Spain. Well, Kay and Olivier saw it. Miranda liked to buy sweets or check her make-up during the newsreels; Miranda never read a newspaper or sat in Mrs Ingram's room, listening to the news on the wireless.

After a month on the Côte d'Azur, a telephone call from Konstantin Denisov ordered his household back to Paris. In August, the city was deserted. Everyone who could afford it had escaped to the sea or the countryside. When Miranda phoned Olivier's office, no one answered, not even sulky Agnès.

Miranda phoned again, every day for a week. It was humiliating – she never chased men, they chased her. Then, one afternoon, telephoning from a café, her heart leaped as she heard Olivier's voice at the other end of the phone.

'Hello, darling,' she said.

'Miranda. Where are you?'

'I'm here, in Paris. Where have you been?'

'Visiting my aunt in Normandy. I slept too much and ate too much. Are you free this afternoon?'

'Perfectly.'

'Then come to the Marais. I'm trying to find a doorway.'

Miranda and Kay took a taxi to the Marais. Olivier was waiting for them in a café; he rose as they came through the door. He was tanned, and he was wearing his old corduroys and a white linen shirt, open at the neck, clothes that on another man might have looked scruffy but which suited him very well.

No time for coffee, he said, they had work to do. Outside, in the Marais, the empty streets were narrow with tall, shuttered houses to either side. Dark shadows, like bruises, gathered in the lee of the walls. There was a solidity to the heat, an airlessness. Miranda was wearing a sleeveless dress; she felt the sun bite into the exposed skin of her shoulders. The sun and the blue-black shadows were hypnotic, making the streets and buildings appear dreamlike, glittering and mysterious.

Lots of doorways in Paris, said Kay, looking round. Ah, but this must be the right doorway, Olivier pointed out, a remarkable doorway, a doorway in which his hero and heroine could kiss for the first time. That's why they were in the Marais, the most ancient district of Paris.

A tall black door, then a brown door with a brass knocker in the shape of a lion's head. A door with peeling grey-green paint that Olivier stood in front of for several minutes, considering. Every now and then he stopped to take a photograph, and so did Kay, with her Box Brownie camera. Another doorway, blue this time, with a fanlight in the shape of a sunburst. Pots of scarlet geraniums stood on the front step.

Kay asked Olivier to take a photograph of herself and Miranda. They posed on the doorstep as he clicked the shutter of her camera.

'Now you two,' said Kay.

Miranda tucked her hair behind her ears and put up a hand to shade her eyes from the sun. Olivier drew her towards him. She felt the pressure of his fingers on her waist. Kay took their photograph and Miranda laughed.

Kay wandered off ahead of them, disappearing round the corner of the street. Miranda, growing hot and a little tired, said what did it matter? A doorway was a doorway.

'Listen,' said Olivier. Gently, he steered her into the shade, where it was cooler. 'Close your eyes. Put your hands over them. That's right. Now imagine it's a bitterly cold night in January. There's ice on the cobbled streets. You're a strong, brave man –' Miranda giggled; he hushed her – 'yes, once you were a soldier but lately you've fallen on hard times. But something has happened – you've been caught up in a conspiracy and now you're hot on the trail of a double agent. You've followed him first from Czechoslovakia and then through Hungary. Now he's in France. He possesses information that's dangerous. If it falls into the wrong hands, it could light the fuse that sparks another war. At all costs you must stop him, but he keeps slipping from your grasp. You know you shouldn't let him out of your sight for an instant, but when you reach Paris, you can't resist going to see a friend.'

'Which friend?'

'The lovely Camille, of course.'

'Why?' asked Miranda, peeking at him through her threaded fingers.

'Because you're in love with her, naturally. Even though you've

41

seen her only a few times – in a nightclub, perhaps, or at the theatre – you adore her. She's the most beautiful woman you've ever known, and you've known a lot of women. She is enchanting, bewitching, the sort of woman men kill for, die for, go mad for.'

'Oh.' Her hands fell away from her eyes.

'Why are you sighing?'

'Because I would so like to be Camille.'

'Well, then.'

'Olivier,' she said seriously, 'my father told me this morning that we're to leave Paris at the end of the week. We're to go to Berlin.'

'And you can't simply say to your father that you'd rather stay here?'

'No, no. Papa would never allow that.'

'If you explained—'

'Darling Olivier, you don't understand. As soon as he knew I wanted something, Papa would be suspicious.'

'I had plans, you see.'

'Did you?' Her heart was beating fast.

His spread fingers rested on the slope of her hips. 'There were things I thought we could do, you and I.'

'The film, you mean?'

'Yes, the film. And, um, other things.'

His eyes were chestnut brown, flecked with gold. You could lose yourself, Miranda thought, in eyes like that.

'Other things?' she repeated.

'This and that.' He kissed her lightly on the lips.

'This film,' she said. 'Your hero, Christophe. You were telling me. He's in love with Camille . . .'

A glance along the street, as if he could see his hero walking through a cold winter's night. 'So,' he said, 'Christophe comes back to Paris and searches for Camille, but he can't find her. Then, one evening, walking through the Marais, he catches sight of her. She plays the coquette at first – she pretends to sulk, to be cross with him for having neglected her. But then – what do you think happens next, Miranda?'

'I don't know.'

'I told you, he kisses her.' This time, the kiss lasted longer.

'Oh,' she said, after they had drawn apart. 'I see. Like that. How forward of him.'

'Isn't it?'

She gave a prim little smile. 'Things are always so easy for people in films and so hard in real life.'

'Oh, I don't know,' he said. 'Kissing's quite easy if you put your mind to it.'

He demonstrated, his lips at first soft and exploring. And then he was holding her in his arms and her breath had caught in her throat and she forgot the sun and the dusty street and the run of piano scales from the open window of a nearby house, and there was only the heat of his body, the taste of his lips and the scent of his skin and she wanted him to go on kissing her for ever and never let her go.

In Berlin, it was autumn. The sky was steel-grey, the drizzle relentless. Leaves drifted from the trees in the Tiergarten and the air was cold. Taking Frou-Frou for a walk one morning, Kay noticed how, when they left the house and went into the street, the little dog shook himself, as if he, too, felt the chill.

The Denisovs were staying in a large flat in Lietzenburger Strasse, south of the Kurfürstendamm. There was nothing interesting to do in Berlin, Miranda complained – no dancing lessons and the dresses in the shops were so prim and proper, with their high necklines and long sleeves. It was no fun going to the park or taking a boat trip on the Spree in such miserable weather. So they ate sausage and dripping from a stall on the Berliner Strasse, or they wandered idly along Unter den Linden, Berlin's main thoroughfare, which was decorated to celebrate the visit of Mussolini with bunting and columns topped with the Nazi eagle clutching a swastika. They ducked into shops to avoid giving, along with the other passers-by on the pavements, the Nazi salute when a man in SS uniform passed. They had tea at Adlon's Hotel, where they amused themselves by making up nonsense about their fellow guests, and they saw film after film at the Ufa-Palast am Zoo cinema — sugary little costume dramas mostly, which they made fun of as they left the picture house, imitating the corny dialogue, earning themselves disapproving glances from other film-goers.

Since they had arrived in Berlin, the household hadn't settled down but had remained in a state of flux, telephones ringing all the time and messenger boys knocking at the door with cables. There was the feeling that at any moment they might all pack their bags and move on again. 'Some dreary thing to do with Papa's business,' Miranda said casually, to Kay's questions.

One afternoon, Kay came across Konstantin's secretary, Luca, on the balcony, smoking and tearing at his fingernails with his teeth. He gave her a wry smile and said something in Italian, which she did not catch. She offered him a peppermint — he wouldn't have any nails left if he carried on like that — and, taking one, he said, 'Take care, Miss Garland, be on your guard.'

Surprised, she stared at him. 'What do you mean, Luca?'

He crushed his cigarette end into a plant pot. 'Appearances

can be deceptive,' he muttered. 'Appearances of great wealth, particularly. There can be a good deal of show on the surface and little beneath to shore it up.' He froze, and flung a furtive glance to the door. 'I tell you this only so that you safeguard your own future, Miss Garland.'

Turning on his heel, he left the balcony. It was the last time Kay saw him. The following day, Mrs Ingram told her that Luca had been sacked.

And then, there was Herr Reimann. At first, they took little notice of him – just another of Konstantin's business acquaintances, another middle-aged man, stocky and red-faced, with a five o'clock shadow and a paunch, someone else Miranda was supposed to dimple and smile at and pretend to listen to – long, pompous stories about the famous people he knew, fat old Nazis, most of them, Miranda assumed.

But Herr Reimann was there when they went down to the drawing room before dinner, and there when Konstantin, Miranda and Tante Sonya dined out in the evenings. One day, he was invited to lunch at the Denisovs' flat. Afterwards, when Kay and Miranda escaped for a walk, they were horrified to find that Herr Reimann insisted on escorting them – how fortunate he was to have the chance to accompany two such beautiful young ladies! He talked about himself all the time and they had to pretend they were going into a lingerie shop to shake him off.

One morning, after breakfast, they armed themselves with raincoats and umbrellas and set off for the zoo. As they walked through the ornate Elephant Gate, Miranda told Kay about the party she had been to the previous night.

'Such a gloomy old house,' she said. 'And the women! Such frumps!'

Rain dripped from the edge of Kay's umbrella. Inside their

damp, puddled enclosures, the animals hid away, put off by the weather. Antelopes shivered beneath the trees; the warthog, searching for acorns with its snout, snuffled as the rain slid off its bristly hide.

'And the men?' asked Kay.

Miranda made a face. 'So boring. They talked about business and politics all the time.' She looked up at the heavy sky. 'Let's go to the aquarium.'

They made their way through crowds of mothers pushing prams and parties of schoolchildren walking hand in hand. Inside the aquarium, crocodiles glided across the water, their eyes and nostrils visible above its surface.

'When I was little,' said Miranda, 'my mother used to take me here. Afterwards, at night, I was afraid there was a crocodile hiding under my bed. I made such a fuss my nursemaid lost her temper with me and slapped me.' Miranda peered into the tank, her eyes narrowed. 'Herr Reimann was at the party last night,' she said. 'I danced with him.'

'Did he stand on your toes?'

'Not too much.' Miranda chewed her lower lip. 'I think he wants to marry me.'

'What a dreadful thought.'

'Isn't it? And – and I'm afraid my father would like me to marry him.'

Kay stared at her, horrified. 'But he's *decades* older than you!'

Miranda gave her well-that's-the-way-of-the-world shrug. They left the crocodile hall and made for the tropical fish house. An octopus clung with pinkish-cream suckers to the glass fish tank and a conger eel threaded itself between stones. A shoal of tiny iridescent blue fish moved through the water like a scattering of sapphires.

'Herr Reimann's very rich,' said Miranda. 'He owns a bank. Papa has some difficulties – mortgages and loans that have gone bad, I don't know, it's all so dull. He needs to borrow money from Herr Reimann.' She gave an odd little smile. 'And in return Herr Reimann wants – me.'

'Has your father talked to you about this?'

'Papa doesn't talk to people, you know that, Kay. He commands, he issues orders. But no, he hasn't said anything yet.' Miranda was fiddling with the buttons on her glove. 'Last night, when I went downstairs before we went out to the party, Papa made me go back to my room and change into a different evening gown. He told me that the one I was wearing – it was my violet satin with the low back – wasn't suitable. He said that Herr Reimann doesn't approve of women who dress immodestly. Immodestly! Have you ever heard anything so ridiculous?' Miranda's voice was calm but there was, in her eyes, a flicker of panic.

'Have you made it clear to Herr Reimann that he hasn't a chance?'

'I don't dare.' Now, Miranda looked frightened. 'Papa would be furious with me. He'd do something horrible to me, I know he would.'

'It's hard to imagine anything much more horrible than being married to Herr Reimann.'

'That's true.' Miranda laughed. 'Always so good at getting to the point, dear Kay. I'll just have to be clever and keep Herr Reimann at arm's length. I'll play the innocent, I'll flutter my eyelashes and say, *Oh Herr Reimann*, and *How clever of you, Herr Reimann*. He likes that. I'll let him dance with me and take my arm when we go for a walk. A little kiss, perhaps, though it makes me sick to kiss him. It's like kissing a horrible animal.'

'A crocodile.'

'No, he's far too bristly for that. Remember the warthog in his pen, eating acorns? Herr Reimann has a bristly chin and he snuffles when he drinks his soup. If he tries to kiss me again I shall imagine I'm kissing a warthog.' Miranda gave a nervous laugh.

Kay squeezed her hand. 'You mustn't worry. It won't happen.'

Miranda lowered her voice. 'Last night, I had an idea. If Papa tries to make me marry him, then I'll run away. I'll become a famous actress. My picture will be on posters and my name will be in lights above the cinema doors.' Her eyes sparkled. 'Wouldn't that be wonderful?'

The Denisovs' apartment was in uproar when eventually they returned to Lietzenburger Strasse. Konstantin had arrived home early, accompanied by half a dozen unexpected guests. Maids were rushing to and fro with table linen and silverware. Tante Sonya, her silk shawl slipping from her shoulders, gave Kay and Miranda a furious look.

'Where were you? I thought you told me you were going to see Fräulein Schmidt?' Fräulein Schmidt was the daughter of a friend of Sonya's. 'I telephoned, but you weren't there.'

'No, you're mistaken, Tante Sonya,' murmured Miranda. 'It's tomorrow we're going to see Fräulein Schmidt.'

Tante Sonya gave her a suspicious look. 'Konstantin was angry not to find you here. He blames me – it's so unfair.' A lock of hair had escaped from Sonya's coiffure and dangled over her forehead like a bleached question mark. 'You must get changed straight away, Miranda. As soon as you're ready you're to join us in the drawing room. Herr Reimann is here.'

Miranda made a snorting noise, like a warthog. Tante Sonya said, 'What was that? What did you say?'

'Nothing, Tante Sonya.' Miranda patted her chest. 'Only a little cough.'

In her room, Kay stripped off her wet mackintosh, kicked off her shoes, and lay on the bed, her eyes closed. She felt tired; every now and then she sank into sleep. Disjointed images flickered through her mind – the shimmering blue of the fish at the zoo, the blank, pitiless eyes of the crocodile, and, unexpectedly, a memory of a beach on the Isle of Wight, where she and Aunt Dot had once gone on holiday, a clear, cool vision of a strand of shiny brown seaweed bobbing in a rock pool. Then the sound of footsteps hurrying along the corridor jolted her awake.

At eight o'clock Kay went to the drawing room. Miranda was sitting on the sofa beside Herr Reimann. She was wearing a frock of crimson silk, cut away at the back and the shoulders. Miranda had evidently decided to disregard her father's – and Herr Reimann's – preference that she dress modestly. Herr Reimann appeared not to have taken offence. Outside, the wind had got up and sharp needles of rain spat against the windowpanes.

Kay was introduced to Konstantin's dinner guests. Herr Neumann and Herr Fischer were employees of Herr Reimann. They were accompanied by their wives. Hands were kissed, champagne poured. At half past eight, they went into the dining room. Candelabra had been arranged on the dining table and on the mantelpiece and sideboards, so that the room glimmered with pinpoints of flickering light.

Kay was sitting between the Neumanns. Herr Neumann was nervous and talked too much. Frau Neumann was more reserved; her small blue eyes darted constantly, inspecting the furnishings in the room. It was a very fine room, said Frau Neumann approvingly; so fortunate to have such a fine dining room in this area of Berlin. The dining room of her own house was much smaller.

There was the whisper of Tante Sonya's taffeta evening gown and Frau Neumann's sniff as she investigated with the tip of her knife the lemon sole on her plate. There was the creak and hiss of a cork being pulled from a bottle of wine and the chink of cut glass. And, throughout it all, Miranda's bright, fast chatter.

Konstantin Denisov spoke little. He had a way of controlling through silence. Konstantin Denisov's silences had a quality that made those who noticed them nervous. As for those who did not notice – the loquacious Herr Neumann, for instance – Konstantin's gaze would every now and then drift to him, settle, and then move on. As though he was taking note in some mental book.

Everyone except Konstantin deferred to Herr Reimann. Konstantin was merely polite, making the appearance of listening while Herr Reimann told them about his ski chalet in Garmisch-Partenkirchen, the wine cellar of his house in the Grünewald, and the improvements that had been made to the city of Berlin since Herr Hitler had come to power in 1933. Herr Reimann seemed particularly keen on the reduction in unemployment and the cleaner appearance of the streets. Kay imagined a broom sweeping along the pavements, gathering up crumpled editions of the *Berliner Tageblatt* along with jobless men in blue overalls.

Herr Reimann had a way of beginning every anecdote with, 'I remember when I was in Cologne' – or Dresden, or Frankfurt – that made Kay careful to avoid Miranda's mocking gaze. During Herr Reimann's monologues, Herr Neumann continued to drink while his wife played constantly with the beads round her neck. Tante Sonya's eyelids drooped every now and then, but Miranda, leaning forward, her chin balanced on a folded hand, every now and then interspersed a, 'How fascinating,' or, 'Did you, Herr Reimann? How clever of you' – all with a look of wide-eyed rapture that made something inside Kay bubble and simmer and threaten to boil over.

Pudding, at last. Only the savoury to endure and then the women, at least, could escape. Herr Reimann began, 'I remember when the bank was in negotiations with the steelworks in Breslau,' pausing only to take, rather noisily, a spoonful of pudding. And Miranda touched the tip of her nose, bending it upwards just the tiniest bit, like a pig's snout – or a warthog's – and the laughter that Kay had been fighting all evening burst out of her.

There was a sudden, appalled silence.

Konstantin Denisov spoke first. 'Something has amused you, Miss Garland?'

Kay flushed. Everyone except Miranda was staring at her. Miranda was looking down at her plate and her shoulders were shaking.

Konstantin murmured, 'I'm sorry, Miss Garland. Was there something you wished to say to us?'

Which sobered her enough to mutter, 'I'm afraid I've something caught in my throat – I beg your pardon . . .' and rush from the table.

In the bathroom, she rinsed her hands under the cold tap and bathed her face. It wasn't even funny – there had been an unpleasant undercurrent to the evening, and she was all too aware that in laughing she had done something very stupid. Yet even now the memory of Herr Reimann's warthog snort made her want to laugh again. She took several deep breaths, checked her face in the mirror, steeled herself, then went back to the dining room.

Konstantin looked up as she came into the room. 'Ah, Miss Garland, I trust you are recovered.' His smile – and the chill in his eyes – reminded Kay of the crocodiles at the zoo. Konstantin turned to his other guests. 'We look upon Miss Garland as one of the family, ladies and gentlemen. She travels with us wherever we go. She likes to sightsee. Isn't that so, Miss Garland?'

'Yes, Mr Denisov.'

'Even in such weather. What took you so long today?'

Kay made herself meet his gaze. 'Miranda and I went to the zoo, Mr Denisov.'

'Ah, the zoo. How pleasing to discover that my daughter has such a keen interest in nature.'

'But the rain, Fräulein Garland,' said Frau Fischer kindly. 'I'm afraid you'll catch a cold.'

Kay turned to her. 'Oh, no, I don't mind the rain. I'm used to it. It rains so much in England.'

'So it does.' Again, Konstantin smiled. 'I insisted on having an English companion for my daughter, you understand, ladies and gentlemen. I have always admired the English. So honest and straightforward. Such – how do they say it? The love of fair play. The good sports. That is the correct expression, is it not, Miss Garland?'

Kay suppressed a shiver. 'Yes, Mr Denisov.'

The next morning, Kay breakfasted alone. Miss Denisov had woken with toothache in the night, Mrs Ingram explained to her, so Madame Sonya had taken her to the dentist. Wednesday was Kay's afternoon off, so Madame Sonya had asked Mrs Ingram to tell Kay she could have the morning free as well.

Kay wrote some letters and then took a tram to the National

Gallery. After a couple of hours looking at paintings, she ate a lunch of bread, boiled egg and salad. Then she wandered round the shops in the Potsdamer Platz. She should have been enjoying herself, but she wasn't. The day had started wrong and had gone on feeling wrong. Tante Sonya never got up early, and if Miranda had had toothache during the night, surely she would not have gone to Tante Sonya? She would have gone to Mrs Ingram, who had the key to the cupboard where oil of cloves and aspirin were kept, or she would have gone to Kay herself, for company.

Kay bought half a dozen postcards and wrote them at a table in a café. One for Aunt Dot, one for Brian at the bookshop in Charing Cross Road, two for schoolfriends, and one for Benoît, with whom she had become friendly.

And one for Olivier. *Cher Olivier*, she wrote, and then her pen hovered uncertainly over the card. She wanted to write, *Dear Olivier, if you love Miranda then you must make her understand this, because I'm afraid that something bad is going to happen and that Miranda will leave it too late to escape.*

But in the end she wrote, *Dear Olivier, We are longing to come back to Paris. It rains all the time in Berlin. Yours, Kay.*

After she had posted her cards, she glanced at her watch. It was almost five o'clock; Miranda must be home by now. She caught a tram back to the Denisovs' flat. In the lobby, she folded her umbrella and put it in the rack. As soon as she went into the entrance hall, she noticed that the flat was unusually quiet. There were no servants hurrying to and fro, no distant sounds of clanking saucepans from the kitchen, no Tante Sonya chattering on the telephone. And no Miranda, rushing downstairs to meet her.

'Home at last, Miss Garland.'

Konstantin Denisov's voice. Kay swung round.

He was standing in the drawing-room doorway. He seemed to fill the opening. As he approached her, he said, 'Tell me, Miss Garland, who is this man?'

He held out a photograph to her. Kay looked down at it. She saw that it was the photograph she had taken of Miranda and Olivier in the Marais.

A moment's blank incomprehension. Then fear. She whispered, 'I took this.'

'I assumed so.'

'But . . . it was in my room.'

'Sonya found it.'

Now her fear was mixed with outrage. 'She's been through my things?'

'I instructed her to. Sonya was packing for you.'

'Packing?' She was bewildered. 'We're leaving Berlin?'

'You are leaving my employment, Miss Garland.'

A ripple of shock ran through her. She followed the direction of Konstantin's gaze to where her small brown suitcase, previously unnoticed, stood beside a marble-topped sideboard.

Konstantin said again, 'The man in the photograph. The man who has his arm round my daughter. I want to know who he is.'

'I can't remember his name.'

'Perhaps if you tried harder.'

Her throat was dry. 'No, I can't remember. He was just someone we met. No one special.'

'I see.' A silence. 'Then it seems we have nothing further to say to each other.'

'Miranda—'

'There is no reason for you to see my daughter again.'

'Please, Mr Denisov, at least let me say goodbye!'

'I thought I'd made myself plain,' said Konstantin softly. 'You are a bad influence on my daughter, Miss Garland, a very bad influence. You are to leave immediately.'

Her heart was pounding, it was hard to speak. '*Now?*'

'Of course, Miss Garland, now.'

'But where shall I go? What shall I do?'

'I have no idea.' He made a dismissive gesture, then turned away. 'It's really no concern of mine.'

No chance to make any arrangements, then, and she was not to be granted the time to reserve a hotel room or book a train ticket. Her movements seemed peculiarly stiff as she crossed the hall and picked up her suitcase.

Kay walked through the lobby, and down the stairs. As she left the building, a cold gust of rain hit her. She had forgotten her umbrella but could not bear to go back to fetch it. She walked for a while and then, catching sight of a tram, climbed on to it. She sat down next to a woman with a shopping basket on her lap, propped her suitcase against her knees and thought, I'll go back to the house and wait till Miranda comes home . . . I'll find somewhere to stay and I'll write to Miranda and tell her where I am . . . I'll telephone . . .

But nothing would work, she saw that clearly. Konstantin would never allow her into the flat. He would intercept any letter, he would forbid Miranda to answer the telephone. He would have Tante Sonya watch her night and day.

The tram deposited its passengers in Pariser Platz. Kay stood irresolute in the rain, her suitcase in her hand, trying to think what to do next. There was the thought of Tante Sonya's fat, pale fingers searching through her chest of drawers, and there was the memory of the cold fury in Konstantin Denisov's eyes.

She felt nausea and shock and perhaps a little shame. She had been dishonest. For a very long time she had disobeyed Mr Denisov's most fundamental instructions.

Yet what was uppermost in her mind was a sense of disbelief that this chapter in her life had so suddenly come to an end. She glanced at her watch. It was half past six. Half past six and she had nowhere to sleep that night. The thought came to her in an instant, accompanied by an almost unbearable yearning, that she must go home. Suddenly, she longed to be in her familiar bedroom in Aunt Dot's house, with the old painted furniture and the shelf of dog-eared books she had known since childhood. She wanted to go home; she wanted to be standing at the sink, peeling potatoes, while Aunt Dot stirred saucepans and they talked about the events of the day.

She set off down Wilhelmstrasse towards the Anhalter Bahnhof. Inside the station there was the shriek of whistles and the acrid smell of smoke. Reaction had set in and her legs were shaking so badly she had to sit down on a bench. She ran a hand through her wet hair. Soldiers gathered in groups around the concourse; a dozen boys dressed in the light brown and black of the Hitler Youth clustered by a sweet stall. So many uniforms – she felt out of place, alien, and tears sprang to her eyes as she rose and crossed the concourse to the ticket office to read the timetable pasted to the wall.

A sleeper train was due to leave Berlin that evening. If she caught it, she could be in Brussels by morning. Then she must take another train to Dieppe before crossing the Channel. And then she would be in England; home.

Returning to the bench, she opened her suitcase to look for the small tin, which had originally contained peppermints, in which she kept the money she saved from her wages. Her possessions – jerseys, stockings, books, writing case – were jumbled together anyhow, as if Tante Sonya had thrown them into the suitcase.

But she couldn't find the tin. She searched through everything again, this time more carefully. She was aware of a rising panic, which she tried to damp down. *It'll be there somewhere, you're just tired and upset and not seeing it.* Tante Sonya could not possibly have overlooked it; the tin had been with her passport, in her stocking drawer. *Passport, oh God, passport.* With shaking hands she scrabbled through her belongings until, with a rush of relief, she glimpsed the navy blue cover, caught between the pages of a book.

She had a sudden inspiration and ran a hand over the lining, in case the tin had slipped through a torn seam. No, nothing. Then she opened the case out flat and moved each item, one at a time, from the body of the case to the lid. It really wasn't there.

She would have to go back to the house. Her jewellery – her mother's engagement ring and the aquamarine pendant Aunt Dot had given her for her last birthday – had been in the tin, along with her money. She had no choice. Without money, she could not go home. She scooped her clothes back into the suitcase.

And then froze in the act of clasping it shut. Miranda's voice echoed. *Sometimes Tante Sonya takes money from my purse.* Kay gave a little moan of horror and several passers-by turned to stare at her.

It was a moment or two before she was able to open her handbag and count out the coins inside her purse. The full gravity of her situation sank in: she was stranded in Berlin without enough money to pay for a hotel room or buy a train ticket and without any idea at all how she was going to get home.

She remained on the bench for a few minutes, gathering up her courage. Perhaps Mr Denisov would speak to Tante Sonya on her behalf. Though she could not imagine that he would. But she must at least try.

Kay picked up her suitcase and headed back to the Denisovs' flat.

Chapter Three

Shortly after finals, Tom Blacklock's tutor, Dr Peacock, invited Tom to his rooms in Trinity. Over tea and Chelsea buns from Fitzbillies, Dr Peacock inquired about Tom's future. Did he intend to pursue further research, perhaps, or was he interested, possibly, in teaching? The questions were put with diffidence, as if such a display of curiosity was not quite the thing. Tom replied, with cheerful honesty, that he hadn't a clue. He had plans for a few weeks in the Cairngorms that autumn, to walk and climb, but apart from that . . . Dr Peacock then cleared his throat and said, 'An acquaintance of mine, a Mr Miles Culbone, who has written an important study on the medieval East Anglian wool trade, is looking for a suitable person to catalogue his library and assist him with his researches. Might you be interested?'

A week later, Tom drove to Suffolk, to Miles Culbone's house, Cold Christmas. The house stood alone, five miles from Lavenham, in woodland. It was raining steadily, and water curled from the tyres of Tom's MG as he headed up the drive.

His first sight of Cold Christmas made him whistle in

admiration. Hidden from the road, the house seemed to have grown out of the soft, damp, dripping landscape that surrounded it. It was large and L-shaped, with three gables of lessening size. Carved barge boards, weathered to a silvery brown, ran beneath the roof. Pictures had been imprinted on the plaster-work between the vertical oak timbers – a bird, an acorn, and a man's face surrounded by wild hair made of leaves.

Mr Culbone's housekeeper, Mrs Bowles, showed Tom indoors. Inside, one end of the great hall was taken up by an inglenook fireplace with stone seats to either side of the hearth. As he walked through the house, Tom had every now and then to duck his head so as not to hit a beam or a door frame. Some doors were so huge they might have been in a giant's house, while others were tiny. Ceilings dipped and floors slanted in a disorientating fashion. Every now and then, looking out of a window, Tom caught sight of an enclosed garden of narrow brick paths and dank, dripping shrubs.

Mrs Bowles introduced Tom to his prospective employer. Miles Culbone was thin, grey-haired and stooped. It was hard to estimate his age any more accurately than to say that he was probably somewhere between fifty and seventy. He had the air of a man who has been elderly since birth. He wore a baggy tweed suit, a grey waistcoat and a maroon bow tie, and his eyes were partly masked by a pair of tortoiseshell glasses. He seemed nervous, as if he found the interview an ordeal.

Their conversation was brief – Mr Culbone disliked having strangers in the house but the job must be done, it had been put off long enough, and besides, his eyesight . . . Dr Peacock had assured him of Tom's sobriety, honesty and industriousness. The work wasn't demanding and he couldn't offer accommodation, he was afraid. Oh, and Tom would be required to travel on Mr Culbone's behalf.

Tom ventured to ask whether Mr Culbone would mind if sometimes he took a week, or perhaps even as long as a fortnight, off, so that he could go climbing. Yes, yes, said Mr Culbone irritably – he found the presence of strangers in the house tiring; it would not trouble him if Tom were to take the occasional holiday. Unpaid, of course.

Then Mr Culbone took Tom to the library. The room was large and high-ceilinged. There must have been thousands of books, thought Tom. Some were bound in gold-tooled leather, decorative headbands woven into their spines. There were tiny, shabby little volumes that looked centuries old, and volumes of letters and copies of court assizes, and county histories – Suffolk, Norfolk, Cambridgeshire – forbidding in their length. Stacks of documents spilled out of folders.

Tom whistled, impressed. 'It's remarkable.'

Mr Culbone flinched at the whistle. 'I would require you to be absolutely silent while you were working, Mr Blacklock. I would be unable to pursue my studies if I were forced to endure a perpetual noise.'

Tom apologized.

Mr Culbone added, rather smugly, 'I believe Cold Christmas's collection of literature on the East Anglian wool trade to be the foremost in England.'

'And it would be my responsibility to catalogue these books and documents?'

'Yes, Mr Blacklock. You would work under my supervision, of course. Some of the volumes on the top shelves are inaccessible to me. My own climbing days being over, you understand.' The mild joke was accompanied by a rusty laugh.

'I would also,' added Mr Culbone, 'require you to make an inventory of my brother's acquisitions. My elder brother Carlyon travelled a great deal during his lifetime. I have no use for the artefacts he collected. I believe they are of some value, and I intend to sell them.'

Tom accepted the post partly because he hadn't yet thought of anything else to do and partly because he had fallen in love with Cold Christmas. He found lodgings in Lavenham and transported his belongings from Cambridge to Suffolk in his old but beloved MG. The following day, he started work. He spent his mornings in the library. Miles Culbone's supervision was characterized by an excess of anxiety and fuss, along with strictures about being *particularly* careful with that volume, and loud sighs or nervous starts if Tom happened to sneeze or drop his pen on the floor. Mr Culbone appeared to find it hard to leave Tom to his own devices. He had a habit of padding silently around the house and materializing without warning in the room in which Tom was working, and peering over Tom's shoulder in a way that those of a more nervous disposition might have found unsettling.

Miles Culbone told Tom that the original hall house had been built in the thirteenth century and had been added to many times over the years. Cold Christmas's period of greatest prosperity had been during the fourteenth and fifteenth centuries, when the East Anglian wool trade had been at its height. Then, the house must have been full of talk and laughter from family, servants and farm labourers. Now, in the library, the only sound to break the silence was the scratch of Miles Culbone's pen.

Mr Culbone appeared to have no friends and few relatives. Mrs Bowles told Tom that a cousin, Mrs Fielding, visited once or twice a year. The majority of Mr Culbone's correspondence was with other scholars and antiquarians. Letters with foreign stamps arrived at Cold Christmas, and every now and then the postman would knock at the door with a parcel.

Each day, at one o'clock, Mr Culbone and Tom stopped work for lunch. Mr Culbone lunched in the dining room, waited on by Mrs Bowles, while Tom ate the sandwiches his landlady, Mrs Hooper, had packed for him, in the garden. Cold Christmas's garden covered several acres. The boughs of the beeches swayed in the breeze, and a river, brown and edged with reeds, ran along the northern perimeter of the property. Tom's midday walk, whatever the weather, was a necessary antidote to the enforced restraint of the mornings. In the garden, he could make as much noise as he liked. He often found himself, as he tramped across the lawn, whistling, or singing aloud. Though sometimes, looking back to the house, he thought he caught sight of Miles Culbone's pale face at a window.

It was on one of his lunchtime walks that Tom came across a circle of marble columns in a clearing in a birch wood. The columns echoed the pale, slender trunks of the trees. At first, he assumed the building to be a summerhouse or folly but, drawing nearer, he glimpsed within the columns a marble oblong. On top of the oblong was sculpted the likeness of a child. A tomb, Tom thought, an effigy.

The marble child lay as if sleeping, his eyes closed and face peaceful. There might have been just a hint of a smile on the curved lips. Fallen leaves, yellowed by the coming of autumn, clung to the folds of marble drapery that lay over the child's body. Along the top of the catafalque words were carved: *Erected in the year of his grief, 1880, CC.* Who was CC? Tom wondered. And what tragedies constituted a year of grief? The loss of a beloved son or daughter, presumably. Anything else?

Miles Culbone, when asked, was uninterested and unforthcoming. The memorial had been erected by his late uncle. The boy had died young – an illness, perhaps, he could not recall. It was long ago.

Culbone's housekeeper was able to tell Tom more. Mrs Bowles explained that the child had been the sole heir of Charles Culbone, who had married for love late in life. Mr Culbone's wife had died of a fever after ten years of marriage. The boy, only eight years old, had perished not two months after his mother. He had drowned in the river, which had been swollen by a heavy rainfall. It had been thought the boy had slipped on the muddy bank while fishing. Ten years after the loss of his wife and child, poor Mr Culbone had himself died, leaving his younger brother, the present Mr Culbone's late father, Mr Stephen, to inherit Cold Christmas.

In the afternoons, Miles Culbone worked alone in his library while Tom set about cataloguing the Egyptian artefacts. Carlyon Culbone, Miles's elder brother, had been an eminent Egyptologist. He had spent most of his life abroad, living in Cairo, engaged in archaeological research, leaving his house in Miles's care. The finds he had brought home with him from Egypt filled three rooms. Some of the fragments of pottery, the jewellery and scarabs, the bronze sculptures, paintings and papyrus, were still in their original packing cases. Tom was to identify and number each item. When the artefacts were properly catalogued, Sotheby's would be called in to value them. Tom found himself wondering what Carlyon Culbone would have thought, if he had known his life's work was to be packed away in tea chests and sold at auction.

Towards the end of his first month at Cold Christmas, Miles Culbone sent Tom on business to London. He had heard of a medieval psalter that was to be sold privately. Tom was to inspect it and, if it was in good condition, offer a suitable price for it. Mr Culbone looked more than usually distressed at the prospect of entrusting Tom with his money, so Tom took pity on him and offered to drive him to London so that he could carry out the transaction himself. 'In a motor car?' Mr Culbone looked alarmed. 'No, no, that would be quite impossible.'

Similar commissions followed in Norwich and Oxford, and then, at the end of October, Miles Culbone told Tom that he required him to travel to Berlin. Did he have any knowledge of German? He was reasonably fluent, Tom said. He had spent a summer in Germany and Austria the year before he had gone up to Cambridge. Mr Culbone explained that a German scholar with whom he had been in correspondence for some years had offered to sell him two books – a rather fine sixteenth-century edition of Aristotle's *Rhetorics and Poetics*, and an early Erasmus. Miles Culbone's eyes, which were the colour of the North Sea in winter, gleamed. His correspondent was most anxious to sell. Tom must secure the books for a good price.

A few days later, Tom travelled to Germany. On his arrival in Berlin, he headed first for the rooms of his old friend, Willi Becker. He had become acquainted with Willi in the summer of 1933, when Willi had been a medical student. He and Willi had spent a month climbing in the Austrian Alps. Now, Willi was a doctor at the Charité hospital.

Over lunch, they caught up with each other's news. Willi – plump, genial and good-natured – had recently become engaged to a girl called Ilona Kruger. 'She's a goddess,' said Willi, as they tucked into black bread with wurst and mushrooms, washed down with beer. 'Hair the colour of butter and skin as soft as a milkmaid's. Lives in Dahlem, with her parents. She's their only daughter and they watch her like a hawk. Ilona believes in keeping herself pure, so I had to ask her to marry me. It was either that or go insane.' Willi took a large mouthful of bread and sausage. 'She drives me wild. A little kiss on the cheek, a little stroke of the hand, then she trots back home to Mutti. So we're to be married next year. Of course, knowing my luck, as soon as she's legally mine, some war or other will break out and I'll be sent miles away, celibate once more.'

'You think it'll happen soon?'

Willi's shrug said, *Look at the posters on the wall, listen to the speeches on the radio, look at the SS officers in the street, with the death's head badges on their black caps. See what the Nazis have done to cynical, civilized Berlin.* Aloud, he said very quietly, 'Everything points to it, doesn't it? We have a year or two, perhaps. And maybe something will happen to prevent it. But I seem to have been hoping that for a long time.'

'And you, Willi? What will you do?'

'I'll be all right. I'm a doctor, after all.' Willi wiped his plate with a crust of bread. He grinned. 'Perhaps it'll never happen. Perhaps Ilona and I will marry and have half a dozen children with hair the colour of butter. Let's drink to that.' He raised his tankard.

At three o'clock that afternoon, Tom called at the flat of Mr Culbone's correspondent, Herr Doktor Bruck, in Charlottenburg. Bruck was in his fifties, Tom guessed. He was short and slight and shabbily dressed, but his English was excellent as he welcomed Tom into the small sitting room.

'I must apologize for having no fire lit – so inhospitable of me.'

Tom assured Dr Bruck that the lack of a fire didn't worry

him at all, that his own family rarely lit fires at home before the evening.

'In which part of England do your family live, Mr Blacklock?' asked Dr Bruck.

'Cambridge. I went to university there as well.'

'Ah, *Cambridge*.' Herr Bruck beamed.

'Have you been there?'

'Twice, to visit a friend of mine at Trinity Hall. And now, let me fetch you some coffee, Mr Blacklock – no, I insist.'

Dr Bruck disappeared into the kitchen. In his absence, Tom looked round the room. He noticed the unmistakable signs of poverty – the frayed patches on the sofa and rug and the wedges of newspaper blocking the gaps where the window frames had rotted. Streams of rain trailed down the panes, seeping indoors, turning the newspaper wedges to pulp.

Dr Bruck returned with a pot of coffee and a plate of biscuits. After he had poured out the coffee, he showed Tom the books.

'They are very fine examples, I'm sure you'll agree.'

Both volumes were in excellent condition. Tom handed Dr Bruck the sealed envelope Miles Culbone had given to him before he had left Cold Christmas.

Dr Bruck opened the envelope and counted the notes inside it. He was silent for a moment, and then he said quietly, 'Mr Blacklock, this is not the amount I agreed with your employer.'

Tom frowned. 'Are you sure?'

'Absolutely certain. The agreed sum was considerably larger.'

'I'm so sorry. Mr Culbone must have made a mistake.'

'A mistake?' A wry smile. 'No, I don't think so.'

Tom stared at Dr Bruck. 'I don't understand.'

The older man sighed. 'I am afraid that Mr Culbone saw the opportunity to strike a bargain.'

'Surely not. Surely he wouldn't do that.'

'I have had some dealings with your employer in the past. He is . . . careful with his money, shall we say. That is his nature.'

Tom was silent. Might Mr Culbone be capable of short-changing a fellow antiquarian who was down on his luck? *Generosity* was not a quality he had come to associate with Miles Culbone.

Dr Bruck was speaking again. 'I am no great collector, you understand. I own a small library of volumes, each of which has particular significance to me. These two books have been in my possession for many years. I found the Aristotle when I was a young man, the first time I visited Florence. I daresay Mr Culbone guessed that expediency has driven me to sell. He's right, of course. I have no choice but to take whatever price is offered to me.'

Tom felt first embarrassment, then anger. 'I'll go back to Cold Christmas,' he offered. 'I'll make it clear to Mr Culbone that you won't accept a penny less than the agreed amount.'

'No, Mr Blacklock,' said Herr Doktor Bruck gently. 'It's kind of you to offer, but it wouldn't work, you see. Mr Culbone can wait, but I cannot.'

'This is wretched – it's outrageous.'

'You are not to blame. Mr Culbone merely takes advantage of a market that at the moment is in his favour. These are dark days, but I am at fault, perhaps, for allowing myself to end up in such a position. I did not see soon enough what would happen. I have continued to hope that the situation would change for the better and instead it has changed for the worse.' He topped up Tom's coffee cup. 'Let me explain. I have lost my position at the university. Officially, it was not because I am a

Jew but because I was deemed surplus to requirements. But . . .'
He shrugged.

'Can't you find another post, if not in Germany then abroad, perhaps?'

Dr Bruck smiled sadly. 'I have tried. I have written endless letters to countless establishments boasting of my many talents, and not one has borne fruit. I'm afraid there are a great many men like me, too many Jewish professors chasing too few positions. If I were a younger man, or if I were a mathematician, perhaps, or a physicist – but a specialist in medieval German literature? German is hardly a fashionable subject these days.'

Tom rose from his seat. 'I'm so sorry. I can only apologize.'

'I'm more fortunate than many. I have a small pension so I will not starve. Stay, please, Mr Blacklock, and let us drink coffee and talk of happier things. Tell me, what did you study at university?'

An hour later Tom left Bruck's flat and headed through the rain for the railway station. He felt furious with Miles Culbone for having used him, and for having placed him in such an invidious position. The dishonesty, he thought – the calculation.

He took the S-Bahn to the city centre, where he walked for an hour or so, visiting familiar haunts. He telephoned friends he had made on his previous visit, but with little success. Rudi was a violinist with the Berlin Philharmonic and was giving a concert that evening, and Stefan was, his wife informed Tom, on business in Hamburg. Another friend, Leni, had left the country. She had been a communist, Tom recalled; life in Berlin was these days little easier for communists than it was for Jews.

The signs in the windows of shops and cafés – 'Aryan store' and 'Jews not welcome' – darkened his mood further. At nine o'clock, he went into a café in a side street off the Alexanderplatz. He was tucking into fried fish and potatoes when he caught sight of her. She was sitting by herself at a table a short distance away. She was young and pretty; he wondered whether she was waiting for someone. Her short, wavy hair, in colour between gold and light brown, was ruffled and windswept. She was wearing an olive-green jersey and a silk scarf was knotted round her neck. Propped by her seat was a small suitcase with a mackintosh folded over it. In front of her, on the table, an open book lay beside a cup of coffee. Tom thought she had a dashing, self-contained appearance, as if sitting in cafés by herself at night didn't particularly trouble her.

What had attracted his attention, apart from her air of self-possession, was the excessive slowness with which she was drinking her coffee. He, too, had often, when particularly hard up, eked out a cup of coffee in a café for an hour or more, just to remain in the warmth. Under the pretext of fetching salt from the counter, he passed her table and glanced at her book. As he finished his meal, he saw her take a purse out of her handbag and begin, under cover of the table top, to count out her change.

Tom had finished his supper. He rose and crossed the room to her. When she looked up at him, he saw that her eyes were not the blue he had expected, but a light greenish-hazel. Her features, which he had seen only in profile, were regular, and her face was open and friendly. There was a dusting of golden freckles across the bridge of her nose.

He said, 'Excuse me, but you're English, aren't you?'

'How did you know?'

He touched the book. '*Dusty Answer*. I've read it.'

'Did you like it?'

'Yes, I did. Though it was a little overwrought, perhaps.'

'Did you think so?' she said coldly. 'I love it.'

He held out his hand. 'My name's Tom Blacklock.'

'Kay Garland.'

'Do you mind if I join you?'

'Um . . .'

'Do say yes. I promise you I'm utterly pleasant and trustworthy.'

She laughed. 'Are you, Mr Blacklock?'

'And I've had a rather trying day, and it's such a relief to come across someone from England. In fact, may I buy you another coffee? I was going to have one myself and it would be good to have company.'

After a little coaxing, she agreed to allow him to buy her a coffee. When he had collected two drinks from the counter, Tom sat down opposite her. Miss Garland asked him how long he had been in Berlin.

'I arrived this morning,' he explained. 'I leave for home tomorrow.'

'A flying visit, then.'

'I'm afraid so. And you, Miss Garland?'

'I hope to go home soon.'

'Are you in Berlin on holiday?'

'No, I was working here.'

She offered no more explanation, but drank her coffee greedily. Tom had a sudden thought.

'It seems a shame to visit Germany and not have a slice of *apfelkuchen*. May I get you some, Miss Garland?'

'No, thank you.'

'Nonsense. It's my treat.' He returned to the counter before she could stop him.

When he came back to the table, Miss Garland was looking annoyed. 'That was very presumptuous of you, Mr Blacklock.'

'I'm sorry, but I don't like to see a fellow countrywoman go hungry.'

She flushed. 'I'm not *hungry*.'

Yet she devoured the cake, picking up the last few crumbs between forefinger and thumb. After she had finished, she sighed. 'That was lovely. So delicious. Thank you, Mr Blacklock.'

She asked him why he was in Berlin. Briefly, Tom told her about Miles Culbone and Cold Christmas.

'Mr Culbone sounds extraordinary,' she said.

'Oh, he is. Untrustworthy too, I'm afraid.' Tom explained how Miles Culbone had cheated Dr Bruck.

Miss Garland frowned. 'How mean of your Mr Culbone.'

'Wasn't it? Mean and despicable. This afternoon, I had every intention of giving in my notice as soon as I returned to Suffolk.'

'And now? Have you changed your mind?'

'The thing is, what would I do instead?'

'For a career, d'you mean?'

'I don't think I'd describe cataloguing Miles Culbone's library as a *career*. If I'm honest it was more a way of *avoiding* a career. I hate the thought of being shut up in an office, you see.'

'What about teaching?'

'That's the obvious route. My father's an academic.'

'I suppose that could be rather off-putting,' she said sympathetically. 'You'd almost feel you were doing what you were *ordained* to do. There's something dreary about that.'

'Exactly. Couldn't have put it better myself. And in some ways, working for Mr Culbone suits me.'

The conversation moved on to their families. Miss Garland's parents were dead. Tom told her about his parents and his younger sister, Minnie. Then he asked Miss Garland what she did.

'I was employed by a family, the Denisovs. I was a companion to Mr Denisov's daughter, Miranda.'

'You were a paid companion? How Victorian.' He frowned. 'You *were* employed by the family . . . ?'

'I've been sacked.' She looked downcast. 'Just this afternoon.' Her long, slender fingers tapped the side of her coffee cup. 'I keep telling myself I didn't do anything wrong, but then, perhaps I did. It's so hard to know.'

'How long were you with them?'

'Since March last year. I thought they liked me. But just to throw me out – and then, there was the money as well. I'm starting to think they can't have liked me at all.'

'Money? What money?'

'Oh, it doesn't matter, it's nothing important. But I'm afraid Miranda will miss me. I'm afraid she'll be lonely.' She looked distraught. 'Oh God, what an awful mess!'

'What will you do now? Will you go home?'

'Yes, as soon as I can.'

'What's stopping you?' He thought of the handful of small change in her purse and the eked-out cup of coffee. He asked bluntly, 'Can you afford your fare home?'

She did not reply. Tom persisted, 'You do have somewhere to stay the night, don't you?'

She seemed to sag a little. 'Actually, I don't. I've only two marks and twenty-two pfennigs left. Do you know of anywhere I could stay for two marks and twenty-two pfennigs?'

'I'm afraid not. And if there was somewhere, I doubt if it would be very pleasant.'

'Oh.' She looked deflated, and then, with an attempt at

73

bravado, said, 'Anyway, I've decided what I'll do. Tomorrow, as soon as the shops are open, I'll sell my camera and my watch.'

'And tonight?'

'I'll stay here as long as possible and then I'll go and sleep on a bench in the Tiergarten.'

'That's a completely ridiculous idea,' he said.

She glared at him. 'Under the circumstances, I should have thought it was perfectly sensible. Besides, I've no choice.' Again, she looked glum. 'I bank my wages whenever I go home to London. There were almost eight weeks' wages in my room in the Denisovs' flat. And it's been stolen.'

'Have you any idea who took it?' He looked at her closely. 'You do, don't you? Then can't you get your money back? Or are you afraid of confronting this person alone? I'll come with you, if you like.'

Her eyes flashed. 'I'm not *afraid*, Mr Blacklock. But it's too late – the Denisovs have gone away. When I realized my money wasn't in my suitcase, I went back to their flat, but when I got there, the caretaker told me that everyone had gone away and that the flat had been closed up.'

'Do you know where they've gone?'

'I've no idea,' she said hopelessly. 'It could be anywhere – Paris, Rome, Vienna – anywhere at all.'

He whistled. 'So you're stranded.'

'Yes, that's about it.'

'You'd better stay with me, then.'

She looked shocked. 'Mr Blacklock, I couldn't possibly do that.'

'Miles Culbone isn't exactly generous with his expenses or I'd offer to lend you the money for a hotel room. I'm staying at a friend's lodgings. Willi works nights at the hospital and

74

he's let me have his bed. You could have the bed and I'll sleep on the sofa in the other room. And then, in the morning, I'll buy you a train ticket and we'll catch the early train to Brussels. I'll give you my address and you can pay me back as soon as you have the cash.'

'It's very generous of you, but—'

'Better than sleeping on a bench, I'd have thought. Better than selling your camera, too, perhaps.'

She was silent for a moment, but then she said, 'I don't understand why you'd do this for me.'

'Because if my sister were stranded in Berlin, I'd want someone to do the same for her.' He glanced at his watch. 'Shall we go?'

Tom Blacklock was tall and athletic-looking. His straight dark brown hair was rather untidy and he had a habit of sweeping it back from his forehead with a quick stab of his fingers. His amused, intelligent eyes were a deep blue. His clothes were scruffy and uncoordinated – brown corduroy trousers, a blue shirt and a grey jacket that had worn at the elbows – as if that morning he had put on the first garments that had come to hand.

And he was very opinionated. He had ambushed her into eating and drinking with him, had dismissed her perfectly rational idea of selling her camera and sleeping in the Tiergarten as if it was beneath consideration, and had dragooned her into spending the night with him. *Spending the night* . . . Walking away from the café, down the darkened street, Kay was horrified at herself. Accepting food and drink from a complete stranger was rash enough, but to go to his lodgings was the height of folly.

And yet, she did not feel afraid. Instinctively, she trusted him, and she did not think her trust was entirely due to the relief one experiences when one comes across a fellow Englishman in a strange and rather frightening city. She sensed that he was honourable. And besides, the camera and bench plan had seemed rather daunting. Firmly, she put aside any worries that she might find herself ravished, murdered, cut up into little pieces and buried in a back garden, and accompanied Tom Blacklock to his friend's lodgings in Wilmersdorf.

There were two rooms and both were very untidy. Mr Blacklock didn't seem to find the untidiness anything out of the ordinary and picked his way through the debris as if it was usual to find a floor scattered with dirty crockery, books and newspapers, clothes, records out of their sleeves, and a skeleton. Kay remembered that Mr Blacklock's friend was a doctor, which accounted for the skeleton, she supposed.

In spite of being tired, she slept poorly that night. It wasn't just the unfamiliar bed and her consciousness that a stranger was sleeping just a few yards away from her – the walls of the room were thin and every now and then she heard the creak of the sofa as he moved in his sleep. Her thoughts were whirling, and she struggled to calm her mind. Images from the events of the previous day repeated themselves over and over again: her horror when she had realized that she had no money, the peculiar and troubling experience of returning to the Denisovs' flat and discovering that it had been abandoned, that she had been so quickly erased from their lives, and, worst of all, the cold contempt in Konstantin Denisov's eyes as he had said, *You are a bad influence on my daughter, Miss Garland, a very bad influence.* No one had ever looked at her like that before. She hoped they never would again. And yet, if one looked at it from Mr Denisov's point of view, she *had* been a bad influence. She should not have allowed Olivier to speak to Miranda. She should not have allowed Miranda to visit the warehouse where Olivier made his films, or dine with Olivier, or fall in love with Olivier. And yet, even now, in spite of all that had happened, she could not entirely regret having done so.

She wondered whether the corrosive, secretive atmosphere of Berlin had contributed to her downfall. Whether the whispering, the fear of saying or doing the wrong thing – of thinking the wrong thing – had been bottled up too long and had found release in that treacherous burst of laughter at Konstantin Denisov's dinner table.

In the early hours of the morning, she slipped into a doze, only to be woken what seemed like a few moments later by Tom Blacklock shaking her shoulder and telling her she must wake and dress if they were to catch the train. Walking to the station, sitting on a bench while she waited for Mr Blacklock to buy her ticket, she felt it again: that dreadful emptiness, that disbelief that this part of her life, which had been so extraordinary, so wonderful, was over. When she thought of Miranda, it was with a pang of misery. Where was she? Where had she gone? What would happen to her? Would her father force her to marry Herr Reimann? And would they ever see each other again?

At least the business of catching the train distracted her. Every seat in the third-class compartment was taken and Kay and Tom were crushed against each other on the wooden bench. Beside them were a mother and four small children; opposite were a middle-aged couple, a sailor in naval uniform, and two men with small suitcases – commercial travellers, perhaps. Tom Blacklock had bought coffee and rolls from the station cafeteria; they ate the rolls and drank the coffee as the train pulled out from the platform. Berlin's houses, offices and factories whirled past and the people in the streets became stick people, blurred by the morning mist and the smoke from chimneys. Eventually, the suburbs thinned out and they found themselves travelling through the countryside, which was brown and grey in the wet autumn weather and punctuated every now and then by a village or hamlet.

The journey would have been pleasant and uneventful enough had they not quarrelled. Mr Blacklock unearthed from his rucksack a crumpled copy of the *Manchester Guardian*. There was a column about the civil war in Spain. Kay read it over his shoulder and made some perfectly innocuous comment about being thankful Britain had decided not to get involved, and Tom said, rather heatedly, 'Well, I think it's damned shameful.'

She glared at him. 'You surely can't want us to sell arms to Spain?'

'Why not?'

'Because it would only prolong the war – it would only make it worse!'

The commercial travellers were totting up figures in their notebooks and the sailor was asleep – it was, after all, not yet nine in the morning. The middle-aged woman was absorbed in her novel and her husband was leafing through *Der Stürmer*. The mother was dividing up apples between her children.

He kept his voice low. 'What about Guernica? Do you think standing aside helped anyone there?'

Earlier that year, the German Condor Legion's aeroplanes had bombed the Basque capital of Guernica in Spain, killing more than one and a half thousand people.

'Of course not,' said Kay. 'It was awful. Sickening. And . . .'

'And?'

'Well, I wobbled a bit, I admit it.'

'Aha!' he said, in an annoyingly triumphant way.

'But,' she added quickly, 'just because another country does something wrong, that doesn't mean *we* should do something wrong as well.'

'How can it be *wrong* to help a democratically elected government that's under attack from a military junta?'

She pointed out to him the obvious. 'Because by selling arms you're helping people kill each other.'

'And if the war goes the Nationalists' way? If Franco's lot wins? Civil wars are the worst sort of war. The repercussions will go on for years – decades, perhaps. And besides, other countries are already involved. Look at Germany, look at Russia. Look at the International Brigades.'

She gave him a quick look. 'You haven't thought of—'

'I've *thought* about it. I've thought about going to Spain.' It was his turn to look annoyed – with himself, perhaps. 'Haven't done anything, though.'

Kay followed up her advantage. 'The situation's dangerous enough already without our making it worse. We shouldn't interfere. Does anyone outside Spain really understand what's going on?'

'Perhaps not. But by saying it's nothing to do with us, aren't we just giving the green light to, well,' he had dropped his voice to a whisper, 'let's say the more aggressive nations, to do what the hell they like?'

'There are other ways of helping,' she pointed out. 'Better ways.'

'What had you in mind?'

'The League of Nations, obviously.'

He gave her a superior look. 'The League of Nations is a spent force.'

His off-hand dismissal of an organization that Kay and Aunt Dot had always keenly supported deepened her annoyance. 'You have to keep trying,' she said passionately. 'You can't just *give up*.'

The inspector came into the compartment and they both fell silent as he checked their tickets. After he had gone, Tom said quietly, 'There are already fewer democracies than there were ten years ago. If we let democracy be thrown aside so lightly, then what hope is there for the future?'

'I just don't want there to be another war, that's all. It would be so terrible. It would ruin all our lives. And it could happen so easily, I can feel it.'

They were travelling through a landscape of farm and field. It was all so neat and tidy – the ploughed fields, the clipped hedgerows, a flock of white goats cropping the grass in a churchyard. 'When I was at the railway station yesterday,' she said, 'I felt it then. It was as though people had *accepted* that there would be a war. Not today, not tomorrow, but sometime in the future, sometime soon, perhaps. All those uniforms. Even the children. And the headlines on the newsstands – they were broadcasting one of his speeches on the loudspeakers. You know.' Hitler's speeches, she meant, but, crowded into the carriage with a dozen strangers, she did not dare even say the name. 'It's as if we're sleepwalking into making war inevitable – or even *acceptable*. It's less than twenty years since the most terrible war the world's ever known. It's as if people have forgotten. I believe we should do anything, anything at all, to prevent that happening again.'

'Yes, of course you're right.' He frowned. 'But it's how best to prevent it, that's the tricky thing, isn't it?'

He seemed then to consider the discussion over. He turned

80

to the crossword, taking a pen from his jacket pocket. Irritated, Kay found her place in *Dusty Answer*. But her eyelids were heavy and she found herself drifting off to sleep.

When she woke several hours later, she felt better. They were coming into Hanover. They shared the last of the rolls and Kay discovered half a bar of chocolate in the depths of her handbag, picked off fragments of silver foil, and divided it between them. A couple of hours later, at the Belgian border, a Nazi official came into their compartment to check their passports. Then they changed trains.

There was relief in leaving Germany, relief that, along with tiredness from their journey, made them dazed and light-headed and eased the slight coolness between them. They played silly word games, I-Spy and My Grandmother's Shop, in English, French and German, and every now and then Kay found herself laughing.

In Brussels, they had a couple of hours to spare before their connection, so they ate supper in a café near the station. In the tiny bathroom Kay pulled a comb through her tangled hair and thought of England, London, Aunt Dot. With longing, she imagined curling up in her own bed and sleeping for as long as she liked.

Then the train to Dieppe, where they boarded the night ferry. They couldn't afford a cabin so they sat, along with other red-eyed travellers, in the passenger lounge. There was a swell on the sea and the ship rose and fell.

It was cold; Kay wrapped her coat around her. She said to Tom, 'I love night ferries. You could imagine you were going anywhere, couldn't you?'

'Where would you like to go?'

She thought hard. 'I'd like to sail round the Greek islands. I'd like to cross the Aegean Sea. Wouldn't that be wonderful?'

'It is, rather.'

'You've done it?'

'In the long vac, when I was at university, I took part in a dig at an archaeological site on Crete. And afterwards I travelled around a bit.'

She said despondently, 'I wonder if I'll ever go anywhere exciting again.'

'Why shouldn't you?'

'Because I have to earn my living. And I shouldn't think anyone else will want to employ me as a companion. I haven't a reference, you see. And anyway, I can't imagine being a companion to anyone other than Miranda.'

'What will you do instead?'

'I don't know.' Kay shivered. 'I haven't thought about it. I don't even know what I'm going to say to Aunt Dot.'

'About losing your job?'

'Yes.' She glanced at him. 'Shall I tell you why Mr Denisov sacked me?'

'If you want to.'

'He said it was because I was a bad influence on Miranda. But actually, I think it was because I laughed at the wrong time. And he didn't like that.'

They talked a little more, and then Tom closed his eyes and slept, wedged up against the end of the seat. Eventually, Kay too drifted off to sleep. At some point during the crossing she woke and was momentarily flustered to find that her head was resting on his shoulder. But it was really rather comforting to feel the warm proximity of another human being, so she did not move, but closed her eyes and slept again.

They arrived at Victoria Station at dawn. Kay had resolved to borrow the money she owed for the train fare from Aunt

Dot and post it to Tom as soon as possible. They exchanged addresses, shook hands and parted. On the underground train, Kay sat, her bag at her feet, as the carriage rattled through the darkness of the tunnel. From Pimlico Station, she walked the short distance home.

She opened the gate and made her way to the back of the house. Through the kitchen window, she caught a glimpse of movement. She was home, and the utter rightness of it, and the immense relief, suffused her as she went into the house. Aunt Dot was dressed in her work clothes, a grey skirt and emerald-green jersey. Her dark hair, greying at the sides, was pinned in a coil at the back of her head. She was standing at the sink, compact in hand, putting on her lipstick. Seeing Kay, her eyes widened and she said, 'Kay. *Darling*.' Then, as her face broke into a smile, she put down the lipstick and, crossing the room, hugged her.

Chapter Four

After Konstantin Denisov sent Kay away, he asked Miranda the name of the man in the photograph, the man with his arm round her waist. *Sonya suspects you have fallen in love with someone. Is this true? Is this the man?* His forefinger stabbed the photograph. *Tell me his name, Miranda.*

No, she said. *I won't.*

Something hard and cruel in her father's eyes. He made a hiss like a snake. *Whoever he is, you'll have nothing more to do with him. You are to marry Herr Reimann.*

No, she said coldly. *Never.* And, when he insisted, she shouted at him that if he tried to force her into marriage she would insult Herr Reimann with such vulgarity that he would never want to see her again. Then her father struck her so hard it made her mouth bleed and tears spring to her eyes.

She hated crying in front of him. She preferred to save her tears for night time, when she missed Olivier and Kay so badly it seemed to scrape at her heart. At night, she wept copiously, shaking and sobbing, her grief and loneliness turning as if by alchemical process to the salt water that poured down her cheeks. She worried about Kay, alone in Berlin, without her, Miranda, for company. She prayed that Kay had got home safely. She liked to imagine Kay living happily in London once more.

A few days later, they left Germany for Switzerland. Miranda and her father shared a compartment in the railway carriage. Staring out of the window, the collar of her fur coat turned up to hide the bruise on her face, the glare from the snow-covered mountains penetrated the dark lenses of her sunglasses. She clutched to herself a crumb of comfort: that her father did not know Olivier's name.

She pieced together the events that had led up to this disaster. The meeting in the park, the filming in the warehouse, the lazy lunches and stolen half-hours. She knew that they had become careless, she and Kay. She should have hidden the joy she had felt when Olivier kissed her. Her happiness must have shown on her face because it had made Tante Sonya suspicious. Tante Sonya, a woman of the world, had quickly and correctly guessed the cause of her happiness: love. Sonya had searched first Miranda's room and then Kay's, looking for evidence. And she had found the photograph and taken it to Konstantin Denisov.

Sonya's mistake had been in believing that Konstantin would congratulate her on her discovery. He had not; instead he had blamed her. Konstantin had recognized that two of his entourage, his daughter and Kay, had begun, surreptitiously, to challenge his authority. And he had acted ruthlessly, as he did in the face of all such challenges. Tante Sonya had been expelled from the Denisov household the day after Kay had been dismissed. Which gave Miranda some satisfaction.

In Geneva, the Denisovs installed themselves in an apartment with fine views of the lake, a short distance from the Botanic

Gardens. Madame Cloutier, a sour woman with steel-grey eyes and an expression as welcoming as a rat trap, was engaged to chaperone Miranda. Miranda's outings were a walk in the park, a visit to a shop or two. Her father had stopped her ballet lessons. She could not, of course, visit the cinema.

At first, she made plans. She would write to Kay, she would telephone Olivier and explain to him what had happened. Or she would run away. But as the days went on, her hopes faded. Madame Cloutier watched her like a hawk. She received no letters, no telephone calls. How could she, when no one she cared about knew where she was? In the flat, all letters were placed on the silver tray on the hall table to be stamped and posted. When she hid a letter to Kay beneath the others it was taken out and torn up by Madame Cloutier in front of her. The telephone was in her father's study, and when her father was not at home, the door was locked. Outside the flat, Miranda was never alone. Madame Cloutier remained at her side, grim, disapproving, limpet-like, from the moment they left home until the moment they returned. An attempt to slip outdoors early one morning earned Miranda a slap from Madame Cloutier and punishment from her father.

Weeks passed. She felt herself sliding back to the boredom of her adolescence, before Kay had come to live with them. The days were made up of small, unengaging events. Time dragged itself out. She could sit for an hour in a stupor, watching through the window the movement of the branches of a tree in a gust of wind.

At night, when she was alone except for her dolls, glassy-eyed and staring on top of the chests of drawers, she knew that the year and a half when Kay had been her companion had been the happiest time of her life. To have that happiness taken away from her was almost more than she could bear. She wondered whether Kay felt as she did, that a part of her had been torn away. She wondered whether Olivier thought of their kiss at all, or whether to him it had been unimportant. And whether he had found another actress for his film.

Though she tried to work out what to do, every avenue of escape was closed off to her. If she ran away, her father would find her. Even if she was somehow able to find her way to Olivier, and even if − a very big if, this − Olivier loved her, they would never be able to stay together. Her father would not rest until he had found them. And then, what would he do to Olivier? He would destroy him, Miranda had no doubt of that. As for Kay − could she remember how to find the little house in London where Kay lived with Aunt Dot? She had visited it twice with Kay, when the Denisovs had been staying in England, but they had travelled to the house by taxi and she could not remember the address. And anyway, Kay would have returned to the life she had had before they had met. Would there be any room in her life for Miranda? In her blackest moods, she was afraid there might not.

She knew that she was trapped. She often imagined that she was walking down a flight of stairs. Down and down she went, and the air became greyer and greyer. When she looked down, she could see only darkness. The foot of the stairs was hidden in darkness.

Her defiance evaporated. She became a dutiful daughter once more, trying to please the clever, cruel, powerful, volatile man who had always dominated her life. Dining with her father and his business associates, she seemed to see herself from a distance, flirting and simpering. Habit, she thought. And fear of her father, of course. She reminded herself of the

88

dolls in her bedroom. She looked unreal, felt unreal, her little red mouth opening and closing, smiling to order, as Olivier had taught her for the camera, her smooth pale limbs worked by someone else. It was as though something vital – brain, heart, soul – had been sliced away and locked in a box.

Sometimes, when she was very, very lonely, she even found herself missing Tante Sonya.

She stopped eating. It made her feel real again – a passing hunger, a fleeting desire for hot, buttered potatoes or *sachertorte* reminded her that she was, after all, alive. And besides, what else could she do? Futile to fight with her father, who could shout louder and twist her words round and fling them back in her face and who could knock her down with a single blow of his hand. In depriving herself of food, she discovered a quiet rebellion that needled Konstantin Denisov, who hated fussy eaters. A self-made man, he still had enough of the peasant in him for the wasting of food to seem an outrage. At dinner, Miranda took a few spoonfuls of this, a sliver of that, and saw how it riled him. It made her feel triumphant. And it was not as if she felt like eating anyway. She felt sick and miserable and any hunger vanished the moment she sat down at the dining table, her father to one side of her and the iron-eyed Madame Cloutier to the other.

After a while, though, it got out of hand. What started as a weapon became a compulsion. Food disgusted her – that frill of white fat around a lamb chop, that twist of bluish gristle across the crimson of a steak. One morning, she fainted in church. A doctor was sent for and she was poked, prodded, lectured, and prescribed a tonic. The following week, the Denisovs left Switzerland for the south of France. Miranda was supposed to get well in Nice, to regain her appetite and put on weight in the milder climate, but all she could think, wrapped up in her fur coat and sitting on a balcony in the pale winter sun, was how different it had been the last time, when Kay had been there and all she had had to do to make herself happy had been to imagine the next time she would see Olivier.

On her return to England, Kay found it hard to settle. Aunt Dot's house seemed so small, and her old life, which she had left behind eighteen months before with hardly a second glance, seemed routine and lacking in colour. She missed Miranda – to be so suddenly separated was disorientating and painful. She had lost the person with whom she had shared her deepest thoughts and feelings, the person who was the nearest she had ever had to a sister. And, if she was honest with herself, she occasionally missed the sense of privilege she had become used to as Miranda Denisov's companion. Tables were not reserved for her in restaurants any more. The best shops no longer welcomed her, smiling.

She was unable to decide what to do next and had taken a series of temporary and rather dislikeable jobs. She went out with a succession of equally short-lived, unsatisfactory boyfriends. Then, one of Aunt Dot's friends told her of a school that was looking for a French teacher. Kay applied for the post and, after an interview, was offered the job.

Oaklands School was in a leafy part of Hampstead. The large, scruffy house was surrounded by an acre of garden. Coeducational, informal and with an unconventional ethos, it appealed to Kay. It was the school's policy never to turn away a child. Some of the children had been sent to Oaklands by their parents because no other school would take them. Some, not yet in their teens, had already been expelled half a dozen times. They were troubled and troublesome, demanding and exhausting. Other pupils were delicate, or they were shy and nervous, unable to cope with the boisterousness of a run-of-the-mill boarding school. You never knew what the day would bring, or what would happen next. Kay rather liked that.

No one seemed to mind that Kay did not possess a teaching qualification. The school's motley staff were oddballs or idealists every one. Roger Lancaster, the headmaster, and his wife, Virginia, fitted into both categories. Kay frequently had to suppress laughter when, each morning in assembly, Roger, who was short and plump and balding, ringingly proclaimed the school to be a beacon of freedom and light. Virginia was her husband's opposite, tall and gaunt and self-conscious. She organized timetables and appointed staff as well as teaching music.

Kay settled in quickly. She started going out with Laurence, who taught art at Oaklands. She enjoyed her work and got on well with both staff and pupils. But still, sometimes at night, in the moments before she fell asleep, she found herself recalling a café in Paris or a beach on the Côte d'Azur. Where was Miranda and what was she doing? Was she still watching the boys in the park, her eyes narrowed with amusement? *Pas mal, Kay, pas mal.*

Her friendship with Tom Blacklock provided some compensation for Miranda's absence. When she had written to Tom to repay him for her train ticket from Berlin, she had offered to meet up with him the next time he came to London. She would buy him coffee and cake. From there, their friendship had flourished. They met up every now and then for a drink. They often argued – Tom was both opinionated and stubborn – and yet somehow they never fell out with each other. She liked him: he was always interesting and he made her laugh, and that, in the rather grey aftermath of her odyssey with Miranda, meant a lot to her.

The Denisovs had returned to Berlin. At a ball, dancing the polonaise, as the long snake of couples followed the leader over chairs, behind curtains, through the garden and back into the house, Miranda caught sight of herself in the mirrored wall of a gallery.

She stopped so suddenly the next couple almost collided into her. She walked to the mirror and put out a hand, touching the glass. This could not be her, this thin, pallid creature. It didn't look like her. Yet it was wearing a white dress with gold ribbon threaded round the neckline, just like hers. And it wore a Russian amber pendant at its throat.

Her partner – she couldn't remember his name, Friedrich von Something? – said, 'What is it? What's wrong?'

'Nothing,' she said. She could not say, *I thought I saw a ghost.*

Taking her hand, he led her to a chair by a window. 'Wait there,' he said.

The polonaise, riotous now, straggling and untidy, had moved on, leaving only the echo of its laughter behind. Through the glass, Miranda could see a balcony. She opened a door and went outside. The air was sharply cold, the night sky speckled with stars. Miranda looked down over the wrought-iron balustrade to the paths and statues and black bulky trees below.

Friedrich von Something returned with a small glass of wine and a little silver dish. 'Drink this,' he said, handing her the glass.

Half a dozen mouthfuls. She counted them to calm herself.

'Here,' he said. 'You'll catch cold.' He took off his jacket and wrapped it round her shoulders.

When she had finished the wine, he gave her the silver dish. *No thank you, I'm not hungry*, she almost said, but the protest seemed too much effort, so she took the dish from him. Inside it was a spoonful or two of ice cream. When she put a tiny morsel on her tongue, it melted, sweet and lemony.

She was aware of the chill of the ice cream, the weight of the man's jacket, the blackness of the garden below, and her sense of panic, almost terror. She had become unfamiliar to herself. She was turning into something unrecognizable.

She made herself focus on the man standing beside her. He must be quite old, thirty at least, as much as forty, perhaps. He was tall and broad-shouldered, fair in colouring, his hair a sandy blond, his eyes a washed-out blue-grey. His features were chiselled and handsome, though a little severe, she thought.

He was looking up at the sky. 'You can see so few stars in Berlin,' he said. 'There are so many street lamps they mask the stars. Where I come from in East Prussia, you can see thousands of stars.'

'Tell me what your home is like.'

'It's the most beautiful place in the world, Fräulein Denisov. There's nowhere else like it.' When he smiled, his features softened. 'But no doubt everyone believes that of their home.'

'I have no home,' she said. 'We never stay anywhere for long.'

'But there must be a place you remember fondly, Fräulein,' he said gently. 'A house, for instance, that you recall with affection.'

'No, there's nowhere like that.'

'Then I'm sorry for you. Sommerfeld Castle stands on the edge of a lake. I wish you could see it. In the sunshine, the lake sparkles. All you can see is the glitter of water and the shimmering of the reeds. I don't believe there's any more beautiful place on the earth.'

Miranda imagined herself sailing on a silver lake. Birds would soar overhead and she would trail her fingertips in the water. How peaceful she would feel.

'The wind makes the reeds move like waves,' he said. 'When you travel the paths through the marshes, their sound is all around you, like a thousand whispering voices.'

He fell silent. Looking down at the silver dish, Miranda saw to her surprise that it was empty.

Afterwards, she felt a certain gratitude, because that dish of lemon sorbet was a turning point. After that day, she forced herself to eat again. It was hard at first, but she persevered. Place a little food in her mouth, chew it, swallow it down, don't let herself imagine it settling heavily around her hips and bust. Fruit was easiest: a slice of out-of-season peach, a segment of an orange.

The ghost she had glimpsed that evening in the mirror had frightened her. It was as if she was gradually rubbing herself away, deliberately erasing her identity. She was making less of herself, she was making herself disappear. Yet she had begun to see that self-denial wasn't much of a victory. If she was weak, she wouldn't be able to fight back. She would have won only when she was able to show her father that she was strong enough to live without him – when she, rather than he, chose her occupation, her friends, her lovers.

It was easier to eat if she distracted herself. If there was no one to talk to, she read a novel. Madame Cloutier muttered about bad manners but Miranda sensed that her heart wasn't really in it. Perhaps Madame Cloutier, like Miranda herself, was tired of those long, dreary meals when her charge did anything to avoid eating. If she was dining with her father and reading was impossible, she pretended to be someone else. It was an old habit, a practised means of escape. She was the fat wife of one of her father's business associates, rippling with flesh and strings of pearls, or she was Mrs Ingram, sitting bolt upright with a creak of corsets. She was a character from a book or a film – a maid, a countess, a foreign spy.

Friedrich, Graf von Kahlberg, called at the Denisov apartment two days after their conversation on the balcony.

'Do you have any family, Count?' Miranda asked him.

'My mother,' he told her. 'My father died in the war. I have no brothers or sisters, but I have a great many aunts and uncles and cousins.'

'I had a friend,' said Miranda, 'an English girl called Kay. Sometimes we used to pretend we were sisters.'

'Did she look like you?'

'No, not at all, she was very English – tall and fair, with a lovely complexion.' Miranda smiled. 'But we liked to talk about the same things – we liked to laugh at the same things.'

'What happened to her?'

'My father sent her away.'

'You must miss her. The friendships we make when we're very young often last for life, I think. I still correspond with friends I made at school.'

She studied him. He was imposing, serious and cultivated. 'I can't imagine you at school, Count,' she said. 'I think you must have been a very solemn little boy.'

'Is that how you see me? Solemn?' Shaking his head, he gave a rueful smile. 'And old, too, I daresay. I must seem very old to you.'

'May I be very impertinent, Count von Kahlberg, and ask you how old you are?'

He made a little bow. 'You may be as impertinent as you wish, Fräulein Denisov. I'm thirty-six.' A silence, then he said, 'Is there too great a difference in our ages, do you think?'

'For what?'

'For friendship, naturally. I may consider myself your friend, mayn't I, Fräulein Denisov?'

'Yes, Count, most certainly.'

His demeanour was sober, earnest, austere, perhaps a little forbidding. But every now and then she caught a glimpse of laughter in his eyes – like catching sight of a rare bird in a tree, she thought. His manners were formal and he had the bearing and self-confidence that went with his background and title. He made informed, thoughtful conversation, but did not chatter and never gossiped. Though he was courteous to Konstantin Denisov when they met at balls and soirées, he was not one of her father's creatures. He had no business dealings with her father, was not part of the fawning circle at the Denisov dinner table. He was icily polite to Madame Cloutier, greeting her at functions with a great deal of heel-clicking and bowing, while making it perfectly clear, thought Miranda, that he despised her.

He showed Miranda a photograph of a white house beside a lake. She counted twelve tall, oblong windows along the front façade of the house. A path led through formal gardens to a classical frontage. There was a glimpse of hedges and trees to one side of the building. Sommerfeld Castle was at the heart of a large property of tenant farms and peasants' smallholdings in Masuria, in East Prussia. Such glorious countryside, Friedrich said, a land of lakes, woods and coppices, meadows and low, rolling hills. Of all the seasons, he loved autumn best, when the leaves on the birches turned gold and the migrating wild geese made their V-shaped processions against the pale blue sky. In the coldest, darkest months of winter, the lakes froze and snow covered the woods and the grasslands.

Friedrich von Kahlberg visited Berlin twice a year, to keep in touch with friends and acquaintances, to speak to his broker and banker, and to purchase books and attend the theatre and opera house. Generally, he kept his visits to the capital short, but this year he had stayed a little longer. When Miranda asked him why, he said, *There are certain affairs that occupy my time.*

At a party in a villa in Grünewald, he brought her sweets, fruit, nuts.

She teased him. 'You feed me like a monkey at the zoo.'

'Not at all. But I've noticed that this is what you prefer — that you don't care for long lunches or grand dinners.'

Which was true. The legacy of years of dining with her father was that she had learned to consume wariness and tension along with every mouthful. It was easier to eat on the move, when her mind was occupied — that way, she could take herself by surprise.

She flushed. 'I'm sorry to be so obvious.'

'There's no need to apologize, Fräulein Denisov.' His voice was gentle, his expression kindly. 'I, too, dislike lavishness and show. I'm sometimes obliged to attend banquets and the like, but I prefer the simple, the honest. I'm glad we agree about such things.'

Mists clung to the woods and fields that surrounded Cold Christmas. The buff-coloured remains of cow parsley and brambles on the verges turned white with frost, and ice crackled round the edges of the ponds. Night fell early, so that Miles Culbone was obliged, grudgingly, to put on gaslights and oil lamps by mid-afternoon. When, at six o'clock, Tom drove home to his lodgings, the country lanes were pitch-dark and the low golden sickle of the moon was crystal clear in the black winter sky.

Tom planned to spend Christmas Day with his family in Cambridge before going climbing in Scotland. A week before Christmas, Miles Culbone's cousin, Mrs Fielding, paid a visit to Cold Christmas. Mrs Fielding was a pleasant, pretty, vague woman in her fifties, who always made sure to stop and talk to Tom, though she could never remember his name.

The day after Mrs Fielding's visit, Tom was working in the library when Mrs Bowles, the housekeeper, came into the room to tell Mr Culbone that she had found two rings, a wedding ring and a diamond engagement ring, on the window shelf in the bathroom. Mrs Fielding must have taken them off to wash her hands and forgotten them. Miles Culbone, looking up from his desk, said, 'Oh dear, how inconvenient,' and then, when pressed by Mrs Bowles, suggested she put the rings in an envelope and post them back to Mrs Fielding. When Mrs Bowles demurred, pointing out the value of the rings and the possible unreliability of the post at Christmas, Mr Culbone said tetchily, 'Then she'll just have to collect them the next time she visits, won't she?'

At lunchtime, Tom went to see Mrs Bowles in the kitchen and offered to take the rings back to Mrs Fielding himself. He had intended to drive to London before Christmas, he explained, and Esher, where Mrs Fielding lived, wouldn't be much out of his way. Mrs Bowles looked relieved, cut Tom a large piece of fruit cake and rattled on about the Culbones' family history while he ate it. Mrs Fielding had three daughters, Laura, Nicola and Edith – pretty little things, all grown up now, of course, and they accompanied their mother to Cold Christmas less often these days. A shame, Mrs Bowles added regretfully; she had enjoyed having the girls in the house.

The day before Christmas Eve, Tom drove to Esher. The weather was rawly cold, with frost lingering in the shadows. Esher was an affluent commuter village, its proximity to London and its green and pleasant countryside making it attractive to wealthy financiers and businessmen. There were golf clubs and a cricket club and detached houses surrounded by gardens of lawns, shrubberies and tennis courts.

The Fieldings lived in Laurel Court, a cul-de-sac off Claremont Lane. The eponymous laurels formed a hedge across the front garden, hiding the house from view. Tom parked the MG, crossed the road, and looked over the gate to the house, which had a red-tiled gabled roof and bay windows.

He rang the front doorbell; when there was no answer, he rang again. He had returned to the street, intending to scribble a note and post it with the rings through the letter box, when a voice said, 'Hello? Can I help you?'

Looking up, Tom found himself face to face with a girl. Her appearance, her breathtaking prettiness, momentarily robbed him of speech. His entire consciousness seemed filled by her heart-shaped face, framed with dark curls that peeped out from beneath the brim of her hat.

Tom heard himself blurt out, 'Have we met? Haven't I seen you somewhere before?'

'I don't think so,' she said with a smile.

He made a wild guess. 'Are you Miss Laura Fielding?'

'I'm Miss Edie Fielding. Laura's Mrs Radcliffe now. Are you looking for her?'

'No, for your mother. My name's Tom Blacklock. I work for Miles Culbone.'

'Poor you,' she said drily.

He noticed that she was carrying a large brown paper parcel. He said, 'Shall I give you a hand with that?'

'How sweet of you.' The parcel dropped heavily into his arms. 'Christmas presents,' she explained as she opened the gate. 'I'm always relieved, aren't you, when the shops close at last and you know that whatever you've forgotten, you can't do anything about it.'

Miss Fielding unlocked the front door and went into the porch. There was an inner door to a hallway, which she opened, calling out, 'Yoo-hoo, Mummy, I'm home!' When there was no reply, she said, 'Come in, Mr Blacklock. You can put the parcel down there. Would you shut the front door? It's freezing outside.'

There was just enough room to put the parcel on the hall stand, which was burdened with coats, scarves, gloves and umbrellas. Holly branches decorated the top of the stand and paper streamers were threaded through the wooden banisters beside the stairs.

Miss Fielding took off her coat. Beneath it, she was wearing a grey wool skirt and a violet-coloured jersey. She took off her hat and shook out her curls.

'What was it you said you wanted, Mr Blacklock?'

'I didn't, actually. But I brought these for your mother.' Tom delved in his pocket and took out the envelope containing the rings. 'She left them at Cold Christmas.'

Miss Fielding peered inside the envelope. 'Oh, my goodness, not again! Mummy leaves her rings in the strangest places. She left them in the powder room at Harrods once. I think they must be charmed because she always seems to get them back. How kind of you, Mr Blacklock. Why don't you wait here while I find Mummy.'

He was shown into a drawing room. Bay windows, framed by floral curtains, looked out to the front garden. There was a bundle of pink knitting on one of the armchairs so Tom sat in the other one.

After a few minutes, Edie came back. 'Mummy's collecting Laura and Helen from the railway station so you'll have to make do with me, I'm afraid. Would you like a cup of tea – or perhaps a sherry?'

'I don't want to put you to any trouble.'

'I was going to have a sherry myself.'

'Sherry would be splendid, then.'

Miss Fielding poured out the drinks. 'I haven't been to Cold Christmas for ages. Mummy visits, though she can't stand Uncle Miles.'

The door opened and a young woman came into the room. Dark and striking, she was unmistakably one of Edie's sisters. She was wearing slacks and a crimson jersey and her hair was tousled.

'Have you an aspirin, Edie?' she asked. 'I have the most frightful head and there's nothing in the bathroom. Where's Mummy? And where on earth is Muriel?'

'Mummy's gone to the station. And Muriel's lying down. She says she's got stomach ache.'

'Muriel's bone idle, that's all that's wrong with her. And Dan's late – too thoughtless of him.' She looked cross. She noticed Tom, who had stood up. 'Who are you?'

'He's called Tom Blacklock,' said Edie. 'Mr Blacklock, this is my sister, Mrs Hetherington.'

'Pleased to meet you,' she said offhandedly.

'Mr Blacklock works for Uncle Miles.'

'Good Lord, how dreary.' There was a wail from upstairs.

She looked harassed. 'Oh dear. Aspirin, darling,' she said to Edie.

'In my bag.'

'You couldn't be a love and give Nanny a hand, could you? Only I simply must have a hot bath, I feel such a wreck, and they always set each other off.'

After she had left the room, Edie said, 'The twins are the most frightful wailers, poor Nicky hardly gets a moment's peace. Hang on, I won't be a mo.' She, too, hurried upstairs.

In the sisters' absence, Tom wandered round the room, glancing at the family photos. There were silver-framed pictures of three little girls in party frocks, wearing ribbons in their hair, as well as more recent photographs. One portrait was of Nicky in a white gown and veil, with Edie and Laura, presumably, as bridesmaids on either side of her. There was a more recent snapshot of Edie, wearing a summer dress and a straw hat, sitting on a beach.

A footstep; Tom turned. Edie was cradling against her shoulder a baby cocooned in a white woollen shawl. 'This is Cherry,' said Edie. 'Isn't she gorgeous?'

Tom made suitably admiring noises. He was supposed to be looking at the baby, but his gaze kept returning to Edie.

There was the sound of a car engine. Edie went to the window. 'Oh look, there's Mummy and Laura.' She waved vigorously. 'Oh, and Dan's turned up at last.' She left the room again. Tom heard her call out, 'Hello, Mummy! Thank goodness you're home, Cherry's working herself up to howl and Nicky's in the bath. So lovely to see you, Laura darling. You look so well. And Helen, my favourite girl. How are you, sweetie?'

Tom saw that two cars, a little Austin and a larger Wolseley, were now parked on the gravel. A longer wait, this time, during which the house echoed with footsteps and babies crying.

Mrs Fielding came into the drawing room. 'Oh!' she said, seeing Tom. 'How lovely to meet you. But how rude of us to leave you all alone.' She was looking at him in a rather puzzled manner. 'Are you one of Edie's friends?'

'My name's Tom Blacklock. I work for Mr Culbone.'

'Oh yes! I remember. How nice of you to call, Mr Blacklock.'

'You left your rings at the house the other day. I thought I'd better return them.'

She beamed at him. 'So silly of me. And so thoughtful of you.'

Edie appeared briefly in the doorway, then rushed off to find Muriel to make tea.

Mrs Fielding said to Tom, 'What are your plans for Christmas, Mr . . . I'm so sorry . . .'

'Blacklock,' said Tom. 'I'm spending Christmas Day with my family, in Cambridge, and then I'm going to Scotland, to climb.'

'Wonderful,' she said vaguely. 'Only I always think, why not have Christmas in January, rather than in December? January is such an unpleasant month, and it would cheer us all up. But could one change the date of Our Lord's birthday?'

Tom was spared answering by the sound of raised voices in the hall. Nicky and Dan came into the room. Nicky was saying irritably, 'Too impossible of you, when you know how awful the twins are at this time of day,' and Dan, who was black-haired, handsome and cross-looking, said rather heatedly, 'I told you, I was chasing the Simmonds contract. What do you expect me to do, leave halfway through a meeting with the managing director?'

Mrs Fielding said soothingly, 'Daniel, dear, you look so tired.

You must sit down and have a rest. Ah, here's the tea. Muriel, why don't we cut the Christmas cake? Mr Hetherington would like some, wouldn't you, Daniel darling? And you'll have some cake, too, won't you, Mr, um . . .'

'That's very kind of you,' said Tom 'but—'

Nicky said sulkily, 'And we'll be late for the Travises. The only decent party this Christmas, I've been looking forward to it for ages.'

'I told you we'd be home in time for the Travises.'

'The twins will never settle – the journey—'

'That's what we pay the bloody nanny for, isn't it?'

'Dan!' said Nicky, looking shocked.

'Nanny and the twins must stay here overnight,' said Mrs Fielding firmly. 'I shall drive them to your house tomorrow morning. You must go to the party and have fun, darlings, and not worry about anything.'

Tom caught sight of a flash of mauve sweater in the hallway. In the bustle of the maid coming into the room carrying a tray of cake and biscuits, he escaped.

'Sorry,' Edie murmured to him. 'It's a bit of a madhouse today.'

'I'd better go,' he said.

'Must you?' She took his coat and scarf down from the stand. As she handed them to him, he caught a breath of her scent, which made him think of beech woods, bluebells, spring.

She gave him a mischievous glance. 'I must say, you don't look the sort of man who'd work for Uncle Miles.'

'How should a man who works for Miles Culbone look?'

'Old and grey and dried up. It must be awfully boring, stuck out there in the middle of nowhere. How do you stand it?'

'It suits me just now. And the house is extraordinary.'

'Isn't it? I've always loved it. Mummy hopes that when Uncle Miles dies he'll leave Cold Christmas to one of us. That's why she visits him, to remind him that we're his nearest and dearest.' She shrugged. 'I'm sorry to be so frank, but I believe in being honest, don't you? By the way, is that your car across the road?'

'Yes. Would you like to see it?'

'I'd love to.'

She put on her coat and they left the house. 'Such an adorable little car,' she said with a sigh, walking round the MG.

'Do you drive?'

'Not yet. Mummy's offered to teach me, but she's such a dreadful driver I'm worried I'd end up doing everything wrong. And Dan offered, but he's always so busy and anyway he has such a foul temper.'

Tom cleared his throat. 'If you'd like to learn, I could teach you.'

She raised her brows, looking at him. 'Do you think you'd be a good teacher, Mr Blacklock?'

'I don't see why not.'

'It might be rather difficult, with you in Suffolk and me in Surrey, but it's a kind offer.'

Seeing her wrap her arms round herself, he said, 'It's cold, you should go back into the house.'

'What, and listen to Nicky and Dan quarrelling?' She frowned. 'Isn't it funny how some people, even though they love each other, seem to set out to annoy each other?'

'They do both seem rather fiery.'

'Nicky is definitely the fieriest of the three of us. Is it a good thing, do you think, to be fiery? Heroines in romantic films are often fiery. And what's the opposite? Docile? Placid?' She made a face. 'So dreary.'

'Serene,' he suggested.

'Yes, that's better.' She glanced back at the house. 'I suppose I ought to go back to the fray. It's been lovely meeting you, Mr Blacklock, and thank you so much for returning Mummy's rings. Especially at Christmas, when you must be busy.'

Get a move on, Tom, he thought, then said aloud, 'Do you like going to the theatre, Miss Fielding?'

'Very much.'

'What sort of thing do you enjoy?'

'Dramas . . . comedies . . .'

'What a coincidence, so do I. Shall I see if I can get us tickets for a show in the West End? We could discuss the driving lessons.'

She was smiling. 'When were you thinking of?'

'I'm away till January the tenth. The twelfth's a Saturday, isn't it? What about then?'

'I'm afraid I've an engagement that night.'

'The following Saturday – no, hang on—'

She laughed. 'Have you a pen and paper?'

He took a pen from his jacket pocket and found a crumpled receipt for petrol in the glove box of the car. She wrote a number on it.

'That's my phone number,' she said. 'Call me after Christmas.'

Hurrying along Piccadilly, Kay paused to check her reflection in a shop window. Pale green polo-neck jumper, grey slacks, navy coat and knitted beret. She rearranged her fringe with her fingers, took her lipstick out of her bag and then put it back in again, saying to herself, 'Well, it's only Tom.' Then she walked briskly on.

Inside the pub, she caught sight of him, sitting in a corner, a glass of beer on the table in front of him. He rose and hugged her.

'How are you, Tom?'

'I'm very well. And you?'

'Fit as a fiddle.'

'What can I get you, Kay?'

She asked for a half of bitter.

When he returned from the bar, Kay raised her glass. 'To the overthrow of tyrants.' Tom echoed her toast. 'How's Mr Culbone?'

'The same as ever. What about you? How's the school?'

She smiled. 'Still a beacon of freedom and light.'

'Are you still a vegetarian?'

'Only when I'm at school. As soon as I go home the first thing I do is make myself a bacon sandwich and devour it at great speed. Then I feel terribly guilty.' She gave him a close look. 'Tom. Are you all right? You look a little . . . well, *dazed*.'

He said, in a bemused way, 'I've just met the most beautiful girl.'

'Where?'

'Esher.'

'Very posh. What's she called?'

'Edie Fielding. She's related to Miles Culbone.'

'But she doesn't take after him, presumably?'

'No, no, not at all. She's utterly lovely. Dark-haired, with the most extraordinary eyes – blue, but not an ordinary blue, a violet-blue. And so sweet-natured, and . . .'

The eulogy continued; Kay said, when she had the chance, 'Goodness, Tom, I don't think I've ever heard you so keen on anyone – or anything, for that matter.'

He blinked, looked surprised. 'What? Is that how you think of me? Half-hearted, apathetic?'

'No, not exactly, but not – not particularly *committed* to anything.'

He looked put out. 'Just because I don't go waving banners and making speeches—'

'I've never thought of you as the *passionate* sort, that's all.'

'I see. You have me pigeon-holed as a dry-as-dust academic. A younger version of Miles Culbone, perhaps.'

'Don't be silly, Tom.'

'A dabbler, then, a dilettante.'

Now, she too was annoyed. 'Well, aren't you?'

He looked affronted. 'Even if I don't spend my time roaring around like you, Kay, trying to change the world, it doesn't mean I don't care.'

Exasperating man, Kay thought. It was his fault, of course – he took offence too easily and, typical man, was incapable of admitting that he had any defects.

He said, 'What about you, then, Kay?'

'What do you mean, what about me?'

'How's whatsisname? The boyfriend?'

'Laurence?' She was forced to admit, 'We've split up.'

'Hah.' It was an irritatingly triumphant *hah*.

'He wasn't right for me, that's all,' she said quickly. 'He was very dear, but too, too *vague*. He never seemed to live in the real world. He was *so* spiritual, *so* gentle, it became rather wearing. Anyway, he's left the school and gone to live in an artist's colony in Cornwall.' Honesty made her add, 'What bothered me most was that it was Laurence who finished with *me*. I was trying to think of a tactful way to break it off but before I could, he told me he'd met someone else.' She looked at her watch. 'I must dash, I'm afraid. Peace Pledge Union meeting – another of my attempts to change the world.' But she could never be cross with him for long so she kissed his cheek. 'Don't forget to write, Tom,' she said, and left the pub.

Edie Fielding had felt attracted to Tom that first afternoon they met in Esher. His dark, dishevelled good looks were of the type she admired, and his kindness in driving out of his way to return her mother's rings had touched her. She had rarely felt so quickly attracted to a man. In the past, she had been as happy spending an evening with a group of friends as she had been dining alone with an admirer. Recently, though, she had begun to feel a little anxious. In November, she had turned twenty-three. Both her elder sisters had been engaged by the age of twenty-three, and she hadn't even a steady boyfriend. Always popular, always sought after, it had come as a shock to realize that there was a danger that she might be left on the shelf. Though she and her mother were close, she did not intend to live at home for ever. She wanted a husband, a home, children.

Edie's previous boyfriends had worked in banks, offices or hospitals. They rented a mansion flat in Highbury or were buying a house in Walton-on-Thames. They played tennis or rugby at the weekends and took her to cocktail parties and nightclubs, and introduced her to their parents over Sunday lunch. They were attentive, pleasant, predictable, and just a little dull.

Tom was different. Tom disliked cocktail parties and night-clubs. On their first date, they went to a play at the Wyndham Theatre. The following weekend, they walked up Box Hill in a rainstorm, which Edie, who had never thought of herself as a walker, found herself enjoying enormously. When Tom took her out to supper the first time, it was to an odd little place in Soho rather than the Ivy or the Connaught. One of the waiters placed his hand on his heart and sang a fragment of opera as he looked into her eyes, and the couple on the adjacent table had a flaming row that ended in the girl slapping her escort's face and walking out. But the food was delicious.

In March, it was Edie's eldest sister Laura's thirtieth birthday. Edie had had to twist Tom's arm rather to attend the celebration, because of his aversion to nightclubs. When she met him beforehand for a drink in the American Bar of the Savoy, she adjusted his tie, smoothed his hair, brushed the rumpled back of his jacket, said, 'You'll do,' and gave him a kiss.

They went on to the Café de Paris in Leicester Square. Sparks of light caught on champagne glasses and diamond necklaces, and the swing band was playing 'Goody, Goody'. Laura and Tony were already there by the time Edie and Tom arrived. Edie made the introductions. She had been looking forward to introducing Tom to Laura, her favourite sister. Laura, who was looking divine in peacock-blue satin, exchanged a few words with Tom, and then gave Edie an approving smile.

Laura's set arrived in dribs and drabs. Champagne was poured, toasts were made, and the band played 'For She's a Jolly Good Fellow' for Laura. After Laura and Tony had danced, Laura crossed the floor to Edie, her hand tucked into the arm of a tall, fair-haired man.

'Edie, Tom, this is my dear friend, Charles Dangerfield. You must tell Edie and Tom about the concerts, Charles.'

Charles Dangerfield had an ascetic look, a long, thin face and pale blue, intelligent eyes. And a monocle. Tom said, 'Concerts?' and Dangerfield, blinking, said, 'Do you enjoy classical music?' and Tom said, 'Yes, certainly.'

'It's something I dreamed up a couple of months ago,' said Dangerfield. 'I hold a concert at my house in Portland Place on the first Wednesday evening of the month. It's a modest affair, about forty guests, but we try to put on something good. Chamber music, mostly, because of the limited space. Have you heard of the Belgrave Quartet? They played for us last week. They're recently formed and very talented. The first violinist is a friend of mine.'

'It sound wonderful,' said Edie.

'It's great fun, actually, you should come along. Half past eight. We serve a light supper.'

'I'd love to.'

'And you, Blacklock?'

'I'm afraid I can't,' said Tom.

'Tom works in deepest Suffolk,' explained Edie.

'Is that so? A shame.'

They stayed at the nightclub until the early hours of the morning and then decamped en masse to Laura's house in Russell Square. After powdering her nose, Edie stole a peek into the nursery. Helen was fast asleep, her favourite doll pressed against her cheek. Edie peered into the crib at the new baby, two-month-old Grace. She was a dear little thing, with fine, perfect features and downy golden hair. A thumb was clamped to her mouth and she was sucking hard.

Laura came into the nursery. 'All's well,' whispered Edie. 'She is so utterly gorgeous, Lo.'

'She's rather a peach, isn't she? Though I'm afraid she'll end up with teeth like a rabbit if she keeps on sucking her thumb.' Laura took Edie's arm. 'Must check my face and have a ciggie. Come and talk to me.'

They went into Laura's bedroom. Laura sat at the dressing table, frowning as she peered at her reflection. She lit two cigarettes and gave one to Edie.

'Biscuits in the ginger jar, if you're ravenous, darling. How's Mummy?'

'Very well. She's knitting a little dress for Grace. It has pink hearts round the neckline, you'll love it.'

'Sweet of her,' said Laura.

'Well?' said Edie, looking at Laura expectantly. 'What did you think?'

'Your Tom?' Laura smiled. 'Divine. Dark and brooding, but not too brooding, if you know what I mean.'

'Oh, absolutely.'

'Are you madly in love with him, Edie?'

Edie did not reply. Laura, who was powdering her face with a swansdown puff, looked back at her. 'Oh. You are, aren't you?'

'I think I might be.'

'How long have you two been together?'

'Three months.' Edie broke a biscuit in half.

'He dances well,' said Laura.

'Doesn't he? I hoped he might, but you can't always tell, looking at a man, can you?' Edie ate half the biscuit, then slid off her shoes and lay back on Laura's bed, her head propped up on her hand. 'I could never marry a man who couldn't dance.'

Laura, who had opened a lipstick, turned round on the stool to face Edie. 'It is serious, then?'

'Oh no,' said Edie, flustered. 'Well, Tom hasn't said anything . . . I only meant . . . and we haven't been seeing each other very long . . .' Then, collecting herself, she explained, 'I have a list, you see.'

'A list?'

'Of the qualities I'm looking for in a husband. Being able to dance is essential, and so is having a good temper. Speaking a foreign language is desirable, but not *absolutely* necessary. I don't mean,' she added quickly, noticing Laura's expression, 'that I tick things off in a little book.'

'Thank heaven for that.'

'I'm only being practical,' said Edie, rather defensively.

Laura had gone back to applying her lipstick. 'How well does Tom score on your list?'

'Quite well. He can dance, he can speak two foreign languages, and he drives a car and has good manners. He's a little untidy but always presentable. I think that's so important.'

'Sounds perfect. I should snap him up.'

'But,' said Edie with a sigh, 'he hasn't much of a job, only working for Uncle Miles.'

'Perhaps Tom doesn't need a job. Perhaps he has a private income.'

'I don't think so. He hasn't mentioned anything like that.' Edie fiddled with her bracelet. 'And I don't want to be poor all my life.'

Laura pressed her lips together to blot them. 'Money is terribly useful. It makes everything so much easier. It's so dreary being poor.'

'You don't think, then,' asked Edie hesitantly, 'that love conquers all?'

'Oh, I'm sure it can,' said Laura, looking doubtful. 'Tell me about Tom's family. What are they like?'

'I don't know. I haven't met them.'

Laura wound her thick, glossy, chestnut hair into a knot at the nape of her neck. 'Don't look so glum, darling, I shouldn't think it means anything. As you said, you haven't been seeing each other long. I didn't meet Tony's parents for ages.'

'Yes, but they were in Singapore.'

'And your Tom's buried in Suffolk with ghastly Uncle Miles.'

'And some weekends he goes climbing.' Edie sighed.

Laura said gently, 'Edie, dearest, a man has to have his hobbies. You know what Tony's like about his wretched fishing.'

Edie sat up, folding her feet beneath her. 'Tom doesn't mind being on his own, Laura. Whether he's working for Uncle Miles or he's on top of some freezing mountain, he doesn't mind being on his own. He hasn't said so to me, but I can tell. And the thing is, I *do* mind. I hate being on my own, I always have done, it makes me miserable.'

Laura gave her sister a kiss. 'Men are such utterly different creatures to us, darling. Just because Tom can sometimes be rather solitary doesn't mean he doesn't adore you. Now, powder your nose and let's go and join the others.'

Edie was staying with Laura that night. At three in the morning, she and Tom said goodbye in the hall.

She said, 'You had a nice evening, didn't you, Tom?'

'Terrific.'

His arms were round her; she liked the fact that the top of her head fitted neatly beneath his chin. She murmured, 'You liked Laura, didn't you?'

'Very much.'

'Isn't she beautiful?'

'Not as beautiful as you are.'

'Sweet of you,' said Edie, fishing slightly, 'but I've always thought she was the prettiest of the three of us.'

'No. You're much prettier.'

'I'd give anything to have hair like Laura's.'

'I prefer your curls.' He kissed one. 'And your face is more expressive.'

'Laura never smiles because she doesn't want wrinkles.'

'Laura hasn't any dimples. I love your dimples.' He kissed both carefully.

'Mr Dangerfield was nice, wasn't he?'

'I thought he was a bit of a stuffed shirt.'

'Oh Tom.'

'And patronizing. And that monocle – so pretentious.'

'Oh, honestly, Tom. He was perfectly sweet.'

But she couldn't get properly cross with him because he was stroking her back and caressing the curve of her neck in a way that sent little shivers up her spine. Then his mouth found hers and they kissed until Tony, who could be rather crass, came out of the drawing room and, seeing them, called out, 'Uh-oh, fetch a bucket of cold water, Laura, the hall's going up in flames,' and they drew apart.

With the coming of spring, recovery. Leaves burst from the branches of the trees and, in the garden behind the Denisovs' rented villa, daffodils and narcissi bobbed their white and yellow heads. Miranda had put on a little weight, regained a little appetite. The softer, warmer air tempted her outdoors. Walking to the shops with Madame Cloutier did not tire her, as it had before. She walked for longer, faster, partly to test herself and to make herself stronger, and partly to tease Madame Cloutier, who huffed along in her wake, black-stockinged legs whirring, protesting at her speed.

Yet, though she was regaining her strength, she knew in her heart that all her difficulties remained, unchanged. This was only a lull, a time in which to draw breath. In the last six months her attitude to her father had hardened. She had always been on guard with him but, until recently, she had tried to be the daughter she believed he wanted her to be: pretty, light-hearted, amusing, decorative. Lately the desire to please had faded. Her father himself had killed it, she thought, when he had sent Kay away, and when he had prevented her from seeing Olivier.

Once, some years ago, on a beach in the south of France, she had seen a girl – eight or nine years old, perhaps – fall and cut her knee on a sharp stone. Her father had picked her up and comforted her and had bandaged her knee with his handkerchief. Watching them, Miranda had felt at first on edge, expecting the father to scold his daughter for crying or for her carelessness. Then, astonishment that he was not angry, that he should comfort his daughter so tenderly. And then, a bitter envy. What would it be like, to have a father she was not afraid of? What would it be like to feel, when he embraced her, perfectly safe?

She knew that her father had not forgiven her for her refusal to marry Herr Reimann. She had defied him and he hated that. There would be other Herr Reimanns, she had no doubt, other men of her father's choosing in whose company she would find herself, with little regard for her happiness or needs. How long would she be able to withstand her father's demands? In another test of strength, which one of them would win?

The atmosphere of crisis in the household persisted. Telegrams arrived at all times of the day and night and the Paris house was to be sold. These days, the men invited to Konstantin Denisov's dinner table were flashily dressed and lean, their accents not the best, hardly the sort to pass in the grand salons and restaurants her father liked to frequent. Their gazes followed her, hungry and bold, and their faces reminded her of the faces of wolves. There was one in particular who frightened her, a quiet, dark man who never smiled, and who once, catching a moth that fluttered round the lamplight, crushed it between forefinger and thumb until the wings turned to powder.

The Graf von Kahlberg, who had returned to Berlin, called at the Denisovs' house to invite Fräulein Denisov and Frau Cloutier to a picnic at Wannsee that Sunday. At the lake, children paddled in the shallows and a few hardy swimmers struck out deeper into the water. Rugs were spread out on the grass, grandmothers dozed in deckchairs, wrapped up in cardigans and coats, their legs encased in thick black woollen stockings.

Miranda wandered a little way from the others, along the shore of the lake. Slipping off her sandals and stockings, she dipped her feet into the water.

Friedrich called out, 'Is it cold?'

'Ice-cold.' She waded a short way into the lake and laughed. 'It takes your breath away. But it's glorious.'

'You remind me of someone,' he said. 'Someone I once knew.'

She returned to the shore. 'Who?'

'She was called Elisabeth. But to me, she was always Elli.'

'Where did you meet her?'

'In my cradle, I think.' He smiled. 'Elli's family estate borders on Sommerfeld. My mother and Elli's mother were great friends. Elli was two years younger than me. When we were children, we played together all the time.'

Miranda sat down on the grass. She patted the ground beside her. 'Sit with me, Count. I can see Madame Cloutier glowering at me, but let's just let her glower. Tell me about Elli.'

He sat down. 'She was so spirited, so full of life. Like you, she didn't care for being told what to do. Her governess would scold her and try to make her study, but Elli would always find a way to escape outdoors.'

'What did she like to do?'

'To swim, to dance, to skate, to play games.' His face darkened.

117

'And to ride. We did everything together, Elli and I. Our mothers were delighted to see us such good friends. They planned that we would marry. We were both only children, our estates lay side by side, and it seemed the ideal outcome.'

'What happened? Did you grow apart?'

'No, not at all. I was sent to school in Potsdam but Elli and I still saw each other in the holidays. After I left school, I toured Europe in the company of my tutor. When I returned, I went straight to the university of Heidelberg. So, what with one thing and another, Elli and I didn't see each other for two years. After my first year at Heidelberg, in the summer, I went home.'

'Did you see Elli again?'

'As soon as I saw her I realized she'd changed. She was no longer a little girl in pinafores and plaits. She had grown into a beautiful young woman. I'd loved her before, but this was different. I adored her, I wanted to marry her, and by some miracle she felt the same. We became engaged, our mothers were overjoyed and a ball was held to celebrate our engagement. We planned to marry as soon as I left university.'

The crowds were thinning out; some of the picnickers were packing up their belongings and scooping up their tired children. Friedrich said, 'Would you mind if we walked, Fräulein Denisov?'

They headed along the shoreline. Miranda carried her stockings and sandals. A rowing boat splashed in the water, the young women inside it shrieking with pleasure. Deeper in the heart of the lake, the white triangular sails of yachts caught the sunlight.

As they walked, Friedrich began to speak again. 'Six months after our engagement, I received the terrible news that Elli had been killed in a riding accident. Her horse had taken a fence clumsily and had thrown her. Her neck was broken. She died instantly.'

'Oh no, how dreadful!' She turned to him. 'And how terrible for you.'

'I went home, I attended the funeral, and then I returned to Heidelberg. What else could I do? I continued to study, I saw my friends now and then. But inside, I was dead. Yes, that's the only way I can describe it. Elli was only nineteen. Her death seemed so senseless. It seemed to make a mockery of everything I believed in.'

'How did you bear it?'

'I did what I had to do. After army service, I returned to the estate and took over much of the work from my mother. My responsibilities, my duty to Sommerfeld and to my country, helped me endure what had happened. Without that, I believe I might have died of grief. And in time I was able to leave my mourning behind me. I listened to music once more. I could read poetry again. I began to live again, a little. Our powers of recovery are remarkable, don't you agree, Fräulein? A cut finger . . . a broken heart . . .'

Cuts left a scar, she thought. Breaks to the heart left their mark. She took his arm as they walked along the shore. The lake was spread out in front of them, the grand villas on the far shore, the yachts and pleasure steamers plying the water.

'It was a long time ago,' he said. 'Now, I find it hard to remember her face clearly. But you, Fräulein Denisov – there is something about you that makes me think of her.'

Leaving his side, Miranda walked across the sand to the shallows, and, crouching, placed the flat of her hand on the surface.

'What are you doing?' he asked.

'Do you see the little fishes? When I was a child – I was about six or seven years old, I think – I went with my mother to visit my grandmother in England. There was a stream at the bottom of her garden. I used to lie on my stomach for hours, watching the fish. I longed to be a part of their world, it looked so calm and green and beautiful. I used to put my hand on top of the water, like this, and close my eyes and imagine that I was swimming through the reeds, like the fish. I thought the stones and the shells were the fishes' homes and the water-weed must be like a forest to them.' She smiled. 'It's the only time I remember travelling alone with my mother. On the train from London, she reminded me of my manners. She told me that I must speak English all the time and that I mustn't curtsey when I met my grandmother because it would be considered affected. I was a wretchedly fanciful child, always imagining myself to be a princess or a fairy, and I expect my mother wanted me to behave like a nice, modest English girl. She told me other things, too – that there were subjects I mustn't speak of. I mustn't tell my grandmother about the way my father lost his temper, for instance, and I mustn't tell her about the irregularities of our household. Of course, back then, I didn't understand what the word "irregularities" meant. I do now, though.' She looked down at the darting minnows. Then she said, her voice low, 'I am not like your Elli at all, Count von Kahlberg. I'm sure that she was good and kind and innocent. I am not like her at all.'

A cloud crossed the sun and, for a moment, the glitter was gone from the lake. Miranda stood up. 'Shall we walk back to the others? Or I'm afraid Madame Cloutier might have a fit.'

They headed back across the sand. Suddenly, Miranda laughed. 'Though I'd promised my mother to be a polite, quiet little girl, I don't think I can have been at all. I remember dancing a tarantella in a room with a pink carpet while an old gentleman with a handlebar moustache clapped his hands. I was always such a show-off. And I'm afraid my grandmother must have disliked me because I never saw her again.'

Later that week, they rode through the Tiergarten, the large, wooded area in the heart of Berlin. Wide, straight avenues cut through the forest and a river meandered, every now and then widening into a pond or lake. Friedrich was riding a short way ahead of Miranda, along a grassy path which led off from the main avenue, narrowing as it made its way deeper into the woodland. Mist greyed the hollows and a pheasant rose into the air with a sudden beating of wings.

Miranda said, 'You're very quiet today, Count.'

Friedrich turned to look at her. 'Am I? Then I must apologize, Fräulein Denisov, for being such dull company.'

'Not at all. Has something upset you?'

The path widened, and they rode side by side. He said, 'I had a letter from my mother this morning. There are some problems with the estate. Nothing serious, but it's made me realize I've been in Berlin long enough.'

'Must you go home?'

'At the end of the week, yes.'

'I'm to go away as well. My father has told me that we're to leave for Paris in a few days' time.'

'When do you expect to return to Germany, Fräulein?'

'I don't know. I never know. A few weeks, perhaps – or a year.'

'Does it suit you, this nomadic life? Is this how you would always wish to live?'

'I used to think so.'

'And now?'

'And now I'm not so sure.' She had learned, she thought, how other people lived. She had learned of the houses they stayed in, perhaps all their lives, and the close friends they'd known for years. She wondered what it would be like to belong somewhere, to a house, a street, a town, a village. To belong to something – or to someone.

'I must be frank with you, Fräulein Denisov,' Friedrich said. 'It isn't only the letter from my mother that's made me thoughtful today. I became embroiled in a foolish argument last night. An old friend from my university days invited me to dinner at his house. There were a number of us – most of us were at Heidelberg together, though there were others with whom Bruno, my college friend, has become acquainted at party meetings. The Nazi Party, naturally, Fräulein – it's the only political party tolerated in Berlin at present. Bruno has become very politically minded in recent years. But then, he was always something of a firebrand when we were at university. Anyway, a great deal of wine was drunk, as it tends to be on such occasions, and the discussion turned to the army, and to the defence of our borders. And then, inevitably, to the Treaty of Versailles, and what it's done to our country.'

She must have looked blank, because he said, 'I speak of the treaty of nineteen nineteen, Fräulein, which apportioned conquered and disputed land after the end of the war.'

'Oh, I see.'

'Prussia was cut in half by a corridor that gives Poland access to the Baltic Sea. East Prussia, where I live, now exists as an island, separated from the rest of Germany. We think of ourselves as a province, set apart. When we travel to Berlin, we say we're going to the Reich.'

'Does that trouble you, Count?'

'In the years after the war, travelling through the Polish Corridor wasn't a pleasant experience. One was obliged to draw down the blinds in the carriage of the train and travel in darkness. Germans were always afraid they would be accused of violating some regulation.' Friedrich sighed. 'The treaty took land away from Germany. In the past, I've felt angry about that, as have many others. But I've come to believe that it was a price worth paying for peace. And I said so last night. But one of the other fellows there — one of Bruno's new friends — was of the opinion that it's a matter of honour to return the land that was lost to Germany.' Friedrich's face darkened. 'The fellow accused me of wanting to avoid war at any cost. He actually said to me, *at the cost of pride and honour*. Honour! What can a man like that know of honour? He was a blustering, conceited fellow who loved the sound of his own voice. It was plain to me that his purpose in Berlin was to secure status and position.' Friedrich put his fist to his heart. 'To honour your family and your country truly is to feel it *here*. To desire above all else to guard them, to protect them.'

'You're very passionate, Count.'

'I'm afraid he angered me. I regret it now. One shouldn't allow oneself to be angered by such men.'

'There's nothing wrong with passion, surely?'

'Passion can take away reason. And,' again, he sighed, 'he had reason on his side, after all. The peace settlement did us no favours.'

They heard voices; a couple, the woman holding a dog's lead, headed towards them down the path.

When they were alone again, Friedrich said, 'I'm old enough to remember the war, Fräulein Denisov. In nineteen fourteen,

Russian troops entered East Prussia. I remember the columns of refugees fleeing the armies of the Tsar, driven from their farmland, their carts and wagons laden with their possessions. Sommerfeld escaped only by the skin of its teeth. War is destruction, it's chaos made actual. And it's the weak – women, children, the old and infirm – who suffer most at such times. Men can sometimes profit by war, but the rest of humanity hardly ever. Of course, there are times when war is unavoidable. But I wouldn't choose for my family to live through such times again.'

Reaching a small, open glade, pocked with rabbit holes, they paused to catch their breath. The air was cool, but Miranda knew that soon the sun would burn away the mist and shafts of light would fall between the leaves.

They dismounted from their horses. She heard Friedrich say, 'May I write to you, Fräulein, when you're away?'

'Yes, of course, if Madame Cloutier permits it.'

'Thank you. I'll speak to her today. And I promise not to write of dull things, such as politics.'

She smiled at him. 'Write whatever you like, Count – I adore receiving letters.'

He frowned. 'This morning, before I came to your house, I was thinking about our conversation at Wannsee.'

'About Elli?'

'Yes, and about you, Fräulein Denisov. I remembered what you said to me that day. You judge yourself too harshly. You *are* good. You *are* kind.'

'I can't agree with you, Count,' she said lightly. 'I have a great many faults. As I told you, I'm a dreadful show-off, and my father often scolds me for spending a ridiculous amount of money on clothes.'

His expression was serious. 'I know – forgive me – that you were very unhappy when we first met.'

Miranda looked away. At the top of a tree, a blackbird sang. She said quietly, 'I was very lonely. I would have liked to wave a magic wand and become a different person, in a different place. But that sort of thing only happens in fairy tales.'

'No, that's not true,' he said. He took her hands, crushing them between his own. 'When I'm with you, I am a different person. With you, I have felt alive again. It is possible to start again. It is possible to have a second chance. You must believe me – I know this now. Share my life, Fräulein Denisov, and you can put whatever unhappiness you have suffered behind you.'

She heard her own quick intake of breath as, raising her hands, he pressed them to his lips, closing his eyes.

'Marry me, Miranda,' he said. 'I will give you my devotion and protection. I will give you a home and a refuge. I will give you anything you want. Marry me.'

Chapter Five

Tom and Edie arrived at the Blacklocks' Cambridge home in time for Sunday lunch. Tom introduced Edie to his mother, who was in the kitchen, and his father, who was working in his study. Tom's sister, Minnie, who had the weekend off from her nursing training at Addenbrooke's Hospital, was in a back room that looked out over the garden, lounging in a chair, reading a novel.

Tom introduced Edie and Minnie to each other. Minnie said, 'How lovely to meet you at last. Tom's been talking about you for ages.'

'And he's told me all about you, too, Minnie,' said Edie.

'Not *all*, surely,' said Minnie. 'I shouldn't think he's told you that when we were little he buried my favourite doll in the garden.'

'No, he didn't tell me that.' Edie turned to look at Tom, who was lying on the floor, rolling a ball to an old labrador dog. 'That was very naughty of you, Tom.'

'And I bet he didn't tell you that he once got so drunk he lost his front door key and ended up sleeping all night in the potting shed.'

'Shut up, Minnie,' said Tom.

'It was snowing, and in the morning he was so cold Ma had to sit him in front of the stove and cover him with hot-water bottles.'

Tom threw the ball at his sister. Minnie shot out a hand and caught it and stuck her tongue out at him. Edie said, 'And how are you enjoying nursing, Minnie?'

'I love it. I'm on men's surgical next week – everyone says it's great fun. What do you do, Edie?'

'Well, I help Mummy in the house—'

'I meant your job.'

'I don't have a job.'

At that moment, Tom's mother came into the room. 'Dinner should be ready in ten minutes,' she said. 'Shall we have a drink? Is there any sherry, Tom?'

Tom opened a cupboard and peered into it. 'Sloe gin . . . something that's lost its label . . . vermouth . . . no sherry.'

'Vermouth, then. You'd like a vermouth, wouldn't you, Edith?'

'Yes, thank you, Mrs Blacklock.'

'It's Dr Blacklock, actually, but you must call me Angela. Glasses, Tom.'

'I'll see if there are any cherries,' said Minnie, and bounded out of the room.

'And call your father, please.'

From the bottom of the stairs, Minnie bawled, very loudly, 'Pa! *Pa!* It's lunchtime!'

Minnie returned with the cherries – glacé, not maraschino, Edie noticed, which was rather peculiar. After they had drunk the vermouth, they went into the dining room. Professor Blacklock carved the beef and Dr Blacklock served the vegetables.

Minnie picked up the threads of their previous conversation. 'Were you sacked, Edie?'

Edie was startled. 'Sacked?'

'From your job. I wondered if that's why you were un-employed.'

'Have you lost your job, Edith?' Tom's mother looked sympathetic.

'I've never had a job,' said Edie.

'*Never?*' Minnie looked disbelieving.

Tom said, 'There's the shop, Edie.'

'It's only a little charity shop, in Esher,' said Edie, who had gone rather pink. 'I do one afternoon a week.'

Minnie was staring at her. 'But if you don't work, what do you do all day?'

'I play tennis in the summer and I'm in a drama club – I'm the secretary, actually.'

'But don't you get bored?'

'No, not at all.'

'I could put you in touch with some voluntary organizations,' offered Dr Blacklock.

'Thank you. It's very kind of you but I'm really very busy.' Edie, who had recovered her composure, spoke firmly. 'I often stay with my sisters and help them with their babies.'

'Edie has four nieces,' explained Tom.

Edie began enthusiastically, 'Helen's four and her sister, Grace, is six months old. She's such a dear. They're my eldest sister Laura's children. Nicky's twins, Cherry and Dawn, have just turned one, and Nicky's expecting again. She and Dan are hoping for a boy this time.'

Edie had anticipated cooing and requests to see photographs, but instead Minnie looked bored and Dr Blackwell said, 'Are your sisters using reliable contraceptives? I do hope so. The female body needs time to recover from the rigours of childbirth. More peas, Edith?'

Edie, who was now scarlet, said, 'No thank you, Angela . . .' and, 'Well, I'm sure . . .' and, 'I shouldn't think they . . .' and then fell silent.

'I don't believe anyone should have more than two children,' announced Minnie.

'I'm a third child,' said Edie, recovering herself a little, 'so I'd hardly agree.'

'Have you read Thomas Malthus?'

'No, I'm afraid not.'

'You should do. I think he was absolutely right. If the population continues to grow, there won't be enough food to go round.'

Tom's father spoke for the first time. 'Populations tend to right themselves, by war or disease or famine.'

'But that's hardly the best way, is it, Father dear?' said Minnie haughtily. 'Surely, in this modern age, we can do better than that. Would you like to borrow Malthus, Edie? It's very interesting.'

'Dr Stopes is perhaps an easier way into the subject,' said Dr Blackwell. 'I'm sure I've a copy of Married Love in the house. You like to read, I assume, Edith?'

'Yes, very much.' Edie felt on much safer ground. 'I've just finished The Stars Look Down.'

'Oh that,' said Minnie scornfully. 'Didn't you find it terribly melodramatic?'

'I enjoyed it. I couldn't put it down.'

'And perhaps,' said Tom, 'melodrama's sometimes necessary to draw attention to a social evil.'

'An interesting point,' said Professor Blacklock. 'But does a strong message excuse bad writing?'

No one answered. Edie wondered whether they couldn't think of a reply or whether they were all so hungry they had at last decided to eat their dinners. In the silence, she muttered, 'I thought it was very beautiful. I thought the love story was really very beautiful.'

Driving home that evening, they quarrelled. The quarrel wasn't about anything important, just a silly cocktail party that Edie had thought Tom had agreed to come to, and Tom thought he had told her he couldn't. The strains of the day made her say (and immediately regret saying), 'Your wretched hobby is more important to you than I am.'

Tom's expression then became set, and he said crossly, 'That's utter rot and you know it.' And then, a few seconds later, 'And it's not a *hobby*. You make it sound like, like knitting or stamp-collecting.'

'Isn't it?'

'No! It's – it's . . .' Being unable to define the difference only seemed to make Tom more annoyed; he said, 'The thought of escaping for the weekend is the only thing that makes your bloody Uncle Miles bearable.'

She didn't like it when he swore. She thought it showed disrespect. She said, her voice as cross as his, 'You don't have to work for Uncle Miles. You could get a better job.'

'I don't want a better job. It suits me.'

She hissed angrily, 'And I suppose you think I'm trivial because I don't have a job. Your sister obviously does.'

'Don't be ridiculous. Minnie doesn't think anything of the sort.'

131

'Oh Tom, she did! She thought I was idiotic, I know she did.'

'What nonsense, she did everything she could to make you welcome,' said Tom, sounding furious.

And so it went on. They were outside St Albans and had reached the silent, sulking stage, when, to make a difficult day worse, one of the tyres blew. Tom fought to control the skid and managed to bring the car safely to the side of the road. Edie stood in the entrance to a field while he changed the tyre. It was a chilly evening and she had only brought a light cardigan and the skid had frightened her, and she found it hard to control her shivering. When Tom had finished, he put his arms round her and said, 'Hey, don't look so woebegone.' Then he whispered in her ear, 'Sorry. I promise I'll come to the next party,' and, ridiculously, she found herself wanting to cry.

They drove on − carefully, after the fright of their near-accident, and careful with each other, mutually aware that their quarrel had touched raw nerves. Tom asked after her sisters and nieces; Edie inquired politely about the mountain he intended to climb.

It was ten o'clock by the time they reached Esher. Tom parked the car on the road outside Laurel Court. Then he took Edie in his arms and kissed her. 'Someone might come along,' she protested, but ended up kissing him back. She didn't know whether it was the relief of being home or the heightened emotions generated by their quarrel, but the strength of her feelings took her by surprise, and she forgot herself and almost found herself letting him go too far. It took a huge effort to push him away and pull down the hem of her skirt, and say, 'No, Tom, you mustn't, you know you mustn't.' Then, rather hot-faced and shocked at herself, she offered him a nightcap, which he refused, and let herself into the house.

'Is that you, darling?' Her mother came out of the sitting room. 'I was beginning to worry.'

'Sorry I'm so late. We had a puncture.' Edie kissed her mother's cheek.

'Isn't Tom coming in?'

'No, he had to dash off, I'm afraid. I'm just going to get changed and have a bath to warm up. These shoes are killing me.'

'Shall I bring you some cocoa?'

'Yes please. Thanks, Mummy.'

Edie went upstairs. In her bedroom, she kicked off her shoes, took out the copy of *Married Love* that Tom's mother had given her from its hiding place in her handbag, and stuffed it in a drawer. Then she lay down on the bed and closed her eyes.

She was so relieved to be home. She felt exhausted and emotional and horribly close to tears. She regretted her complaining tone of voice when they had quarrelled – she did not want to be a nagging sort of girlfriend. And it had been foolish of her to criticize Minnie when she knew how loyal Tom was to his sister. But then, Tom might have helped. He might have warned her that his mother worked part-time at a Planned Parenthood clinic. He might have warned her about his family, described them to her, because, heaven knows, they were not a *usual* sort of family.

What a family and what a home! She was sure she had not betrayed her astonishment – her dismay – at the state of the Blacklocks' house, but it had been a battle. The house had been large and spacious and had overlooked a common and

133

lay only a short distance from the river. It could have been a nice house. But it had not been a nice house. The mess! The dust – and, it had to be said, the dirt! Everywhere there had been piles of books and papers, on tables, cupboards, chairs, window sills and floors. She could understand the books – Tom's father was an academic – but she had noticed vases with browned papery flowers so old they seemed to have fossilized, and an enormous weeping fig, almost leafless, festooned with spiders' webs. Upon one of the branches, someone – Minnie, Edie suspected – had hung a red velvet hat. In fact, clothing seemed to have been abandoned at random throughout the rooms, coats piled on the end of the banisters, cardigans bundled on sofas and armchairs, and a pair of wellington boots left for no obvious reason in the middle of the sitting-room floor. The Blacklocks' pets – the dog, a budgie, a bundle of fur in a cage on a dresser and several cats – had also left their mark. There had been pet hairs everywhere and the grubby feeding bowls on the kitchen floor had made her shudder. Edie had had to stop herself looking for cat hairs in her dinner.

And then, Tom's family. Edie was sure his parents must be perfectly sweet beneath their eccentricities. But Professor Blacklock's cardigan had had so many holes, Edie had expected it to dissolve into shreds on the dining-room floor at any moment, and though the professor had been a quiet man, when he had spoken it had generally been to issue a difficult question or sharp contradiction. Tom's mother had been unnervingly direct – impertinent, actually. *Are your sisters using reliable contraceptives?* What on earth had she been supposed to reply? Had she been expected to detail the most intimate details of Laura's and Nicky's lives over the roast beef and Yorkshire pudding?

And then there was Minnie. Try as she might, Edie couldn't take to Minnie. She did not think she had ever met such an opinionated girl. Minnie, who was tall and slim and rather pretty, had worn, in the manner of her parents, a selection of ill-matched garments – a purple silk skirt, a yellow blouse, a striped jersey and a fringed Spanish mantilla. Minnie's voice had been loud and she had not walked, she had bounded. All too easily, Edie could picture her on the men's surgical ward, bossily organizing her patients.

The Blacklocks hadn't conversed, they had *challenged*. Over lunch, Edie's opinions, her achievements, her entire existence, it seemed to her, had been held up to the light and examined and found wanting. It had been utterly exhausting. Her head ached with it. After dinner, she had been required to play a game. She had done her best – she was not a fool, she read the newspapers and had a reasonable general knowledge – but she knew that she had not acquitted herself well.

Her mother arrived with a mug of cocoa. Edie hugged her – it was such a relief to be back home with her nice, *normal* mother – then found her pyjamas, slippers and dressing gown and went to the bathroom. There, she ran the bath, sprinkling into the water a large handful of the expensive bath salts Laura had given her for her birthday. When the bath was run, Edie peeled off her clothes and stepped into the perfumed water.

Cheer up, she told herself, as she reached for the soap and flannel. Tom had taken her to meet his family at last. Which surely proved some seriousness of intent.

But as she drank her cocoa in the bath, she felt unhappy and disappointed. Part of her disappointment was with herself – it was a matter of honour to her to be cheerful in the most trying circumstances. But the truth was that the Blacklocks were not the family she would have chosen Tom to have. That messy, dirty house – she could not live like that. Their lack of tact and the abrasive, teasing way they addressed each other was alien to her.

Edie's father had died when she was nine, in a railway accident. He had left his widow and daughters only the house and a small pension. Once school fees had been paid, there had been barely enough for four people to live on. Edie's mother managed by continual scrimping and saving. They had only the one servant, Muriel. All the Fielding women were handy with a needle and made most of their own clothes. A man came once a fortnight to cut the lawns and the hedges, but otherwise Edie's mother cared for the large garden herself. Mrs Fielding was very clever at saving seeds and taking cuttings, so the garden always looked delightful in spite of never having any money spent on it. They let the decoration of the house go as long as possible in the rooms that were not on public view. Edie herself had painted the drawing room and the dining room, had enjoyed the sweep of the paintbrush, the refreshing appearance of a newly decorated room.

But whatever their financial constraints, the house was always clean, tidy and welcoming. They were a close-knit and affectionate family. They must have had the knack of making people feel comfortable because they were never short of visitors. Laura had married well, which had eased matters. If Dan, Nicky's husband, was not yet comfortably off, he had the ambition and drive that meant he would be successful in the future. It was a matter of pride to the Fieldings that not one of their friends or neighbours appeared to suspect the hard labour that went into preserving appearances. But it was hard, and often Edie's mother looked exhausted. And wretched Uncle Miles, their only relative who could be considered affluent, never offered a penny to help. And so typical of Uncle Miles, Edie had once or twice guiltily reflected, to appear to be heading comfortably into a stingy but healthy old age.

Edie's upbringing had taught her to fear poverty – the unpredictability of it, the anxiety of it, the shame of it. Her instinct was to protect her mother, who so often looked tired and fragile. She shared with her mother some things, but not others. Tomorrow, perhaps, she would tell her mother some of the more amusing incidents of her visit to Cambridge, making a joke of them, but she would not worry her by confiding in her how she had felt when she had kissed Tom.

There were things she had to face up to, she thought, as she lay back in the hot, scented water, closing her eyes. Tom might be handsome and clever and good fun but it had always been obvious to Edie that he hadn't two pennies to rub together. A part of her knew she was wasting her time, dating Tom Blacklock.

Edie climbed out of the bath and wrapped a towel round herself. Her thoughts drifted to Charles Dangerfield, whom she had first met on Laura's birthday. She had attended two or three concerts at Charles's Portland Place house. Every so often she went to a theatre or a restaurant with his set, who were urbane, intelligent and cultured. She had known for some time that Charles was attracted to her. The previous week, he had asked her out to dinner, just the two of them. She had refused him, reminding him that she was seeing Tom, and he had said, 'I had assumed you two weren't serious.' She must have managed some sort of reply but she couldn't for the life of her remember what it had been. But his words had remained with her. *I had assumed you two weren't serious.* She was horribly afraid he might be right.

And yet, when Tom had kissed her . . . She thought of their leave-taking. She had never felt like that with any other man. It disturbed her to recall how close she had come to losing control – and in the front seat of a car! It made her feel ashamed of herself.

A stroke of good fortune: leaving the train at the Gare du Nord in Paris, Madame Cloutier slipped and fell, spraining her ankle. During the day, while Madame Cloutier recovered, Miranda was dispatched to the home of an acquaintance, Madame Robert. The Roberts had known the Denisovs for some years and Madame Robert had agreed to chaperone Miranda while Madame Cloutier was incapacitated.

The Roberts lived in the Fourth Arrondissement. Madame Robert, who was in her early forties, had strong, mannish features that might have seemed ugly had she not dressed immaculately and had her face not been perfectly made-up. She wore suits of lavender linen and frocks of polka-dotted lime-green silk. Her glossy black hair was immaculately curled and tucked beneath a chic straw hat with a half-veil. She was kind and brisk and always very busy. In the mornings she darted between the grocer's and the baker's – she didn't trust the maid to choose the cheese or the dessert, she told Miranda. In the afternoon, she called on friends or visited her dress-maker.

Miranda felt deeply envious of Madame Robert. A married woman, Madame Robert had a freedom that she, Miranda, who must live in her father's house, lacked. Madame Robert was not required to have a chaperone. She might drive wherever she liked, unaccompanied, in her little Renault. She might spend as long as she wished at the shops, or she might remain in the house all day, writing letters or preparing for a dinner party. She might travel to Lille, to visit her sister, or spend a day at the races in the company of friends. Miranda, an unmarried girl, could do none of these things.

One afternoon, they were sitting in the drawing room, drinking coffee and eating pastries. Dabbing crumbs from her mouth, Madame Robert explained to Miranda that Monsieur Robert – *cher Maurice* – always worked late into the evening. Five o'clock was a convenient time for Madame Robert to visit her friend. It was a long-standing arrangement. Miranda understood, didn't she? She would be able to amuse herself, *n'est-ce pas*?

Oh yes, said Miranda. She'd be able to amuse herself very well.

Madame Robert gave her a close look. 'If you have a friend of your own you wish to see, then of course I understand. Only be sensible, mind, and you must always be back here by seven o'clock.'

Which gave Miranda two hours' freedom. Directly after Madame Robert had left the house in a flurry of silk, face powder and Guerlain, Miranda went outdoors also. In a telephone booth in a café she gave the operator Olivier's number. Her heart was pounding and she felt breathless with fear, anticipation and longing. A few moments later, the operator put her through. A girl's voice answered the phone. It wasn't Agnès, realized Miranda.

She asked for Olivier Roussel. Madame had the wrong number, said the girl briskly. To Miranda's inquiries she explained that the warehouse was now leased by a Monsieur

Barthou, who imported whisky from Scotland. Monsieur Barthou had been leasing the warehouse for the past six months. No, she did not know where the previous owner had gone.

Miranda put down the phone, left the café, and walked to the Seine. There, she sat down on a bench. Ferries and barges glided along the glittering water. Paris looked the way she loved it best – bright and shining and confident and happy, and with a sense of promise.

She thought of how, these past ten months, she had longed for the moment when she would speak to Olivier again. How she had schemed and plotted to begin with, and how, later, she had despaired. Yet ten minutes ago she had put down the telephone and walked away. Why was she not using her precious hours to try again? Why had she not asked the operator to phone every Roussel in Paris until she found Olivier? Why was she not searching the streets until she discovered where he had gone?

Because she would only break her heart all over again. She might reach him on the telephone and say, *Olivier, it's Miranda*, and he might say, *Miranda . . . Miranda qui?* in that questioning tone of voice one uses when one has forgotten someone's name. After all, what had taken place between them? A little flirting, a kiss, nothing more. A relationship that had meant so much to her might have meant little to him. Olivier was older and more experienced than she was. Good-looking and charming, he had probably kissed dozens of girls.

He might believe she had left Paris of her own free will. He might think he had not been important to her. He would certainly have found another actress for his film. No sense in waiting around for a girl who never turned up. Plenty of girls would leap at the chance to act in a film. Money was tight, and time, as Olivier had often pointed out, was money. He would have had no alternative but to find another Camille, another girl to walk through the old, dark streets of the Marais, arm in arm with her lover.

He might, in the months since they had last met, have fallen in love. He might even have married.

And if he hadn't forgotten her, what then? What if she found him, and what if, by some miracle, he felt as she did? What if they met for an hour a day and then, in a fortnight's time, or perhaps a month, she had to leave Paris again? Could she survive the pain of another such parting? She did not think she could. She knew now that if passionate love transformed, it also burned. She had been burned, she had almost been consumed. She should forget Oliver. She must forget him.

They had found a buyer and were clearing the house. Tall carved armoires and pretty little gilt chairs had been labelled up for sale or for storage. Curtains had been taken down, folded and packed away with mothballs. The house was in confusion, in a state of flux. Madame Cloutier hobbled about on crutches, her nose wrinkled in perpetual disapproval of the noise and mess. Mrs Ingram supervised the packing, always with a long list to hand. Tables and chairs and long sausages of rugs were carried out of the house. The bare, echoing rooms seemed to retain little impression of the years the Denisovs had occupied them. An era was coming to an end, a line was being drawn. What now, Miranda thought, what now?

In her bedroom, she put away her jewellery in a tortoiseshell chest. She dropped her amber pendant in a velvet pouch and locked that away too. As she packed up her dolls, she felt as if she was putting away her childhood. Silk and cashmere shawls protected the fragile wax and porcelain faces. She laid them side by side in their coloured cocoons inside a packing case. She should give them away, she thought. She was far too old to play with dolls.

In her pocket was a letter from Friedrich von Kahlberg, reiterating his proposal of marriage. That morning in the Tiergarten, she had prevaricated. He had taken her by surprise; his declaration was too sudden, she needed time to think. And she had thought, at length. *It is possible to start again*, Friedrich had told her. *It is possible to have another life, a second chance.* Was he right? If she married him, could she make for herself another life, a better life?

Her father would give his permission for her to marry Friedrich, she thought. The title, the estate, his position and status: all these would make him a suitable match for the only daughter of Konstantin Denisov. She remembered the photograph Friedrich had shown her, of the white fairy-tale house by a lake. East Prussia was separate from the rest of Germany, a remote and, to Miranda, unknown land. Off the beaten track, you might say. A long, long way from her father.

Could she love him, this intense, serious man? She liked him, she admired him, she felt safe with him, so why should she not be able to love him?

She read the final paragraph of the letter again.

There is one more thing I must make clear. You would, of course, be free to pursue your own interests. I have no wish to confine you. You would be able to travel and to see your father and your friends. My mother runs the house and I look after the estate, so you need not fear that you will be burdened with domestic duties.

At the foot of the letter, he had written over and over again, *I love you. I love you. I love you.*

Tom's phone calls to Edie were made from a draughty phone box in Lavenham. Late one rainswept Thursday evening, he left his lodgings to call her. There was a queue; he had mislaid his umbrella and rain dripped down the collar of his coat.

Eventually, it was his turn. He asked the operator to put through his call. Edie answered. She had been to a concert, she explained, which was why she hadn't been in when he had phoned earlier that evening.

'Was it good?' he asked her.

'Yes, very.' A silence; Tom could hear rustling on the line. The operator unpeeling the foil from a chocolate biscuit, perhaps – his landlady had mentioned to him that she liked to listen in.

They talked for a few moments, and then Edie said, 'Tom, I must dash, it's late and I'm rather tired.'

'I've forgotten what time I said I'd pick you up tomorrow night.'

'A quarter to eight.' There was a touch of impatience in her voice. 'I told you when I booked.'

Walking back to his lodgings, Tom ran over their conversation in his mind. He sensed a distance between them, something not quite right. It wasn't anything Edie had actually said, more the spaces between their phrases. Of course, the line had been bad, and she too may have been aware that their conversation was not private. And she had said that she was tired. But he slept badly that night.

His restlessness remained with him the next day. Miles Culbone chose that morning to have Tom search for a missing book. There was an undercurrent of accusation as Tom went through the library shelves, an implication that Tom was somehow to blame, which he found himself resenting.

The uppermost shelves of the library could be reached only with stepladders as old and rickety as Miles Culbone himself. Spiders' webs were slung between the spines of books that had not been opened for decades; over time, dust had settled on the grey ropes of the webs.

Miles Culbone watched from below. He had taken off his glasses to polish them and was glaring myopically up at Tom. He was hoping, Tom guessed, that he might discover a forgotten treasure. As Tom reached the highest shelf, there was a creaking, tearing noise as the topmost tread of the stepladders gave way beneath his weight. He found himself leaping the six feet to the floor below as the stepladders crashed to the ground and books slithered out of his arms.

'Careful! You must be careful!' Miles Culbone's voice had an hysterical edge. 'These are valuable books, and you are rampaging about like a gorilla!'

'These books?' Tom had got himself upright again; he had jarred his ankle painfully and splintered pieces of stepladder lay scattered around him. 'You're worried about these books?' One by one, he thumped them down hard on Miles Culbone's desk, sending up clouds of dust – *Farming Annals, Wanderings in the Italian Alps by A Yorkshire Gentleman, A Clerical Life*. 'I doubt if any of these would earn you more than a few pence from a second-hand bookseller!'

'Mr Blacklock,' squeaked Miles Culbone furiously, 'you forget yourself!'

Tom wanted to punch him. Instead, he walked out of the room, slamming the door behind him. It was one o'clock, lunchtime. He took his sandwiches and Thermos from his haversack and went outside.

It had stopped raining, the sky was blue and Cold Christmas's garden and grounds sparkled, clean and refreshed, in the sunlight. The green and blue beauty calmed him as he limped out of the kitchen gardens and across the lawn to the woodland. Sitting down on the edge of the circular dais that held the catafalque and its sleeping marble child, he decided that he would hand in his notice at the end of the month. He had known for a long time that working for Miles Culbone was only a stopgap; he had stayed too long. And Edie would be pleased. He was aware that things had not gone so well between them recently. And he was sick of Miles Culbone, the man was an ass.

When he returned to the house at two o'clock, Mr Culbone was already sitting at his desk in the library. Tom was about to start work when Culbone gave a cough and said, 'A word, Mr Blacklock, if you please.' Then some shuffling of papers. Then, 'I'm afraid I don't require your services any longer.'

Tom stared at him.

Mr Culbone bit at a hangnail. 'The bulk of the cataloguing is complete and my brother's artefacts have been sold. I have no further need of an assistant.'

'You're *sacking* me?'

'Yes, that's it. You may go, Mr Blacklock.'

'You want me to leave *today*?'

'Yes, of course, today.'

'Now? This minute?'

Mr Culbone gave a heavy sigh. 'I see no point in delaying matters.' A bony hand held out to him a manila envelope. 'Your outstanding wages, Mr Blacklock.'

Tom opened his mouth to speak, shut it again, and then walked out of the library.

That evening, he took Edie to a restaurant in Esher. In the car, after he had explained to her what had happened, she said, 'Sacked? Uncle Miles sacked you?'

'Yes.'

'Goodness, Tom, what on earth had you done? Doodled in the margin of one of his precious books?' She touched his hand. 'I'm sorry to be flippant, darling, but you must admit it has its funny side.'

'Has it? I hadn't noticed.' He realized he sounded pompous, and added furiously, as he parked the MG near the restaurant, 'I could have broken my leg. The only thing he cared about was his damned books.'

He opened the car door for her and they went into the restaurant. The waiter showed them to their table, then held out chairs, flicked napkins on to laps, and, with a flourish, presented tasselled, leather-bound menus. Tom's temper worsened as he ran his gaze over the fussy furnishings and the equally fussy dishes on the menu, all in French, of course. It was the sort of place he hated.

'Suburbia with pretensions,' he murmured to Edie, when the waiter had gone.

'Tom. You can be so arrogant.'

Startled, he protested, 'That's not true. I'm not arrogant.'

The waiter returned with their wine. During the palaver

of the wine being opened and the tasting and offering his approval, Tom remembered that it was Edie who had chosen the restaurant.

Eventually, the waiter left them alone. Tom said, 'I'm sorry, Edie. This is fine, of course it is. But I don't see how you can say that I'm arrogant.'

'You are, Tom. It just isn't the usual sort of arrogance. You don't mind the lower classes and you don't mind if things are old or worn out, but you hate it when you think people or places are trying to make out they're something they're not. You're contemptuous of what you think of as poor taste – an attention to how things look, to appearances and manners which you think are superficial.'

'You're probably right,' he admitted. 'I dislike pretentiousness.'

'It isn't wrong to try to better yourself, surely? Just because Esher's in the suburbs, why does that mean it can't have a good restaurant?'

He tried to explain. 'So often these sorts of places ape the good restaurants without getting the important things right. They spend a fortune on silver cutlery and tailcoats for the waiters and yet the food's lousy.'

'You haven't eaten a mouthful yet,' Edie reminded him, rather stiffly.

'True. So we'll see. The proof of the pudding's in the eating, isn't it?'

Edie didn't reply. After a few moments, he reached across the table and squeezed her hand. 'I'm sorry. Your Uncle Miles has put me in a vile mood.' He whistled. 'Do you know, he didn't even pay me up till the end of the week. Not even for this *afternoon*.'

'When we were little,' said Edie, 'he used to send us a postal order for a guinea at Christmas. Not three guineas, just one between the three of us. And he never remembered our birthdays. You must have annoyed him, Tom.'

'Yes.' He scowled. 'I suppose I must.'

The waiter served the soup. They drank a few spoonfuls, then Edie whispered, 'It is rather awful, isn't it?'

'Pretty frightful. Like dishwater.' He topped up their glasses. 'There, drink up, it'll take the taste away. Tell you what, I'll take you to Carlo's next Friday to make up for this.' Carlo's, in Piccadilly, was their favourite restaurant.

But she said sharply, 'Not next Friday, Tom.'

'What, are you busy?'

'Tom. The play.'

'Oh God, yes, I'd forgotten.'

'Yes, you had, hadn't you?' Her voice was tight.

He said quickly, trying to retrieve things, 'It slipped my mind for a moment, that's all.'

She looked hurt. 'I don't know how you could forget. It's the biggest role I've ever had.'

'Darling, it was very stupid of me. I'm looking forward to it enormously. Wild horses wouldn't keep me from seeing you play Titania.'

'I suppose that to you it's just another little am dram production. It may not be important to you, but it's very important to me.'

'It is important to me, terribly important. And it'll be great fun.'

Too late, he realized he had chosen his words poorly again. Edie said coldly, 'That's exactly what I mean. You may pretend to be fair-minded, but unless something is absolutely top-notch you look down on it.'

Tom was stung into saying, 'That's rather harsh. You can't just forget your critical faculties – you can't metaphorically leave them at the door, like a coat and hat. And naturally, I wouldn't expect the same standards of an amateur production as I would of a professional one.'

'Too kind of you, Tom,' said Edie, with heavy sarcasm.

He gave a short, angry exhalation of breath, and took out his cigarettes. Edie, who disliked smoking in restaurants, said, 'Must you?' and he put them back in his pocket.

The waiter came to take their soup bowls away. When he had gone, Tom said, 'I only meant that, for instance, I'd hardly expect your Oberon to be up to Olivier's standards.'

Edie, who could never be cross for long, gave a half-smile. 'Our Oberon works in an insurance office in Guildford. And he has dreadfully bushy eyebrows. I never imagined the king of the fairies to have bushy eyebrows.'

He said gently, 'Forgive me.'

She looked down. 'It's not just you. I'm rather prickly today, I'm afraid.'

'Are you worried about something?'

'Well, the play . . .'

'You'll be marvellous, I know you will.'

'No, I won't be marvellous,' she said crisply. 'I'll be all right, but no more than that. I know my lines and lots of people have told me I look the part, but I know I'm not much of an actress. But it isn't only the play. I feel – I feel *unsettled*, Tom.'

'What's bothering you?'

She gave a little laugh. 'That's the thing, I don't really know. Silly, isn't it? I'm worried about Mummy. She hasn't been very well recently – nothing serious, just colds and coughs, but she does too much, I know she does.'

The main course arrived. Tom had ordered steak, Edie Dover sole. She said, 'I suppose Uncle Miles sacking you might be a blessing in disguise.'

'Because it frees me up to do something else? To tell the truth, I've been there long enough. I need to move on. I suppose I've needed a shove. I had a few ideas while I was driving up from Suffolk.'

'Did you, Tom?' Edie looked more cheerful. 'I had an idea of my own, actually. If you like, I could ask Laura if she'll speak to Tony on your behalf. Perhaps he'll be able to find you a job in the bank.'

'I can't see myself in a bank. I was thinking of going abroad for a while.'

'Abroad?' Edie echoed.

'Yes, I thought I might explore the Massif Central. I've never been there. Or the French Alps, for that matter.'

'How long are you going away for?'

'I don't know. I haven't decided yet.'

'But what will you do?'

'Walking . . . climbing . . . If I need money, I can turn my hand to most things. I spent a summer in France when I was at university. I washed up in cafés, picked grapes, helped on a fishing boat.'

'I assumed you'd look for a *proper* job now that you've left Uncle Miles,' said Edie irritably. 'I hoped you wouldn't be wasting your time any more.'

'I haven't been wasting my time,' he replied, needled. 'And what do you mean by a "proper" job? Commuting to London with all the other drones?'

'I meant something with a future and a decent salary.'

'I've never been too bothered about money.'

'No,' she muttered, 'I can see that.'

'A lot of my school or university friends have taken proper jobs, as you'd see them. They work for the Civil Service or a bank or a business, nine to five, five days a week. They expect to go on working, perhaps for the same firm, until they're sixty-five. Forty years doing the same thing. I don't want that, Edie. I can't help feeling life has more to offer. Is that so wrong?'

She gave up picking bones out of the sole and put down her knife and fork. Then, looking him in the eye, she said, 'And what about us, Tom?'

'You could come with me.'

'Oh, don't be so silly!' she said furiously.

His smile disappeared. 'Why not?'

'Where would we live? In some horrid little attic room, I suppose? What would I do all day? Wait on tables while you washed up? No, Tom, never. I'm not a Bohemian and I never will be.'

He sawed at the steak, which was tough. 'Washing-up was only an example. I'm sure I could find something better than that. If you don't fancy the mountains then we could do something else. We could hire a boat, perhaps, and take our time sailing round the Mediterranean. You'd like to do that, wouldn't you?'

'Not particularly,' she said coldly. 'I like living here.'

'How can you know you wouldn't be equally happy living abroad if you've never tried it?'

'No, Tom.' Her voice was sharp. 'I have my own life, and I'm quite content with it. I have my family, my sisters and my nieces and I love them and they need me and I won't leave them to go wandering around the Continent like a gypsy. Oh, I wish you were more ambitious!'

151

'Well, I'm not, so there it is.' He, too, was annoyed. 'I take it you admire ambition?'

'Yes, I do, I've always admired people who get on in life.'

'Getting on in life often involves trampling over other people. I daresay your brothers-in-law have elbowed a few aside in their race to the top.'

'Tom, that's a horrible thing to say! You seem to be suggesting there's something morally wrong in having aspirations!'

'Sometimes there is. What's wrong with being contented with what you have? The trouble with materialism,' he added bitterly, 'is that people will always want more.'

'I'm not materialistic!'

'I didn't say you were.'

'No, but you implied it,' she said, with equal bitterness.

They fell silent. After a few moments, Edie said quietly, 'We've turned into one of those dreadful couples you see arguing in restaurants. How sad.'

The waiter came to take their plates and to offer the pudding menu. 'No, thanks,' said Edie. She looked pale and miserable.

'Coffee?'

'No, I'd like to go, actually.'

Tom paid the bill and they left the restaurant. In the car, on the short drive back to the Fieldings' house, they did not speak.

Parking outside Laurel Court, Tom said, 'I'll see you next Friday, then.'

'No, I don't think so.'

'The play—'

'I'd rather you didn't come, Tom. Actually, I don't think I want to see you again.'

Something was tearing at his heart. He had always thought

himself good with words, but now he fought to find the right ones. 'Edie,' he said. 'Edie, for God's sake. I'm sorry this evening's been a washout. And I'm sorry if I've been in a foul mood – and that I've hurt you. But please, please don't do this.'

She shook her head slowly. 'It isn't just this evening.'

'Then what is it?' When she did not reply, he whispered, 'Edie, darling, *please*.'

'No, Tom. I won't change my mind.'

She got out of the car. Tom, too, stepped outside. He could see that she was on the verge of tears.

He said, 'I don't understand.'

Edie bit her lip. Then she flung him a defiant glance. 'It's quite simple. You're just not a good bet, Tom.' Then she went into the house.

Johnny Gilfoyle wasn't the sort of man Kay had expected to fall in love with. She met him at a party, one of the many impromptu parties that sprang up at night in Fulham. Someone had decided to make a bonfire – indoors – and it had got out of hand and the curtains had caught fire. Kay had found herself out in the street, brushing ash from her clothes. Johnny – evening dress slightly rumpled, hands in his pockets and laughter in his eyes – had emerged from the house at much the same time and had asked her whether she was all right. And whether she fancied a drink.

His name was St John Gilfoyle, but everyone called him Johnny. He was tall and handsome with patrician features and wavy hair the colour of autumn leaves. His blue eyes looked at her in a way that made her heart beat faster. His childhood had been one of nannies and public school and his adult life an easy slotting into a place that had been made ready for him. He said things like 'Good show' and 'Right-oh' and 'Wizard', and should have been ridiculous, but somehow wasn't. He moved with equal assurance between two worlds, working for the family business by day, partying or playing the piano in jazz clubs at night.

He was at the centre of many social circles. *You must know Johnny Gilfoyle, everyone does.* He introduced Kay to his old school-friends, who had neat little moustaches and slicked-back hair and might have stepped, she thought, out of Wodehouse. His musician friends were a different kettle of fish entirely. They were from this place or that place, some old, some young, some exuberant, some introverted, a few always out of kilter on drink or drugs. Everyone knew Johnny and everyone loved him. No one had a bad word to say about him. Cast-off girl-friends fluttered their eyes seductively or wept a little.

They had been seeing each other for two months when they became lovers. Johnny was staying in a cottage in the Norfolk Broads for the weekend, fishing, shooting and boating. It was a funny little wooden house, paint peeling from its ornately carved bargeboards, the River Bure lapping only a few yards from the front porch. Friends of Johnny's gave Kay a lift from London; as the evening lengthened and the sun sank gold into the reeds, Johnny's friends drifted away. She made to go with them; he caught her hand and said, 'Stay.'

So she stayed. Johnny made love like he played the piano, with such obvious pleasure that his delight delighted Kay. She couldn't, at first, quite see what the fuss was about, but then the second time, when they woke together in the middle of the night, she began to. In the morning, while he still slept, she wrapped herself in a blanket and walked outside to the river. Light made diamonds on the water. Bliss and anxiety mixed with equal measure – what if she fell pregnant? He had been careful, but what if something went wrong? She let fall the blanket and dived into the cold, silky water. When she emerged, shaking drops of water from her hair, she looked up and saw that he was sitting on the porch, smoking a cigarette. He smiled his lovely slow smile and waved at her.

A week later, she got herself fitted for a Dutch cap by a doctor that Johnny knew of. She didn't tell Aunt Dot that she and Johnny were lovers – she had an inkling that Aunt Dot mightn't approve of Johnny – but sometimes she suspected that her aunt had guessed. Happiness, now that it had found her, stayed with her through the summer of 1938.

But by late September, she had two lives. There was Johnny, and all the bliss, and then there was the other life, the everyday life, that had fallen beneath a darkening shadow. Like everyone else, she tried not to think about it, but it became impossible to escape. A line of darkness ran along the trenches the men were digging in the parks; anti-aircraft guns, like predatory black insects, perched on the roofs of the highest buildings. On the tube, the passengers were even more silent than usual, and blazoned across their folded newspapers was the word *Czechoslovakia*.

It had been brewing all year. In March, six months earlier, Hitler's armies had marched into Austria. In Vienna, crowds had cheered the Nazi dictator; the international reaction, though one of disquiet, had been muted to verbal protests.

Next, Czechoslovakia. After the Great War had ended in 1918, the country had been cobbled together from territory that had once been part of the Austro-Hungarian empire, a hotchpotch of nationalities – Czechs, Slovaks, Hungarians, Ruthenians – that had never quite gelled, but a nice little democracy nevertheless. The Sudetenland was a mountainous area of Czechoslovakia bordering on Germany, populated largely by German speakers. A shortsighted gym instructor, Konrad Henlein, leader of the Sudeten German Party, had chummed up with Hitler, complaining of ill-treatment at the hands of the Czechs. Perhaps Hitler, turning his angry, greedy gaze towards the Sudetenland, had been inspired by his success in Austria. Or perhaps dictators kept lists headed *Ripe For the Picking*. What next? wondered Kay. Poland? France?

France was Czechoslovakia's ally and Britain was France's ally. Perhaps the Czechs were cheered by the thought that the western democracies would stand by them if it came to the crunch. But the French, headed by Edouard Daladier, and the British, under Neville Chamberlain, didn't want war, weren't ready for war.

Which made things difficult for Czechoslovakia and difficult, too, for Kay. She didn't want war either, loathed and feared war, had some idea of what war could do – a grave in a foreign land, a life half lived. But then, on the other hand . . . There was something craven about it, all this flying off to Hitler's weekend place in the Berchtesgaden. The newsreel photos of Chamberlain setting off from Croydon airport, the solemn faces, the hats raised in salute as the fragile aeroplane drew away from the earth, had a desperate look, she thought. It seemed, well, overly obliging. Submissive. *Cowardly*, even.

And then, as tensions rose and the fleet was mobilized, other dilemmas. Should she join those queueing in schools and factories for their gas masks, or would that mean she was contributing to the war, going along with the build-up to war, making it yet more inevitable? But it was not much of a protest, to be suffocated by poison gas. Who would know, picking her out of the dead, that she had died for her principles? In the end, she collected the thing, hating the rubbery smell of its khaki snout, hiding it beneath her coat on the peg on the door of her room. And should she volunteer for air-raid precautions? After all, it wasn't fighting, was it, to learn first aid and how to put out a fire. It would be useful, it would help people, it would save lives. But by doing so, weren't you egging disaster along, weren't you accepting the inconceivable?

Why should we go to war for some far-off country? Of course, she didn't think they should. But it was the going to war she objected to, not the far-off country. Too fine a dilemma for the girl at the newsagent's. The girl at the newsagent's couldn't spell or pronounce Czechoslovakia and didn't see why they should risk life and limb for 'them Czechs'. This said with indignation, as if it were the Czechs who were at fault, who were doing the bullying. Wasn't it a luxury, this rarefied distinction of principle and reason? It wouldn't matter a jot to the Czechs themselves, that was for sure.

In the end, Neville Chamberlain returned from Munich, waving his piece of paper with its promise that Britain and Germany would never go to war again, and the country gave a collective sigh of relief and they all tried not to notice that the sandbags were still around the Houses of Parliament and the scars still ran through the lawns of the royal parks. And when Germany began to occupy the ceded parts of Czechoslovakia, as agreed, Kay tried to tell herself that now it would be all right. A sacrifice worth making, et cetera, et cetera. Only it wasn't *her* who had made the sacrifice.

The unease: that remained. She saw it reflected in the eyes of her fellow passengers on the tube and her friends in the pub, the knowledge that something shameful had taken place. She couldn't talk about it to Johnny, because she and Johnny didn't talk about things like that. They had a different language. Her sigh as he stroked the curve of her hip. His small intake of breath as she brushed her mouth across the base of his stomach. Her moan of pleasure as they lay entwined, their bodies fitting together as neatly as jigsaw pieces.

A month later, out of the blue, a letter was delivered to her after a long and tortuous journey. The letter was from Miranda, and the address on the envelope – sadly dog-eared now – was, 'Miss Kay Garland, c/o Brian, The Bookshop, Charing Cross Road, London.'

In her letter, Miranda expressed the hope that Kay was well and happy and that she had reached London safely. Miranda wrote how she regretted their sudden parting, how much she had missed Kay, and how foolish she had been to forget Kay's home address. She trusted that her letter would reach Kay's dear friend Brian and that he would deliver the letter to her. She trusted that Kay would forgive her, that she would not have forgotten her.

Then Miranda wrote that she had married, and that she was living in a castle in East Prussia. How grand, thought Kay. And then she thought of the lilacs in the park, and the way Olivier had looked at Miranda, and felt sad.

Something else troubled her. East Prussia – she had to look it up in the atlas. It was a long, long way away, separate from the bulk of Germany, not so very far from the Russian border. A great distance from all that had once been familiar to Miranda.

But, such a great pleasure to hear from Miranda at last, and such a relief to know that she was well and that she appeared to be content, and that she was free of her father at last. Reading the letter, Kay could hear Miranda's voice, light, amused, faintly mocking. *So, me, a countess — this is the most ridiculous thing, don't you think, Kay?*

Miranda and Friedrich had been married in Paris. She had worn a dress by Coco Chanel, sewn over with hundreds of seed pearls, and a filmy veil, also dotted with pearls. After the brief civil ceremony, entering the church on her father's arm, she had seemed to see the world through a snowstorm. Once they were properly married, Friedrich had raised the veil and kissed her, and she had seen clearly again.

After their marriage, Friedrich had taken her to Sommerfeld. There, he had shown her the places he had loved since childhood. Formal gardens of hedge and pathway stood at the front of the house. Behind the house was a terrace, then more gardens and lawns, and behind that a stand of birches. You walked through the birches to reach the lake, with its creeks and small, sandy beaches. The water reached to the horizon, and was a deeper blue than the blue of the sky. When Miranda walked along the wooden jetty, the reeds in the shallows made the sound of a thousand whispering voices.

One day, Friedrich drove her through the villages and tenant farmlands that made up the Sommerfeld estate. The roads were lined with tall trees, so that the car passed through a corridor of green shadows and shifting sunlight. Sunlight shone across a field of grain and made a flash of luminescence on the stalks and seedheads. Emerging into a village, Miranda saw thatched wooden barns, small red-roofed houses and a church built of brick. A woman pegged an embroidered cloth to a line, a goat glared with yellow eyes, and, on top of the chimneys, storks nested.

They went to Rastenberg, to see its great, red-brick castle, and to Angerberg, a small, bustling town at the top of Lake Mauer. One day, they drove for a long time through gentle, wooded countryside that was as still and quiet and mysterious as the landscape of a fairy tale. Miranda caught herself wondering whether they had slipped back in time, whether one of the long, tree-lined avenues might have somehow spat them out in an earlier century. Only the low, purring engine of the Daimler broke the silence. On and on, and she hardly saw a soul – an old woman, once, with a bundle of firewood on her back, and two children, paddling in a stream. And silence and greenness and stillness, as though this deep, distant place was waiting for something. The forests, seen through the car windows, glittered darkly. A rainshower shimmered around a stone figure greened with moss, heavy-bodied, hunched, almost as tall as Miranda herself – and then, as the car sped along the road, the figure was lost in the trees and the hills.

They visited Königsberg, at the mouth of the Pregel River. Königsberg, with its cobbled streets and tall, narrow, many-storeyed houses, was the capital of East Prussia. To its south-west lay a lagoon, the Frisches Haff, enclosed between the Vistula estuary and the long, narrow sandbar that separated the lagoon from the Bay of Danzig and the Baltic Sea. Roses and fir trees covered the steeper side of the sandbar, where it looked out across the Baltic, yet walk only a very short distance and you reached the inner edge and the lagoon with its still water and fringe of reeds. Miranda bathed in the cold, grey Baltic and searched the pale, silky sand for drops of amber. Afterwards, they dined at a hotel in a nearby resort.

At night, at Sommerfeld, they made love in a room furnished with painted chests and huge, dark, carved cupboards. The bedroom ceiling, with its ornamental cornices and centrepiece, was twenty feet high. Crimson damask curtains hung at the tall windows that looked down over the long, straight alley of lime trees.

Friedrich's lovemaking was thoughtful and considerate, just as Friedrich himself was. Thoughtfulness and consideration she could accept, feel grateful for, try to give back in return. But, now and then, in his eyes, she glimpsed a dark fire that unsettled her and seemed to point out a lack in her.

She had everything she had always wanted – a home, family, security and a husband who loved her. Why, then, did she still feel such emptiness? She knew that it would disappear as soon as she had a child. She longed for a child. She longed for someone she could love without limit, who would never be taken away from her.

In her youth, Friedrich's mother, the dowager Gräfin von Kahlberg, whom everyone called 'the Countess', had been a famous horsewoman, but now her rheumatism prevented her from riding. If she wished to visit Angerberg or Rastenberg, the chauffeur drove her in the Daimler. The Countess preferred to sit in the front of the car, beside the chauffeur, rather than in splendid solitude in the back. It was more interesting in front, she told Miranda. You could see more and she liked to have someone to talk to.

The Countess had been almost forty years old when Friedrich was born. She had despaired of having any children; Friedrich had been her miracle. Her marriage, though neither unpleasant nor ultimately without affection, had always retained a certain austerity. Friedrich's father had not been a demonstrative man, even in private, and she herself had found the physical side of marriage distasteful. She had been relieved when, at the age of fifty-five, Paul had found himself a mistress in Danzig (a sudden inclination to wear cologne and silk waistcoats had conveyed to her his secret) and *all that*, as she had called it to herself, had no longer been an obligation.

Paul had died during the last year of the Great War and she had mourned him sincerely. He had been a good man and they had shared a sense of duty both to the von Kahlberg name and their social position. More than fifty years ago, obedient to the desires of her parents, she had had no expectation of romantic love. A good marriage was one that reinforced or improved her family's position. Her union with the Graf von Kahlberg had been an excellent marriage. Her parents had been distant, alarming creatures, given to going away on long tours of Italy or Bavaria and sudden homecomings that ruffled the placid routine of the household. Her childhood – she had been born and brought up in Vienna – had been, on the whole, solitary. Her brother, Stefan, had been eight years older than her and away at school for much of the time. All her childish affections has been given to her nurse, an Irishwoman called Connie. Connie had told her stories about her homeland, a place of silver lakes and emerald hills. The first time she had seen Sommerfeld, with its shining lakes and gently rolling hills, she had remembered Connie's stories.

Love, when it had come to her on the day of Friedrich's birth, had almost overwhelmed her. Love had made her blossom, but it had also uncovered a rawness inside her, and afterwards that part of her had remained open to wounding. Her serenity had become dependent on Friedrich's well-being. The inevitable illnesses and accidents of childhood had brought with them terror — yes, one would have to call it terror, that falling away, that dreadful perception of the possibility of loss. Taught from an early age not to give way to her feelings, the Countess had hidden her vulnerability well, masking over the distress she had felt when she had seen Friedrich off first to school and then, years later, to university. In private, though, she had wept bitter tears.

Friedrich had become a son of which any woman would have been proud. In many ways, Friedrich took after his father — there was a certain asceticism, a severity in his nature. But there was another side to him, a capacity for passion that his father had lacked. Paul had never once looked at her in the way that Friedrich looked at Miranda. There had been someone else, long ago, who had looked at her in that way, but she had been married by then and had never let him know how his glance had melted her, and she regretted that only a little now.

Now in her mid-seventies, the Countess had recently begun to fear that Friedrich would never recover from the death of his fiancée, that he would never marry, that he would be the last of his line. So she had received the news of his engagement with relief as well as pleasure. Because her rheumatism had prevented her from attending the wedding in Paris, she had met her new daughter-in-law for the first time at Sommerfeld. A part of her, as she welcomed Miranda to the house, might have preferred that Friedrich had chosen a girl less ethereal in appearance. A beauty, without doubt, but she did not look robust.

The Countess showed Miranda around her new home. Friedrich's bride must know all the important things: who was in charge of the wine cellar and where the medicines were kept and which china should be used on which occasion and in which bedroom a visiting dignitary should sleep. They took their time over their tour of the castle – 'I don't want to exhaust you, my dear,' the Countess said. 'I realize all this may seem rather daunting. But one day it will be yours, so you need to know where everything belongs and what it means.'

There was an entire room just for the best dinner service, used only for weddings and christenings and visiting royalty and the Countess's birthday. The cream bisque porcelain was painted with bright flowers and insects. On the side of a dish, a bee buried its nose in a honeysuckle trumpet; in the centre of a plate, a dragonfly perched on a water lily. The silver and glass cupboards held goblets whose stems were twisted like barley sugar and threaded through with pale filaments, as if strands of silk had been woven into the glass. Inside the linen cupboard – not so much a cupboard as a small room – there were stacks of neatly folded bedlinen, tablecloths and towels. Plain cotton pillowcases for the servants, monogrammed linen for the family, and a set of pillowcases embroidered with the coronet of a prince who, eighty years ago, had stayed at the castle.

Upstairs, cupboards and wooden chests contained blankets, eiderdowns, fur coats, hunting jackets, army greatcoats, children's and babies' clothes. Lift the lid of a painted chest and the room became redolent of cedar chips. Part layers of tissue paper to find a silk gown, pale blue and embroidered with gold thread, corseted into a tiny waist. And then, the hat boxes. There were top hats and homburgs and ladies' wide-brimmed straws; there were extravagant hats crowned with satin bows and ostrich feathers and even – dreadful – a small bird, glass-eyed and faded. In a small, oblong box nestled a pair of lace gloves, yellow with age and perfumed with lavender.

There were rooms the family used every day and rooms which were never used at all, where a carved mahogany chair leg peeped out from beneath a dust sheet and the rugs had faded to pink and grey. In these rooms, the air was still and quiet, as if waiting for someone. In a dark red room, dust motes floated in the narrow strips of sunlight between the drawn blinds. 'I've never liked this room,' the Countess told Miranda. 'A child died here, Friedrich's father's little brother. He was only an infant. I always feel such sadness lingers, don't you?'

The Countess quickly became fond of Miranda. She would have loved her anyway, because her son loved her, but she discerned the girl's good qualities – an eagerness to please, as well as courage and spirit and generosity. Gently, she attempted to mould Miranda's less favourable attributes – the lack of rootedness that the Countess discerned in her, and not coarseness, exactly, but a guardedness, a knowingness, the air of someone who has seen too much, too young.

The Countess's hair was white and she wore it in an old-fashioned style, piled up in frosted loops and coils on top of her head. The lineaments of beauty could still be seen, however, in her finely drawn features and the narrow bones of wrist and ankle. Often her blue eyes sparkled with laughter, but the laughter might die away in a moment and be replaced by an icy hauteur. The Countess had the most perfect manners Miranda had ever seen. She never raised her voice, knew exactly what to say to put anyone, from a gawky village lad to an ancient scion of the nobility, at ease. Or, equally, to put them in their place. She reserved her scorn for the social climber, the ill-mannered, the crude. Miranda set about trying to copy her, to walk with the Countess's soft, assured step, to give orders in a firm modulated tone, to express displeasure with the lift of an eyebrow.

Some of the rooms at Sommerfeld were intimate, like the octagonal white and green room that led off from the orangery, but others were designed to impress, to awe, to intimidate. In the largest of the ceremonial chambers, Miranda's voice echoed in the wide, empty space and her high heels click-clacked on the marble floor. Standing in the centre of the room, she smiled and made a gesture of the hand, as if she were on stage. She curtseyed to the stern gentlemen in wigs and the porcelain-cheeked ladies in shimmering satin dresses who looked down at her from the walls. She felt their painted eyes watching her and paused to glance at her reflection in an ornate silver mirror.

Over centuries, the von Kahlbergs had filled their house with treasures. A library of leather-bound books here, a jewelled Fabergé egg there. Miranda remembered her father telling her of his escape from Russia during the turmoil that had followed the Revolution, how he had worked his passage on a merchant steamer across the Baltic Sea to Sweden, disguising himself as an ordinary seaman. Before he had boarded the steamer, Konstantin Denisov had taken a shell and a pebble from the beach, to remind himself of Russia. They were his good luck talismans: wherever the Denisovs were living, the shell and pebble always stood on the mantelpiece in Konstantin's study.

Miranda's favourite rooms were to one side of the house. The kitchens, laundry and pantries were always so pleasantly busy. There were rooms for washing and rooms for drying, rooms for bottling and rooms for baking and rooms for making cheese and storing eggs in isinglass. There were dried mush-rooms, strung on to long grasses like beads on a thread, and sides of bacon, hanging from hooks, and fish from the lake, drying on racks like leathery brown rags. There were the cellars, which were cold and clammy and mysterious, and where dusty, cobwebbed bottles of wine were stored beneath brick arch-ways. There was a larder, with jars of apricots, raspberries and peaches and pickled onions like clouded eyeballs and honey the colour of Baltic amber. There were golden pats of butter and pails of milk and vats of cream. The high, stone rooms with their wooden tables and vast sinks and stoves were always noisy with the chatter of the maids, the rattle of washboards, the clatter of dishes in the sink, and the chorus of a folk song as the women ran the sheets through the mangle or put up carrots in sand for the winter.

Tea, coffee and wine had to be bought in, but almost everything else consumed by the family, their servants and guests, was grown on the estate. The home farm's produce was supplemented by tithes from the tenant farms. Little money exchanged hands – the labourers who worked on the broad, placid fields were paid in kind, the tithes likewise. At Sommerfeld, they hunted for deer and hare, fished for pike and trout, and shot snipe, duck and pheasant. The estate was a little country of its own, a province within a province, Friedrich's kingdom. Friedrich was intimate with every part of Sommerfeld, every room in the house, every event in its long history, every field and forest and lake and tenant farm. You could have said that Friedrich loved Sommerfeld, but it was more than that: Friedrich *was* Sommerfeld, they were each a part of the same whole.

The estate had its own rules and customs. Every morning, Miranda was woken by the maid drawing the curtains and bringing her coffee. Friedrich kissed her good morning and asked her how she'd slept, and then she bathed and dressed and went downstairs. There was a brief religious service to begin the day, the family and servants present as Friedrich read out a prayer and a psalm or a few verses from the Bible. Over breakfast, they conversed about this and that, the events of the day, the social calendar, any weddings, births or deaths. Never gossip; the Countess never indulged in gossip.

After breakfast, while Friedrich was working on estate matters, Miranda walked her bloodhound, Gisela. Then, back to the castle, where she wrote letters or read until it was half past one and time for lunch. In the afternoon, if someone in the village was unwell, then the Countess visited, taking medicines with her. Miranda sometimes went with her – not, in all honesty, because she liked to tend the sick, but because she enjoyed visiting the houses in the village, was fascinated by their dolls' house neatness. Even the smallest of the thatched, wooden buildings had an allotment with rows of vegetables and half a dozen hens and a cow grazing the grass. The ground-floor room would contain a tiny recess with a stove, tap and cooking pot. There would be wonderful smells of baking and coffee. Sometimes Miranda and the Countess were offered bread and curd cheese or a pancake, dripping with honey.

Miranda watched and learned. The manners of her father's house wouldn't quite do here. No flirting with the gentlemen at the dinner table, no rages or raised voices or angry blows. Sometimes she seemed to catch sight of herself, as if from a distance, and know that she was acting a part – but then she had always been good at acting a part.

A great many guests visited the castle. Some stayed for weeks. It took Miranda a while to work out who was who. Once, discovering a shabby old man wandering round the ceremonial rooms, assuming him to be a servant, she sent him to the housekeeper to fetch candles. He returned, happily enough, with a box of candles, but later, at dinner, she caught sight of him sitting a few seats down from her and, inquiring of her neighbour, discovered he was the proprietor of a neighbouring estate. In his youth, he had been a friend of Hindenburg.

And then there were the von Kahlberg relatives, the great-uncles and great-aunts, the aunts and uncles and cousins. They arrived at Sommerfeld in a Mercedes Benz or perhaps a racy little sports car, or on horseback or in an old, black-and-gold carriage and pair. Great-Uncle Leo sported a majestic beard and wore shiny black boots and an equally shiny top hat, and strode around the house as if he were inspecting a battlefield. Great-Uncle Helmut was untidy and shambling, a pleasant, inoffensive old man, who ate his food with gusto and said little. Oskar and Katrin were brother and sister, the children of Uncle Georg and Aunt Klara. Both were tall, with reddish-blond hair, fair, freckled skin and blue eyes. They lived in Königsberg. Uncle Karl, Klaus, Max and Anna lived at Waldhof, a house of such haunted, fading charm that Miranda, visiting, felt as though she had stepped into an enchantment. The brothers Klaus and Max were handsome and dashing, wonderful dancers, and their sister, Anna, was small and dark, four foot ten in her stockinged feet, with a scar on her cheekbone from when she had fallen from a horse, and brown eyes that became bright with laughter at the least thing.

Getting to know Friedrich's cousins, Miranda admired their toughness, their disregard of the cold and fatigue. They bathed in chilly lakes, they hunted all day and then strode back into the house, red-cheeked and tousle-haired, rubbing their hands together and asking whether there would be dancing that evening. Miranda felt hugely grateful to all of them for accepting her without question, for drawing her into their warm, lively circle and including her in their picnics and jaunts to the seaside.

Walking on the Sommerfeld estate one day, Anna linked arms with her as they headed back to the house. 'We're so pleased Friedrich found you, Miranda,' she said. 'We had all begun to despair of him. We were afraid he might live like a monk for the rest of his life. Constancy is a virtue, of course, and what happened to Elli was a tragedy, but to remain bound to someone who has been dead for fifteen years . . . My cousin is a good man, Miranda. He loves rarely, but when he does, he loves deeply. If you can love him as he loves you, then you'll be blessed indeed.'

When the cousins were staying at Sommerfeld, every evening was a party. Someone would put on the gramophone or Aunt Klara would play the piano and they would dance round the ceremonial rooms, making the spun glass goblets quiver in their cases.

When Miranda sang for them they applauded loudly. When she recited Miranda's speech from The Tempest ('I do not know One of my sex; no woman's face remember, Save, from my glass, mine own') there was a silence after she had finished, during which she wondered whether she had somehow offended, or perhaps they had not understood the English. Then the Countess said quietly, 'Thank you, Miranda. That was so beautiful. Recite something more for us, would you, please?'

'What would you like?'

'Anything. Anything at all.'

So: Juliet, Desdemona, and then, just for a change, Hamlet, scowling tempestuously round the battlements of Elsinore. Afterwards, she was elated, as if she had drunk an entire bottle of champagne. She had Aunt Klara play a quickstep, and she and Klaus whirled like dervishes around the room.

In quieter moments, she thought: so this is how other people live. This is normal life, this peaceful, timeless fairy-tale land. The predictability of it all, the safety of it. No *irregularities* at Sommerfeld. She liked that.

On their way to the party, taking a short cut across Lammas Land, Tom told Minnie about Edie.

'She's engaged to be married. I ran into her sister yesterday in Piccadilly and she told me.'

'Who's she going to marry?'

'A chap called Charles Dangerfield. He's an idiot.'

They had to step carefully: a mist lay over the low-lying land and, in the darkness, it was hard to see the path. The air smelled brackish, of the river.

Minnie said, 'You were in love with her, weren't you, Tom?' and Tom said shortly, 'Yes, I expect so.' Then they walked for a while in silence.

A week after he had broken up with Edie, Tom had left for France. At first, he had walked and climbed in the Alps, but he had soon realized that his heart wasn't in it. He had spent the past five months working in Paris for an agency that supplied financial institutions and legal firms with translators. He had returned to England two days ago, in time for Christmas.

Minnie said, 'I liked her, actually. You could tell, just by looking at her, that she was the sort of person who knows how to do everything properly. She was – capable. Yes, that's the word.'

'Capable of marrying a complete ass,' said Tom bitterly. 'Looks like I'm well out of it, doesn't it?'

Minnie gave him a sideways glance. 'What happened between you two?'

'We had a row, that's all.'

A fallen tree lay over their path. Minnie hoiked up her long skirts and clambered over it. Following her, Tom said, 'Bloody Miles Culbone didn't help. Do you ever have days when everything goes wrong?'

'Oh God, yes. My first day on Maternity, I almost drowned a baby. It slipped out of my hands while I was bathing it. And of course Sister was watching.'

'Culbone sacked me that morning. It made me angry.'

They had reached the road; they headed along the pavement, not speaking for a while. Then Tom said, 'It was about time I left, anyway. Edie was right about that, at least.'

'Tom, you don't have to be noble about it, no one likes being sacked. It must have been humiliating.' Minnie hooked her hand through his arm. 'I suppose, in our family, we're rather used to being good at things. We're put out when we don't succeed at something.'

They had almost reached their destination. In the light from the street lamps, Tom saw that the hem of Minnie's long, scarlet skirt was coated in mud. He pointed it out and she said airily, 'It doesn't matter, it'll dry off. It's one of Ma's old ones anyway.'

* * *

172

Kay to Miranda: Johnny says that his mother buys him and his brothers and sisters exactly the same Christmas presents each year, an umbrella from James Smith and Sons and a Waterman fountain pen. He says that his sister, Louise, who is rather poor because she made an unfortunate marriage, plans to set up a market stall selling umbrellas and fountain pens.

Miranda to Kay: The snow, darling — I would so love you to see the snow . . .

Map of East Prussia, pre World War II

Chapter Six

On the morning of the first snowfall, Miranda took her dog, Gisela, for a walk through the forest of firs. Inside the forest, the trees grew so tall and so close together they shut out the light. It was dark and cold and the scent of pine resin perfumed the air. Where the branches threaded overhead, no snow had reached the ground, so she trod on a soft path of pine needles. Gisela remained at Miranda's side, making a low growl when clumps of snow slid to the ground. Miranda gathered fir cones to take back to the castle, so that she could watch them spit and burn in the fire. The lower branches of the trees were leafless, brown and brittle. When she brushed against them, fragments of wood scattered to the forest floor, like spent matchsticks. Catching a flicker of movement in the distance, she thought she glimpsed a deer, running through the tunnel of trees. Behind her, the path disappeared into darkness. Other paths criss-crossed her way. It would be so easy, she realized, to become lost, so she turned back.

The snow made the castle look grubby, Miranda decided. When, as a new bride, she had first seen Sommerfeld Castle, she had thought how white it looked, how pale and beautiful against the green of garden, trees and grass. But the snow was whiter than anything, whiter than the castle walls, whiter than Friedrich's favourite horse, whiter than his mother's fox fur coat. Whiter, even, than the sky. Standing at the window, Miranda watched the flakes whirl and dance. First the snowstorm erased the distant lake, then the birch wood, then the paths and parterres of the garden, until everything was bleached white.

Waking the next morning, a cold bright light penetrated the room. The maid had drawn aside the curtains. As far as the eye could see, the landscape was white. The snow had sculpted itself into drifts, some ridged so sharply they had the look of a frozen wave, others sweeping up the walls. The gleam of the low winter sun sparked jewelled light on the spun sugar shapes.

That afternoon, the cousins arrived. They had brought their skates. Max carried a gramophone down to the frozen lake, and the dogs came with them, running between the birches, panting, pink tongues out, until they stood on the edge of the ice, yelping.

Klaus wound the handle of the gramophone and put on a record. The 'Blue Danube' waltz started up and Anna shrieked.

'Klaus, you know I hate this song!' Whirling across the ice, she planted her hands on her brother's chest and gave him a shove. 'They used to make me play it on the piano when I was at school. Pom, pom, pom, pom, pom, plink-plink, plink-plink. It used to drive me mad!'

Max, Oskar, Katrin and Anna circled and glided on the frozen lake. The dogs ran back to the birch wood, darting between the trees. Klaus led Miranda out on to the ice and took her in his arms.

'Where's Friedrich?'

'He had to go to Königsberg on business.'

'Good, then we can run away together. You know that I'm madly in love with you, don't you, Miranda? Look, I kiss your hand.' Klaus did so, his other hand to his heart.

'Don't be silly, Klaus,' she said indulgently.

The sun was spreading its dilute light across the ice. 'I love the snow,' she said, as they danced.

'In a few months you'll hate it, I promise you. We call it "reading time", when the day's too short and the snow's too deep to leave the house.'

'I can't imagine you sitting over a book, Klaus. You're too much of a fidget.'

Max and Anna, dancing together, were roaring in time with the music, 'Pom, pom, pom, pom, pom, plink-plink, plink-plink!'

Klaus grinned. 'Aha. Maybe I don't read. Maybe I have a very odd pastime for the winter months, like Great-Uncle Leo.'

'What does Great-Uncle Leo do?'

'He stuffs birds and arranges them in glass cases. Would you like to do that, Miranda?'

'I don't think so. The poor birds.'

'And of course,' Klaus went on, 'there's Uncle Karl. In the winter, he writes letters to every railway station in Europe and asks them to send him a photograph.'

'What does he do with them?'

'He pastes them in an album. You should ask him to show it to you some time.'

She laughed. Glimpses, as they danced, of the plain and the birch wood. The sky had taken on a heavy, brownish tinge: it would snow again that night. The dogs barked excitedly; looking to the shore, she saw Friedrich.

She skated across the ice to him. 'How was your business, darling?'

'Very dull. I won't bore you with it.'

He took her in his arms and held her close to him as they skated in the cold twilight.

When it became too dark to skate, they all went back to the castle. After dinner, Oskar played Chopin, and Miranda curled up on the corner of the sofa nearest to the fire and felt herself floating off into a dream, pleasantly tired by the exertions of the afternoon.

Then, to wake them all up, Oskar switched to jazz, and the beat made it impossible for Miranda not to dance. They danced for hours, until the cousins, remembering they had promised their mother they would go to church with her the next morning, gathered themselves up and drove off into the darkness before the snow began to fall again.

Every day after that, it snowed. The frozen lake seemed to go on for ever, blurring into the pearly light of the horizon. Miranda liked to listen to the creak and whine of the ice. Inside the stables, there was an old dog sled. She thought how lovely it would be to ride on it, wrapped in furs, bells jingling, across the snow-covered fields. The Countess had told Miranda that this winter wasn't too bad at all, that one year the snow had covered the stone steps and had drifted over the front door. They had had to dig themselves out of the castle. It was not uncommon in the winter for the thermometer to show in the coldest months twenty degrees of frost.

The days became shorter, the snow deeper. When she went outside, the bitter air stung her face. Ice glazed the cobbles; icicles hung from the gutters. The cousins no longer rode over to Sommerfeld, and the trees beside the avenue were silvered with ice, as if they had been coated with a thin layer of glass.

They were enclosed in the castle, waiting out the months till spring. *Reading time.*

In March 1939, Hitler's armies invaded the remaining defence-less rump of Czechoslovakia. Turning the pages of the *Manchester Guardian* in the school staffroom, Kay learned of the long queues of Czechoslovakian Jews and political dissidents outside the British Consulate in Prague, all seeking passage to England. She read of the subsequent round-up by the Gestapo of 'harmful characters' and their incarceration in gaol. Though she still attended meetings of the Peace Pledge Union, it was with an increasing sense of futility. In the staffroom at school, and in the streets of London, the sense of dread was almost palpable. You went about your daily life because you couldn't think what else to do, and because you might as well go on living normally because, realistically, it didn't look like *normal* was going to last much longer. But the fear was there, dark and gelid, bobbing to the surface every now and then.

They tried not to let their apprehension infect the atmosphere of the school, though sometimes it boiled over in a sudden bitter argument in the staffroom. Kay wasn't the only pacifist at Oaklands. Kay thought she saw apprehension even in the nightclubs and parties she went to with Johnny. As if people were trying to blank out the fear with the noise they made or the cocktails they drank so they wouldn't have to think about what was just round the corner.

They were so rarely alone, she and Johnny. Everyone was Johnny's friend. Meet up at the Trocadero – Johnny loved the Troc – and she'd be part of a crowd of ten or a dozen, fun, glamorous, rather fast. But. Though Johnny always had a good reason for turning up late or not being around for a while – he had bumped into a friend he hadn't seen for years at his club, or he was playing the piano in Paris – and though she always said, How nice, or Paris, you lucky thing, afterwards she found herself adding it up, the time they spent together. As if you could work out these things mathematically.

She glanced into her pigeonhole one Friday lunchtime, thinking there might be a letter or even a postcard from Johnny waiting for her. But there was nothing. Passing Virginia's office, it crossed her mind that she could phone Johnny at his office – easy enough, Gilfoyle and Sons, at the Surrey Docks – but something, pride perhaps, stopped her doing so.

Lunch, then lessons until ten to four, then a break for tea and buns, and afterwards she had to supervise prep. Then supper. No phone call, and the afternoon post had brought her no letters. She had promised to help Virginia sort out the music for the school concert, which she did, sitting on the floor in Virginia's study, copying out the parts and gathering them into folders. By the time they had finished, it was ten o'clock. Kay asked Virginia whether she could use the telephone.

She dialled the operator and gave her the number of a club in Soho. After a long wait, she was put through to the proprietor. She could hear in the background music and raised voices and laughter. She asked for Johnny.

Another long wait. Then Johnny's voice said, 'Hello?'

Always, that shiver up her spine. 'It's Kay.'

'Kay! How are you, my darling?'

'I'm very well. Are we seeing each other tomorrow?'

'Tomorrow?'

'The party . . .'

'Ah yes, the Hunts' bash. Actually, old thing, I'm not going to be able to make it. It's a blighter, but the old man needs me to go to Portsmouth.'

'Oh.' A sinking feeling inside her. 'That's a shame.'

From the other end of the line, muted voices – Johnny's and someone else's. Then a girl's voice shrieked, 'Shall I tell you the truth about Johnny Gilfoyle? He's an utter swine, you know!'

'Shut up, Serena,' said Johnny. Then, to Kay, 'I say, are you doing anything now? Why don't you hop into a cab and join us here? Everyone's here – we're having such a wizard time.'

'Shall I?' Her spirits lifted.

'Of course. Hurry up, the fun's just getting going.'

Upstairs in her room she scrubbed the ink off her fingers and put on her make-up. No time to wash her hair, so she brushed it furiously until it gleamed golden-bronze, falling in feathery waves. She changed into the green chiffon dress she had bought in Paris an age ago, with Miranda. She had only a small mirror, but if she stood on a chair she could look at sections of herself.

Cabs were expensive, so she caught the tube instead, in her green chiffon and her raincoat, and dashed through the rain from the station to the club. Narrow stone steps led down to a basement and, at the door, a large chap in ill-fitting evening dress looked her over and waved her inside. A woman with gingery hair frizzed up in a permanent wave took her coat.

Music, urgent and sensuous, drew her into a dark, crowded room. The dim, pinkish light revealed walls decorated with silver zigzags, and half a dozen small, round metal tables, each with a candle in a jar. There were cigarette stubs on the floor and rings of liquid smeared the bar. A fug of smoke clouded the tiny dance floor. The band – piano, sax, double bass and a singer, a tall, slender black woman wearing a sheaf of glittering silver sequins, who stooped her shoulders to caress the microphone as she sang – were crushed in a corner of the room.

And then there was Johnny, taking her in his arms and kissing her and saying, 'So glad you could come. Isn't this simply the most marvellous place?'

'One of your seedier dives, isn't it, Johnny?'

His dark eyes glittered. 'But I *like* seedy. I *adore* seedy, you know that, Kay.'

Johnny and his friends were drinking champagne – well, something fizzy that masqueraded as champagne. More than half a dozen of his friends had squeezed round a table; every now and then someone drifted away or another couple arrived, shrieking about the rain or a party they had been to. Johnny played the piano, and the evening lifted; even the drunk at the adjacent table stirred and opened an eye. Later, dancing with Johnny, it seemed to her that everything that mattered – love, desire, intimacy – was distilled into one pure moment.

But as the night went on, her contentment ebbed away. A couple of dances and then Johnny would drift away to chat or dance with someone else – some blonde who'd come to the nightclub after dinner at Claridge's, some brunette who'd spent the day in bed and got up at five to have a leisurely bath and dress herself for an evening of cocktail party, dinner and nightclub. Not one of these girls, Kay supposed, had had to scrub the ink from her fingers with a pumice stone or dash through the rain to the tube. Not one was struggling, at three in the morning, to keep her eyes open because she had been up since seven the previous day.

And sometimes she found herself hating them, these Rosamonds and Evelyns and Angelas who insisted on having *just one teeny dance* with Johnny. Sometimes she was surprised by the rage that boiled in her at the sight of their smooth, powdered faces and the sound of their cut-glass, upper-class vowels. Girls who had never had to do a day's work in their lives, girls who had progressed from being the most popular girl at the school to deb of the year. Kay disliked herself for hating them; she hadn't thought she was the jealous type.

Miranda had received a letter from her father, telling her that he was unwell and asking her to visit him in Paris. *Asking* . . . for the first time in her life, her father had made a request instead of issuing an order.

Miranda took Gisela out for a walk, trying to make up her mind. Ragged white clouds scudded through a cornflower-blue sky. She walked through the garden, beneath the birches, with their dappled, shifting light, and then out along the narrow peninsula of land that protruded into the lake. She sat down on the grass, looking out over the water while Gisela ran along the bank, disturbing a flock of ducks who flew quacking into the sky. The breeze whipped up waves and the reeds moved restlessly, whispering to each other. In the lake, a heron stepped gracefully along the shore of an islet. She could see no boats, no houses or farms. No people. She might have been the only person in the world. Everyone else might have fled, leaving East Prussia to the storks and the hares and the deer.

She owed her father nothing. And yet, to her surprise, every now and then, she missed him. Life sometimes seemed – what was the word? – *flat*, without him. Like meat without salt.

A part of her still expected this life of hers to be transient, liable to disappear at any moment. Waking in the morning, it always seemed possible that Friedrich might turn to her and say, *We've been here long enough, today we go to Paris*. Or Vienna. Or Rome. If she had had a child, she might have felt differently, she thought. But it was the end of May, she had been married for nine months, and still she was not pregnant. The sun emerged from behind a cloud, shedding silvery light on the far side of the lake. *Paris*, she thought, with longing.

Her father wanted to talk to her about money. The apartment in which Konstantin Denisov had been staying for the past few months had rooms of turn-of-the-century elegance. Always the best for Konstantin Denisov, who lay in bed, propped up on pillows, recovering from a seizure. His colour was poor and his face and hands puffy, his voice lacking in strength. Some of the energy, some of the life had been drained out of him. That he was truly unwell shocked Miranda; she had assumed his letter to be some sort of ruse.

Before he spoke to her, Konstantin dismissed his nurse. When the woman had gone, he said to Miranda, 'There is the house in London and I have recently bought a villa in Nice. There are bank accounts in Paris, Berlin and London and there is the safe deposit box in Switzerland. Kowlowsky, give the Countess von Kahlberg the numbers of the accounts.'

Her father's accountant, Monsieur Kowlowsky, a devious man with bad teeth, handed a sheet of paper to Miranda.

'There is cash, gold and bonds in the Geneva bank,' said Konstantin. 'The cash is in Swiss francs. Water . . .' Miranda helped him with the glass. 'I have transferred the title deeds of the London house to you, Miranda.' Konstantin snapped his fingers; the accountant handed her more papers.

Miranda looked down at them. 'Papa—'

'It is of the utmost importance that you keep these safe, do you understand? I have sold the grain business – a pity, but there were some bad debts. I shall keep my interests in the mines and oilfields for as long as possible. When the war comes, armies will need coal and oil.'

'You're going to get better, Papa,' she said. 'I know you are.'

He shot out his hand, grasping her wrist, his grip stronger than one would have expected from a sick man. 'You don't know any such thing, Miranda. None of us knows anything of the future.' Then he lowered his voice. 'If Germany invades Russia, then you must leave that husband of yours. Germany will never conquer Russia's armies on Russian soil. If Germany chooses to fight Russia, then Germany will be destroyed. And they will fight, sooner or later.'

A week passed. Miranda wrote to Friedrich, explaining that she must remain with her father. The mornings she spent at her father's flat, and the afternoons, while Konstantin rested, were taken up by visits to acquaintances and fittings at her couturier. Silks and linens were held out for her inspection, pretty models walked up and down in front of her to display a frock or a summer coat. Paris was hot, busy, on edge, a shock after the dreaming countryside of East Prussia. Every now and then she felt as if she were coming alive again.

After a long lunch with a scriptwriter at the Café de Flore, Olivier Roussel walked back to his office. He was carrying a canvas bag containing a fishing net, several glass floats and a couple of dozen rubber fish. The bag, though not heavy, was bulky and awkward to carry as he wove through the crowds of tourists and shoppers on the Pont de la Concorde. Hurrying through traffic, darting round a motorcycle spewing out black smoke, he almost lost the rubber fish.

On the Champs-Elysées, his eye was caught by a girl in a black straw hat. She was twenty yards or so ahead of him, walking in a purposeful manner, a black patent leather handbag swinging from her arm and black patent leather high heels clacking on the pavement. Olivier slowed his pace, admiring her legs and the sway of her hips. She was wearing a cream-coloured backless dress, edged in black: very chic. At the window of a shop selling silk scarves she paused. Then she gave a little toss of the head and walked on.

That little toss of the head seemed familiar. It reminded him of the way Miranda had tossed her head when she had disapproved of something or disagreed with something or simply thought something not quite important enough to trouble herself with. This girl had legs like Miranda's, was small and slim like Miranda, and, though her head was hidden by the hat, he had caught a glimpse of a fall of black hair as she had turned to look in the shop window.

He drew level with her, glanced at her, and said, 'My God, Miranda.'

She stopped, turned to him. Her black-gloved hand flew to her mouth. 'Oh.'

'You're very late,' he said.

'Late?'

'Two years late, in fact.' He couldn't stop smiling. 'But then, you're always late.'

'Yes, I am, aren't I?' She made a sound somewhere between a sob and laughter. 'Oh, *Olivier!*'

He kissed her, left-right, left-right. A cloud of Shalimar and for some reason her hair always smelled of lemons. Her cheek, which he brushed with his lips, was cool and fine-grained.

She said, 'Tell me how you are. I must know everything. Where are you going? Are you busy?'

'I have to take this back to my office and make a phone call.' He held up the canvas bag. 'But then I'm free. What about you? We could have coffee together.'

'I have an appointment at my couturier.' A mischievous look. 'But I can always be late, can't I?'

Olivier's office was in the tangle of streets between the Place de la République and the Marais. On the Métro, they talked. Miranda told Olivier that she had been in Paris for a week. She was having such a lovely time. And it was so marvellous to see him! She had tried to phone him when she had last been in Paris a year ago, but he had moved away. He looked just the same – no, he looked *almost* the same. He looked – and she studied him in a way that made his mouth go dry – more *successful*.

'Oh, I'm hanging on by the skin of my teeth,' he said, with a grin.

'What's in your bag?'

'A fishing net, some floats and a couple of dozen rubber fish.' She giggled. 'Why do you have fish, *chéri*?'

He loved the way she said the endearment. It made his skin tingle.

He explained, 'I'm working as an assistant to René Clair.'

'Who's he?'

'A very famous film director, you ignorant girl. We're filming a gangster movie – Jean Gabin's playing the hero. Very moody, lots of menace. There's a scene in a fisherman's shack at the harbour in Marseilles. And the bright lights make real fish smell appalling, so . . .'

They walked from the Métro station to a building in the

Rue Dupuis, between a greengrocer's and a shop that made bows for violins. As they climbed the narrow stairs to Olivier's office on the top floor, they drew apart, but their hands remained linked together, tying them one to the other.

Two of the girls from the typing pool on the first floor called out to him as they passed. They had to squeeze against the wall as a woman carrying a mop and bucket plodded downstairs.

Olivier's office was on the top floor. He unlocked the door. The blinds were down; the air was hot and dusty. 'Miranda,' he said, and as he closed the door behind them she put up her face and he kissed her.

And then he had dropped the bag and they were tearing at each other's clothes and the glass floats were rolling across the floor and the fish had tumbled together in a little silvery heap.

They made love standing up, and then on the sofa. Then sitting on his lap.

She had never made love like that before. She and Friedrich made love decorously, in bed.

After the third time, he pulled on his trousers and left the room, returning with a glass of water. They lay on the sofa, side by side, sharing the water. He ran the palm of his hand over her breasts, her stomach, her thighs. 'Like silk,' he said.

The next time he made love to her it was slowly, tenderly, lovingly. The phone rang several times but he took no notice. His mouth caressed every part of her: the soles of her feet, the soft skin of her inner thigh. This time, when she came, she cried. He asked her why she was crying but she shook her head, because she didn't understand it herself.

She said, 'I suppose you're always making love to women here.'

'Every day. I find them walking along the street and I ask

them back to my office.' He kissed the lobe of her ear. 'No, I promise you're the first. Though once or twice I've slept here when I've been working late.'

'This room is such a mess.' The desk was heaped with papers and there were strange things piled on the floor and on the shelves – papier-mâché masks, half a dozen brightly coloured parasols, a lion's head, a couple of revolvers – replicas, she assumed.

Idly, his fingertips stroked her stomach. 'I'll tidy up next time.'

'Next time we'll go to my room.'

'Where are you staying?'

'The Crillon.'

He wriggled round so that he could look at her face. 'Why didn't you come back to Paris?'

She shrugged. 'My father.'

He took her left hand and kissed it. Then he touched with his thumb her engagement and wedding ring. 'Tell me.'

'He's called Friedrich von Kahlberg. Count Friedrich von Kahlberg.'

'So you're a countess?'

'Yes. And I live in a castle. Isn't that extraordinary?'

He laughed. 'But then,' he said, 'you always were extraordinary.'

'Yes,' she said complacently, 'I am, aren't I? And you, Olivier? Are you married?'

'No.' His mouth nuzzled her neck.

'A fiancée, perhaps?'

'No.'

'A girlfriend, surely?'

'One or two.'

'Are they pretty?'

'Very.'

'Prettier than me?'

Propping himself up on his forearm, he looked at her consideringly. 'Mmm . . .'

'*Olivier.*' A little punch to his chest.

He caught her hands and wrapped them round his neck. 'How could they possibly be prettier than you? But you're not pretty, Miranda, you're beautiful. You are the most beautiful woman I've ever seen. I thought so the first time I saw you, in the Parc Monceau.'

Then he kissed her on the lips and in the hollow of her throat and she closed her eyes and gave a sigh of pleasure.

It was dark when at last they dressed and went out for something to eat. Olivier took her to a restaurant in the Marais, not her usual sort of place at all. There was one big table, around which everyone sat, elbows jostling. At the far end of the table, a woman suckled her infant; the man to the other side of Miranda was wearing blue overalls and rolling cigarettes.

But the food was divine. She hadn't thought she was hungry – she was satiated; surely she was incapable of any sort of hunger? – but the artichokes were succulent and slippery with butter and the lamb in the navarin swam in a rich, dark sauce. And Olivier's arm was round her waist so that they could only use their forks, and their bodies pressed against each other, her head leaning on his shoulder, and she could smell the salty, soapy scent of his skin and she would have liked to have bottled the moment and kept it for ever.

Every morning, she went to see her father. Still the dutiful daughter. As he grew a little stronger, Konstantin Denisov tried, just the same, to impose his will on her.

Why was she staying in a hotel? She should be here, with her father.

No, Papa.

Why not?

The honest answer would have been, *because then I wouldn't be able to spend the afternoons in bed with my lover.* Instead, she said, 'I like the Crillon. It suits me.'

She should dine with him, at least. He would soon be well enough to go out to a restaurant in the evening.

No, Papa. It would tire him too much. He must be sensible. At that, he growled. She would lunch with him, here in the flat, if he liked. Besides, her evenings were busy. She had friends to see, old friends.

She was a married woman now, which meant that she was free to see whomever she liked. Her father had no hold over her now. The mornings were his, but her evenings – and the afternoons when his work permitted it – belonged to Olivier. Sometimes they dined in this or that restaurant. Once, they went to the cinema and now and then they walked in the park. But mostly they stayed in bed. Her bed at the hotel or his bed in his apartment in the Marais. Or the sofa in his office, for old times' sake.

You could fit, she was discovering, a lifetime into a day. Every hour, every minute and every second were precious to her.

Her room in the Crillon, with the *Do Not Disturb* sign hanging on the door, at that time when late afternoon turns to early evening. They had made love slowly and luxuriously, aware of all the people in the city hurrying home from work and their good fortune in not being among them.

She climbed out of bed and went to the window.

'If some lucky cab driver should look up from the road below,' said Olivier, 'he'd see a magnificent sight.'

Naked, she was looking down to where the traffic wove itself into knots on the Place de la Concorde.

She turned and smiled at him. 'Do you think I should put some clothes on, darling?'

'Certainly not. I love to watch you walk around like that. So unconcerned.'

'I'm really very modest. Usually I reach for my robe as soon as I step out of bed. But perhaps that's because it's always so cold in the castle.'

She came back to bed and lay down, her head resting on his taut stomach. He lit two cigarettes and gave one to her. She liked smoking in bed, it made her feel deliciously decadent.

He said, 'Tell me what you're thinking.'

'That I adore you.'

'That's just as well, because I adore you too.' His hand stroked her hair. 'I love you, Miranda. I've never felt like this about anyone before. I love you with all my heart.'

There was the rumble of the traffic through the open window and, outside the room, the clink and clatter of a trolley wheeled along the corridor. When she was with him, she didn't want to be anywhere else or become anyone else. When she was with him, she could be naked, body, heart and soul.

She needed to know all about him. His favourite film, his favourite novel, the dishes he most liked to eat.

He considered. 'Boiled crab,' he said. 'I like taking it apart. I'd like to think that's because I enjoy the technical challenge but I'm afraid it's because I'm a savage at heart.'

Here, he scooped her up in his arms, and she gave a little shriek.

'When, in your entire life, Olivier, were you most bored?'

'Military service,' he said. 'We were in a field somewhere in the Marne. We had to dig a trench and defend it against another company's assault. But they got lost somewhere so we just sat there all day, at the ready, waiting. It was winter and very cold.' He gave a theatrical shiver and then kissed her. 'And what about you, Countess? Tell me what bores you.'

'Once, when I was young, everything. I remember the exact day. I was thirteen years old. We were on the train, travelling from Berlin to Hamburg. When I was a child, I loved to go on the train, but then, all of a sudden, I was tired of it, it was so boring. I thought I would die of boredom. I don't think I stopped being bored until Kay came to live with us.'

Her last question. 'When were you happiest? You must think very hard about this, Olivier.'

'Now,' he said.

He told her that his Belgian backer, Monsieur Charlier, had pulled out not long after she and Kay had left for Berlin, leaving him with insufficient money to make his film. Poor Olivier, she said, though she was secretly pleased she had not been replaced by another Camille. And then, for a while, things had been difficult. He'd tried to keep going, had filmed one or two advertisements and a great many weddings, but in the end he'd had to give up the warehouse. But then, out of the blue, a stroke of luck – René Clair had seen a short film Olivier had made a couple of years before and had offered him work. Many of his day-to-day tasks were run-of-the-mill, but he was learning so much, watching a master. It was an invaluable experience, and when the film they were making was finished, he would revive his own production company, find a backer and make something of his own, something wonderful.

She told him about Sommerfeld. The long, cold winter, the blossom in the orchards in spring and a cormorant, like a black arrow, diving into the lake behind the castle. Friedrich's cousins, the parties and the dancing. Visits to great manor houses to see Friedrich's friends and relatives. 'Such extraordinary houses, darling,' she said. 'So *stately* and they've been there for ever, and they never buy a new piece of furniture or a new ornament to put on the mantelpiece. Everything is just *there*. I now see that my father and I are disastrously *nouveau riche*.'

She never talked about Friedrich to him. It would have seemed disloyal. Talking about Friedrich was perhaps the least of her disloyalties, but there it was.

The courtyard outside Olivier's apartment was guarded from the street by heavy double doors, twelve feet high. The Marais was old, old Paris, weighted with history and perhaps even a little tired, damp plaster in the apartment building and shadows on the walls where there had once been oil lamps. In Olivier's rooms, there were movie posters and ceramics in iridescent colours – turquoise, fuchsia, gold.

'Your mother made these?' she asked him, touching a statu-ette of a woman in a blue dress, all sinuous curves and dark, almond-shaped eyes.

'Yes, all of them.' He was making coffee in the kitchen. 'Do you like them?'

'Very much. Though, this . . .' She pointed to a vase incised with angular red and black lines, some of them broken.

'My mother was very ill when she made that. She was in a lot of pain.'

'Poor lady. How old were you when she died, Olivier?'

He put the coffee pot on the table and took from a cupboard two tiny cups painted with multicoloured stripes.

'I was fifteen,' he said. 'My father died a year later. When I was growing up, my parents often quarrelled. They were both people who had a very decided way of looking at the world, who found it hard to compromise. But in the end, they couldn't live without each other.'

She stroked his face. 'We'll never quarrel, will we?'

'Never.' He kissed her palm.

'Ah, these are wonderful!'

Near the window, two fat-bellied ceramic bluebirds with golden beaks spun, their wings outstretched, from cotton threads, moving in the gentle breeze.

He came to stand beside her. 'My mother made them when she was expecting me. They used to hang over my cradle.' When he touched a string, the birds bobbed and danced.

'They're beautiful,' she said. 'How lovely to fall asleep watching the bluebirds flying.'

They had so much in common. They both loved long, lazy lunches and browsing the bookstalls on the Seine and they both disliked grey, gloomy weather and adored the sun. They liked eccentric people who had peculiar interests – people who bred parrots or collected antique door knobs or who made photograph albums of railway stations, like Uncle Karl. They both loved the cinema, of course, though they had a slight difference of opinion as to whether gangster films or romances were best. A gangster movie with a romance, said Olivier, and Miranda said, yes, the very thing.

They considered the qualities they admired. 'Courage,' said Olivier.

'Courage, of course,' said Miranda. 'But kindness, too. I sometimes think it's as hard to be kind as it is to be brave.'

They were sitting at a pavement table in a café. The rays of the sun, shining through the striped awning, cast shadows on the pavement.

She said, 'That was one of the things I first loved about you, Olivier, that you were kind. I could tell, you see, from the moment I met you. The same with Kay. Kay is a kind person. Me – no, I try to be, but I'm not really. I look at myself all the time and I try to work out what other people are thinking of me, what impression I'm making, whether they like me. And if I'm afraid they don't like me enough then I change myself a little. My father tells me I'm cunning. I expect he's right. After all, he should know. You can't be kind if you're always thinking about yourself.'

A pause, while she crumbled her bread between her fingers and threw crumbs to the sparrows pecking beneath the tables. Then she said slowly, 'But when I'm with you, I'm a better person. I don't try to work out what you're thinking of me because I know that you love me. It's funny; because I'm not afraid you won't like me, I find I don't dislike myself.'

A fortnight passed. Her father grew stronger each day. He was no longer in his bed when Miranda came to his flat in the mornings, but had progressed to a chair in the drawing room, the newspapers and the telephone on a table beside him. She wrote to Friedrich, telling him of her father's recovery.

Far too soon, it was her last evening in Paris.

They dined in a quiet restaurant and afterwards went back to Olivier's flat. They made love and dozed a little, then woke and made love again and dozed a little more. And then the dawn showed, a pale light creeping through the slatted blinds into the room.

She had to go, she said. Friedrich had arranged to meet her in Berlin; she must pack and then she must catch her train. She sat up in bed, looking at Olivier.

'What are you doing?' he asked.

'Memorizing you.' Perhaps her eye would act like a camera lens. Perhaps if she looked long enough, in times to come she would blink and he would still be there, recorded on her inner eye. The triangle of his torso, broad at the shoulders and tapering at the hips, his hands, strong and well-shaped, the curl of his upper lip that she loved to kiss, and his eyes, the colour of caramel and Corsican honey.

'Stay with me,' he said.

'Chéri, you know that I can't.' The words were soft, like a sigh.

He climbed out of bed, pulled on his trousers, made them coffee, lit two cigarettes and gave one to her. Sitting on the bed beside her, he said, a little bitterly, 'We should have run away together two years ago, shouldn't we?'

She squeezed his hand. 'Darling, we didn't know. We didn't understand.'

He threaded his fingers through hers. 'When will I see you again?'

'I don't know.' She thought. 'We have obligations – a holiday, visits to Friedrich's relations, a trip to Berlin. September, I should think. Yes, I'm sure Friedrich will understand if I need to visit my father again in September.'

He brushed back a lock of hair that had fallen over her face. His gaze rested on her, intent, serious, full of love. 'If there's a war,' he said, 'you should go to England.'

'Darling, if I was to go anywhere at all, I would come to Paris.'

'No. In the last war, the Germans were within this much,' he put his finger and thumb a very short distance apart, 'of taking Paris. And now, I'm afraid we're going to have to go through the whole thing all over again.' His shake of the head expressed resignation and anger. 'Miranda, if, God forbid, Paris were to fall, what would your father do?'

'Darling—'

'I mean, whose side would he be on?'

'Whichever side paid him the most money, I should have thought.'

He frowned. 'I hope, I *believe* we'll be safe, but I can't be sure. But if it does come to war, I'll be called up. I'm in the reserve. You mustn't come to Paris. You would be safe in England. You have a house there, don't you? And there's your friend, Kay, so you wouldn't be alone.'

'Olivier,' she said gently. 'I won't leave Friedrich. I've thought about this, and I won't. What I've done is bad enough, but I won't make it worse by leaving him. Not if there's a war and not even for you. So, my darling Olivier,' she made herself smile, 'come back to bed and hold me until it's time for me to leave.'

Later, he walked back with her to the hotel. The sky was a very pale blue, the air soft and cool, though she could sense the promise of the day's heat. The streets were almost empty. Only a few vehicles hurried along the road – a horse pulling a cartload of squealing pigs, an open truck crowded with workmen, heading for a building site or the docks. They crossed the Place des Vosges, then walked along the Rue Saint Antoine and down by the Hôtel de Ville to the river. Paris, Miranda thought, had never looked more beautiful.

On the quayside, resting her arms on the stone parapet as she looked across to the Île de la Cité and the great bulk of Notre-Dame, she said softly, 'Until a week ago, until I saw you again, I thought I was happy.'

He stroked her cheek with his finger. 'Do you regret it?'

'No, not at all.'

She heard him say, 'Miranda, I wish—' and she put her finger to his lips, silencing him.

'No, don't say it.'

'The next time you come to Paris—'

'You'll have married, darling.' She made a stab at lightness. 'You'll have married one of your dozens of girlfriends and you'll have a dear little baby. Twins, perhaps.'

'Twins, that would be nice. Boys or girls?'

'Boys, of course, with curly hair and brown eyes, just like yours.'

He held her in his arms, whispering that he loved her, and she closed her eyes, trying to stem the tears.

'If we should ever lose touch again . . .'

'We won't.'

'If, though. You must look for me in the Parc Monceau, Miranda. I'll wait for you there.'

'You promise?'

'I promise.'

He took a small parcel from his pocket and placed it in her hand. She was not to open it, he said, until she was on the train.

Inside the Crillon, she bathed and put on her travelling clothes and packed her cases. Everything seemed charged, brilliant – the glitter of the brass buttons on the porter's uniform as he carried her luggage downstairs, the morning sunshine as they stepped out of the hotel and into the waiting taxi. At the Gare du Nord, a porter took her cases and hat boxes and put them in the luggage van and an attendant offered to show her to her seat.

On the platform, Olivier embraced her. Smoke plumed from the funnel and the guard blew his whistle. Miranda stepped into the carriage.

A jolt as the train began to move. She put her hand to the glass of the window; he pressed his own hand against it. The train pulled out of the station; for a while he ran beside it, and then he was gone.

'Do you regret it?' he had asked her.

'No, not at all,' she had replied.

Sitting in the carriage, she covered her eyes with her dark glasses and felt her heart as heavy as a stone. Had she told Olivier the truth? Or was there a small part of her that wished that afternoon on the Champs-Elysées he had walked by a little later, or she had left for her couturier a little earlier, and that they had never seen each other again. Then she would never have learned what was possible. Then she might have been content with her kind husband and her beautiful castle.

Just when everything was going so smoothly, she thought. Just when she was safe. This, like a thunderbolt. Well then, she would have to make sure everything went on running smoothly. Olivier must be a part of her life, a most precious part, but a secret part. She could do that; she was used to having secrets.

She took from her bag the package he had given her and unwrapped it. In her palm lay a small ceramic bluebird. There was a note with it: *I have the other bluebird. I shall keep it with me always and think of you*. Closing her eyes, she pressed its cool body against her cheek, and thought of him. *My God, Miranda . . . You're very late. Two years late, in fact.* The look in his eyes. The way the corners of his mouth curled when he smiled. The way his fingers had brushed against the bare skin of her forearm, making her shiver.

She thought of the letter she would write to Kay.

The most wonderful thing has happened to me, she would say. *I can't tell anyone else, but I must tell you. That way it will seem real.*

Chapter Seven

It was Friday night. Kay had received a postcard from Tom, telling her that he was returning to England, suggesting they meet that evening at their usual rendezvous. Waiting outside the pub, she looked for him among the crowds on the pavement. When she caught sight of him, she waved and called out.

'How lovely to see you, Tom!'

'And you.' He put down his rucksack and kissed her cheek.

'You smell of the sea.'

'It was such a glorious crossing, I spent most of the time on deck.' He ran a hand over his chin. 'I apologize if I look a little rough and ready.'

Inside the pub, it was crowded. She perched on the end of a bench while Tom went to the bar. It cheered her up to see him again.

'You're very brown,' she said, as he came back with the drinks.

'I was in Provence until a couple of days ago.'

'Provence. Lucky thing.' Her gaze washed over the people in the pub, the city men in suits, a sprinkling of girls in bright cottons. 'I wish I could go away,' she said wistfully. 'I'd love to go to France again.'

'How are you, Kay?'

'I'm very well.'

'And Johnny?'

'Oh,' a little shrug of the shoulders, a quick glance down at her glass, 'we've broken up.'

'I'm sorry. That's rough.'

'It was, at the time, but I'm over it now.'

'What happened?'

'Nothing much, really. Nothing much changed. We were just as we always were. Only I started wondering whether he said the same things to the other girls that he said to me. Whether, when he danced with them, he held them like he held me.' She smiled at Tom, though she didn't feel like smiling inside. 'So no blazing row, nothing dramatic. I suppose I realized that I wasn't as special to him as he was to me. And then it just rather fizzled out.'

'When Edie finished with me we were in a terrible restaurant in Esher. She told me I wasn't a good bet.'

'Oh dear, how crushing.'

'It was rather. But she was probably right.'

She thought he looked gloomy, which wasn't like Tom. Touching his hand, she said comfortingly, 'I think you're a good bet. Goodness knows what would have happened to me if you hadn't rescued me that time in Berlin.'

The crowd round the bar had swelled; there was a roar as someone came into the pub and then a ragged rendition of 'For He's a Jolly Good Fellow', which for some moments removed all possibility of conversation. When the singing had died down, Tom said, 'I still think about her a lot. I try to tell

204

myself it was for the best, that we wouldn't have lasted anyway, but I don't really believe it. In here,' he touched a finger to his heart, 'I know that it was me who messed it up, that it was my fault. If I'd been quicker off the mark – if I'd been more decisive and I'd made it clearer to her what I felt for her – then she mightn't have looked at Dangerfield.'

'Why don't you talk to her, Tom?'

'There'd be no point. I phoned her sister, Laura. The wedding was a couple of weeks ago.'

'Oh, Tom,' she said.

Another cheer from the crowd, and the throng moved, like a many-limbed monster, pressing against Kay, on the end of the bench.

'It's funny, isn't it,' she said to Tom, 'how you can know perfectly well that something isn't right at all, and that it hasn't been right for rather a long time, but it's still awful when it comes to an end. I hated myself for ending up doing all the things I never thought I'd do. Waiting indoors in case the phone rang and mulling over every word Johnny said to try to work out whether he really loved me. You know. Or perhaps you don't. Perhaps men don't do those things.'

'Perhaps we don't,' he agreed. 'Perhaps we make a mess of it too, but in a different way, not noticing what's going wrong until it's far too late. I have a horrible suspicion I'll always regret losing Edie. I'm afraid that night in the restaurant was a turning point and I just happened to take the wrong turning. And I'm not ever going to be able to go back.'

She said hesitantly, 'But if she didn't feel the same . . .'

'It's obvious that she didn't, isn't it? Or she wouldn't have married Dangerfield.' Frowning, he cast a glance round the pub.

'I'm not really in the mood for this, are you? We could walk in the park, if you prefer.'

He shouldered his rucksack and Kay followed him outside. She took his arm as they crossed the road and headed to St James's Park.

'Do you think anyone will ever want either of us?' she said. 'I mean, really want us, fall madly and deeply in love with us?'

He did not reply. Sunlight fell through the heavily leaved branches, dappling the path as they walked. It had not rained for weeks and the grass edges were pale with dust. The heat had a heaviness, a solidity; she felt as if she pressed against something unyielding.

She said suddenly, 'Oh Tom, why do I always get everything so *wrong*?'

'Johnny, you mean?'

'No, not Johnny. Sometimes I've wondered if I was so head over heels over Johnny *because* of the rest of it – because war's looking more and more possible. I'm so frightened, Tom. Most of the time, I feel frightened. I can hardly bear to read the newspaper or see the newsreels. When I was with Johnny, I stopped being frightened. But it was only ever for a while.'

'It's still possible that it may not come to war.'

'Oh Tom, it'll happen, we both know that! Maybe not now, but sometime. It's like that first time we met, in Berlin – I can feel the same thing here, now. That sense of apprehension, that something terrible is going to happen, which none of us can stop. And when it does come, I don't know what I'll do.'

'You and I – all of us – may not have much choice about it.'

They stopped at a bench beneath a lime tree. Tom slid off his rucksack; a few yards away, a woman stooped and rubbed ice cream from her child's face with a handkerchief.

He said, 'We may be lucky. Hitler may wait a while before turning to Western Europe, until forty-one or forty-two, perhaps, and by then we'll be ready.'

'But that's the thing!' she cried. 'That's what I feel so awful about! We're not ready because of people like me!'

He looked at her, astonished, then gave a bark of laughter. 'You're not blaming yourself for our failure to rearm, are you?'

'What if pacifism has *allowed* the Nazis to become powerful? What if it's actually *encouraged* war?'

'Kay, you're being ridiculous.'

'Am I?' She sat forward on the bench, her hands tightly clasped. 'By now, Hitler must be utterly convinced that no one will ever stand up to him. He must believe he can do whatever he likes. Think of Kristallnacht, when all those Jews were murdered. Think of Czechoslovakia. We couldn't *do* anything because we weren't *ready* to do anything! And if appeasement's been shabby – and it has, Tom, it has – then what does that say about pacifism?'

'It's easy to look back with hindsight. At the time, none of us could tell which way it was going to go.'

'You could. On the train, when we were coming home from Berlin.' He looked blank. She said, 'Don't you remember? We quarrelled. We were talking about Spain. You said that if we let democracy be thrown aside so lightly, then there wouldn't be much hope for the future. And you were right.'

He stretched an arm along the back of the bench. 'And we could have charged in, guns blazing, stirred up a hornet's nest, and still fought and lost.'

'Some people – Churchill, for instance – have been telling us for ages that we should rearm. It's been people like me who've been against it. What if I've been wrong all the time? What if the very thing I've believed in most strongly all my life has done such enormous harm? What if my judgement is so lousy? How will I ever be able to trust myself again?'

'You can only do what most of us try to do – follow our instincts, our principles.'

'I'm not sure I think much of my principles any more,' she said bitterly. 'They seem to me rather – rather *disreputable*.'

'I've a feeling that whatever any of us does, it isn't going to make much difference now.'

'But Tom,' she cried, 'what shall I *do*? If there's a war, what shall I *do*?'

He gave her a half-smile. 'You'll think of something, Kay. I know you. You'll do what you have to do, and you'll make the best of it, even though you hate it.'

'But I don't know what's *right* any more! I don't know what I *ought* to do! I feel as if I'm being forced to make a choice that's quite impossible, that I don't want to take, and that I don't even *understand*!'

And then suddenly she was crying. He looked shocked, but then, so was she. She hadn't meant to cry, had had no warning that she would cry. 'Sorry,' she gasped, delving into a sleeve to search for a handkerchief. 'Sorry, I'm so sorry . . .'

He drew her to him, stroking her hair and patting her back and saying *hey, come on, it's not as bad as all that*, and *we'll get through it, you'll see*, while the tears poured down her face. When, eventually, she managed to stop, she said, in a choked voice, 'How awful of me – so embarrassing – it must be the heat . . .' and turned away from him, scrabbling in her bag.

She found a handkerchief at last and blew her nose. 'Sorry.' She produced a smile. 'What an awful homecoming for you . . .

It's OK, I've pulled myself together. Give me a kiss, Tom, and show me you're not cross with me.'

He kissed her cheek. And she found herself holding him, running her fingers through his hair and turning her face so that his next kiss brushed against her mouth. He tasted of the sea. They kissed again.

Then, suddenly, he moved away. 'No,' he said. He sounded angry. 'You don't want this, Kay. You're missing Johnny and you're upset, that's all.' He stood up. 'Come on, it's time to go home.'

Dazed, she rose shakily and followed him out of the park. Now, they walked apart, a careful space between them. Outside the Ritz, he hailed her a taxi and insisted on giving the cab driver the money for her fare. Glancing out of the window as the vehicle drew away, she saw his form diminish against the evening crowds. Then she made a half-hearted attempt to tidy her hair with her hands and took her compact out of her bag and peered quickly at her pink-cheeked, red-eyed reflection. She caught sight of Miranda's letter in her bag, the open envelope, the slanting black script on the cream-coloured notepaper.

The most wonderful thing has happened to me. I can't tell anyone else, but I must tell you, Kay.

Oh God, she thought – to know something – *anything* – to feel as certain as Miranda felt . . .

Berlin: 28 August. Friedrich and Miranda had been staying for a week at the Hotel Adlon. She was due to travel to Paris the next day. Suitcases were packed; in the afternoon she went to the shops and bought toothpaste, stockings, a new scarf.

Friedrich was waiting for her in the lobby when she returned to the hotel. 'Darling,' she said, and kissed him. She felt feverish; her hands shook as she put down her packages.

He said, his voice low, 'I'm afraid you must cancel your journey, Miranda. We must return to Sommerfeld tomorrow.'

Her heart hammered. Did he, somehow, *know*? His expression was peculiar – shocked, grim, even angry. Had she made a mistake? Had she given herself away?

Then he said, 'This news – it will mean war.'

At his words, it was hard to restrain a smile. *War? Is that all? I was afraid it was something much worse.*

She said soothingly, 'Surely not, darling. Whatever's happened, surely it won't come to that.'

'It will, this time.'

He scooped up her packages. They wove through the noisy throng of men in the lobby who were queueing for the telephone, and took the lift.

When they were inside their suite, Friedrich told her that Germany and the Soviet Union had signed a pact, agreeing to remain neutral should the other country become involved in war.

Still, she was sure it would be all right, that it was only a matter of explaining, reassuring. 'But I don't see,' she said to him, 'why this matters to *me*.'

'This is part of Hitler's preparation for war with Poland. It is, for him, the final piece in the jigsaw. He couldn't invade Poland while there was any risk at all that Russia might come to her defence. And now there is not.'

She saw that he was deeply worried and took his hand, trying to comfort him. 'But even if there is to be a war, not *yet*, surely?'

'Any day.'

Now, she felt a frisson of fear. But she said calmly, 'Even if what you say is true, I can't see that makes any difference to us. It needn't prevent me going to see my father.'

'It makes every difference to us. France and England are bound by treaty to defend Poland. This will not be how it was with Austria or Czechoslovakia, Miranda. It will not be *easy*. The Poles will fight. There'll be war in Europe.'

'But not *overnight*, surely?' Troubled, she stared at him. 'Perhaps I'll have to cut my journey short. Perhaps not a fortnight, then, but a week—'

'No, that's not possible.'

'Friedrich, I must see my father.'

His mouth set, he gave a quick shake of the head. 'It's out of the question.'

She had never before seen him like this – curt, severe, immovable. Always before, in any little disagreement, she had been able to coax, to persuade.

'I don't understand you,' she said. 'It was all arranged. I *have* to go.' Her voice rose, just a little. Olivier, she thought. I've waited so long.

She heard him say, 'I hadn't thought you so fond of your father.'

Careful. He was looking at her in a way that made her feel uneasy. She remembered Herr Reimann, and how she had given herself away, and the disaster that had followed. She tried to compose herself, to speak coolly as she said, 'Whatever our differences in the past, he is still my father. I have no other relatives. Papa has been very ill and I must go and see him. I'll be perfectly safe. I'm used to travelling, you know that. If you're concerned, Friedrich, then I'll stay in Paris for a shorter time.'

'No. There may not be any trains. They will have been

commandeered for military use. I'm sorry. I realize you must be disappointed.'

With a renewed sense of shock, she remembered Olivier's flat in the Marais: the bed, the warmth of his body. *If it should come to war*, he had said to her, *I shall be called up. I'm in the reserve. You mustn't come to Paris.*

She couldn't speak. She put her hand to her mouth, as if to hold back a cry of pain, and went to the window, struggling to compose herself. She made herself look out of the window and focus on the scene outside. A few leaves from the lime trees – straggling little saplings, replacements for the much older trees the Nazis had had cut down several years ago – had begun to brown and fall, lying on the pavement like crumpled, dirty scraps of paper. The roads, always busy, were busier than usual, cars jammed nose to tail, a policeman directing them with a sweep of a hand. Crowds clustered round a newsstand and there were queues at the tram stop and taxi rank. Through the open window she could hear a noise, like the buzz of bees about to swarm, a murmur of unease and apprehension.

Where was Olivier now? Was he already in army uniform, crushed into the carriage of a train or the back of a lorry, heading north, to the border? A small sound escaped her, she could not hold it back.

She heard Friedrich say, 'Miranda, are you all right?'

'Yes, of course.'

She made herself turn and look at him, but something in her expression must have betrayed her, because he said, 'You would tell me if you were unhappy, wouldn't you?'

'I'm not unhappy, Friedrich. Though, all this . . .' She glanced back at the window.

'I remember how you were when you came back from Paris. You were happy then – I saw it in your eyes.'

She gave a little laugh. 'You know how I love Paris.'

'No, there was something more than that – you were transformed.' He was standing at the fireplace, watching her. He said, and his tone of voice remained conversational, 'I wonder, if you were to go to Paris this time, whether you would come back to me.'

He took his cigarette case out of his jacket pocket. 'When I first met you, Miranda, it was as though you were looking out at the world through a pane of glass. You had retreated behind a barrier. We could look at you and admire, but you scarcely noticed us. I wondered what had happened to you to make you feel like that, so young. I thought of my own loss, of course, and wondered whether you had endured something similar. You never spoke of it, and I thought it intrusive to ask. Or perhaps I dared not ask. I imagined there were experiences we had in common and I flattered myself that because of that, I alone would be able to break through to you. And so I've waited, throughout our engagement and marriage. I've waited such a long time. Once or twice I've glimpsed the beginnings of an alteration in you – when you recited poetry to us in the evening at Sommerfeld or that time I watched you skating on the lake with Klaus. There it was, I could see it on your face, a moment of being completely alive. I feel it whenever I'm with you, and I have waited so long to see it in you. But it always dies, and you retreat behind the glass again.'

He tapped a cigarette against the silver case, then lit it. 'When you came back from Paris in the spring, you had changed. Something happened to you there, Miranda. Something changed you.'

'Friedrich,' and her laughter sounded false even to her, 'doesn't everyone love springtime in Paris?'

But he continued implacably, 'I think you met someone. Perhaps you knew him already – perhaps it was he who was the cause of your grief when I first met you. I've thought about this for months now.'

'No, Friedrich,' she murmured.

Everything about him remained the same, his stance as easy and elegant as always, his straight fair hair brushed back from his face, his voice level and low. But in his eyes – she could not look into his eyes, because in their blue-grey depths she saw a terrible pain.

She said, 'When I met you, I felt imprisoned, that was why I was unhappy. My father gave me no freedom, no life of my own.'

'I won't ask you to tell me his name,' he said. 'To tell the truth, I don't think I could bear to know for certain that he exists.'

'There's no one.' She shook her head. 'You're mistaken, Friedrich.' Yet her voice seemed flat, lacking in colour.

A loud blare from a car horn, cutting through the silence that lay between them, and he rose, saying, 'I regret that we have not had a child. It would have made a bond between us.'

They had been married over a year and there had not been a baby. Not even her passionate affair with Olivier, when they had not always remembered to be careful, had made a baby. Her womb, she thought, must be cold and unwelcoming, offering little succour.

Friedrich glanced at his watch. 'We should dine.'

'I'm not hungry.'

'You must eat. You must keep up your strength.' He opened a wardrobe, took out a shirt.

Only one evening dress remained in her wardrobe. All the others had been packed. In the bathroom, running water into the basin, she held her hands under the cold tap and then pressed them against her face, holding back the tears, shutting in the pain.

When she had agreed to marry Friedrich, she had had a vision of herself as the serene, untroubled chatelaine of Sommerfeld. So different to her previous life. She had thought it would suit her. And it had, for a while.

Yet these past four months, certain triggers had made something inside her leap and burn. Words: *Paris*, and *September*. A phrase in a novel, a glass of French wine, the scent of lilacs – these she had held closely to herself.

She changed into her evening frock, then put up her hair, powdered her face, put on lipstick. Painted on a mask – who knew how long she must keep it there?

When she went back into the other room, Friedrich had gone to his desk and was sorting through papers, tearing some and dropping the fragments in the waste-paper basket, putting others aside. Her gaze drifted to her suitcase, standing by the door. *Oh Olivier*, she thought with a searing pain, *how will I bear this?*

She heard Friedrich say, 'I truly believe you'll be safer at Sommerfeld than you would be if you were still wandering around Europe with your father. Sommerfeld has survived many wars. It has survived for centuries. But while I'm away—'

'Away?' she echoed.

'I shall have to return to my regiment.'

'Oh. I didn't realize . . .'

'While I'm away you must be careful, Miranda. You must be

circumspect. We must all watch what we say nowadays. You may speak as you wish among family, of course, when you are at Sommerfeld. But outside, and when you are in company, you must be careful, because you are not German.'

'Yes, Friedrich.'

He went on, 'I have little admiration for this leader of ours. His vulgarity – his crudeness – offends me. There are many who see Hitler as our saviour, who believe he'll make Germany great again. There are those who see themselves as victims of injustice, and others who have no interest in politics, who think that what's taking place is no concern of theirs. And, of course, there are the bullies, the sadists, the Jew-haters, who'll make the most of the opportunities the regime offers them. And those men who are at heart so vain, so puffed-up, they'll stab a man for looking at them the wrong way. It's convenient, I suppose, to blame all Germany's troubles on the Jews, it's useful to the regime to keep old hatreds alive, to incite fear and loathing of what's different and foreign.' He made a contemptuous sound. 'As always, there are those who, though they may dislike what's happening, fear for themselves and their families. They'll keep their heads down, hoping to survive until it's over. I must place myself in that category. My loyalty is to my family and my estate. I'll fight, if I must, but I fight for Sommerfeld, and for you, Miranda. And yet,' his voice dropped, 'and yet I remember the last war. The agony of knowing there were foreign armies on our soil. I am still, in the end, a patriot.'

He picked up her silk shawl and wrapped it round her shoulders. His hands stilled; he kissed the curve of her neck. 'I love you,' he said. 'No one could love you as much as I love you.

No one. I won't let you go easily, Miranda. I'll wait for you and I'll fight for you. I'll never let you go lightly.'

She caught his hand as he kissed her again and pressed her cheek against the back of it, closing her eyes. Then, without speaking, they went downstairs to dinner.

Part Two

Sowing the Wind

1940–1945

Chapter Eight

O livier did not know where he was. He had an idea of the date – around 26 May 1940, in which case it was sixteen days since the German army had invaded Holland and nine days since it had entered Brussels. Every now and then, Olivier spotted a milestone. Many of the villages they came across were deserted, but there were a few that seemed to exist in a different time, unaware of the disaster that was about to overtake them, where there was still a baker's shop with plump loaves in a window, or an old woman in black coming out of a church. Curious gazes watched them from behind the shutters as they drank from the well; a small boy ran through the street and then came to a halt with a skid, staring at their dusty uniforms and the machine gun. Then, their thirst slaked, they headed back to the main road.

Today, tramping across empty fields, they had seen hardly a soul. In the afternoon, they came across a farmhouse surrounded by sheds and tumbledown barns. A dog barked and hens pecked at the scrubby grass. Entering the yard, they called out, but there was no reply. Gaston hammered on a door then disappeared round the back of the house.

There was an archway in a red-brick wall; going through it, Olivier found himself in an orchard. Blossom drifted across lush green grass and the air was still and warm and filled with light. Olivier unlaced his boots, kicked them off, and then lay down on the grass. Pierre did likewise. Beneath Olivier's hot, sore feet the grass was cool and soft. When he looked up, he saw blue sky clouded with white blossom. A few petals floated and a bird sang; elsewhere, there was silence. He wondered, before he closed his eyes and fell asleep, whether he could sit out the war here. Whether, perhaps, the armies that marched over France would divide around the farmhouse, not touching it, in the way that a stream divides round a rock.

That evening, they cooked the chicken that Gaston had caught and drank a couple of bottles of red wine from the farmhouse's cellar. The next morning, waking at dawn, they left the farmhouse and the orchard behind them and walked on.

Olivier had spent the winter in northern France, one of a company of reserves in an infantry regiment. It had been the coldest winter in decades. They had hacked trenches in frozen soil and marched here and there. And had waited, huddled round a stove in a barn which they fed with damp wood, the determination and resolve that had sustained them when they left their homes at the outbreak of war in September 1939 chilling in the snow and the fog and the waiting.

In April, with the better weather and the news of the German invasion of Norway and the occupation of Denmark, they were moved north, closer to the Belgian border. Then, 10 May, and the Luftwaffe attacked Holland, Belgium and Luxembourg, following up the air bombardment with a ground offensive.

Olivier found himself in the hills above the Meuse while

Stukas screeched through the sky, pounding them with bombs. Not far away, a French artillery battery kept up an incessant barrage. Machine guns were fired at the German planes, to little effect. In the evening, two French aircraft turned up and chased away the Stukas and a cheer rose up from the men. Not long afterwards, they received orders to fall back to a village three miles south – the Germans had broken through to the east.

Olivier was in a detachment of six, from all over France – two from the Midi, the others from Marseilles, Normandy and the Alps. They wound between rocks and trees, hauling their heavy equipment, keeping away from the roads whenever possible. They had run out of water; after a few hours, Olivier found it hard to think of anything other than his thirst. When, around dawn, they reached a village, they went first to the well and drank deeply.

There were other soldiers in the village, sleeping at the road-side or standing in groups, smoking. There was an air of confusion everywhere, the junior officers glancing at watches and maps and now and then walking back to the road, as if looking for something. Orders hadn't been received or orders hadn't been sent. The field telephones were in the trenches they had been forced to leave behind and they had not been issued with wirelesses.

A few hours later, catching sight of a German reconnaissance plane, Olivier's detachment left the village, which was too easy a target, and made for the hills to the south, where they dug in and waited. Later that day, the soldier from Normandy returned to the village to refill their water bottles. In his absence, they sighted the first German tank rumbling through the woodland to the left of them. They stubbed out their cigarettes and checked the gun sighting. Tanks rolled through the undergrowth. Olivier felt the reverberation through the earth. Beneath their treads, saplings and bushes flattened. A mortar shell struck a tank, which burst into flames. The heat burned their faces and they scrambled out of the foxhole.

In the early hours of the morning, a lieutenant appeared and gave the order to retreat. He had a wild look in his eye, Olivier thought. There was, in the words he used, a touch of *every man for himself*.

At around midday, they took shelter in a deserted mill and Olivier headed off to find rations. By the time he returned, less than an hour later, his comrades had vanished. Though he tried to find them, taking the main road and searching through the crowds for familiar faces, he never saw them again.

The exodus: vast columns of refugees that clogged the main roads, hindering the passage of the vehicles of the French army. A counter-attack could not be mounted because the roads were blocked by a torrent of exiled men, women and children. All northern Europe, it seemed, had taken flight.

No one had told the citizens of Holland, Belgium and northern France what to do in the event of invasion, and so, pursued by the Luftwaffe, they had taken matters into their own hands, loading family and possessions into cars, carts, prams and wheelbarrows, before fleeing south. Their cars ran out of petrol and were abandoned at the roadside, and the belongings that had seemed so precious at the outset of their flight — an ornate mirror, a grandfather clock — became too cumbersome, too useless, and were jettisoned also. The verges took on the air of a Surrealist exhibition, an accordion rubbing shoulders with a set of dining-room chairs, a birdcage, its door opened to free its occupant, perched on a tower of encyclo-paedias. Livestock wandered abandoned in the fields, the cows lowing because they had not been milked. A child in a grubby pinafore wept at a crossroads, tears pouring down his dirty red face.

Since losing his regiment (careless that, soldier), Olivier had latched on to other detachments whenever he could, taking part in a series of desperate little battles. You bunkered down on the bank of a river or behind a hill, trying to hold back the columns of German tanks, armoured cars and motorcycles that poured through the widening holes in the Belgian border. When it became obvious you were about to get killed or captured, you retreated a couple of miles and found the next river or hill.

He had been walking alone when he had met Pierre. The village was deserted, as most villages were, except for a French soldier sitting at a table outside a café beneath an advertise-ment for Gitanes. Pierre was short, dark, stocky, fortyish. His uniform was, like Olivier's, torn and dusty. He wore a straw hat.

They shook hands.

'Lost my glasses near Sedan,' said Pierre, in an explanatory way. 'Can't see a thing. Still, I found this hat.' Raising the hat, he revealed the bald patch on the top of his head. 'Stops me getting sunburned. I used to have a good head of hair.' He shrugged, then added, with a nod towards the interior of the café, 'I made some coffee. If you'd like some . . .'

The scent of fresh coffee pervaded the small, dark room. Olivier poured himself a cup then went back outside to the table and sat down.

'I had an excellent brandy a few days back. Someone found

it in some château or other. Do you think that when this is over, we'll go on living just as we always did?'

'It depends,' said Olivier, 'on what you mean by "this". This battle or the war.'

Pierre gave a sardonic smile. 'Aren't they both the same?' Then, with a glance over the cobbled village square, he said, 'I'm an accountant for the Galeries Lafayette. People always need shops, don't they? Even Germans need shops. In war or in occupation, people still must buy things. My work's routine, but steady, and a great many pretty girls work at the Galeries Lafayette. What about you? What do you do?'

Olivier gave him a brief résumé of his career. He thought it sounded thin, insubstantial. Then they shouldered their knapsacks and walked on.

The next day, they came across Gaston, asleep at a crossroads. Gaston came from a farm near some little town Olivier had never heard of, somewhere near Auxerre. He possessed several useful talents – he could fall asleep straight away whenever the occasion permitted it, he was an expert shot and a good cook. After linking up with Gaston, they ate surprisingly well, Olivier thought, considering they were taking part in a huge, chaotic retreat. Most of the time, they kept to the byroads and footpaths. The main roads, choked by refugees, were too easy a target for dive-bombing Stukas. The periods of calm, while they walked through empty fields and woodland, were punctuated by instances of intense fear. Once, turning a corner, they found themselves a few feet away from a Wehrmacht motorcycle and sidecar. One of the German soldiers was relieving himself against the wall; the other – tall, black-booted, young – was repairing the tyre of the motorcycle. He looked up and saw them. There was a widening of the eyes, a twitch of the fingers towards the machine gun propped against the wall before Gaston shot him in the head. Then his compatriot.

There were Germans to every side of them. Not just north, east and west, but south as well. They popped up when you were least expecting them, motorcycle riders heading along a road like a column of dusty brown beetles, or a Stuka overhead spraying them with bullets as they dived into a hayrick. Whenever they ran into French or British troops, they stopped and chatted, trying to find out what was going on, what they were supposed to be doing, where they were supposed to be going. Joining together the snippets of information, there was no escaping the conclusion that much of the French army had been encircled, cut off from the larger part of France. On the north-west coast, Allied troops were being taken off the beach by ship to England. Other regiments, fortunate enough to find themselves south of the westward German sweep to the coast, were continuing the fight for France.

At a crossroads, Olivier and Gaston parted from Pierre. Along with another Parisian, Pierre had decided to make for the capital. He had exchanged his army uniform for civilian clothes, taken from an abandoned cart. Olivier and Pierre shook hands and wished each other luck. Pierre said, 'When you're next in Paris . . .' and touched his forehead in salute. Olivier watched him disappear round a bend in the road.

Olivier and Gaston became part of one of the many impromptu detachments of infantry soldiers that had sprung up out of the tattered army of France. As they headed towards the Dunkirk pocket, the engagements became more frequent. One of their company was shot in the leg and they took it in turns to carry him on a makeshift stretcher.

Towards the end of the afternoon, they took shelter in a farmhouse. That evening, they watched the progress of the enemy troops through the upper window of the farmhouse. The German soldiers ran then crouched, ran then crouched through the marshy fields to the rear of the farm. Gaston picked off a few, and they seemed to pause. Leaving the owners in the farmhouse, Olivier and the others took up position in the stables. Watching from the window the dash and bob of the German troops — a glint of sunlight on a belt or buckle, a movement in the reeds — he felt peculiarly dehumanized, no longer an individual, no longer Olivier who made films, or Olivier who loved Miranda.

But after the reeds stopped swaying and the sun died, he must have slept for a while, and in the morning, when they left the stable block, the landscape appeared empty of people. They walked on, keeping to the shelter of ditch and hedge whenever they could, heading north-west, towards the coast. A brightness in the sky told them of the approach of the sea, which cheered them; after all the days of wandering, they were finally reaching their objective. Olivier imagined being on a ship, heading for England. Perhaps Miranda had gone to England, as he had told her to. Yes, perhaps she had.

Some French and British soldiers joined them; there was a brief exchange of news and then they all fell silent, too exhausted to talk. A couple of hours later, heading up a narrow wooded track, there was the rattle of machine-gun fire and they dashed for cover. Crouched in a ditch, it took them a while to pinpoint the location of the enemy soldiers, who were hiding in a shack — a henhouse, perhaps — on the far side of the road. After several brief exchanges of fire, there was nothing more from the henhouse. Cautiously, they climbed out of the ditch.

And then, speeding towards them, along the road they had just travelled, a dozen motorcyclists. Tyres squealed, engines roared, and the soldiers in the sidecars sprayed them with bullets as they scrambled for the shelter of a hedge.

It was over in minutes. One of the British Expeditionary Force soldiers was lying on the road, bleeding, and others were draped over the ditch or curled up motionless at the foot of the trees. An officer stepped forward, spoke first in English and then in very bad French, and one by one they emerged from their hiding places.

For a second or two, Olivier thought he might get away with it. He was that little bit further away than the others. They might not have seen him, they might overlook him, scoop up their prisoners and go away without him, leave him to go on to England, and Miranda, as he had intended.

Then, a footstep, the sound of a pistol being cocked, and he stood up, his hands above his head.

'For you, the war is over.'

He actually said it, thought Olivier. A bubble of some inexpressible emotion – horror, fury, amusement – rose in his throat.

For you, the war is over.

In October 1939, Kay applied to join the Auxiliary Territorial Service.

She did so for a variety of reasons. Because everyone else seemed to be busy and she had never liked to be left out. Because, in spite of the efforts of the Peace Pledge Union and other pacifist organizations, war had been declared, and perhaps if she did her bit, it might come to an end a little sooner. And because, if you were going to throw aside everything you had ever believed in, then you might as well do it with flair and go the whole hog.

But perhaps her principal reason for joining up had been embarrassment. Could one join the services out of embarrassment? *She* had. Every time she remembered the evening she had kissed Tom Blacklock, every time she recalled his tone of voice — *You don't want this, Kay. You're just missing Johnny and you're upset, that's all* — she had wanted to curl up, or preferably hide in a dark corner and die. What on earth had possessed her? In the absence of dark corners and death, she had done the next best thing. Joining the army would take her out of London, she had reasoned, it would occupy her, and it would take her mind off things. She had opted for the ATS rather than the WAAF or the WRAC because Roger Lancaster had taught her to drive when she had been at Oaklands and she had thought the ATS might be able to use someone who could drive.

Aunt Dot had supported her decision. The evening before Kay left home, they talked about Aunt Dot's experiences, nursing in Étaples during the Great War. Kay kept to herself the fact that she felt sick with nerves and was half certain she was making a dreadful mistake. Her sense of dislocation had remained with her as she travelled to the training camp. So many people's lives were changing — Oaklands School had been evacuated to Devon, her friend, Brian, from the bookshop, had volunteered for the navy, and other friends were in the forces or helping on the home front or were making a different sort of stand as they struggled to adhere to their pacifist principles.

Then, basic training, and at least she no longer had time to think. She was training or she was sleeping, and in the rare moments when she wasn't training or sleeping, when she was cleaning her teeth, for instance, or eating her lunch, she was invariably late for something, so had little chance for reflection. To her surprise, the worst thing, the most lowering thing, was that she wasn't any good at it. She had always been good at things. Never brilliant, but always capable. Her incompetence dismayed her. PT wasn't too bad, and she was no worse at marching than most of the others – better, in fact, than the girl from Bolton who was unable to distinguish her left from her right and one morning ran off the parade ground, howling. She didn't mind the communal living, the Nissen huts and canteens, could cope with it after her year and a half at Oaklands; nor did she mind – much – the horrible scratchy uniform with its unbecoming cap that had to be soaked and stretched overnight to get it into any semblance of shape.

It was the spit and polish, the inspections, the saluting, the orders barked out at this unfamiliar creature, Private Garland, whom she had become on joining the ATS, that grated on her. She hadn't realized quite how much she would resent being told what to do, especially when so much of what she was told to do seemed to her stupid and pointless. And the attention to detail, to the petty, futile detail that the army demanded, confounded her. Her bed, an iron frame with three unyielding 'biscuit' mattresses, was glanced at, sneered at, then ordered to be remade. Her uniform was never quite right, her skirt was creased or there was a ladder in her stocking. Her shoes and brass buttons did not shine brightly enough, and her hair wriggled itself out of whatever style she put it in, even though her head was as spiky as a hedgehog with hairpins.

One morning, when Kay had failed yet another kit inspection, the sergeant said to her with lip-curling contempt, 'Think yourself above all this, don't you, Garland? Well, you're not. You're rotten, pretty useless, one of my worst recruits. If I could pass you on to someone else, I would.' The threat shook Kay, as did the dislike in the sergeant's eyes. She felt first anger, then resentment, and then, as she faced the truth, shame. The sergeant was right. She *did* look down on the army. She *was* contemptuous of routine and drill. Unthinking obedience was alien to her, and a large part of her thought that only a fool would put up with it. She resented the humiliations the army heaped on its recruits: the foot inspection, the hair inspection, the tiring, degrading punishments and the mindless discipline, all of which were designed to eat away at individuality. The qualities she prided in herself – independence of thought, originality, spontaneity – were not valued by the army. Both Sylvia, who had worked at Boots in Liverpool before joining up, and Jeanette, who had been in service before the war, were better soldiers than she was.

In the third week, two of their intake deserted. Why did she, Kay, not do as she longed to do, admit she had made a mistake, pack her bags and go home? There would have been few consequences; women soldiers were not subject to the same military discipline as men. She stayed mainly because she could not bear the ignominy of failure, of admitting she had made a mistake. But there was another reason. By then she had found friends. Along with Sylvia with her raucous laugh and foul mouth, and Jeanette, who kept a scrapbook devoted to Clark Gable, there was also Josephine, who in another life had been presented at court, and Louise, who in peacetime had worked in a solicitor's office in Cardiff. In the brief spaces between the various torments the army chose to hurl at them, they talked. They talked about their families and their homes, their jobs and their boyfriends, their tastes in clothes, films, books, music. They shared their common loathing of Sergeant Preston and army food. They sighed as they disclosed their longings – to wear a pretty frock again, to eat a home-cooked lunch, not to be woken at half past six in the morning by the blare of a cornet.

And they helped each other. They lent each other coppers for the phone, hairpins, aspirins, darning needles and cigarettes. They comforted each other, cheering up whoever was the most fed up, giving her a chocolate from a parcel sent from home or sometimes just a hug. Jeanette, who had once spent entire mornings polishing silver, showed Kay how to do her buttons. Sylvia, a cigarette dangling out of her mouth, knelt on the bed behind Kay and teased her hair into shape. Josephine, who as an ex-deb was used to spit and polish, checked her over before parade.

Kay made a huge effort, crushed down her rebellious spirit, and let the army batter her into whatever shape it wanted. It was, she realized, as much an attitude of mind as anything else. You accepted it, the shouting and the orders and the nonsensical tasks. You forgot that there had ever been anything else. You forgot that you had ever sat on a sunny beach in the south of France and watched the men go by. You got on with it. You stuck it out. Then you didn't end up peeling bucketfuls of potatoes quite so often. And by the end of basic training, no matter how hard she glared at Kay's kit, laid out on her perfectly made bed, Sergeant Preston could not find fault with it. When they drilled on the parade ground, Kay and her intake made their turns with a single clean movement. Now, when she looked in the mirror, Private Garland stared back at her.

Along with a dozen others, Kay was sent to the Transport Training Centre at Camberley. There, she learned how to drive army trucks, how to start the vehicle by winding the handle and how to double declutch without crashing the gearbox. She learned to read a map, to fill in a worksheet and logbook, to maintain the truck, changing the oil and filling the radiator with water in winter. Though it was hard work, there was satisfaction in the acquisition of new skills. This, she could see the point of. One day, she might even be useful. She sent a postcard to Tom, a cheery, breezy sort of postcard, apologizing for not having been in touch and conveying her best wishes. A week later, to her great relief, she received an equally cheery, breezy postcard back.

She spent the bitterly cold winter of 1939/40 transporting army vehicles to sites in southern England. Then in April, the phoney war came to an abrupt end with the attacks on Denmark and Norway, quickly followed by the invasions of Holland, Belgium and France. And then, Dunkirk, and the nation watched with horror as the BEF and a large part of the French army were trapped on a small pocket of land and encircled by the enemy. Horror changed to hope, and everyone seemed to hold their breath as, day after day, naval vessels and a vast flotilla of small boats crossed the Channel, rescuing the stranded soldiers from the beaches while undergoing continual bombardment. Transported to the southern ports of England, the men, ragged, mauled and dead-eyed with exhaustion, were ferried inland by train.

The shock of the fall of France – the battle over, lost in such an unbelievably short time – crashed like a cold, grey wave over Britain. When she considered France's fate, Kay felt the sort of grief one might feel for a friend one has always admired, perhaps envied a little, who has suffered something truly appalling. She thought of Olivier and Agnès and Benoît, and wondered how they would bear it. In that

234

jarring moment between waking and hurling herself out of bed in the morning and reporting to the garage for her orders for the day, she had to remind herself that nothing – *nothing* – was the same, and that, quite possibly, nothing would ever be the same again.

But there was no chance to reflect because all the changes they had so far endured – rationing, conscription, the blackout, the evacuation of children to the countryside – were dwarfed by this newest alteration in their circumstances, that they teetered on the brink of invasion. Pamphlets entitled 'If The Invader Comes' were sent to every household. 'When you receive an order, make sure you know it's a true order and not a faked order.' And how on earth, Kay wondered, was one supposed to establish *that*? The things she saw, things she had never thought she would see, as she ferried her lorries and trucks. A Local Defence Volunteers checkpoint in a narrow Hampshire lane, its guards armed with Molotov cocktails. Barricades made of hayricks, empty cider barrels and fallen trees outside sleepy country villages. Concrete pillboxes and tank traps along a coast where cliffs and beaches bristled with barbed wire. Rusted machinery, cattle troughs and farm implements scattered as if by the hand of a giant over the newly harvested fields to prevent planes and gliders from landing.

The sky had become a battleground. In Portland harbour, beneath a speedwell blue sky, a Stuka plummeted like a bird of prey towards a destroyer, straightening out of its dive only at the very last moment as a dark plume rose from the stricken ship, smudging the blue. The silver flash of a Spitfire's wing as it turned in the sky as dogfights were fought over the Kent and Sussex countryside. At an airfield in the aftermath of a raid, the hangars were ablaze and thick black smoke jetted from the burned tangles of metal on the runway. This splendid summer, and yet, pausing for a cigarette and a sandwich en route from somewhere to somewhere, Kay looked out to sea and saw a plane fall in a ball of fire, to be consumed by the waves. No sign of a parachute. She couldn't eat her sandwich, there was a metallic taste in her mouth. She smoked with a steady intentness, then kicked the stub into a ditch and drove on.

On a train journey to London, men and women in uniform were crushed into corridors and compartments. The boy in air force blue in the seat next to Kay's told her that it was his first evening off in London in two months and he was going to paint the town red. The day before, he had baled out of his plane. 'Saw the wing was on fire, and the next moment there I was, floating on my brolly. Can't remember anything about getting out of the cockpit and opening the chute, nothing at all. Funny, isn't it?' Then he fell asleep, his head on her shoulder, waking only when she nudged him at Victoria Station. She bought him a cup of tea at the station café and promised to meet him in the bar of the Berkeley. Sometime.

At first, the Luftwaffe bombed the airfields and the southern ports. But you were never *safe* – a returning plane, off course perhaps, might dump its load of bombs anywhere, on the most remote farmhouse or hamlet, or on the most undistinguished, unremarkable town. Then, in mid-August, the raids were stepped up, clawing further inland to the towns and cities. The first of the major bombing raids on London was on the night of 7 September. That evening, Kay was driving in convoy through Sussex. From the Downs behind Brighton, she saw the crimson glow on the horizon, the red shadow in the sky as London burned.

After that night, bombs fell on the capital for fifty-seven consecutive nights. People sought shelter wherever they could – in basements, in the tube, beneath viaducts, in caves, as the docks and factories went up in flames and the cramped tenements of the East End were reduced to rubble. It was the domestic detail that saddened – wallpaper that had once been carefully chosen peeling from wet plaster, birthday cards fallen from a mantelpiece, sodden and smeared among fragments of ceramic tile and broken brick.

Now, when Kay and Josephine hitch-hiked up to town for a night out, their progress was slowed by the heaps of debris and craters in the streets and the signs warning of impassable roads and unexploded bombs. They had a routine, she and Josephine, slick, fast, to get the most out of an evening. They headed first to Josephine's parents' flat in Clarence Gardens, where they changed out of their uniforms. Josephine's parents were sitting out the war at their country house in Wiltshire. A gin, a bath, dress and make-up. Kay kept an evening frock at the flat, which was furnished with deeply polished mahogany tables and velvet-covered, button-backed Chesterfields, and must once have been immaculate. One evening, in the fireplace, they discovered a dead bird, papery and fragile, shaken loose from its resting place by the force of the bombardment and cast down the chimney. There were cracks in the windowpanes and sand had hissed from the ceiling on to the dressing table, forming tiny pyramids among the bottles of foundation and Elizabeth Arden 'Blue Grass'.

As soon as they were ready, they went first to the Berkeley Hotel, on the corner of Piccadilly. There were always people they knew in the bar of the Berkeley. And at the Dorchester and the Ritz. They'd have a drink or two, and then they'd head on to the Mirabelle, perhaps, to dine, and then to a nightclub, the 400 or the Café de Paris.

Of course, she didn't always spend her evenings off with Josephine. The Mirabelle and the 400 were expensive. And anyway, the people at the West End hotels and nightclubs were Josephine's old friends, not her old friends. They had their own customs – in peacetime, their own social calendar, and a penchant for killing animals, which disgusted Kay. They had their own codes – Not Safe in Taxis, Nice Girls Don't. But she had with Johnny Gilfoyle, so did that make her not such a nice girl? Though they were always courteous and good fun, she suspected that Josephine's friends could look you up and down in an instant and know you didn't quite belong. Kay admired their cool heads in a crisis, their seemingly limitless ability to put up with physical discomfort, but she knew she wasn't one of them.

Other evenings, she went to an East End dance hall with Sylvia, where she danced with wiry, thin-faced boys with slicked-back hair, who offered her Woodbines and asked her to write to them when they went back to their ships. Or she went to the cafés and pubs of raffish Fitzrovia or intellectual Bloomsbury, which had been her haunts before the war.

Sometimes the raid started while she was walking to the café or queueing to get into the nightclub. There would be the howl of the siren, then the distant crump and thud of falling bombs. The long, white beams of the searchlights would criss-cross the sky and barrage balloons would float up into the air, bobbing like giant silver beads. One evening, she was in a restaurant when the room began to rock and the bottles and glasses jumped off the tables and smashed on the floor. Then there was an explosion so intense the vibration seemed to pass

238

through Kay's body, and she found herself sitting on the floor, surrounded by broken glass. Running outside, she saw that everything glittered: the shards of glass on the scorching-hot pavement, the sequins on the girls' dresses, the arcs of water from the fire hoses. There was a hot, dusty smell and an acrid taste in her mouth. And she was trembling; she couldn't stop trembling. The shuddering came from the core of her, the heart of her, like a fever.

When the raid was bad, she ducked down into the tube or into a public shelter. Inside the shelters, there was often, in this different, jumbled-up London, an odd mixture of people. Old ladies in shabby coats and knitted berets, sitting on the benches, their bandaged, swollen feet propped up on bricks. Men in army uniform standing near the entrance, talking about government bonds. Women in evening dress, out for the night, like Kay. She would squeeze on to a bench, take a paperback out of her pocket, turn on her torch, and try to read, try not to mind too much about the wail of the siren, the judder of the ack-ack guns, the whirr and roar and thunder of the bombs.

The friends she made in that strange, dislocated autumn and winter of 1940: the girl in Holborn who beckoned her in from the street when she was caught outside during a heavy raid; they sheltered beneath the kitchen table and exchanged stories about the ATS and munitions factories. The boy from Balham who had lost his entire family when a bomb had made a direct hit on a rest centre. He told her about his brothers and sisters, about the day in the mid-1930s when his father had died in an accident at the docks, and how, afterwards, his mother had kept the family together by charring, and how he had left school at fifteen to work in the docks, like his dad. Kissing him outside a dance hall, she would almost have married him, just

239

to see him smile. Then there was the American journalist who had watched the Battle of Britain from the south coast and who told her that Britain would eventually win the war, but that it would take many years – ten, perhaps. And the Polish officer, Franciscek: when the Germans had invaded the previous year, his family had fled Warsaw, travelling east to stay with relatives. Two weeks later the Russians had invaded Poland from the east. Along with other remnants of the Polish army, Franciscek had made his escape through Romania, arriving in England at the beginning of 1940. He knew nothing of the fate of his family. In bed with him, she curled up against him as he stroked her thigh and murmured soft, incomprehensible endearments to her.

In January 1941, Kay was ordered to transport a lorry from Yorkshire to a camp at Amesbury. By the time she reached Salisbury Plain, it was dark, and she was very tired. A mist shrouded the plain, surrounding her with opaque whiteness. She could see only the few feet of road ahead of her through the narrow slits of greyish light from her headlamps, all that was permitted in the blackout. She drove very slowly, hugging the verge, yet though she had spread out the map on the seat beside her, she was unable to match the inked lines to the pattern of road and field. There was nothing to hold on to, only an awareness of the swell of a hillside to one side of her and the black shadow of a tree to the other.

The cab of the truck was open-sided. In spite of her great-coat and leather gauntlets, she was very cold. Her fingers were numb, and she seemed to feel the hard metal of the clutch pedal through the sole of her shoe. She headed on, hoping to come across a village or hamlet where she might be able to ask for directions. But there were no houses, no buildings, not so much as a barn. She had lost both her sense of direction and her sense of time. She glanced at her watch and was surprised to see that it was only nine o'clock. It felt like midnight.

She stopped the lorry, peeled off her gauntlets and lit a cigarette. She wondered whether she should park up, wait till dawn. But then she would be late, and it was a cardinal sin to be late in the army, a cardinal sin not to rush everywhere, because only if you hurried would the war be won. Yet if she drove on, she might end up heading further and further away from her destination. She felt a sudden rush of fury at her helplessness; all she wanted was to complete her job and find warmth and shelter and a hot meal. That was not too much to ask, surely? She longed with a savage intensity for the war to be over, to have back the life she had lost.

As she peered into the whiteness, a strand of mist drifted aside and she saw out of the windscreen a circle of immense stones. They were so tall and magisterial that she gazed at them for a moment, awed. Then she grabbed the map, shone her torch on it, and found Stonehenge. Her destination, Bulford army camp, was only a few miles away. She put the lorry into gear and set off. She reached the camp, delivered the vehicle and someone gave her a plate of food and mug of cocoa as she warmed her hands on the oil stove.

A few days later, she had a weekend's leave. After an evening in town, she walked home. But the Blitz had altered the familiar geography of London, erasing a row of houses and offices, knocking the spire from a church, jumbling up shops, gardens, parks and roads, so that their constituent parts were stirred up like a pudding. An old woman, clucking and crooning to her cat inside the ruins of a house, and a sailor, looking out over the span of Blackfriars Bridge, his face pale in the moonlight, loomed out of the darkness like ghosts. The river, with its black loops and coils, was the only constant. She found herself drawn towards it. Then she turned towards home, needing its continuity, longing for her small room with its containment of her past, longing for safety and security.

Chapter Nine

April 1941, and Tom spotted her on the platform at Waterloo: Edie Fielding – no, he reminded himself, she was Edie Dangerfield now, had been for more than a year and a half. Married, but his heart still sang, seeing her, and he knew that if there had been ten times more people there he still would have picked her out of the crowd.

He hesitated only a second, and then he pushed through the milling people to her side.

'Edie,' he said.

She looked up, startled. 'Tom. Goodness me. Fancy seeing you here.'

'How are you?'

'I'm very well. And you, Tom, you look well.'

'Where have you travelled from?'

'Cricklade. I'm staying with Charles's people.'

The crowds jostled her; he said, 'Here, let me take that,' and took her case from her. His hand lightly touched her shoulder to guide her through the throng.

Outside the station, Edie said, 'Such a crush.' She gave him a brisk smile. 'So kind of you to help, Tom.'

'How long are you in London?'

'Only a day or two. My mother's unwell, and I worry about the house and . . .' She glanced towards the queue at the bus stop.

'Let me take you out to dinner tonight.'

Her gaze flicked back to him. 'Tom—'

'You haven't other plans, have you?'

'No, but—'

'For old times' sake.'

He thought she might refuse, but then she murmured, 'For old times' sake.' She looked up; her eyes met his. 'Yes, why not?'

Tom had joined up at the beginning of the war. After basic training, he had been drafted into Military Intelligence and attached to the staff of a brigade based in Buckinghamshire. His day-to-day work consisted of liaison duties as well as the interpretation of signals.

That night, he booked a table at a restaurant in Park Street. Edie was a quarter of an hour late, time enough for him to begin to think she had changed her mind. He rose when he saw her come through the door.

'I'm so sorry,' she said, as the waiter took her coat and hat. 'I wouldn't want you to think – well, that I was late out of spite, anything like that.'

'I don't believe you've a spiteful bone in your body, Edie.'

'Of course I have,' she said, sitting down, taking off her gloves. 'In fact, this war seems to bring out the worst in me. But I walked, and they'd found an unexploded bomb in Wigmore

Street, and there was a diversion, and it seemed to take me for ever.'

She was wearing a silvery grey dress and had knotted a silk scarf, cream scattered with pale pink and blue flowers, about her neck. He thought she looked lovely, and said so.

She made a downward, disparaging glance. 'This was all I could find. Most of my clothes are in Gloucestershire – though why I took them there I can't imagine, as I never go anywhere.'

The waiter arrived and they ordered drinks and food. Edie's gaze darted round the restaurant. There was a touch of discontent in her eyes that Tom could not recall having seen before.

'So nice to be somewhere civilized,' she said.

'You're living in Gloucestershire now?'

'Yes, at my mother-in-law's house, Taynings. I've been there since August, Charles insisted.' She grimaced. 'That's eight months. Eight dreary months.'

He laughed. 'It can't be that bad, surely?'

'Oh, it is, Tom, it is. Not that Charles's mother, Honoria, isn't perfectly sweet. His sister, Catherine, is a nightmare, though. I'd always thought I could get along with anyone until I met Catherine. Charles admits she's impossible. She doesn't even seem to like Rosalind very much. I thought all women liked babies.'

'Rosalind?'

'My daughter.'

'Congratulations,' he said.

'Thank you.'

'How old is she?'

'She's almost thirteen months old.' Edie beamed. 'She's terribly advanced for her age – she's begun to walk already. She's with Nanny, at Taynings, just now. I didn't want to risk bringing her here. That's why I agreed to go to Taynings, for Rosalind's sake. I'd have stayed in London otherwise. I sometimes think I'd prefer bombs to boredom.'

'Does she look like you?'

'Everyone says so. Would you like to see a photograph of her?'

'I'd love to,' he said.

Edie took a snapshot out of her handbag and passed it to him. A plump, smiling baby in rompers and cotton hat sat on a sunlit lawn.

'She's going to be a beauty,' he said. 'Takes after her mother, of course.'

'Oh, Tom, still so smooth,' she said mockingly. But her hand had darted to her face, as if checking something.

Their drinks arrived. Edie raised her glass.

'Chin-chin.'

'Your health. It's good to see you, Edie.'

She sighed. 'I'm very lucky and I shouldn't complain, not when so many people are homeless.'

She sounded, he thought, as if she was reciting something she had learned by heart.

'And you, Tom?' she asked. 'Are you stationed in London?'

'No, though I come here fairly often. I move around quite a bit.'

She said, rather sharply, 'Don't tell me, stationed somewhere unspeakable, doing something unmentionable.'

'Yes, I suppose that's about it. Truly, it's very dull, I just shove bits of paper around. What's Charles up to?'

'He's at the War Office. He wanted to join the navy but they

246

wouldn't let him because of his eyesight. He's always so busy, I hardly ever see him.'

The waiter put a plate of pâté in front of her. Edie stared at it and said softly, 'I'm sorry. I mustn't moan.'

'You're permitted to moan,' he said, with a smile. 'Defeatist talk is strictly forbidden, of course, but moaning's allowed.'

'It seems to have gone on so long. When it started, I thought six months, at worst a year. Stupid of me. And every now and then you think something good has happened, that we've won something, but then, the next day, there always seems to be something unbearable.'

'Tell me about Taynings,' he said gently. 'Tell me why you hate it so much.'

'Well.' She made an exasperated face. 'There's the house itself, for a start. Before I went there for the first time, before I became engaged to Charles, I thought it would be glorious. I imagined it would be like Uncle Miles's house.'

'Cold Christmas?'

'Yes, like Cold Christmas. When I was a child, I used to adore Uncle Miles's house. He was perfectly dreadful, of course, but I loved his house. But Taynings isn't like Cold Christmas at all. It's in the dreariest valley in Gloucestershire and it always seems to be cold and damp and foggy. The old house was knocked down fifty years ago and the new place is an absolute monstrosity, red brick and crenellations and ugly little turrets and vast, gloomy rooms, and of course there's never enough coal to heat them. Honoria and Lilian don't seem to notice – they have their philosophy to keep them amused – but Catherine hates it just as much as I do. I could almost feel sorry for her, except that she's such a misery, so she just makes me cross.' Edie gave Tom an apologetic look.

'Oh dear, I'm afraid I'm going to end up like Catherine, miserable and lonely and bitter.'

'Philosophy?' asked Tom.

'Yes. Honoria and Lilian — Lilian is Honoria's friend, she's lived at Taynings for years — they share this — I'm never sure whether it's absolutely a religion, or more a kind of theory — they call it the Philosophy. With a capital P, I always think. I don't really understand it. I've never been terribly good at theoretical things. Honoria did try to explain it to me once, but when she began talking about Being and Greater Consciousness, I'm afraid I stopped listening. Anyway, it's terribly worthwhile, I'm sure. They support seamen's missions in Liverpool and Glasgow. I knit hats and socks for them.' Edie frowned. 'I daresay Taynings might be easier if I could become enthusiastic about the Philosophy. It seems to keep Honoria and Lilian happily occupied. They do a Gestetnered newsletter, which they send to all their friends, and Mr Stockfish comes to Taynings for exercises and meetings. Don't laugh, Tom.' There were crinkles of amusement round Edie's eyes. 'Mr Stockfish is a perfectly pleasant man. He lives a few miles away. Most mornings he walks over the fields to Taynings. He wears gaiters, because of the wet grass.'

Tom snorted. 'And your sister-in-law? Does she subscribe to the Philosophy?'

'Not at all. Catherine thinks it's ridiculous. And she hates gardening and knitting, which is what we mostly do with ourselves at Taynings. I didn't think anyone could knit angrily, but Catherine does. She's never married — she's a bit of a bluestocking. She loves doing crosswords. She does The Times crossword in a few minutes — it's awfully impressive, I suppose. Apparently, when she was younger she wanted to go to university, but girls don't in Charles's family.'

There was a silence while the waiter took away their empty plates. Breaking it, Tom said, 'But you're finding it lonely? You said you were lonely.'

'I suppose it's ridiculous to say that, when there are half a dozen other people in the house. I think what I meant to say is that I don't have much in common with any of the others. It's made me realize how lucky I've always been to have people I'm fond of and could talk to close to hand.'

Their main courses were served. 'At least at Taynings we eat very well,' said Edie, surveying her fricassée. 'There's a huge kitchen garden. It's not as if we're having to live off rations, thank goodness. How are your family, Tom? How are your parents and Minnie? Are they well?'

'Very well, thank you. My mother's working at Addenbrooke's now and Minnie's nursing at the London Hospital. And your sisters?'

'Nicky and the girls are in Yorkshire. They're living in a cottage near the camp where Dan is stationed. But the army keeps moving him, so they have to keep moving too, and Nicky's getting rather fed up with it. Laura's in Ayrshire, staying with a friend. Tony's in the navy, on the Atlantic convoys – I know Laura worries about him dreadfully.' Her eyes darkened. 'That's the worst thing, of course, the way this wretched war separates us from the people we love. I haven't seen either of my sisters for months.' Edie gave Tom a rather cool look. 'I suppose it's not the same for you, Tom. You've always preferred not to have ties, haven't you?'

He suspected she was implying something he didn't much care for, and which contained an uncomfortable truth. 'Yes,' he admitted, 'I suppose I have. It must be hard for you.'

'Mustn't grumble,' she said lightly. 'That's what Mrs Parrish, who cleans for us at Taynings, always says. And as I'm housed and fed and I don't have a husband or a brother in the forces, I've nothing to grumble about, have I?'

Yet he could tell that she did mind. He thought she had changed; she was thinner, and a little harder, perhaps. No less beautiful, though – the curves and planes of her face had fined down and the softnesses of youth and inexperience had been rubbed away, revealing the delicate structure beneath.

Dangerous ground, he thought. He found a different subject. 'How is your mother?' he asked. 'I'm sorry to hear she's unwell. I hope it's nothing serious.'

Edie looked worried. 'Some rather ghastly women's trouble, I'm afraid. Mummy has to have an operation but she keeps putting it off. I'm going with her to the specialist tomorrow. I do worry about her, all on her own. If Taynings was a little more bearable, I'd ask Honoria if Mummy could come to stay.'

'The Philosophy doesn't appeal to your mother, then?'

'I'm afraid not. And Mummy's always been a town person, like me.'

'And your uncle? How's dear old Uncle Miles?'

'You don't think a little thing like a war would make Uncle Miles change his ways, do you, Tom?'

He grinned. 'No, probably not.'

The conversation drifted on to other topics, books and films and the often discouraging progress of the war. They had been served coffee when the air raid siren sounded. Though many of the diners remained where they were – hoping for a false alarm, Tom assumed, as there had not been a heavy raid for some time – he offered to take Edie to a shelter.

'I'd rather go home, actually, Tom.' She cast a nervous glance out at the street. 'We have a basement. Charles told me I was to go there if there was a raid.'

He paid the bill and they left the restaurant. As they crossed Wigmore Street they could hear the crump-crump of bombs, coming closer. Along the skyline was a band of fiery orange. They walked fast; she took his arm. When they passed a public shelter, he glanced at her but she shook her head.

'I want to go home.'

'You'll be there in two ticks, I promise.'

They turned up the criss-crossing of streets that led to Portland Place. Now the noise of the guns and the explosions and the screaming of the dive-bombers made conversation impossible. Shrapnel hit the pavements with a ping, scattering like grey, misshapen hail. Tom took Edie's hand as they ran. Above them, the sky was lit up with star-shaped white, yellow and scarlet lights, great coloured chandeliers that illuminated the city for miles around. Bombs and sticks of incendiaries were tumbling through the air, and Tom felt Edie grasp his hand tightly as, looking up, they glimpsed with perfect clarity the round, rushing dark bellies of the planes overhead. The pavements were awash with fragments of broken glass and the air was acrid with the hot, dusty smell of burning masonry.

A loud, booming crash made Edie cry out. Tom glanced quickly from left to right, searching for shelter. Edie looked up and froze. Following her gaze, Tom saw what she had seen – that directly above them the sky itself appeared to be on fire. Flames burned in the air, tongues of fire leaping and darting in the hot wind. Then, with horrifying speed, the conflagration of smoke and flames seemed to plummet down towards them. Tom swung Edie into a doorway, shielding her with his body. There was the pop and tinkle of windows shattering in the heat and the air was too hot to breathe. He could feel the searing heat on his back. When he glanced back to the road, he saw that it was dotted with flames, little columns of fire that twisted and danced. Fragments of scorched cloth were being blown along the pavements, swooping and plunging like fiery swallows.

'It was a barrage balloon,' he said. His heart was hammering. 'It's all right, we're fine, it was only a barrage balloon.'

Edie was shaking. 'Oh God, Tom, I thought we were going to be burned alive!'

'It's all right,' he repeated.

Then he kissed her. She seemed to respond instinctively, her hungry mouth seeking out his, her body close to his, her breath coming fast. He no longer noticed the heat or the noise, was aware only of the softness of her skin and the springtime scent of bluebells.

Then, suddenly, she pulled away from him. 'No,' she said angrily. 'No, no, we mustn't. I didn't want this to happen.'

Freeing herself, she stumbled down the steps and ran away from him. Pieces of blackened cloth, dotted with glowing orange embers, floated spectrally through the smoke-filled air. Though he called out to her, she did not look back. Beneath the light provided by the smouldering fires, he saw her stumble through the debris to a house in Portland Place. At the front door, she fumbled in her bag, the door opened, her grey coat was a sliver of silver in the darkness, and she was gone.

Tom noticed something pale on the step beside him,

among the charred remains of the barrage balloon. He picked it up. It was a cream scarf, scattered with pink and blue flowers.

The next day, London seemed dazed, stunned and traumatized by the severity of the raid. The Admiralty had been hit and craters had been gouged out of Hyde Park. More than a thousand people had died, and more than fifty thousand houses had been damaged or destroyed. Walking through Mayfair, Tom passed teams of heavy rescue men searching through the rubble for victims and survivors.

He thought of Edie, remembered their kiss. Had it been only a reaction to the drama and fear of the moment, as one might grasp at a stranger's hand in a time of danger? Or had it signi-fied something more? Throughout the day, he had wondered whether he should go to see her again, had known he should not, had known also that he must, and would. In his mind's eye, he retained a clear image of his last glimpse of her as she had entered the house. She had seemed so small, so fragile.

Walking along Portland Place, he saw a house reduced to broken masonry and splintered wood, where a bomb must have scored a direct hit. Instinctively, he touched the silk scarf in his pocket, as if it were a talisman. As he neared the Dangerfields' house, he noted the broken windows and missing tiles. He rang the doorbell, then rapped on the door.

Edie opened the door; seeing her, he felt a rush of relief and pleasure.

He said, 'I came to check you were all right.'

'I'm fine.' She was wearing a grey skirt and a short-sleeved blue jumper. Both were dusty. There was dust in her hair and she looked pale.

'I found this.' He held out her scarf.

'Thanks,' she said. She took the scarf from him, adding, rather ungraciously, 'You'd better come in.'

He followed her into the house. It looked, he thought, as though it had been picked up, given a good shake, and set back down clumsily. There were cracks in the ceilings and along the tops of the walls. Books had tumbled out of their cases and a stack of framed prints lay on the floor.

'I'm sorry,' Edie said, with a wave of her hand. 'It's all such a mess. I've been trying to clear up, but it's impossible. Most of the windows are broken and there's glass everywhere. I think I've got all the pieces up and then I find fragments between the floorboards. And the dust just keeps falling. As soon as I've got it up, it comes back again. I tried going over everything with a damp cloth but now it just looks dusty and smeary. When I think of all the trouble I took, choosing curtains and things, and now look at it.'

'I tried to phone,' he said.

'The phones aren't on.' She looked distracted. 'It's a wretched nuisance.'

He followed her into the drawing room. Large and high-ceilinged, it had a dismal air to it, every surface greyed with dust and the darkening outside showing through the cracked windows.

Edie drew blackout curtains with an angry flick of the wrist. 'This was where Charles used to hold the concerts, before the war. It was such a beautiful room. We took all the good things to Taynings, of course, but Charles has to come to London sometimes because of his work, so we had to leave some furniture here. They've even broken the *clocks*.' She stared up at a deep fissure that snaked across the chimney breast. 'And this,' she said. 'Do you think I should do something about this?'

'What were you thinking of?'

'Well, that's the trouble, I don't know. Should one fill it with something? Or would it only come apart again? Do you think the chimney might collapse? I haven't been able to get a workman because of the phone, and anyway, everyone says they're booked up for years ahead.'

'I thought you might have gone back to Gloucestershire.'

'No, not yet.' Edie went to a cupboard, took out two glasses, and poured gin into both. 'Have you any cigarettes, Tom?' she asked. 'I've run out and I haven't managed to get to the shops.'

He lit cigarettes for both of them. Attempting reassurance, he said, 'It doesn't look too bad. Nothing that can't be fixed.'

'Oh yes, at least the house is still standing.' Her eyes had narrowed and she was looking at him with a contained fury that took him aback. 'These days, I seem to spend my entire life saying "at least". At least my house isn't a pile of rubble. At least my husband isn't in the army. At least my child is safely in the countryside.'

'I didn't intend—'

'I'm supposed not to mind the fact that nothing, absolutely nothing, is how I wanted it or planned it, aren't I? I *hate* what they've done to my house. I *hate* it that Rosalind and I are separated from Charles.' She took a swift pull on the cigarette. Her eyes were blazing and her mouth curled in an angry smile. 'And shall I tell you what I hate most of all, Tom? That I'm not useful any more. In fact, I'm the opposite of useful, I'm just another mouth to feed, another mother who must be bundled off to the middle of nowhere because she's getting in the way. Oh, I'm worse than useless – I'm a nuisance, to be shunted aside and never told anything important. Sometimes this war feels like a club that people like me aren't invited to. Mothers and children are supposed to spend their time mouldering in the countryside, having their heads patted every now and then while someone tells them to do what they're told because it's good for them. Well, I hate it, Tom, I hate it!'

'I can see it might feel like that,' he said reasonably, 'but you're wrong. Of course you're wanted. Of course you're still needed. Surely the war's being fought for women like you and for children like Rosalind.'

'No.' Pursing up her mouth, she shook her head slowly. 'No, you're wrong, Tom. Mothers and children can't contribute anything to the war so that makes us a burden. Shall I tell you what a woman on the train said to me yesterday? We got chatting and I showed her my photo of Rosalind and I mentioned that I'd like Rosalind to have a brother or sister soon. And she said that she didn't think people should have babies in wartime. She said that it was inconsiderate and selfish. She actually said that to me. It's funny, but I think she upset me even more than this. I didn't say anything – one can never think of the right thing to say at the time, can one? – but it made me furious. Before the war, the only thing I ever wanted was to get married and have children. I've never wanted anything else. We weren't brought up to go out to work – it seems rather idiotic now, when you think how poor we were, but that's how it was. And now I'm supposed to forget all that, I'm supposed to wait for however long this wretched war goes on and not mind that I hardly ever see my husband and my mother and sisters are miles away and my daughter and I can't even live in our own home.' She stared at him, challenging him. 'Go on, point out to me how fortunate I am compared to so many people.'

'I wouldn't dream of it. A slightly batty mother-in-law and a grumpy sister-in-law doesn't sound a lot of fun.'

She didn't smile. Instead, she made a derisive sound. 'I don't know why I'm saying this to you, of all people. It can't be of any interest to you at all. I expect the war suits you very well.'

'Well, no, it doesn't,' he said, annoyed.

'Oh Tom.' She gave a mocking laugh. 'I should have thought it was just what you wanted. Moving around all the time and the odd bit of derring-do. Although I suppose you've always prided yourself on being unconventional, haven't you? That must be rather tricky, in the army.' Her voice was bitterly sarcastic.

Stung, he said, 'You and me – it was never a question of not wanting to be tied.'

'What was it, then? Wasn't I pretty enough? Wasn't I clever enough?'

'Don't talk rot, Edie. You dropped *me*, remember?'

'Only because you'd made it perfectly plain that you didn't think about *us* at all.'

'What utter nonsense, of course I did!'

'No, Tom, you didn't,' she said crisply. 'You wanted to go on in exactly the same way you always had. Climbing, travelling, never settling down. You didn't think for one second about what I wanted.'

'That's not true,' he muttered. But inside he felt uneasy.

She had turned her back on him. He saw her throw her cigarette stub into the fireplace, and heard her say, in that same hard, clipped tone, 'Last night – what happened – I was just frightened. People do funny things when they're frightened. I hope you haven't read anything into it.'

'No, of course not.'

'That's fine, then.'

A silence, then he said, 'That night at the restaurant in Esher, we seemed so far apart. Until then, I'd thought we wanted the same things.'

'Women can't wait for ever, you know, Tom. It's easier for a man, he can marry a woman half his age and no one thinks anything of it. Charles is ten years older than me, actually. But a woman hardly ever marries a man ten years younger than herself. Women haven't the luxury of waiting, we need to marry before we're twenty-five or thirty, or people start saying we're on the shelf. I've known women who've left it too long, who've spent their twenties having fun, and then they find there are no decent men left. Or perhaps they do meet someone, and then they discover they're too old to have a baby. Women have to be practical. We can't afford to have all these airy-fairy ideas. You thought I was materialistic and ambitious. That's why we quarrelled. You know you did.'

The hurt, anger and resentment of their break-up bubbled up inside him, still raw and unhealed. 'Materialistic and ambitious?' he repeated angrily. 'If we're telling home truths then, weren't you, Edie? Charles is well-connected, isn't he? And he has a few bob, I believe. And you didn't exactly wait long after dropping me, did you?'

'Perhaps you should leave, Tom,' she said coldly.

'Perhaps I should.' His voice was bitter.

But as he made to go, she seemed unexpectedly to falter. In a flat, subdued tone, she said suddenly, 'Yes, I suppose I did want to marry well. I wanted to feel safe, I've always wanted that. But I would have put it all aside for you.'

He stared at her. 'No, I don't believe you.'

'Have it your own way.' She looked deeply upset. 'It's true, though.'

His heart seemed to be contracting. Appalled, he said, 'But why didn't you *say*?'

'Because I wanted you to work it out yourself. It would have shown me you'd thought about it, that you cared.' She had picked up a cloth and began to run it in a mechanical fashion along a window sill. 'I was never sure. And after we broke up, I was so certain you'd write or something. It hurt me so much that you just forgot me.'

'But I didn't,' he protested. 'I didn't forget you! Never!'

'The truth is,' she said wearily, 'I never felt important enough to you, Tom.'

He felt winded and a little nauseous. 'When I heard you were engaged I could hardly bear it. Oh God, Edie, if only you'd said all this to me before!'

'Oh Tom, if only you'd *listened*,' she said sharply. Then she gave a small shake of the head. 'How silly we both were, then.'

In the silence, he heard the hiss and clatter as she swept fallen plaster into the dustpan. Bleak and unspeaking, he watched her pick sooty shards of glass from the fire surround. If, before, he had wanted a kind of vengeance, an admission from her that she, too, had been at fault, he now felt drained of any emotion other than regret.

'But now, your marriage, it's happy, isn't it?' But he was unsure what he wanted her answer to be.

'Very happy.' She smoothed her hair behind her ear – he noticed a dab of grey dust on her curls as she emptied the dustpan into a cardboard box.

To see her and not touch her. To see her and to be aware of her contempt. To see her and to know what a fool he had been.

He picked up his cap. 'I should go.' Then he remembered something. 'Your mother,' he said. 'Weren't you going with her to the doctor today?'

'Yes.'

'Did you, then?'

'Yes.' Suddenly, she looked stricken. She put down the dustpan and brush.

'How did it go?'

'Awful – it was simply awful. May I have another cigarette, Tom?' He offered her the packet, lit her a cigarette.

She took a deep breath. 'I went to the station to meet Mummy but when I got there I found out the trains weren't running. So I came back here and tried to telephone but of course the phones had been cut off. I couldn't think what to do so I stuck a note on the front door, explaining that I'd gone on to the hospital and would wait for her there. It took me an hour to get there – there were no buses, so I had to walk. Anyway, eventually Mummy turned up. She'd driven all the way from Esher, round all the blocked roads and craters. She must have had a teaspoon of petrol in the car – she ran out in Chelsea. Then we had to wait for hours anyway because all the appointments were late. Poor Mummy was exhausted, I could tell that she was. And then the specialist told us she has to have an operation in a week's time. They won't let her wait any longer.'

'I'm sorry,' he said. 'That's rotten luck.'

'I asked her to come back with me to Taynings, but she refused. She said she'd rather be in her own home. I couldn't even invite her to stay the night here because the house is such a mess.'

'I'm so sorry,' he said again.

She looked small and lost; he made to go to her, but she said, a warning in her voice, 'No, Tom.'

He gave a quick nod of the head, accepting the rebuff, then said, 'I hope things look up for you, Edie. Please give my best wishes to your mother. I was always very fond of her.'

He left the room. He had reached the front door when he heard footsteps behind him. He turned.

She was standing in the hallway. 'Sorry,' she said. 'Sorry I've been such a bitch.'

'I don't doubt I deserve it.'

'Perhaps you do.' She pressed her lips together. Then, 'Hold me, Tom,' she said suddenly. 'I want you to hold me. All I've been able to think about, since last night, is how much I want you to hold me again.'

He took her in his arms. There were specks of dust in her hair; tonight, she smelled not of bluebells but of chalk and cleaning fluid. Her eyes were closed and her long, black lashes made fine shadows against the blue-white skin beneath her eyes. He slid his hand beneath her jersey, brushing his palm against the cool silk of her slip. She gave a little moan, and moved slowly, urgently, pressing herself against him.

There were French prisoners of war working on a farm near Rastenberg. In the autumn, riding home after visiting Friedrich's cousin Anna, Miranda caught sight of the men labouring in a field. Her horse stepped elegantly over a ditch scattered with red and gold leaves. At the side of the field, she called out to the men. As they walked towards her, she saw how their eyes lit up at the sound of their own language. She asked them whether they knew Olivier – Parisian, thirty years old, honey-brown eyes. Whether they had seen him. Whether they could tell her what had happened to him. And they frowned and shrugged, shaking their heads.

At first, she had been certain they would meet again soon. The war would end, because surely Hitler must be content with the conquest of Poland, which had reunited East Prussia with the rest of Germany. The war would end and she would travel to Paris, and she and Olivier would be together again, if only for a week or two. In Paris, it would be possible, if not openly approved of, for a married woman to see her lover, as Madame Robert had done. And afterwards, she would return to Sommerfeld, and Friedrich.

But after the battle for France in the summer of 1940, everything had changed. In September, she had written to Madame Robert. She had pictured Madame Robert, in her lime-green dress with the polka dots, ringing the doorbells of Olivier's flat and office. A fortnight later, she had received a letter telling her that Olivier's office had been unoccupied for more than a year and that his flat in the Marais was now lived in by a German officer. *Désolée*, Laure Robert wrote, but she had been unable to discover anything more. Olivier had escaped to England, Miranda told herself, and was now with the Free French army. Or, after the fighting had ended, he had returned to France, to a different address and a different occupation. He might be living much as he had in peacetime. Though, somehow, she did not think so.

There were possibilities, of course, that she could not bear to contemplate. That he had been injured in the fighting. That he had been captured. That he was dead. Yet inside her, there remained a kernel of hope, a conviction that, if something had happened to Olivier, she would somehow know. She remembered his promise to wait for her in the Parc Monceau, if they should be separated. In her bedroom she took the ceramic blue-bird out of a drawer and touched its cool solidity.

Friedrich had been stationed in Paris throughout the winter. The irony of it, Miranda often thought, as she watched the snow fall and the long, crystal spears of icicles form from the gutters, that Friedrich should be in Paris when she could not. He had had a week's leave at Christmas before returning to France. They exchanged letters, affectionate, courteous – who, reading them, would have guessed that a distance had existed between them since that afternoon at the Hotel Adlon?

Spring came and the snow melted, and the white fields were replaced by the sparkling colours of the new season, the green of the new leaves on trees and a flash of yellow irises beside the lake. On fine evenings, at twilight, she liked to walk out to the terrace behind the castle and watch the swallows swoop and dive – the glitter of a blue feather and the turn of a wing as the sun dipped to the tops of the trees. Often, listening to the news from the west, she was thankful for Sommerfeld's tranquillity. The fertile farmlands meant that they were not short of food. Lying far to the east, out of the range of British bombers, East Prussia had been spared the air raids that Berlin, Hamburg and other more westerly cities endured.

One evening in early May, Miranda and the Countess were sitting after dinner in the drawing room. Miranda was reading aloud to the Countess. There were sounds of a distant commotion in the house – voices, a door opening – and the Countess smiled and said, 'Anna, perhaps. Though it's rather late.' Then, footsteps in the corridor, and the Countess's expression stilled, and she whispered, 'Friedrich . . .'

He came into the room, tall and tanned. A bow to his mother as he kissed her hand, then his lips brushed against Miranda's.

His orders had been unexpected, he explained – he had not had time to warn them of his homecoming, and besides, he had wanted to give them both a surprise. He was not hungry; he had eaten en route.

A pot of coffee and a glass of brandy were fetched. Friedrich produced from his pocket two small parcels. For his mother, a cameo brooch, and for Miranda a necklace of black pearls. He clasped them round her neck; looking at her reflection in the mirror, she saw how they set off her ivory skin.

'Shall I write to the cousins and ask them to dinner this Friday?' the Countess suggested. 'It would be like old times.'

Friedrich gave an apologetic smile. 'I'm afraid I won't be here on Friday, Mother. I must leave tomorrow.'

'Tomorrow . . .' The Countess put her hand to her mouth.

Friedrich touched her shoulder. 'But I've brought good news. I'm to be stationed nearer to home, for a while, at least, so you may be seeing more of me over the next few weeks. So much better, don't you think, that I'll be closer to home?'

'So much better,' said the Countess. She pressed Friedrich's hand to her cheek.

They talked of family matters, of the recent bad weather and the harm that the heavy spring rains had done to the crops. At ten o'clock, the Countess retired to bed. After Friedrich had seen his mother upstairs, he dismissed the servants and returned to Miranda.

'My mother looks tired,' he said. 'And frail.'

'She's almost eighty, Friedrich. And she worries about you.'

'My Miranda . . .' he murmured. 'My beautiful Miranda. Do you know how much I miss you when I'm away?'

'A great deal, I hope. As I miss you too, my love.'

She kissed him lightly on the lips. There was dust on his

shoes and he smelled of the outdoors. She said, 'Why have you been posted back here, Friedrich?'

'Perhaps at last my superiors are taking my wishes into account.' He gave a cynical smile. 'Perhaps they know how homesick I am. Perhaps they've realized how much I've missed you and feel sorry for me.'

'It would be nice if that were so. But I doubt it, somehow.'

'One is pushed around from pillar to post in the army. We're not always given a reason why. We should enjoy our good fortune while it lasts.'

Friedrich rarely expressed his feelings openly, believing that to do so was distasteful and vulgar, cowardly even, especially in a man. But Miranda had learned to read the small signs.

'Friedrich, I understand that you don't want to worry your mother. But you must tell me the truth. You must tell me everything.'

'Everything?' His eyes, clear, light, translucent blue-grey, held hers. 'As you have always told me everything, Miranda?'

She looked away. She heard the hiss of his outward breath. 'I'm sorry,' he murmured. 'I shouldn't have said that. I'm tired, it was a long journey.'

Miranda sat down on the sofa. 'Anna has told me about the troop trains coming into Rastenberg. A few at first, but then more and more. Hundreds of them, Anna says, and each one is packed with soldiers. I'm not a fool, Friedrich, and I'm not a child either.'

'Of course, I know that.' He sighed. 'I only wish to save you anxiety. This wretched war — this damnable war! I should be here, with you.'

'Soon, perhaps.'

'No, I don't think so.'

'Friedrich, you must tell me.'

'I hope it may not happen,' he said softly. 'I pray it may not happen.'

'What? What do you hope may not happen?'

A silence, then he said, 'At this moment, there are hundreds of thousands of our troops stationed in positions along the Russian border, all the way from the Baltic to the Black Sea. Their tanks are concealed in the forests and their field guns are hidden in barns behind the lines. Why else would they be there, except to attack Russia?'

'There have been rumours. I've heard people talking in the village, and at church. I hoped it wasn't true.'

'It isn't easy to hide an army. It's hard to believe that Stalin himself hasn't noticed.'

Miranda recalled the lobby of the Hotel Adlon, the crowd of reporters queueing for the telephone, and Friedrich explaining to her that Germany and the Soviet Union had signed a pact, agreeing to remain neutral should the other country become involved in war. She remembered the despair she had felt as she had understood that she would not be able to travel to Paris, and Olivier.

'But there's a treaty, isn't there,' she said 'between Germany and Russia, a treaty of friendship? Before the war, that day in Berlin, you told me.'

'A treaty of friendship?' Friedrich's lip curled. 'I wouldn't call it that. Convenience, or expedience, perhaps. Besides, our Führer doesn't care for treaties, you know that, Miranda. He tears them up without a second thought.'

'Is it certain?'

'Not yet. I still hope it may not come to war. It's possible that Stalin isn't yet ready for war. Perhaps he'll offer the

Ukraine, as a sop. Perhaps Hitler will be content with that. And yet . . .'

'Tell me.'

'You can't hide an army and neither can you keep it waiting. Armies have to be supplied and they have to be fed. They have an impetus of their own. If it happens, it'll happen soon. The generals will hope for a summer campaign, a short, sharp attack that quickly overwhelms the Russians.' He sat down on the sofa beside her. 'The optimists speak of our being in Moscow in four weeks' time. Some of the men are convinced of this. They're confident. Our victories in Europe have made them believe we can do anything.'

'And you, Friedrich? What do you think?'

'Anything's possible. I've little faith left in my ability to predict the outcome of events.'

He looked tired; close up, she could see the threadwork of lines around the corners of his eyes and the silver hairs among the sandy gold.

'Perhaps it's inevitable that we'll end up going to war with Russia. Perhaps, if we wait, Stalin's armies will become strong again and attack Germany. We East Prussians fear the Russians, Miranda. We're afraid that they hunger after our land.'

'My father once told me that Germany could never destroy Russia's armies on Russian soil.' She remembered the last time she had seen her father – his illness, and the plans he had made to secure the Denisov fortune should there be war.

Friedrich gave a bitter smile. 'You only have to look at the example of history to see that your father may well be right. Remember Napoleon's fate. The Russian winter may yet pose a greater threat to us than Stalin's armies. Russia isn't the same as Western Europe. It's vast, unimaginably vast, and the climate's merciless. And there's another thing. The Russian people have always lived in servitude to one tyrant or another. What have they left to lose except their homeland? When a man has nothing left to lose, that's when he fights most fiercely.' His voice lowered. 'I'm afraid we're about to embark on a disaster. I'm afraid this will destroy us. I'm afraid – most of all, I'm afraid of what I'll become.'

'You?' She smiled at him. 'You'll always be Friedrich. You'll always be good and kind and brave.'

'Will I?'

His expression disconcerted her. Impossible to read, this time.

He said, 'I want you to promise me something, Miranda.'

'Yes, if you wish.'

'I want you to promise me to remember that whatever happens, wherever I go and whatever I do, the only thing I cared about was to protect you and Sommerfeld.'

'Yes, of course. I promise.'

The darkness in his eyes vanished; he was urbane and controlled once more. 'I hadn't meant to speak of this to you, my dear,' he said lightly. 'And I've often been accused of pessimism. It's a bad habit of mine. You mustn't worry. Will you step outside with me for a few minutes? I'd like to smoke.'

On the terrace at the back of the house, the light from the orangery flooded out on the flagstones. The sky had faded to grey and, high above them, Miranda could see the darting black shapes of bats. Standing at the stone balustrade, Friedrich looked out over the garden. Friedrich's domain, Miranda thought, Friedrich's little kingdom. Beyond the lawn, the trees cast their long blue-grey shadows on the grass. A full moon was rising, a disc of white gold.

She heard the click of Friedrich's lighter and saw the glimmer of a flame. 'It hasn't changed,' he said. 'It's still exactly the same.'

'We're looking after Sommerfeld for you, Friedrich, the Countess and I.' Though there were changes, Miranda knew — some of the manservants and farm labourers had left Sommerfeld for the army, and she and the Countess were able to travel less often to Königsberg and Berlin.

'You can't imagine how pleased I am to be home,' he said. 'Paris was a pleasant posting, of course, but they hate us, I can see it in their eyes.'

'Were you able to see my father?'

'I called on him a couple of times. He looked well enough.' Friedrich gave a short laugh. 'He seemed to be prospering.'

'Papa's a survivor. Wherever he is, he manages to make the best of things.'

'That's not so easy, nowadays. Even your father may have found his wings have been clipped.'

'Papa's always been clever. If Paris no longer suited him then he'd find somewhere else.'

She could feel his gaze on her. 'And you, Miranda?' he said. 'If Sommerfeld no longer suited you, would you, too, find somewhere else to go?'

'Friedrich—'

'Every time I come home, I wonder whether you'll still be here.'

She felt a rush of anger. 'And where would I go?' she said bitterly. 'To my father, who betrayed me a long time ago? To my family? I have no family other than you and the Countess. Or shall I go to a friend — shall I buy myself a train ticket and travel to London, to visit my dear friend Kay? Do you think your armies would permit me to do that, Friedrich?'

'Is that why you stay? Because you have nowhere else to go?'

'No.'

Her anger left her as suddenly as it had come, and was replaced by melancholy. 'I married *you*, Friedrich,' she said. 'I *chose* to marry you.' Though there was something counterfeit in her self-defence, she thought, something shoddy in a choice born of fear and desolation.

'So you did.' He held out a hand to her. 'Come, let's not quarrel, Miranda. I shouldn't tease you. I apologize. Come here.'

After a moment, she took his hand.

'You're cold,' he said. 'Shall we go back inside?'

'Not yet. I like it here.'

'Here.' He took off his jacket and wrapped it round her. He put his arm round her shoulders. She could feel the beating of his heart. 'My beautiful Miranda,' he said. He ran his fingers down her long fall of black hair. 'Perhaps we're more alike than you think, you and I. Neither of us loves easily. I've loved with passion only twice in my life. And you, Miranda – how many times have you truly loved?'

She held up a hand, touching the tip of each finger in turn. 'There was a puppy when I was a little girl. And my favourite doll. She had big blue eyes and I called her Celestine because I thought it was the most beautiful name in the world. And of course there's Gisela . . .'

'Minx,' he said, drawing her tightly to him. 'I talk of undying love and you speak of dolls and puppies.'

They kissed for a while, and then she said, 'There was a time when you saved me, Friedrich. I was losing myself and you saved me. I'll never forget that.'

'Gratitude . . .' he murmured. 'Then I'd better be content with that, hadn't I?'

270

'No, more than gratitude.'

He dropped the stub of his cigarette into the flower bed below and took her in his arms. 'I shall persevere,' he said. 'I can be very patient, you know.'

She rested her head against his chest, closing her eyes. 'I wish I'd been able to give you a son. The best gift I could have given you, and I've failed.'

Every Sunday, at church, she prayed for a son. She prayed for a son, as she prayed for Olivier, for Kay, for Friedrich and for her father, that they would survive the war.

From the woodland, an owl's cry. Friedrich's kisses were quick and passionate, bruising her mouth, her throat, the hollow beneath her collarbone and the curve of her breast. She felt herself responding to his hunger.

'It's late,' he said. His voice was rough and low. 'We should go in.'

Six weeks later, on midsummer morning, 22 June, Miranda walked to the lake with Gisela. As they headed across the lawn, the dog ran ahead of her, her paws marking dark tracks in the dew. Overhead, the sun was a blurred, luminous globe.

In the cool silence of the birch wood, the pale columns of the trees shimmered and strands of mist curled in the hollows. Leaving the woodland behind her, she made her way through the long, wet grass to the shore of the lake. Reeds rose blade-like out of the shallows. The world seemed to be beginning again, reborn that morning, full of expectation and promise.

In the afternoon, after lunch, Miranda and the Countess drank their coffee while they listened to the radio. That was when they heard the news that, in the early hours of the morning, on the shortest night of the year, German troops had entered Russia. First, there had been the artillery barrage, then bridges had been seized and rivers crossed. Planes had taken off from bases behind the line to bomb Russian airfields and military emplacements. The war in the east had begun.

If Germany invades Russia, you must leave that husband of yours. Miranda told herself that her father had exaggerated, seeing the world as he always did, through greedy, rapacious eyes. They would be safe at Sommerfeld. And besides, she must not allow her anxiety to unsettle her. She must be careful with herself.

Because at last, the miracle had happened. She seemed to have held her breath for days, but she was sure now, certain that she was pregnant, that she was expecting a child, the child both she and Friedrich longed for.

On the way back to his hotel, Tom dropped into a pub on the Strand. He was standing at the bar when he noticed someone sitting at one of the tables. It took him a second or two to place the face: it was Charles Dangerfield.

He turned to leave – too late. Dangerfield rose and crossed the room to him.

'Blacklock? It is you, isn't it?'

'Yes.' Tom heard himself give an overly hearty laugh. 'Well spotted.'

'Always had a good memory for faces. May I buy you a drink?'

Actually, I'd rather you didn't because I'm having an affair with your wife. He said, 'Decent of you,' and asked for a Scotch.

They sat down at a table in the corner of the room. The private bar was an old-fashioned, wood-panelled affair, with separate booths. Dangerfield said, 'Are you stationed in London now?' and Tom shook his head.

'I come up to town every now and then. What about you?'

'I'm at the War Office. They wouldn't let me join the forces – my eyesight, you see. I hate it, not being in uniform like everyone else. It makes me feel second-rate. But I shall keep plugging away. I've a friend or two in the Admiralty – I'm trying to pull a few strings.' Dangerfield gave a quick smile.

'Well, good luck.'

Dangerfield glanced round the bar room. There were cracks in the ceiling and the glass in one of the windows had been replaced by a sheet of hardboard. 'Poor old London,' he said. 'She's looking awfully battered, isn't she?'

Tom echoed, 'Awfully.' And then, because he thought it would have looked odd not to, he asked, 'How's Edie?'

'In the pink,' said Dangerfield. 'Glad to be back in London.'

Since the German invasion of the Soviet Union, the bombing raids on London had largely ceased. People were drifting back to the capital, picking up the threads of their old lives.

They talked about the war – the Axis invasion of the Balkans and Greece, the loss of Crete, the Allied occupation of Persia to secure the oil pipelines, and the continued march of the Wehrmacht deeper and deeper into the Soviet Union. Then, just as Tom was thinking he might decently be able to make his excuses and leave, Dangerfield said suddenly, 'Do you think perhaps it's worse for women, all this?'

'The war, do you mean?'

'Yes.' Dangerfield pulled at his long, thin nose. 'I think women mind more about leaving their homes and their families being broken up, that sort of thing. Whereas we men – if we're honest, I think most of us would have to admit that there's something in war we find exciting, something that suits us.'

'Perhaps.'

'I know that Edie minds. She doesn't talk about it, but I can tell that she does. I can tell she's not happy.'

Tom felt a prickle of danger. He glanced at his watch. 'I'm afraid I must head off.'

Dangerfield rose and offered his hand. 'Well, thanks for the company. And best of luck.'

Tom left the pub. Outside, the sky was grey and rain was falling. As he headed along the Strand he was waylaid by a woman with a collecting box. Orphaned children or sailors' widows, he didn't bother to find out, but emptied his pockets of change as if in expiation.

The last time he and Edie had met, he had been staying in a small hotel in Maida Vale. They had dined at the hotel – the food had been awful, a watery stew followed by a heavy currant sponge notably lacking in currants. Edie had been nervous, looking up whenever anyone came into the dining room, but then she had relaxed and they had laughed together about the food. After dinner, they had gone up to his room. When, an hour later, she had left, all that had remained was the faint drift of her perfume and a hollow in the pillow.

I can tell she's not happy, Dangerfield had said. Walking through the rainy London streets, Tom acknowledged that the joy he and Edie found together was always limited, on her part, by anxiety and guilt. Their meetings had a pattern: her initial worries, his reassurance, and then the wordless communication of their love-making. He knew that what they shared was trapped in a bubble, that it had no life outside the walls of a hotel room. A part of him knew that the affair was making her unhappy, yet the depth of his need for her rode over all other considerations. Her need of him was less, he thought. Perhaps he compensated for the absences in her life – her family, her husband, her home.

They rarely talked of anything serious. When, once or twice, he had tried to speak to her about the possibility of her leaving Charles, she had cut him off. He had not pressed the subject because he had been afraid to. Which amounted, he thought, to cowardice.

Chapter Ten

Miranda's life had narrowed, confining her more and more to Sommerfeld. Friedrich, Klaus, Max and Oskar were far away, fighting on the Russian front. Anna was working as a nursing auxiliary at the hospital in Rastenberg. Though food was still plentiful in East Prussia, petrol was now rationed. The Daimler had been confiscated by Nazi Party officials a month ago for use at the Eastern front, leaving the family only the small Volkswagen. The chauffeur had been called up; fortunately, Herr Bernard, Friedrich's secretary, who had been spared army service to run the estate, was able to drive. Because of her pregnancy, Dr Kornblum had forbidden Miranda to ride on horseback, and, since the invasion of Russia, the railways had become less reliable. Letters from Friedrich and the occasional missive from her father, in Paris, were her only connections to the outside world. Except for the radio, of course, which that autumn blared out Hitler's triumphs as the Wehrmacht pressed deeper and deeper into Russian territory. *A victory which is without parallel in history . . . the complete annihilation of the Soviet army.* Smolensk had fallen, then Kiev and Kharkov, and Leningrad was under siege.

Sometimes Miranda found herself wondering whether she had changed one sort of prison for another, much more agreeable, one. The war must be over soon, she reminded herself, and then Friedrich would come home and the new year would come and her baby would be born. And she would no longer feel the walls of this great house pressing in on her, so that sometimes, when she was lying alone in bed at night, the silence seemed to speak to her, to remind her of the precariousness of life, and how, in the flick of an eye, everything might change.

The movement of her baby in her womb was at first a slight, feathery fluttering. Miranda pictured it twisting and turning, like a fish swimming in an undersea cave. What did it think of, waiting and growing in the darkness? What did it feel? What did it long for?

If she had a girl . . . She would be a good mother to this daughter of hers. She wouldn't leave her for weeks on end with a nursemaid who would slap her for crying because she was afraid of the dark. She wouldn't engage a governess who rapped her knuckles and told her she was stupid. She wouldn't dress her in frills and ribbons and parade her to sing and dance in front of party guests on one day and on the next punish her for showing off. She wouldn't make her share the dinner table when she was fourteen years old with gentlemen who pinched her cheeks and told her jokes she didn't understand. Her child wouldn't have to learn, far too young, how to keep those gentlemen interested by bestowing on them a kiss, and neither would she have to learn to repel them with an icy hauteur when they demanded more. Her daughter wouldn't learn to watch herself, to try to please, to gauge the mood of the company as soon as she entered a room. She wouldn't go to bed in the early hours of the morning and curl up with her doll, her head filled with the echo of her own tinkling laugh and simpering smile. She would not learn to hate herself.

Her daughter would have a home. Her daughter would know Sommerfeld as intimately as Miranda herself had come to know the capitals of Europe. Sommerfeld would be her world, as it was Friedrich's world. And if that meant quelling her own restlessness, that need for novelty that slipped too easily into boredom and depression, then so be it. She would manage, somehow. She would forget Olivier, forget Paris, forget the Miranda she had once been, with her dreams of love and fame and the dark attentive eye of the film camera, that had allowed her to speak in a way she had so rarely been permitted. Again, so be it. She would do that for her daughter.

And if she had a boy . . . Perhaps this son and heir for Friedrich would be fair, like his father. Perhaps, in the summer, she would take him to the lake and show him the fishes that darted in the shallows and the wildfowl that hid between the reeds. They would picnic in the meadows among the poppies and ox-eye daisies. When he was older, she would teach him to ride and to skate.

On cold winter afternoons, Miranda sat in the orangery, sewing, warmed by the winter sun. A long time ago, a Swiss governess had taught her how to embroider. Her baby would be a child of the north, who knew snow and ice and grey seas and chilly grasslands. Later, when he or she was old enough, they would travel to the Mediterranean, to warmth and sun and white sands licked by a turquoise sea. Until then, she would breathe in the scent of oranges.

On Wednesday afternoons, Edie worked in a Women's Voluntary Service shop near Bishopsgate. Heading home after work, walking past St Paul's, she was surrounded by devastation. Sometimes there was an appearance of normality, a street of houses almost untouched, just a few chips and cracks, and yet the next street might be a wasteland. Paternoster Row, where the publishing houses had once stood, had been obliterated, and buildings remained only on the left-hand side of Cheapside. In the ruins, plants had taken root, rosebay willowherb, brambles and nettles, now browned by the first frosts. On a derelict wall, someone had painted a V for Victory. Inside the roofless shell of a church, autumn leaves had gathered, their gold, red and bronze burnishing the stone flags that were incised with the names of the dead. The sight of a bombed church always produced a particular melancholy in her. Edie shivered.

She had felt rushed all day. After breakfast, she had left the house to queue at the shops while Mrs O'Brien, who did the rough work, mopped the floors. Then, Mrs Lumley, who lived in domestic chaos but smocked beautiful little nightgowns for babies, had phoned to tell her that she had half a dozen items for collection but could not leave the house because her eldest had gone down with measles. They were low on stock, so Edie had hurried over to Battersea before making her way to the WVS shop at two. The shop sold small gifts and garments made by WVS members to raise money for the war effort. Edie had taken on the task of collecting items produced by women who were housebound, either because they were elderly and incapacitated, or because they had aged relatives or babies and small children to look after. Sometimes she took Rosalind with her on her excursions, wheeling the pram down London streets she had never seen before.

On Wednesday afternoons, her shop afternoon, she always

left Rosalind with her nanny. It had been a busy few hours, with plenty of customers looking in, and all Mrs Lumley's night-gowns had sold. Edie glanced at her watch. She liked to be home by six, in time for Rosalind's bath. She would dine alone that night, because Charles was away. And then she would leave the house and go to a hotel to meet her lover.

She and Tom met in hotels whose names – The Excelsior, The Carleton – would before the war have been blazoned in gold on the fanlight above the front door, but had since been covered over with blackout material or blown out by the Blitz and replaced by a sheet of plywood. The hotels were in not so poor a district that if an acquaintance were to catch sight of her entering the building it would be impossible to explain, and nor were they the kind of establishment where someone she knew might be sitting in the bar or dining room.

The first time she and Tom Blacklock had made love, the day after the air raid, she might have blamed it on the Blitz. Their close proximity to death and the loss of the normal struc-tures of everyday life had seemed to diminish the importance of everything but feeling and desire. It had been as though the extremity of those nights – the noise and the destruction and the terror – had given them permission. If you were about to die, then what difference would it make if you went to bed with an old boyfriend? Afterwards, she had felt a mixture of euphoria and guilt. As time had passed, the euphoria had shrunk away and the guilt had intensified.

But then, the second time. By then, the worst of the London Blitz had been over. Hitler's attention had turned to Russia, and Edie, Charles and Rosalind had returned to the London house – the poor London house, battered and scarred, no longer the grand, elegant thing it had been before the war. Then, one evening, Tom had phoned. Charles had been away and Rosalind had been teething. It had been a WVS day, and the twenty-year-old son of one of the regular helpers had been lost at sea – poor Mrs Rice was pale-faced and quiet, though she did not break down, but Edie kept an eye on her and made cups of tea. And she had been worried about her mother, who had not yet really recovered from her hysterectomy and had sounded tired and weak over the phone. Edie had offered to take a train to Esher, but her mother had said no, Mrs Phillips had promised to look in, she mustn't worry.

But none of that was any excuse. She had been eating her dinner when Tom had called. He was staying at the Adelphi in Earl's Court – would she join him for a drink? She had said no, I'm afraid I can't, and had put the phone down. And had had to force down the remainder of her food, reminding herself of the merchant sailors who might have died transporting it across the Atlantic – Mrs Rice's son among them, perhaps. And the house had seemed so empty, so quiet, and she had thought of Tom on his own, in a dreary hotel bar, and had found herself putting on her coat and hat and leaving the house, telling herself as she sat on the bus that they'd just say hello, have a drink and a chat. And then, at the hotel, meeting her in reception, he had taken her hands in his, and had murmured, 'I've missed you,' and they had gone upstairs to his room.

No, no excuse at all, because she was deeply thankful to be back in London, even this altered, wounded London. She loved working for the WVS, had surprised herself with the energy and enthusiasm she had discovered for her various responsibilities. And she was not, after all, the sort of woman who conducted adulterous love affairs, was not the sort of woman who made assignations in public telephone boxes. She was not the sort of woman who lied. The affair was wrong, and it was dangerous, and it threatened not only her own and Charles's well-being, but Rosalind's too. Sometimes, waking in the night, remembering, she felt a sickening horror. Why did she do it? Was it only because of the colour of his eyes and the sound of his voice?

Only in one thing had she been honest, she considered. She had never allowed herself to say to herself that she hadn't had a choice. *We got carried away, and then . . .* She despised that sort of self-deception. She *chose* to meet Tom and she *chose* to go to bed with him. The exhilaration of their love affair did not rob her of the power of thought. She saw him because to do so made her happy, and made her experience – and *this* was true – a passion she had never felt before. Each time they met, they made no further arrangement to meet again. Each time, when Tom telephoned to tell her that he was in London, it came as the most delightful surprise, a wonderful gift, lifting her out of the day-to-day routine. And there she was, an evening or so later, heading off to The Excelsior or The Carleton.

Over the past seven months, she had discovered a great deal about herself. That she was capable of the worst sort of deception, and that sex, which she had looked upon as a dreary marital duty, could be glorious, breathtaking and joyful. She had discovered that a touch could ignite a desire so compelling that almost all other considerations – sense, loyalty, even dignity – could be put aside. And that love – she supposed this was love – could transform.

But if this was love, then what did she feel for Charles? The evening they had first become lovers, Tom had accused her of marrying Charles for his money. It was true that the Portland Place house had enchanted her when she had first attended Charles's Wednesday evening concerts, and it was equally true that had Charles been penniless, she probably would not have married him. But she had not married him for the house. If she had not liked him, liked him a great deal, found with him a contentment that she had not, until then, known she was searching for, then she would not have married him. If she appreciated beautiful houses, then was that so reprehensible? After her marriage, she had taken a particular pleasure in transforming Charles's house into the home of a married couple rather than a bachelor. It irritated her that the arrangement of a home, a room, seemed commonly regarded as trivial, women's work. Yet a dusky peacock-blue damask cushion on an ivory silk sofa, and the echoing of a gold curtain by the tassels of yellow laburnum that showed through a French window: these were important to her, and gave her greater contentment than the architectural prints Charles liked to collect.

But contentment had vanished a long time ago, with her exile to Taynings. Charles had been the opposite of Tom, reasonable, straightforwardly adoring, established in a senior post in the Civil Service, cultured, organized, grown-up. She remembered thinking that about Charles the first few times they had conversed, how very grown-up he was, with his proper house, proper job, proper life. There was a wildness, an unpredictability about Tom, which she had distrusted. She had finished with him because of that uncertainty – and she had fallen in love with him all over again because, in spite of herself, some part of her seemed to long for it.

She often thought that they had not had much of a chance,

she and Charles. She must have fallen pregnant with Rosalind on their honeymoon. She had been horribly sick for the first few months, during which time Charles, who was a kind and considerate man, had slept in his dressing room. By the time Rosalind had been born, Hitler had invaded Norway and Charles had been working long hours at the War Office. He was very conscientious, and Edie knew that he hated the fact that his poor eyesight had up until now prevented him from joining one of the Forces. She suspected that he had compensated by overworking.

But even if they had not spent so much of their married life apart, she would still have sometimes found Charles hard to understand. It might have been easier had her father not died when she was so young, or if she had had brothers – then she might have understood men better. Charles had a way of involving himself so deeply in a task that he became oblivious to the outside world. He had a capacity for concentration that she herself lacked and that she sometimes felt excluded her. He liked to talk about things, was erudite, well-read, spoke several languages, adored Italy in particular – he had regretted deeply that the political situation had forced them to honeymoon in Cornwall rather than Tuscany – and had a range of interests that was both wide and deep, as well as a variety of hobbies that, while he was engaged in them, absorbed him completely.

Sometimes she wondered whether she had fallen in love all over again with Tom because of the drabness of wartime life, the unending gloominess of the news, the far too frequent defeats and retreats and stalemates. The invasion of Russia had opened a new front, and had given Britain an ally at last, yet the news from Russia was discouraging, and the Wehrmacht now threatened Moscow itself. Fear of the future and a lack of fun and pleasure and privacy and time to oneself had to be compensated for somehow. Why not in a hotel room with one's lover? And then, there were the absences she felt so keenly – her sisters, of course, and her friends, many far away, some dead, lost on a beach at Dunkirk or buried beneath the ruins of a house in Chelsea.

Yet if this had been merely an entertainment, a distraction, she knew that she could have ended it. It unsettled her deeply that she did not seem able to do so; it forced her to feel differently about herself. Sometimes the elation and the desire were glorious and transforming, but at other times, in cooler moments, she disliked herself intensely. Guilt and self-loathing were her constant companions. Sometimes she wondered whether she kept herself busy so that she did not have time to confront her guilt. It ate at her, gnawing away at her former image of herself. She had lost control of herself, and control had always been so important to her. Her desires and emotions were no longer neat, confined, brought out for this or that occasion; instead, they were disorderly, unpredictable and demanding.

Edie caught sight of a bus, ran for it. Standing crushed in the aisle on the crowded lower deck, clutching tightly the metal rail of a seat, she reproached herself for not being firmer yesterday. She should have told Tom that it was over and put down the phone. But then, Mrs O'Brien had been dusting in the next room, and it was a coward's way out, wasn't it, to finish with someone by phone – cruel, really, and she couldn't do that, not to him.

But she must end it tonight. She no longer had any choice – choice had been taken away from her. Before supper, sitting in front of her dressing table, she stared at her reflection and was almost overcome by a sudden premonition of loss. She ought to wear her most unflattering dress, she ought not to brush her hair or put on lipstick. Perhaps that would make it easier – then he wouldn't want her. But instead, rising from the dressing table, she chose a dark blue crêpe frock, edged with velvet, and swept her hair back from her face, pinning it in a tumble of curls on top of her head. Her reflection stared back at her, blue eyes, white skin, crimson mouth. Duplicitous. Desirable.

'I won't be long,' she called out to Mrs O'Brien as she left the house. 'If Mr Dangerfield phones, please tell him I've just nipped out to a WVS meeting.'

She took a bus to Paddington Station and walked from there. The temperature had fallen since the afternoon; there would be a frost that night. The hotel was in Bayswater. A quick glance over her shoulder and she went inside. There was no one at the reception desk. Then Tom appeared from round a corner and her heart leapt.

'Edie, darling.' He kissed her, drawing her to him with the flat of his hand on her back, and they went upstairs.

The room was pink and yellow – pink walls, yellow curtains and lampshades, and a pink and yellow eiderdown. He said, 'It's rather like being inside a blancmange, isn't it?' and then, in a different tone, 'I'm always afraid you won't come. Every time, I'm afraid you won't come.'

When he threaded his hands beneath her coat, she shuddered.

'If only you'd let me take you out somewhere decent for dinner,' he said, 'it wouldn't be quite so, quite so—'

'Tom, you know we can't.' Edie took off her coat, took a

deep breath. She was about to say it – *Tom, we can't see each other any more* – but he spoke first.

'Still, I've brought the next best thing.'

On the small, glass-topped dressing table there was a bottle of champagne and an oblong red and yellow tin. Edie peered at the tin. 'Smoked mussels,' she said, and laughed. 'Where on earth did you find them?'

'At my parents' house, at the back of the larder, mixed in with a lot of junk. My mother can't remember where they came from.'

'You've been home?'

'Just for an evening. I'll open the champagne, shall I?'

She watched him as he cut away the gold foil. She heard him ask, 'What is it? Are you all right?'

'Yes, of course.' She kicked off her shoes and sat down on the bed beside him, one leg tucked beneath her. 'I'd love a drink, darling.'

They drank champagne out of an enamel beaker, then they lay down on the bed and curled up close to each other.

He stroked the curve of her hip and thigh. 'What sort of a day have you had?'

'Pretty average. I was at the shop this afternoon. Oh, and Bronwen's given her notice.'

'The nanny?'

'Yes.' Edie sighed. 'I was expecting it to happen so I can't say it was a surprise. I've had to almost *bribe* her to stay with us this long. Everyone's saying women will be conscripted soon – Charles is sure of it – so she's decided to go now, before it's compulsory, so that she'll have a choice and won't end up working somewhere ghastly. I can't blame her.'

'Won't that make things rather difficult for you?'

'Well, yes, it will. Rosalind will miss her dreadfully.' Say it, she told herself. Go on, here's your moment, say it. Yet she remained silent.

He had unzipped the back of her dress; his hands slipped round her waist to stroke her stomach. 'God, how I've missed you,' he murmured.

She closed her eyes – there were tears burning in them. One last time, she thought, let him love me just one last time. She turned to him and they kissed, deeply and slowly. He eased her dress down over her shoulders and hips. Undoing her bra, he cupped her breast in his hand and she felt herself melt with desire. Then there was the awkward moment of getting out of her girdle – she had never found a way of doing it elegantly – and then he was inside her, and they were moving together on the pink and yellow eiderdown.

Afterwards, she found that she was crying and, when he asked her what was wrong, she shook her head and let him kiss away the tears. Then they lay, wound together, on the bed. He fed her smoked mussels from the tin – she liked their salty, rubbery taste.

'Charles phoned last night,' she said suddenly. 'The navy have taken him at last. I think he must have persuaded someone to pull some strings. He knows he won't get a ship because of his eyesight, but he says he doesn't mind, at least he'll be in uniform. Anyway, he's being posted to Plymouth for training. He asked me if I'd go with him.'

His fingers, which had been tracing her spine, stilled. 'What did you say to him?'

'I said yes. What else could I say? Charles doesn't want us to be separated again. He's trying to find us a hotel in Plymouth.'

Tom propped himself up on an elbow. 'So you're leaving London again?'

'Yes, I'm afraid so.' She managed a smile. 'It's a blow, I was so pleased to come home, but it can't be helped.'

'But when you come back—'

'Tom, I think that this is the end,' she said gently.

'Please don't say that.' He had flinched. 'You'll come up to London sometimes, surely, and I travel all over the place. I was in Bristol only last week. We'll still be able to find a way to see each other.'

'No, Tom.' Edie looked down at the pink and yellow eiderdown. 'Even if this hadn't happened, I still should have finished it. It can't go on. It's wrong. What I'm doing is so terribly wrong.'

'If no one knows – if no one's hurt – then how can it be wrong?'

It was an argument they had had half a dozen times before. This time, she said flatly, 'It just is. And it's tearing me apart.'

He climbed out of bed and began to pull on his clothes. She said quietly, 'Don't be angry, Tom, please. I don't want us to part badly.'

'The thing is,' he said, 'I love you.'

A silence, broken by her saying softly, 'Then, if that's true, please don't make this hard for me. Let's just pretend. Let's pretend we're parting as usual. I hate goodbyes.'

With his thumb, he gently wiped the tears from her cheeks. She caught his thumb and kissed it, tasting the salt of her tears.

Half an hour later, she went home. Taking off her coat, hat and gloves in the hall, she felt dazed and exhausted. Through the closed door of the drawing room, she heard the low rumble of the wireless and felt a stab of alarm.

She went into the room. Charles was sitting on the sofa, and the low table in front of him was covered in papers.

'Darling,' she said. Her voice sounded hoarse, unsteady. 'I didn't think you were coming home until tomorrow.'

'My meeting finished earlier than I'd expected so I rushed for the train. I wanted to get back to you and Rosalind.'

The wireless was murmuring of Russian military defeats. Edie kissed Charles's cheek, then said mechanically, 'Such a lovely surprise. Have you eaten?'

'Mrs O'Brien made me a sandwich. You're late, darling, I was starting to get worried.'

'I'm sorry.' She gave a little laugh. 'I lost track of the time. These wretched meetings . . .'

'Did it go well?'

She had a mental image of herself and Tom, entwined on the pink and yellow quilt. 'Yes, quite well,' she said.

'I nipped up to see Rosalind but she was fast asleep. With a bit of luck, I'll catch a few minutes with her tomorrow, before I have to go out.'

She was moving around the room, tidying a pile of books, straightening a cushion. 'Bronwen's given her notice,' she said.

'That's a blow. Poor old you. I'll have a word with Mother, if you like, see if she knows anyone in Cricklade.'

'Yes. Thank you, Charles.'

His gaze had returned to the papers and he was writing in his bold, neat script. He had taken out his monocle to rub his eyes, which were darkly shadowed.

She said, 'You look done in, darling.'

'It's been a long day.'

'Can I get you anything? Cocoa or anything?'

'No, no.'

'You should come up to bed, have some proper rest.'

A murmur. She could tell he wasn't listening. Had she said, *Actually, I've spent the evening in bed with my lover and we've just broken it off and I feel utterly awful* – would he have heard her?

'I might have a bath and an early night,' she said. 'Are you coming up, Charles? Charles, are you coming to bed?'

She had raised her voice; he looked up, startled. 'You sound pretty whacked yourself, darling. You go ahead. I have to get through all this, I'm afraid. I'll come up soon.' He began to write again.

Climbing the stairs, she felt drained, the effort of putting one foot in front of the other almost too much for her. She went first to the nursery to check on Rosalind. Her head ached horribly. Surely one was not supposed to get a headache after drinking champagne? Perhaps she was sickening for something. Yes, she felt unwell, every muscle ached.

It was for the best, she told herself. Tomorrow she would be thankful that it had ended.

But tonight the thought gave her no relief. Instead, she felt destroyed. She pressed her hands against her face but was unable to staunch the flow of tears. They poured down her cheeks as she ran a bath. Scoured, hollowed out, she recalled her last glimpse of Tom as they had parted outside Paddington Station, before she had caught her bus. She had asked him not to come with her, had preferred that they part at the hotel, but he had insisted. In the darkness, they had kissed and they had clasped hands tightly, afraid of letting go.

She climbed out of the bath, towelled herself dry, and put on her nightdress. In bed, she curled up under the sheets, shivering. She wanted Charles to join her, she wanted the warmth and solace of the proximity of another person. Unreasonable, given the circumstances, but so. But he did not come, and the hands of the clock moved slowly round until at last she fell asleep.

'It doesn't hurt so much now,' said Klaus. 'At the front, at the field station, they gave me morphine and I had the most extraordinary dreams.'

The news that Klaus had been sent home to convalesce from a wound he had received on the Eastern front had reached Sommerfeld at the beginning of December. One morning, Herr Bernard drove Miranda to Waldhof, Uncle Karl's house. The first of the winter snows had fallen and a smooth layer of snow iced the verges. Black, charcoaled stubs of trees stood out starkly against the chalk-white fields. Herr Bernard drove slowly and carefully, keeping to the main roads.

In the bedroom, a fire burned in the grate and Klaus lay in bed with a cage over his leg to keep the weight of the blankets off the shattered bone. There was a bandage to one side of his forehead and dark smudges beneath his eyes. Anna, who was sitting on the window sill, swinging her legs, was wearing a dark green silk dress and had tied back her black hair with a scarf. Miranda perched on the edge of Klaus's bed as they ate the sugary little almond cakes and drank the rich, spicy wine the Countess had sent to restore Klaus to health.

Miranda said, 'I expect you'll have the most romantic scar.'

'I hope so.' Klaus gave a lopsided grin. 'What's the point of getting wounded if you don't end up with a good scar? Will you fall in love with me, Miranda, if I have a scar?'

Anna picked fragments of sugar off a cake. 'I don't expect Miranda will come to visit you again if you don't behave yourself, Klaus.'

'Then I'd have a relapse. Then you'd feel sorry for me and then you'd fall in love with me, wouldn't you, Miranda?'

'No, darling Klaus.' She kissed his wan cheek. 'And truly, I can't think how anyone could possibly fall in love with me now, I'm so fat.'

'Hardly *fat*.' Anna's gaze rested on Miranda's stomach. 'You must have a very neat little baby tucked in there, Miranda.'

'Dr Kornblum says it's small for my dates. But then, I'm rather small, aren't I? I expect it'll be a girl, a small girl like me. Poor Klaus. Are you feeling utterly dreadful?'

'Not half as dreadful as I was a couple of weeks ago.' A hand fluttered to his forehead. 'I can't remember what happened. There we were, in the bloody awful cold and snow and the Ivans were taking pot shots at us from all directions, and then, there I was, in the field hospital. I can't remember the bit between at all. And I can't even remember the hospital clearly, because of the morphine. The surgeon told me they had to take out a dozen pieces of shrapnel from my leg. They've left one or two in my head because they were too difficult to get at. So if I ever go a bit cracked it'll probably be because of that.'

'You always were a bit cracked, Klaus,' said Anna. 'I doubt if we'll notice much difference.'

Klaus threw a grape at her. 'How's the Countess?'

'She's been rather unwell,' said Miranda. 'She had a bad cold and it went to her chest. She sends you her love, Klaus, and hopes you feel much better soon. She's writing you a letter but it takes her rather a long time because of her arthritis.'

'And Friedrich? Have you heard from Friedrich?'

'He seems well. Mostly he asks about me and the Countess and Sommerfeld. He doesn't say much about himself.'

'Well, he can't, can he? He can't write the truth. He knows

his letters will be censored.' Anna's black brows had straightened into an angry line. 'I hate living like this. Unable to speak my mind, afraid to write what I really think because I know my letters might be read. I hate it.'

'*Anna,*' said Klaus softly.

Anna shrugged. 'If we can't be honest with each other, then what's the point of anything?'

'And the others?' asked Klaus. 'The Königsberg lot? Have you seen them at all, Miranda?'

'Uncle Georg and Aunt Klara and Katrin came over to Sommerfeld on the Countess's birthday. They seemed well.'

'Katrin has become engaged to some horrible Nazi.' Anna took another cake. 'I can hardly bear to speak to her. I shouldn't be surprised — she always had lousy taste. You're slipping down again, Klaus. Let me help you sit up.'

She hooked her arm around her brother and helped him sit more upright, plumping his pillows and handing him his wine glass. 'There, that's better, isn't it?' she said. Tenderly, she wiped the beads of sweat from his forehead.

Miranda said, 'And Max? How is Max?'

Anna looked worried. 'We haven't heard from him for ages.'

'He'll turn up,' said Klaus carelessly. 'You know Max. He was always damnably lazy. He probably can't be bothered to put pen to paper.'

'Will you still be at home at Christmas, Klaus?'

'I hope so. It depends how quickly my leg heals. They'll put me on light duties for a few weeks, I should think. And then, I suppose they'll send me back.'

'In that case, I hope your leg doesn't ever get better.' Anna, who was tidying up the pile of books on Klaus's bedside table, spoke sharply. 'I'm sorry, Klaus, perhaps I shouldn't say such things but I can't tell you how much I hate the thought of you going back to that. Conditions on the front are terrible, Miranda, the wireless and the papers don't say what it's really like, of course they don't.'

'Anna, please,' said Klaus again.

'What? Am I supposed to keep silent, like a good little German woman? Did you know, Miranda, that it's so cold that sentries who fall asleep at their posts at night sometimes freeze to death? Did you know how many of our soldiers have had limbs amputated because of frostbite?'

'Friedrich never speaks of it . . . Poor Klaus.' Miranda touched his hand.

Klaus said slowly, 'If it isn't the mud – and the mud's like black treacle and you're afraid of being sucked down into it and never being able to free yourself – then it's the cold and the snow. You can't see more than a few feet ahead of you in the blizzards, and in the morning your tank won't start and your gun won't fire because the temperature's dropped overnight to minus thirty-five degrees. You wrap up every inch of yourself because any part of you that's exposed to the elements will freeze. And your men are suffering because they haven't the right boots or warm coats because this was supposed to be a summer campaign, wasn't it? Moscow captured in a couple of months, and none of this mess and cold and snow.'

He sank back on the pillow, his eyes closed. Miranda stroked his hand. 'It'll be over soon. Surely, Klaus.'

'No, I don't think so.' His eyes opened again, tired blue slits. 'It was fine in the summer – there we were, happily marching on, the conquering heroes. Only it didn't quite work out, did it, the original plan, and now there's their unutterably endless winter. And there's the partisans, too. We have to look over our shoulders all the time, because if we don't then we get a bullet through our heads.' He gave a raw laugh. 'I'd never have thought a few peasants on skis could cause so much trouble. They're like a swarm of hornets, coming at you wherever you don't think to look for them. And there're millions of them, that's the thing, millions of damned Russians, popping up all over the place, like the bloody Hydra. Kill one of them and fifty more spring up to take their place.'

Klaus's eyes closed once more and his breathing calmed. After a few minutes, Anna rose quietly and beckoned Miranda to follow her downstairs.

In a back room, Anna lit a cigarette. She looked thin, pale, on edge. 'He keeps doing that,' she said. 'I'm talking to him or reading to him and then I look up and he's fallen asleep. The rest is good for him, I suppose. Thank you so much for coming, Miranda. It was so good of you to make the journey. I hope it hasn't tired you too much.'

'Not at all.'

'The doctor dressed his wounds this morning. His leg has become infected. It was awful for him – I heard him cry out.' Anna tucked a loose strand of hair back beneath the scarf. 'And what I said to Klaus is true. I find myself hoping he won't fully recover, that his leg won't ever mend properly. Then he won't have to go back to the front. Do you think that's dreadful of me?'

'It's understandable. Poor Anna.'

Anna gave a strained smile. 'Sit down, Miranda, and talk to me. I've been going mad with anxiety these last few days. There's Klaus, of course, but I'm starting to worry about Max as well.' She sighed. 'The trouble is that I don't seem to have anyone to talk to. I mean, *really* talk to. I have to be careful what

I say at the hospital and my father lives in a world of his own these days. It's as though he can't admit to himself what's happening.' Suddenly, she sprang to her feet. 'Oh, I'm such a rotten hostess. Can I get you something, Miranda? Coffee? Or biscuits and cheese?'

'No, thanks, honestly. And Anna, when things get better—'

'Do you believe that they will?' Anna went to stand at the window.

Miranda said carefully, 'Not completely, no.'

'Nor do I. And actually, I'm not sure they should.'

Through the window, they could see the woodland that surrounded Waldhof, the dark greenish-black of the firs, the slender silver branches of the birches, all frosted with snow.

'In his letters,' said Miranda, 'Friedrich talks about Sommerfeld all the time. I can tell how deeply he longs to come home. Anna, what do you mean when you say you're not sure whether things should get better?'

Anna was resting her palms on the window sill, staring out at the tiny flakes of snow drifting through the still air. 'Sometimes I wish I was like stupid Frau Hirsch,' she said softly. 'Sometimes I wish I could rattle on about how wonderful it'll be when Russia is ours. I might be happier then.'

'If you said that, Anna, I'd know you were lying.'

There was a silence. Miranda waited. Then Anna said, 'I heard something. Something terrible. I have friends, you see, who think the same way as I do, who share my political views. We can't see each other very often and we don't dare write or phone, of course. But I met up with one of them when I was staying in Berlin a few weeks ago and I can't forget what he told me.'

'What? What did he tell you?'

Anna glanced at the door. She said quietly, 'My friend, Dieter, is a doctor. He works in a hospital behind the front line. He was given a week's leave earlier in the year so we arranged to meet each other. He told me that Jews and partisans are being slaughtered every day in Russia. I don't mean in battle – I mean shot in cold blood. And not just a few, but hundreds – thousands – of them. Dieter told me that one day, he was looking after a soldier who was very badly wounded. He couldn't do much for his patient except make him comfortable and try to reassure him. But the man insisted on telling him something. It was as if he wanted to get it off his mind. He told Dieter that, a few months before, he'd been part of a company of soldiers who'd been ordered to keep guard over two hundred Jews from a nearby village. The Jews had been made to dig a trench. When it was finished, they were ordered to stand beside the trench, and then they were shot. Not only the men, but the women and children as well. And the most terrible thing – some of them didn't die straight away. Yet they were still thrown into the trench and covered with earth.' Anna sighed. 'Perhaps I shouldn't have told you. Pregnant women are supposed to think happy thoughts, aren't they? But I have to speak of this to someone and who else is there? Not Klaus, when he's so ill. Not my father. Not Katrin and her SS boyfriend. And anyway, you should know the truth.'

Miranda said, 'I have heard . . . *rumours*.'

'Haven't we all? Those of us who care to listen, that is. And why should I have been so shocked? After all, they weren't only Jews, they were Bolsheviks as well.'

'But *Klaus* – and Max and Friedrich. *They* wouldn't do anything like that.'

Anna's face was in shadow. 'No, of course not. None of them

would do such a terrible thing. But I find myself in an impossible position. I dread us losing the war, because what will happen to us if we do? But how can I possibly want us to win?'

She sat down beside Miranda. Taking Miranda's hand in hers, Anna said, 'I've another reason for feeling glad you came today. I haven't been able to face telling Klaus yet, but as soon as he's better, I'm going away.'

'Where are you going?'

'Berlin.'

During her three years at Sommerfeld Miranda had become fond of Anna. She cried, 'Oh, Anna, must you?'

'Yes, I think so.'

'But I'll miss you so much!'

'And I'll miss you too, Miranda.' The strain disappeared from Anna's face and she smiled. 'You make me laugh, and I treasure that, especially these days.'

'But why are you leaving? And why Berlin, when it's so dangerous, now, with the air raids?'

'I'm going to train to be a nurse. I want to learn how to nurse properly – I need to learn how to do more than sweeping floors and emptying bedpans.' Anna's straight black brows lowered. 'We've been so sheltered here, so protected. And I find myself feeling ashamed of that. I need to be in the heart of things. How else can I know what to do? And besides, I don't have much of a choice. Have you heard that Hitler has built himself a little fortress in the forest near Rastenberg? It's supposed to be a great secret, of course, but everyone knows about it. I know that forest well – we used to go there when I was little, to look for mushrooms. I remember that I always disliked it. It wasn't nearly as pretty as our own woodland, the trees are so dark and so close together and I got bitten almost to death by mosquitoes. Anyway, a party official visited us a week ago and it seems that one of Hitler's toadies has rather taken to Waldhof. So our house is to be requisitioned.'

Miranda stared at her, appalled. '*Anna.*'

Anna wound the ends of her headscarf round her fingers. 'I was furious at first but I've got used to the idea now. I've had to play the grieving sister of the war hero so that they'd allow us to remain here for another couple of months, until Klaus is better. Oh, and they've generously offered to let Father and me stay on in one of the wings.' Anna's voice dripped sarcasm.

'Couldn't you?'

'My father will. Papa can't imagine living anywhere other than at Waldhof. He was born here. As I was – as Klaus and Max were. But I couldn't bear to stay here with them in the house. I truly couldn't bear it.'

'You must come to us – you must all come to us. We've plenty of room.'

'No.' Anna gave Miranda a hug. 'It's sweet of you to offer, and I shall miss you all dreadfully, but no, I shall go to Berlin. I've made up my mind.'

Rumours. These days, they sought them out, or shied away from them, or fed off them.

Driving away from Waldhof, Miranda recalled a rumour of a massacre in Kovno, in Lithuania, around a hundred miles from Rastenberg. More than nine thousand Jews had been murdered in one day, the rumour said. The inhabitants of the ghetto hospital and the Jewish orphanage had been locked inside and the buildings set on fire. Watching the snowflakes float down from a heavy, gun-metal sky, Miranda remembered that rumour, and thought of the terror the orphaned children must have felt, as the first flames began to lick the building.

There were other rumours, too. And there were oppressions and horrors they all knew about. The Jews must wear the yellow star and so were constantly at risk of insult or physical assault. Their homes were confiscated, their rations curtailed, and they were allowed to visit the shops for only an hour a day. They were beaten by the Gestapo, and if they had transgressed – or if they had done nothing wrong at all – they were imprisoned or transported to concentration camps.

Some of the visitors to her father's house in Paris had been Jews. Konstantin Denisov had regarded them with a mixture of distaste and respect for their intellect and their business acumen. How far, Miranda wondered, as she gazed out of the car window at the falling snow, was the distance between distaste and loathing? How far must you travel before you could bury a man alive or put a torch to a building with children trapped inside it?

Shivering, she wrapped her fur coat tightly about herself. She found herself remembering her long-ago childhood visit to her grandparents' house in Wiltshire. The gentle warmth of the air, the scent of her grandmother's garden after the rain. If she concentrated hard she could almost feel the soft grass on the river bank, almost see the fish swimming in the cool, green water, alien, in their own world, which was nothing to do with hers at all. She supposed that to light that torch you would have to believe the Jews to be something less than human. She supposed that to dig that grave you would have had to have heard year after year the angry, accusing speeches on the wireless, and you would have had to have watched the films and read the gutter press that told you that the Jews were the agent of all your miseries, that they had brought their troubles on themselves, and that it had been the Jewish-Bolshevist conspiracy that had started the war.

The wariness that had been essential in her father's house was useful to her now. She was careful, cautious, discreet. The von Kahlberg name gave some protection, and naturally she never told a soul that her father had been Russian, her mother English. She, who had loved to be the centre of attention, now tried to melt into the background. If she did not hate the conspiracy of silence that enclosed them all as much as Anna did, then perhaps it was only because she was used to it. She had learned to watch what she said in childhood – good practice for living as they all did now.

She looked out of the car window at the chill, bleached countryside. For a few moments she allowed herself the luxury of thinking of Olivier. She treasured her memories of him: each memory had become polished like a jewel, by time and use. She permitted herself to glance at them only every now and then, as if she was afraid of wearing them out. She recalled how she had been walking down the Champs-Elysées, and how she had heard a voice say, *My God, Miranda*, and how she had turned and had seen him. The miracle of that moment. The indescribable joy of finding him again, after so long.

Yet this time the recollection gave her no comfort, and instead, a great surge of fear and longing for him welled up inside her. Even if he had survived the battle of France, how would he bear it, he who had belonged so completely to Paris, living in an occupied city? Olivier would not stand idly by, she knew that. He would fight, in whatever way he could.

She had thought that Sommerfeld would provide her with a refuge, but she had been wrong. It was as though she had been placed on a chessboard, and left alone at the margins while great and terrible things happened elsewhere. Now, though, she was being drawn closer to the conflict. The war was reaching East Prussia, for so long quiet and remote. Military vehicles dominated the roads and trains left the station at Rastenberg daily, filled with fresh troops going east and the wounded travelling to hospitals in the west. Once, tuning the wireless, she had come across a broadcast from the BBC Foreign Service. There had been the ticking of a clock and, at every seventh tick, a voice had said, *Every seven seconds a German dies in Russia. Is it your husband? Is it your son? Is it your brother?*

A few days later, they received the news that Friedrich's cousin Max had been killed on the Eastern front. During the funeral at Waldhof chapel, Miranda thought of Max, twenty years old, handsome and dashing, dancing with her in the ceremonial rooms at Sommerfeld. She remembered Max carrying the gramophone down to the frozen lake and waltzing with Anna to the tune of the 'Blue Danube'. Both had been laughing. Now Anna, standing in the pew a few yards away from her, didn't look as if she would ever laugh again. The von Kahlbergs' circle, which had seemed, when Miranda had first come to live at Sommerfeld, to reflect the timeless rural landscape in which they lived, was being torn apart.

Not long afterwards, they went to the forest to choose the Christmas tree. The men, Polish forced labourers and French and English prisoners of war who had replaced the farm workers of East Prussia who had been conscripted into the army, dragged it back from the forest and put it up in the great black-and-white tiled vestibule of the castle. Miranda decorated the tree with the painted wooden ornaments and candle-holders the family used each year. On Christmas Eve, they would light the candles. Whenever she brushed against the pine branches, she caught their scent, the cold, resiny scent of the forest.

Kay hadn't heard from Tom for ages, and then, in early December, a letter arrived at barracks, telling her that he was on embarkation leave.

The Piccadilly nightclub where he had told her that he would wait for her was small and intimate, with fewer than a dozen tables. Kay caught sight of him as soon as she entered, sitting in a corner of the room. She waved, and wove through the tables and chairs.

'Tom!'

He rose and they kissed. 'Sorry I'm so late,' she said. She sat down opposite him. 'I had to drive to Catterick and back today. It took hours and hours. I'm afraid I didn't have time to change out of my uniform.'

'You look lovely, as always.' He glanced at her stripe. 'Lance corporal, eh? Congratulations.'

'I'm a staff driver now. I drive cars instead of lorries – such a relief. I had a rather nice Humber Snipe the other day.'

He ordered drinks. A mouthful of gin and lemon and she gave a sigh of pleasure. 'How lovely and civilized. So, tell me how you are, Tom.'

He talked about his work and his family and how pleased he was to be going overseas at last. She said, 'I hope you'll write a bit more often when you're in the desert or wherever. You really have been a lousy correspondent.'

'Sorry.' He looked sheepish. 'I've been busy.'

She gave him a look of mock disapproval. 'It's all right, I forgive you. I was worried for a while that it was because of what happened, but then I thought, not Tom, he wouldn't be like that.'

He looked blank. 'Because of what happened?'

'You know. In the park.'

He still looked confused, and then his face lightened, and he grinned and said, 'Oh yes. St James's Park. I remember. Actually, I assumed you'd had too much to drink, Kay.'

'Did you know that I joined the ATS because of you?'

'Seriously? Why?'

'I felt so mortified. You were very stern and disapproving and bundled me off home in a taxi.'

'Did I?'

'Well, so long as you haven't been sulking.'

'Me? Good Lord, no.'

They fell silent for a while, listening to the band, as a man with slicked-back hair sang 'The Last Time I Saw Paris'. In repose, Tom looked less cheerful – grim, almost, and rather strained. But then they were all strained, she supposed, after two and a half years of war. She herself had risen at five that morning to drive to Catterick. On the way back, her passenger, a Major Lansdowne, had insisted she tell him her Christian name, and had then talked to her at length about his wife, who didn't understand him. She had had to pinch herself every now and then to keep awake as he had listed his wife's failings. Reaching London, the major had offered to take her out for a drink; after she had refused, he had gone off in a huff.

She touched Tom's hand. 'Cheer up, old thing.'

'I'm fine. Do you want anything to eat, Kay? Can I buy you supper?'

She shook her head. 'Better not. I seem to be eating vast quantities of bread and potatoes these days.' She ran a hand over her hips. 'Why do NAAFI canteens make such lovely puddings? If the war goes on much longer I shall be hideously fat.'

'You? Fat? Never. You don't sit still long enough to get fat.'

She smiled at him. 'I'll tell you what I'd like to do. I'd like to dance.'

He held out a hand to her. 'Come on, then.'

The song ended; the raucous cry of a trumpet and then the swing band burst into 'Boogie Woogie Bugle Boy', and the small dance floor was full of couples dancing.

Afterwards, the music slowed again, and Tom took her in his arms and she rested her head against his shoulder. Fractured thoughts drifted through her tired brain. She had never danced with Tom before . . . she must be up early tomorrow because she had to drive back to Aldershot . . . Tom was really rather a good dancer . . . lovely to dance with a man who was tall enough for her . . . good old Tom, she'd missed him . . .

'Hey,' he said. 'You're falling asleep. Come on, I'll take you home.'

They collected their coats and left the nightclub. Kay was staying at Aunt Dot's house that night. Aunt Dot was in the north of England, giving talks for the Ministry of Food to WVS groups. They took a bus part of the way, and then walked. It was a dark, murky night, with a hint of rain in the air. They talked of Pearl Harbor: the previous Sunday, Japanese planes had bombed the American fleet where it lay at anchor in Hawaii. More than two thousand people had died, many ships had been sunk or badly damaged, and a large number of American planes had been destroyed on the airfields. But the Japanese action had brought America into the war at last; Germany and Italy had declared war on the USA.

'So awful,' she said, as they picked their way over a bomb site, 'about the *Prince of Wales* and the *Repulse*. Why are naval defeats always so much worse than other defeats?'

Tom gave her his hand to help her over a broken wall. 'Because that's what we've always been good at. Britannia rules the waves and all that. We can tolerate a few reverses on land, but losing a ship always seems a particularly hard blow.'

'Every now and then,' she said, 'I catch myself thinking that this is normal, and that this is how life's always going to be. People say the war will be over sooner now that the Americans are in, but I'm not so sure. Perhaps it'll only mean that the fighting spreads, and that more countries will have to go through what we're going through. Sometimes I'm afraid it'll go on for ever.'

They had reached the road; the dimmed light of Tom's torch lit their way. 'We *will* win,' said Tom. 'It might take years, but we will.'

'How can you be sure?'

She expected him to confide in her some strategy, some plan or other, but instead he said, 'Because we have to. It's as simple as that. And I believe that in the end, good will win out. However long it takes. In my heart, that's what I believe.'

They had reached the house. Opening the side gate, Kay led the way to the back of the house, warning him of familiar obstacles – the honeysuckle tendrils that reached over the path, the empty milk bottles.

She let them in through the back door. The kitchen was cold, so they kept on their coats. Kay made cocoa; Tom rested against the dresser, long and lean, too tall, she thought, for the small room. He would travel to Cambridge tomorrow morning, he told her, to spend a few days with his family before leaving the country. He couldn't wait to be gone.

She was suddenly anxious for him. 'Tom, you will be careful, won't you?'

'Course I will.' A quick grin. 'I've fallen off mountains, I've crashed cars – I bounce, my mother says. I'll be fine.' He paused; the smile slipped, and he muttered, 'Anyway, I had to go. I had to get away.'

'Is something wrong?'

He shook his head, made a small, hopeless sound, and then, after a few moments, said, 'Edie and I were seeing each other again.'

She stared at him, surprised. 'Edie? I thought she was married.'

'She is. And she has a child, a daughter.'

Oh Tom, she thought, what a tangle. And felt a flicker of resentment towards the unknown Edie – Kay had never met her, but she imagined her to be sweetly pretty, vain and indulged. Why couldn't the wretched woman leave him alone?

She heard him say, 'It's all over now, anyway. She finished it a month ago.' His voice was flat. 'It should probably never have begun.'

'Poor old you.'

'Do you think so?' He looked up at her and shrugged. 'My own bloody fault, I'd have said.' He gave a short laugh. 'Madly and deeply – that's what you said, that day in St James's Park, would anyone ever love either of us madly and deeply. The thing is, that's how I loved Edie.'

Kay put the cocoa and some biscuits on to a tray; Tom carried it into the sitting room. He said, 'When we were seeing each other, no matter what else was going on, I didn't mind, it didn't seem to matter. However bad the news was, I felt as if nothing could touch me. The night Edie finished it, I couldn't take it in. After I saw her on to her bus, I walked for hours and hours. It started raining but I just kept on walking. Every now and then, something would catch my attention and I'd forget it – I mean, forget what had just happened, but only for a second or two – and then I'd remember all over again. I was afraid to stop walking and I was afraid to let it sink in. I remember once when I was climbing in the Cairngorms, I slipped off a rock ledge. I remember falling, not having anything to hold on to, and just this blind terror. That's what it felt like, as if I'd been cut loose and was plunging into darkness. Anyway, in the end, I was soaked and I had to go back to my hotel to change. I must have got about half an hour's sleep before I had to go and meet my CO. I was useless that day – he tore me off a strip.'

'People do say,' she said tentatively, 'that these things get less painful in time.'

'Yes, they do, don't they?' He frowned. 'I wonder whether that's true.'

Once, Kay recalled, she had asked Aunt Dot whether she minded not having married. Aunt Dot had told her that, as the years had passed, her work at the magazine and her correspondence with her readers had taught her that though sexual love could be nourishing and joyful, it could also be destructive, exhausting and debilitating.

Destructive, exhausting and debilitating. Much of what had originally charmed her in Tom, that first time they had met in Berlin – his humour, his energy, his enthusiasm – now seemed diminished.

Kay put his cocoa in front of him. He asked her whether she had met anyone special, and she shook her head.

'Oh dear, we're a rather hopeless pair, aren't we?' She wound her coat around her and stretched her legs along the couch. She was very tired, and her eyelids were heavy.

'Pretty disastrous,' he agreed.

'When we're old, Tom, and I'm a spinster who keeps cats, and you're a mad old bachelor with a pipe and holes in your sleeves, we can share a house, like brother and sister.'

The picture pleased her. A cottage, roses round the door, a ginger cat sitting on a fence post, delphiniums, hollyhocks, sunlight . . .

Kay slept.

Chapter Eleven

One morning, Miranda slipped on the ice, crossing the courtyard to feed Gisela, who lived in comfortable quarters at the far end of the stables. Her foot shot out in front of her and she found herself sitting rather painfully on the cobbles. A stable lad rushed to help her, and for the remainder of the day she lay on the sofa in the Countess's little green-and-white sitting room, her swollen ankle propped up on a pillow, with a book and some sewing on a table beside her.

In bed that night, she woke and realized that her back was hurting more than her ankle. It had been hurting on and off for days, but now the pain had come to have a rhythm to it, a rise and fall. She put on the light and took out of the drawer of her bedside cabinet the booklet that Dr Kornblum had given her. She had studied the booklet conscientiously, though it had sometimes made her laugh with its comparisons of expectant mothers to ships in full sail. At other times it had unnerved her by recommending that women distract themselves from the pain of labour by reminding themselves that motherhood was the crowning glory of a woman's life. There had been some practical advice mixed in with the homilies. Labour pains came and went, the booklet said, steadily increasing in intensity until the mother was ready to push the baby out through the birth canal. Miranda's pain was intermittent and it was certainly increasing in intensity.

She wondered whether, if she lay very still, the pain might go away and she might doze off again. Yet she could not find a comfortable position in which to lie. There was a squirming restlessness in the pit of her stomach which made her feel she had to move about. Cautiously, she sat up. She put her good foot on the floor first, and then the other, gingerly, one hand holding the bedstead for support as she stood up. There was a whoosh of fluid from between her legs and she cried out.

Then, after she had rung the bell for help, there was a lot of busy rushing around. Two of the maids were woken to boil water and fetch linen, Herr Bernard was dispatched to Angerberg to collect Dr Kornblum, and the Countess came to sit with her. In the middle of all this, Miranda alternated between the continuing need to walk round the room, holding on to a maid's shoulder because of her sore foot, and then, when the pain started up again, lying on the bed because when it hurt, it hurt so much she couldn't think about anything else, not even walking. She wondered why it hurt so much and whether it was supposed to hurt so much, and if so why no one had warned her, and concluded, quite sensibly she felt, given the circumstances, that it was because women wouldn't have babies if they knew beforehand how much it would hurt. She seemed to be surrounded by conspiracies of silence, by things that should have been said but weren't, because perhaps they were too horrible to contemplate.

They went to close the curtains but she wouldn't let them because she wanted to see the falling snow through the window. Being able to see the snow made her feel a little less frightened. Whenever a contraction began, she stared at the snow, at the patterns it made against the night sky – floating, whirling, or shooting so fast the blots of white smeared together. Between the contractions she watched the clock, a large, complicated edifice encrusted with porcelain fruit and insects. The first time she looked at it, it was half past one in the morning. She longed for Dr Kornblum to arrive, willed herself to hear his car heading down the driveway. Dr Kornblum must be able to stop it hurting so much, she was sure he must. But what if the baby came before Dr Kornblum arrived? What if the snowstorm turned into a blizzard? What if Dr Kornblum was away, attending another patient? She gave a whimper of fear, and the Countess, sitting beside her, squeezed her hand and murmured soothingly. A pain gathered, growing in strength, sweeping over her like a great, dark wave. When it subsided, she looked at the clock and was horrified to see that only five minutes had passed.

Dr Kornblum reached Sommerfeld shortly before three o'clock in the morning, accompanied by a stout, middle-aged woman wearing a nurse's uniform and fur-lined boots. Dr Kornblum said, 'Ah, my dear little Countess, so your baby has decided to come a fortnight early, has he?' and beamed at her, and Miranda felt immensely relieved. His nurse would assist him at the birth, Dr Kornblum explained, so perhaps the Countess might prefer to return to her bed. The Countess left the room.

Then, after examining her, which was both painful and distressing, he told Miranda that all was well, and she mustn't worry. To her inquiries, he said that the baby wouldn't be born for some hours and that she must try to rest as much as possible between the contractions. 'Some hours?' Miranda repeated. She had expected him to say an hour or, at the very worst, two. 'How many hours?' It was impossible to tell, said Dr Kornblum. He hoped the baby would be born by midday.

Hours and hours more of pain – it was unendurable. The hands of the porcelain clock were moving very slowly now. She tried to distract herself by fixing her gaze on a smooth pink and yellow apple or the shiny black coil of a ceramic snail, but they made her feel nauseous and she closed her eyes and the nurse placed a cool cloth on her forehead.

And so she was dismissed, the Countess thought, and for that she could only feel thankful. Leaning heavily on her stick as she walked slowly down the corridor, she acknowledged that her own memories of childbirth had become hazy. One could remember that it had been unbearable without being able to recall what the pain had felt like. Her recollection of her own ordeal had become thinner, less substantial, like a piece of cloth that had worn away over time.

It had been Dr Kornblum who had attended her when she had given birth to Friedrich. Like herself, Dr Kornblum had been born in the eighteen sixties – a more gracious age, the Countess thought, without the stridency of this modern era. Dr Kornblum had come out of retirement because the younger medical men were now working in the military hospitals or at the front. The Countess would have preferred to have a younger man attend her daughter-in-law. Dr Kornblum was kind and gentle, which was so important to a woman in labour, but the Countess feared he might not be abreast of the most modern medical techniques. And besides, there was no denying that, as one grew older, physically one *failed* a little. The Countess narrowed her eyes, struggling to see in the ill-lit corridor, and felt the tremor of her hand as she placed it on the stair rail. She sighed. He would do his best. They shared a great deal, she and Dr Kornblum. They had lived through war and defeat and revolution.

And it was because she remembered what war could do that, after a scant four hours' sleep, the Countess rose as usual at seven o'clock to carry out her daily round. After prayers and breakfast, she went to the kitchens. Not a day passed when she did not run her experienced eye over the work of Sommerfeld's kitchens, checking that the food was stored correctly and ensuring that economy was constantly practised. War and deprivation went hand in hand, and it was her responsibility to see that no one on the estate starved.

At mid-morning, she drank coffee with Herr Bernard, Friedrich's secretary, while they discussed any questions arising from the farms and tenancies. Afterwards, she wrote letters to Friedrich, to Anna in Berlin, and to her late brother Stefan's daughter, Susanne, who lived in Switzerland. Because the arthritis had spread to her hands, writing was a slow and painful business. The Countess persisted because she had always found pleasure in describing the life of Sommerfeld, and because she was reluctant to give in to the greedy demands of her illness.

This morning, though, it was hard to concentrate. A part of her listened constantly for footsteps in the corridor. First labours were often long, she reminded herself. She must be patient. Her thoughts drifted to the hopes she knew Friedrich cherished for his child, that he would carry on the traditions of

Sommerfeld, that he would share the qualities Friedrich himself had always striven to uphold – an appreciation of his country's culture and intellect, and an awareness of the responsibilities that came with rank.

At one o'clock, the Countess had a message sent to Dr Kornblum; shortly afterwards, he came to the dining room.

'You must eat, Herr Doktor,' said the Countess. 'And you must rest, if only for half an hour.'

She had the servants bring Dr Kornblum a bowl of soup, white rolls, sausage and cheese and a glass of wine. Only when he had finished did she inquire about her daughter-in-law.

Dr Kornblum blotted his moustache with a napkin. He would have preferred the Countess's labour to progress a little faster, he said. He was afraid that the Countess was tiring.

She said, 'As soon as you have news . . .' and he bowed.

'Yes, Gräfin, naturally.'

After he had gone, the Countess closed her eyes and prayed, for Friedrich, for Miranda, and for the unborn child. Sitting in the green-and-white octagonal room, she watched the dusk fall. Night came so early in this, the dark heart of the year. She must have dozed, then, because she dreamed she was a child again, and she was walking through the Rathauspark in Vienna with her nurse.

She woke suddenly, confused. The room was in darkness – no servant had come to turn on the light – and Dr Kornblum was standing in the doorway.

She fumbled for the lamp switch. 'The baby—'

'Not yet, I'm afraid. My apologies for disturbing you, Countess.' Dr Kornblum gave a little cough. 'The Graf von Kahlberg . . . can he be sent for?'

'I'm afraid not.' The corner of the Countess's eye was caught, through the orangery, by the swirl of the blizzard outside. She added, 'I believe that conditions on the front are very difficult. I can write a letter, but . . .' The remainder of her sentence she left unvoiced.

They had drawn the curtains. She was too tired to tell them that she preferred the snow, disliked the colour of the crimson damask, which enclosed her in a hot, red box which matched the hot redness inside her head whenever she closed her eyes. Sometimes, she seemed to sleep for a moment or two, and then the pain jolted her awake, gathering like a black beast, ready to spring. She tried not to cry out, having a vague idea, picked up from who knows where, that it would be wrong to cry out, but then Dr Kornblum told her to push and she wept as she tried to tell him that she couldn't possibly push, it hurt far too much, and if she pushed, she would split in half like an overripe fig. Then the nurse wiped her face with the cool cloth and told her that her baby was coming, and that she must push him out, and from somewhere she found a scrap of courage and did as she was told.

But they kept telling her to push and she kept trying, and still the baby would not come. After a while, no matter how hard she tried, and though she didn't care any longer whether she lived or died, she couldn't push any more. She was crying, and she was apologizing for her failure and she was aware that she was speaking French when she should be speaking German to Dr Kornblum, but she was too tired to remember any German. But Dr Kornblum patted her hand and said, 'There, there, my dear, you've been very brave and now I'm going to give you a little help.' Then she heard Dr Kornblum say to the nurse, 'Yes, now,' and a square of white gauze was placed over her face and there was a sweet smell and she felt herself drift away somewhere safe and dark.

It had gone on too long. The Countess still prayed, but she knew in her heart that it had gone on too long. She waited, surrounded by history. It echoed, bore in on her, could be seen in the painted faces of the gentlemen in the portraits and in a silver christening spoon emblazoned with an enamelled crest. History was in the fabric of this house, in its brick and wood and tile, ingrained, ineradicable. History would wash over them all, she reminded herself; it would take her, soon enough, and it would even erase, in time, Friedrich's grief if he were to lose his wife and child.

Hearing footsteps in the corridor, she stiffened and composed herself. And then Dr Kornblum was in the room, grey-faced and old, like her, standing though she beckoned him to sit. And he was telling her that though he believed that her daughter-in-law would survive, he had had to deliver the baby by forceps, and the child, a boy, had been born blue, with the cord round his neck, and though he had fought for it, had done every-thing in his power, he had been unable to save it.

'Edie? It is you, isn't it?'

Edie was riding up the escalator at Oxford Circus. At the sound of her name she looked round and stared, puzzled, at the face of the young woman two steps down.

'Good gracious,' she said. 'Minnie Blacklock.'

'I saw you in the carriage but it was too crowded to speak to you. How lovely to see you, Edie. It's been ages. You haven't changed at all. I knew you the minute I saw you.'

There was a large gentleman standing on the step that

separated them. When she reached the top of the escalator, Edie stood aside to let Minnie catch up with her. Minnie, who was in her nurse's uniform, wore her light brown hair parted to one side and smoothly coiled at the back of her head. She was tall and slim, thinner than Edie remembered. She had Tom's eyes, dark blue, thickly lashed and straight-browed. Edie felt a stab of loss, seeing Tom in his sister.

'You've changed, Minnie,' said Edie. 'You look quite different to how I remember you.'

Minnie smiled. 'I seem to remember I was going through my Bohemian phase when we met.'

'Are you working in London?'

'Yes, I'm at the London Hospital in Whitechapel. What about you?'

'Charles and I are living in Liverpool just now. I'm staying in Esher for a few days, with my mother.'

Minnie glanced at her watch. 'I say, what are you doing now? Are you in a rush? Or have you time for a coffee?'

'I came in to buy knitting wool,' Edie explained. 'But I'm perfectly certain none of the shops will have quite what I want and I'm rather tired, so it would be lovely to sit down and talk.'

They left the tube station and made for a café Minnie knew behind the shattered edifice of John Lewis. A waitress brought coffee for Minnie and tea for Edie. She drank it carefully, taking little sips.

'Actually,' she told Minnie, 'I'm expecting a baby.'

'Congratulations.'

Edie gave Minnie a wary look. 'You're not going to lecture me on my contribution to the population explosion, then?'

'Did I do that the last time we met?' Minnie grimaced. 'Dear me, what a frightful prig I was. No, I'm delighted for you. When's it due?'

'September. I did hope I wouldn't feel so sick this time, but even tea's a struggle. Everyone tells me I'll stop feeling sick after the first three months are over, but I didn't the last time so I can't feel very optimistic.'

'You poor thing. It must be grim.'

'I may feel rotten,' said Edie resolutely, 'but at least there's a happy event at the end of it. I shouldn't complain when so many people are having a much worse time.'

Minnie gave her a quizzical look. 'Do you think that sort of reasoning ever works? I don't find it does with me. If I'm feeling blue then I'm feeling blue and I'm not at all sure that thinking about people who are more miserable makes me feel any better. In fact, it might even make me feel worse.'

Minnie herself did not look happy, Edie thought. She looked tired and thin and rather sad.

'Tell me about your work,' she said.

'Are you sure you want to hear? All I seem to think about these days is nursing, and I can't help feeling it's rather a bore for other people.'

'Not at all. I used to help at a WVS shop, but I had to give it up. I miss it rather a lot. So please do tell me about nursing. It always sounds so interesting.'

'It is. I love it. I'm a ward sister now, which means I can boss all the poor little VADs around. I thought it would mean no more bed-making and bedpan emptying, but I still have to muck in if there's a rush. I'm on men's surgical. They are so terribly brave. Even when they're in pain they always try to smile or crack a joke.' Minnie fell silent for a moment, and then she said, 'It's funny. We were hit by quite a few bombs in the Blitz, and it was frightening, of course, but in a peculiar way I seem to miss it now. Life seems, I don't know, flat. Dreary and tiresome and just going on and on.'

Edie was shocked to see that there were tears in Minnie's eyes. She had a sudden thought, which cut through her like a knife, and could not stop herself saying, 'Minnie, what is it? What's wrong? It's not Tom, is it?'

'Tom's fine, as far as I know.' Minnie stirred her coffee. 'My boyfriend was lost at sea a couple of months ago, you see.'

Edie found she had been holding her breath. Letting it out, she said, 'I'm so sorry. How terrible for you. What happened?'

'Malcolm was on the *Matabele*. They were escorting a convoy to Murmansk and they were torpedoed. Only two of the crew survived. The sea was so cold, even if he had managed to get off the ship before she sank, he would have frozen to death.'

'Oh, Minnie. Had you been together long?'

'Six months. Malcolm was twenty-five, the same age as me. It was very on and off, of course, what with Malcolm being away so much.' Minnie smiled. 'We met on a bus. I was going to the hospital and he got on and asked me if he was on the right bus for Piccadilly. Well, he wasn't, of course, but we got talking. He was from Aberdeen – he'd never been to London before.' She scrabbled in her bag, took out a packet of cigarettes, and then put them back again, saying, 'No, I mustn't smoke, not if you're feeling rotten. Anyway, we were going to get engaged on his next leave. I wish we hadn't waited. A girlfriend's nothing. His parents didn't even invite me to the memorial service. They said it was just for close family. They didn't count a girlfriend as close family. And of course all his things were sent to them, so I haven't even much to remember him by.'

Edie squeezed Minnie's hand. 'I'm so sorry.'

'I don't think Malcolm's parents approved of me. They're very stuffy and old-fashioned and they don't think girls should work. They seemed particularly to disapprove of nursing. All those *bodies*, I suppose. Anyway, there's just this awful nothingness. No proper grave, of course, because they never found his body. And there aren't many people I can talk to about him, because almost all his shipmates were drowned as well.' She frowned. 'I keeping thinking how awful it must have been for him, alone in the water. I can't get it out of my head.'

Knowing that anything she said must be inadequate, Edie ventured, 'It must be so difficult for you.'

'It was, at first, but I'm fine now.' Minnie gave a brisk smile. 'My work keeps me busy, thank goodness. Tom's in North Africa, by the way. So far as I can tell, he's fine apart from stomach bugs. I told him to boil absolutely everything. What about you? How are all your sisters and nieces?'

'I've two more nieces than when we last met. Which means there are seven cousins, all girls.'

'*Seven*. Gracious.'

'We Fielding women only seem to produce girls. Mummy despairs of ever having a grandson.'

'What do you think your next one will be?'

'Oh, a girl,' said Edie, laughing. 'I'm sure it's a girl.'

Shortly afterwards, Minnie left for the hospital. Edie drank another sip or two of her tea, which had gone cold, and wondered whether she should order a sandwich – oddly, she sometimes felt hungry as well as sick – and decided not to risk it. Instead, she caught a bus to Sloane Square and went to Peter Jones, where she bought pink wool for a cardigan for Rosalind and a marled grey for a sweater for Charles, for his birthday. Then she made her way to Esher.

On the train, she thought about the conversation in the café. She had liked Minnie a great deal better than the previous time they had met; she remembered how, that Sunday at the Blacklocks' house, Tom's sister's bounding boisterousness had irritated her. She found herself considering something Minnie had said. *We were hit by quite a few bombs in the Blitz, and it was terribly frightening, of course, but in a peculiar way I seem to miss it now. Life seems – I don't know – flat.* Though she could not have said that she herself missed the Blitz – her one exposure to its fury, that night with Tom, had been terrifying – she thought she understood what Minnie had meant. All around them was the feeling, which went largely unvoiced, that they were in the middle of a long, gloomy tunnel, without even a pinpoint of light visible at the end of it. She wondered whether she, too, seemed somehow *lessened*, whether the string of appalling defeats and the rationing of food, clothing and fuel – of so much that made life comfortable and pleasurable – had affected them all.

The first three months of 1942 had been a disaster for the Allies. In January, Rommel had made gains in North Africa, and in the Far East Manila had fallen and the Japanese had invaded Burma, a British possession. Then, in the middle of February, there had been the body blow of the fall of Singapore. She had been in the very early stages of pregnancy – she and Charles had conceived their second child when celebrating Charles's fortieth birthday that January, Edie suspected – and she had felt particularly unwell. They were in Plymouth, staying in a hotel on the far side of the town from the docks – safer, Charles had pointed out, not to be too near the docks, because Plymouth had been badly bombed the previous year. The hotel seemed always to have a fuggy, meaty, oily sort of smell, which Edie found intolerable. She spent most of her time lying down, trying to amuse Rosalind with stories and colouring books, trying not to be sick. In the middle of the day, which had been her best time, if she could have been said to have had a best time, she took Rosalind out for a walk. Those streets which had not been ripped open by the bombing were dreary, and it was rawly cold. As the radio was in the hotel sitting room, she missed the announcement. Charles hadn't said anything when he returned to the hotel, but in the dining room – she always tried to dine with Charles, even if she had to bolt upstairs halfway through the meal – she noticed an atmosphere. The other guests seemed subdued; there was not the usual ripple of chatter. Haven't you heard, Charles said, about Singapore? She thought she would remember that moment for the rest of her life – a dribble of gravy on the cloth, the heavy plum-coloured swags of the dining-room curtains, the tired-looking waitress in her black dress and white cap, and Charles telling her that the Japanese had taken Singapore.

And nothing since had cheered. Rangoon had been occupied, Java had fallen, convoy ships were daily being sunk on the Atlantic and in the Mediterranean, and there was not the slightest sign that the second front, to liberate the occupied countries of Europe, which everyone so desperately longed for, might be opened any time soon. Charles said that American arms and manpower would eventually make a difference, but it would take time. Meanwhile, they must battle on.

They were all battling on, she supposed, one way or another. Before Christmas, she had visited Charles's family at Taynings. Catherine had left home and was now working at Bletchley, and the two young maids had gone as well. Edie's mother-in-law, who had a rheumatic hip, and Lilian, were both in their seventies. The remaining servants were similarly aged. Most of the rooms in the house were unused, and the poor construction of the building, all unnecessary little turrets and excrescences, had begun to show. Damp bloomed darkly on some of the walls and the house, which was always cold, had acquired a stale, musty jumble-sale smell. Edie had done what she could, had had a go at the kitchen garden and had thrown out when no one was looking some saucers of mouldering leftovers she had discovered in the larder. She had also tinkered with the ancient Olympia typewriter on which the Philosophy's newsletter was composed, and had managed to get it working again. Though Honoria and Lilian had both been resolutely cheerful, they had seemed frail and over-burdened, marooned in a house that was far too big and difficult for them. On the train back to Plymouth, Edie had felt depressed, and a little guilty, as if she had abandoned a sinking ship.

Her decision to try for another baby after her affair with Tom had ended had been partly, she acknowledged, an attempt to defy the gloom. A new baby was hope personified, living proof of a belief that things would, in spite of all evidence, improve. But she had also recognized that she must make a new start. She needed to make her marriage work. Charles adored Rosalind and was a good father. When he was home on leave, he was always happy to take care of Rosalind if Edie needed to go out. Not all men would do that; Edie knew that Laura's husband, Tony, for instance, refused to be left on his own with the children.

Charles was a good father, but not, perhaps, such a good husband. He was not − and she put it bluntly to herself − good in bed. She suspected that physical passion wasn't important to him. The trouble was, it was to her. Sometimes she wondered how would she bear it, the rest of her life without passion. She hadn't thought, before she married, that sex would be important to her – but how could she, when she had known so little about it?

A wave of nausea washed over her. Edie looked out of the carriage window, trying to distract herself, but the rush of the scenery only made her feel worse. She thought of Tom in the desert, of the heat and the flies. The nausea pulsated and rose. Oh God, she wasn't going to be sick on the train, was she? Tripping over the other passengers' feet, she mumbled apologies, and dashed along the corridor to the lavatory.

In early May, Tom was invited to dinner at a villa in the Garden City area of Cairo. Beneath a sky of dark blue velvet, the house nestled like a white pearl in its bower of palm and acacia and jacaranda trees. The night was warm and windless and, as he made his way through the garden, he noticed that there was a perfume in the air, rich and heady, perhaps a little nause-ating. Sprinting up an entranceway of wide marble steps and columns, he took a deep breath, hoped he wasn't in for another bout of bellyache, and rang the doorbell.

A servant showed him into a drawing room, where he was presented to his hosts, Colonel and Mrs Brooke-Smith. Colonel Brooke-Smith, who was nut-brown and wizened, as if shrunken by the intensity of Cairo's sun, exchanged a few words with Tom about mutual acquaintances at GHQ. Mrs Brooke-Smith, in blue satin, was taller than her husband. Diamonds glittered regally on her magnificent bosom. Her features were patrician, her eyes light blue. She bestowed on Tom a fleeting, chilly smile before turning to her next guest. The Brooke-Smiths' daughter, Delys, an attractive but sulky-looking girl of twenty or so, who was dressed in greenish-grey chiffon, looked Tom over in an uninterested fashion.

Tom had been given an introduction to the Brooke-Smiths by Dr Peacock, his former tutor at Cambridge. Dr Peacock and Colonel Brooke-Smith had known each other since Harrow. Tom had written to the Brooke-Smiths not long after his arrival in Cairo; he had received in reply a brief note welcoming him to the city and hinting vaguely at a future invitation to dinner. He wondered why the invitation had at last materialized and concluded that a male guest had had to cancel his acceptance late in the day and that Mrs Brooke-Smith had found herself with an empty seat to be filled.

There were fourteen to dine that night, all of the men in uniform. Tom was seated between Delys Brooke-Smith and a Mrs Fairbairns. His attempts to engage Miss Brooke-Smith in conversation were met with shrugs and monosyllables, so Tom turned to Mrs Fairbairns. She was plump, middle-aged and friendly, and worked for the Red Cross.

As the first course, a chilled tomato soup, was served, Mrs Brooke-Smith, who was seated at one end of the table, addressed Tom, asking him about his family. Tom explained that his father, who was a colleague of Dr Peacock's, was a professor of history and his mother was a doctor.

'A *doctor*,' said Mrs Brooke-Smith, and gave Tom her cool, questioning smile. 'How unusual. You mean, a *medical* doctor?'

'Yes, Mrs Brooke-Smith. My mother trained at the Elizabeth Garrett Anderson Hospital in London.'

Mrs Brooke-Smith digested this information. Then she said, 'Your family are from Cambridge, aren't they, Lieutenant Blacklock? You must know Giles and Hilary Potter.'

'My mother plays bridge with them.'

'Giles Potter's brother, Alexander, served with my husband in India. Are you acquainted with Major Potter, Lieutenant Blacklock?'

'I'm afraid not,' said Tom.

Mrs Brooke-Smith made a disappointed sound. Colonel Brooke-Smith said, 'Haven't seen old Lionel Peacock for years. I hope he's keeping well.'

'He was very well the last time I saw him,' said Tom.

Mrs Brooke-Smith's attention moved on to another guest. Tom's neighbour, Mrs Fairbairns, glanced at his plate. 'Are you off your food, my dear? Newcomers so often find our climate a strain. One becomes accustomed to it in time. I find a cup of mint tea last thing at night to be helpful.'

'I'll give it a try.'

'How do you find Cairo, Lieutenant Blacklock?'

Impossible, he thought, to distil his impressions of this vast, beautiful and chaotic city down to an adjective or two. 'Fascinating,' he said. 'Extraordinary. And very hot and very busy. I'm still finding my way around.'

They talked about Cairo until Mrs Brooke-Smith's precise, penetrating voice broke once more into their conversation. 'Do you play tennis, Lieutenant Blacklock?'

'A little.'

This time, there was a touch of satisfaction in her chilly smile. 'I hope to get up a party in the next week or two. I shall put you down.'

Later, after coffee and brandy, after Tom had thanked his hostess and was about to leave the house, Delys Brooke-Smith drew him aside.

'You must have passed muster, Lieutenant Blacklock.'

'What do you mean?'

'The tennis.' They were alone apart from the servants in the large, marbled hallway. Miss Brooke-Smith gave one of her unconcerned shrugs. 'You can make some excuse, if you like. Say there's a flap on or something.'

A fan spun on the ceiling, making the fronds of the palms in the brass pots sway. Startled, Tom said, 'I don't mind — if you can't find anyone better.'

'Mummy's trying to find out whether you'd do to marry me. You don't want to marry me, do you? It's all right, you don't have to pretend, I don't mind. I certainly don't want to marry you.'

Her light, greyish-green eyes were the same colour as her dress. There was something appealing about the sullen downward curve of her full mouth, yet her languor, her air of weariness, repelled. In twenty years' time, he thought, she would have turned into her mother.

'Mummy's rather scraping the barrel nowadays,' she said. 'To begin with, it was only majors and honourables. I'm going to marry a Polish friend of mine, actually. Mummy doesn't approve, so I have to wait till I'm twenty-one.' She frowned, studying him. 'You know Coral Portman, don't you?'

'Yes,' he said.

She nodded. 'I thought so. She told me about you. Goodnight, Lieutenant Blacklock.' She swung away in a blur of chiffon.

Tom walked back to the flat he was sharing with another officer. At midnight, Cairo was still busy. Taxis took the streets at breakneck speed and half a dozen squaddies, singing drunkenly, hove into view.

He had arrived in Cairo at the end of the previous year and had been assigned to GHQ, where his work involved collating intelligence about General Rommel's troop movements in the desert. The hours were long and he had been frustrated to find himself confined to an office again. He sometimes thought that if it had not been for Cairo itself – hot, scented, hypnotic Cairo – he might as well still have been in Buckinghamshire. His request for a transfer into 'The Blue' – the desert – had so far been denied.

After the fall of France, North Africa had been the only remaining land on which the Allied and Axis armies could meet in battle. Since 1940, the two forces had conducted a vast, inconclusive dance back and forth across the desert. There had been a series of victories that were not consolidated and defeats that never quite turned into a rout. The prize for which they fought was mastery of the route to Egypt and the Suez Canal. Without the canal, troop ships carrying men and equipment to India and the Far East had to make the far longer journey around Africa and the Cape of Good Hope. In the Mediterranean, British naval vessels were forced to run the gauntlet of German and Italian warships and bombers as they transported weapons and food to the island of Malta, which had been under siege since 1940. Malta, which was needed to supply Allied troops in North Africa, was taking a pounding. All too often, ships, fuel, materiel and men ended up at the bottom of the Mediterranean.

To begin with, the Allies had won a series of victories over the Italian army, but since Rommel's arrival in North Africa in February 1941, it had been the Allies' turn to retreat. At the beginning of the year, Rommel's Afrika Korps had recaptured western Cyrenaica. His troops were now within seventy miles of the garrison of Tobruk, which Allied troops had taken from the Italians almost a year and a half ago. There had been a lull in the fighting for several months while both sides scrambled to re-order and re-supply their positions. Desert war, Tom's superiors had drilled into him, was primarily a war of supply. The huge distances and the harsh nature of the terrain meant that whichever side could more quickly and efficiently provision their armies with fuel, vehicles and weapons had the advantage. Now, there was a pervasive feeling of edginess at GHQ. They knew the lull couldn't last.

Each defeat suffered by the Allies had been accompanied by a progressive loss of confidence. They needed to win. They needed to believe they could win. When the next battle came – and it would come very soon – the need for a decisive victory would be even more pressing. The Soviet Union, which was fighting desperately to hold Axis troops at bay, must be kept in the war. If Moscow and Leningrad were to fall, and if advancing German troops were to take Stalingrad, then Germany might capture the oil fields of the Caucasus. The ultimate nightmare was that Cairo and the Suez Canal might be trapped in the middle of a gigantic pincer movement as the Axis armies currently fighting in the Soviet Union overcame the Russians and were able to cut a swathe south through the Caucasus, and, at the same time, General Rommel's Afrika Korps succeeded in breaking out of Libya and entering Egypt. Then the British presence in Cairo and the Middle East could be crushed.

The North African front must be used to distract Germany and to absorb Axis troops that would otherwise be fighting on the Russian front. Far too often in the course of the war, the Axis powers had had their own way. Victory in the desert could change that.

Desert war was also a war against heat, lack of water and flies. Tom had been ill more or less since he had arrived in Cairo at the end of the previous year. Rarely ever ill before, he had considered himself a reasonably seasoned traveller when he had embarked for the Middle East, and the discovery that Egypt didn't agree with him made him feel disappointed in himself. He had come down with a severe bout of gyppy tummy as soon as he had arrived in the capital and had been plagued by fevers and stomach bugs ever since. It took the enjoyment out of anything that should have been pleasurable – even his first sight of the Pyramids, emerging out of the desert in the moonlight, had been accompanied by memorable stomach cramps.

He had met Coral Portman at the Gezira Club, Cairo's most exclusive sporting club. Popular with officers, the Gezira was surrounded by gardens and set on an island in the Nile. Someone from GHQ had taken him there – 'This is Miss Portman,' his friend had said to Tom, introducing a sweetly pretty girl with brown curls and hazel eyes. 'Why don't you buy her a drink?' So he had. In the ensuing weeks, he had taken Miss Portman to the cinema and they had gone to a dance or two. He had extracted himself from the friendship when he had realized that she was falling in love with him. She had wept, and several of her friends – Coral had a lot of friends – had cold-shoul-dered him since.

He had thought that dating Coral Portman might help him forget Edie. To the same end, he had had a brief affair with an older, more experienced Levantine Frenchwoman, who lived apart from her husband and held little soirées for officers in her flat in Quba Gardens. The affair hadn't lasted long. 'The thing is, chéri,' she had said to Tom one evening, 'I don't think your mind's ever quite on me.' She had given him a cool, appraising look and swung back her long blue-black hair. 'And when we're in bed together, that's really rather insulting.'

Tom crossed the road and let himself into the building in which he lived. As he ran upstairs to the flat, a phrase of Delys Brooke-Smith's came back to him. *Mummy's rather scraping the barrel nowadays.* Bloody cheek, thought Tom.

On 21 June General Rommel's armies captured the fortress of Tobruk, taking tens of thousands of Allied prisoners. After the fall of the garrison, German and Italian troops poured across the Egyptian frontier to within seventy miles of Alexandria. The British Army, in full retreat, came eventually to a halt between the Qattara Depression and the coast, near the village of El Alamein. In Cairo, Europeans crowded into boats and trains, fleeing the city for the safety of Palestine and the Lebanon. Classified documents were burned at GHQ and in the British Embassy. The clouds of ash generated by the fires fell in a grey shroud over offices, mosques and the gardens of the villas of the wealthy, earning the day the soubriquet of 'Ash Wednesday'. Mussolini arranged to fly to Africa, taking his favourite white stallion with him, so that he might ride at the head of the Axis's victory parade through Cairo.

Yet somehow, the Allies scraped themselves up from the shock of defeat and fought back. A British artillery barrage kept the Afrika Korps at bay. Rommel had outrun his supply lines and air forces. Those who had left the city began, after a while, to travel back to Cairo, hauling their dusty, battered suitcases with them, some a little shamefaced, perhaps. Mussolini returned to Italy, and, at the beginning of August, Churchill visited Cairo to assess the situation. Sweeping changes in the army's leadership were made: Lieutenant-General Sir Harold Alexander took over Near East Command in place of General Sir Claude Auchinleck, and Lieutenant-General Bernard Montgomery was appointed to command the Eighth Army. In early September, Rommel's forces were rebuffed by the Eighth Army at Alam el Halfa. After the catastrophe of losing Tobruk, there began, under Montgomery's firm, decisive leadership, to be a sense of optimism at last. Yet Rommel was still only a short distance from Alexandria: Alam el Halfa was only a prelude to the much greater conflict, still to come.

In the shake-up, to his delight, Tom's request for a transfer had come through. He was in 'The Blue' at last. Assigned to Brigade Headquarters as an intelligence officer, he discovered that the desert was not, as he had imagined it to be, a series of endless, undulating reddish-gold sand dunes, but was made up of grit, stones and rock, speckled every now and then with a sandy terrain dotted with tough, thin-leaved shrubs. Sometimes the desert was flat and sometimes it rose in ridges or dipped into salt lakes. The wind sculpted extraordinarily shaped columns from the sandstones. Shimmering mirages, as well as the sheer immensity of the expanse, played tricks with the mind, making it hard to estimate distance. By day, the pale earth contrasted with a burning blue sky. As August turned into September, Tom learned to survive the searing heat of the day and the bitter cold of the nights. Worse even than the extreme temperatures were the flies. They swarmed around you as you slept, dressed, washed, worked. It was impossible to eat without taking a mouthful of flies. Some of the men adopted elaborate routines of swathing themselves in jackets or sleeping bags before eating, but the flies always found their way inside.

After Alam el Halfa, the multinational forces of the Eighth Army – Indian, Australian, New Zealand and South African as well as British – were sent for rest and recreation to the beaches of the North African coast before returning to the lines for training. El Alamein itself was a railway station, two miles inland from the Mediterranean. From the coastal road you could see for miles across the open desert. Forty miles south, the Qattara Depression was a seven thousand square mile area of salt marsh and hill, almost impassable to tanks and armoured vehicles. To the west were the Axis positions and Rommel's 'devil's gardens', vast minefields laid beneath the sand.

On 21 October, all leave to Cairo and Alexandria was stopped. Allied troops took up their positions. Some remained hidden in narrow slit trenches throughout the day. In the evening, under cover of darkness, they crawled out of the trenches to eat. Conversation was intermittent; some men wrote letters, others read or smoked. The desert was a silent, tranquil sea, bathed in silver moonlight.

It was now a year, Tom reflected, since he and Edie had parted. During that year, his emotions had lurched from anger and grief to regret and then acceptance. He had come to acknowledge the flaw in his character that had led to him losing Edie, his fatal tardiness in recognizing what was of importance. He had not offered her what she had most wanted – security. He had since learned his lesson, but it had been a bitter one.

The extremity of the desert, and the way it forced all who lived there to focus on the essentials of survival, had made him see their relationship more clearly. It seemed to him that they had not always been well-matched. They had not held the same things to be of importance, there had been some division between them that had jarred and which had provoked their quarrels and their differences. Desire and liking had not, in the end, been enough. He thought less often of her now. All his attention was directed to the coming conflict.

Part of him welcomed it. Part of him longed for the challenge and distraction of pitting himself against something extraordinary and perilous. He felt apprehensive too, of course. Every now and then he found himself wondering whether he would have what it took – courage, endurance, strength, nerve – to get him through the days and weeks ahead. And then there was the analytical part of his mind, which was simply curious. The names of battles learned when he was a schoolboy rattled through his head like a drum roll: Agincourt, Malplaquet, Waterloo, Passchendaele. Would this battle at El Alamein someday be spoken of in the same breath?

Later that evening the silence of the desert was broken by the thrum of aeroplane engines, bombers on their way to pound enemy positions. Then, pinpricks of light in the sky. Searchlights, crossing in the darkness, briefly formed a St Andrew's cross.

And then, in a flash of fire, the bombardment erupted. The ground shook and the rending, raw, intolerable noise seemed to pass through Tom's body. White and orange explosions lit up the sky as the artillery barrage was augmented by naval guns fired from the ships off the coast.

The battle had begun.

On 15 November, the sound of church bells, reverberating across the bare fields, reached Edie as she was pegging out the washing. The distant chimes rose and fell on the wind. A flurry of brown leaves danced across the long grass of the lawn. It had rained the previous night, and there were puddles in the deep ruts on the track that led from the cottage to the road.

Edie went indoors. She was staying with Nicky, who was renting a cottage in the Forest of Bere, to the north of Portsmouth. In the sitting room, Nicky was standing by the radio, twiddling buttons, but there was only static. The cottage was surrounded by tall trees and radio reception was poor.

She looked up when Edie came into the room. 'Did you hear them? The bells?'

Edie glanced at the children, who were playing Schools. The younger children and half a dozen dolls were lined up in a row on the rug; Cherry was shaking a finger at them.

Edie lowered her voice. 'You don't think it could be an invasion, do you? Not now, surely, not after all this time?'

'I'll cycle down to the village and find out. You'll be all right with them for half an hour, won't you, darling?'

'Of course.'

Nicky left the house. Edie checked on Henry, who was asleep in his pram in the hall. She still found it hard to believe that she had had a son. Henry had been born on 7 October, and when, at the nursing home, they had told her that her baby was a boy, she had at first thought they must have made a mistake. She had protested – rather feebly, because her labour had been long and hard – and the nurse had said briskly, 'Well, he certainly is a little boy, Mrs Dangerfield, and he's a fine little fellow.' Then they had given her a pill and she had fallen asleep. The next day, when she was feeling somewhat better, she had unwrapped her baby's shawl, nightgown, vest and nappy, and had known that he was, indisputably, a boy.

Edie had left the nursing home after a week, still a bit wobbly, and Charles had driven her and the baby to Nicky's cottage. Nicky had been looking after Rosalind while Edie was in hospital. The cottage was secluded, primitive and very inconvenient – the diesel pump that took water from an underground stream was liable to ice up on frosty mornings, and the nearest shop, the village store, was two miles away. Days could pass without them seeing a soul other than the milkman and the postman.

Edie loved it. They kept to their own rhythm, she and Nicky, a rhythm dictated by the needs of the children. They rediscovered their old, close relationship, which became closer still through the sharing of the pleasures and anxieties of bringing up their children. Edie didn't mind that the radio didn't work very well, or that they didn't always buy a daily paper because, with five small children to look after, there often wasn't time to nip into the village. She discovered that she liked to feel cut off from the war. It allowed her to concentrate on the delightful process of getting to know her new son. Great lengths of time could pass by just in revelling in his beauty. He had blue eyes, like her, and a high forehead, like Charles. During the last few days, he had learned to fix on her gaze and give her drunken little smiles.

Isolated in the cottage, she had begun to realize how much the constant flow of war news, most of it bad, had preyed on her nerves. Recently she had found it even more nerve-racking to listen to the radio news or to read a paper. This was because the Allies seemed to be winning at last. In the North African desert, Montgomery had forced Rommel to retreat, and then, a week ago, Allied – largely American – forces had landed at Algiers, Oran and Casablanca. Axis battalions had found themselves trapped between the two Allied armies. At the same time, in the Soviet Union, the besieged city of Stalingrad was putting up a ferocious defence, dooming the Wehrmacht to endure another bitterly cold Russian winter.

At the possibility that the tide might have turned at last, Edie found herself afraid to open a newspaper. If the recent victories were to be followed by yet more setbacks, as they had been so often before, and if the hope that had begun to gleam inside her were to be crushed, she did not know how she would bear it.

But if there had been an *invasion* . . . She had a momentary and terrible vision of herself and Nicky defending the cottage against invading troops, with hoes and rakes, perhaps. As soon as she glimpsed Nicky's bicycle crest the rise of the hill she hurried outside to meet her sister.

But it wasn't an invasion: they were ringing the bells to celebrate the victory of the battle of El Alamein. A *victory*. Edie and Nicky hugged each other, then went back inside the house and poured themselves a drink.

Chapter Twelve

Miranda was in the pantry, inspecting the sides of ham that hung on hooks from the ceiling, when the butler came to tell her that they had visitors. 'Official visitors,' he murmured, and she said, 'Thank you, Georg. Tell them I'll be with them right away,' and he shuffled off down the corridor.

There were two of them, and they were from the Gestapo. The short, fat one chattered and smiled a lot; the taller, thinner, younger one said nothing at all. They had become lost – the snow, and these little country roads all looked the same. Could the countess – the fat one hoped it was not too much trouble – give them directions?

With pleasure, she said. But perhaps first she could offer them some refreshment?

The fat one made delighted noises of acceptance. It was a beautiful house, he said, looking round, and she said, yes, it was.

Was she alone here? No. Her mother-in-law also lived at Sommerfeld, but unfortunately she was unwell just now. And her husband? The Graf von Kahlberg, she explained, was fighting on the Eastern front.

Murmurs of approval. Georg returned, carrying a tray, and, as the men looked away to take their wine and sandwiches, Miranda wiped the film of sweat from her upper lip.

While they were eating, they asked her questions about Sommerfeld – its size, the number of its tenant farms and other properties, the yield of its land. A small cough – the fat one had thought that, driving down the avenue to the house, he had caught sight of a man on horseback. A brother or a cousin of hers, perhaps? She had no brothers, Miranda told them, and her husband's surviving cousins were in the army. They had seen Herr Bernard, she expected, who had been spared army service to run the estate. He was the only able-bodied man left at Sommerfeld – the officers must understand that there were tasks a woman (she simpered) was unable to carry out.

He quite understood, the fat one said as he scribbled in his notebook, but in these difficult times one had to be sure . . .

Miranda diverted the conversation, offered more wine, told them amusing little anecdotes – a tale about a feathered hat of hers nearly having been mistaken for a fowl on a duck shoot, that sort of thing, and the fat one laughed. When they had eaten, she gave him directions to Rastenberg and he rose and bowed and thanked her again.

They had reached the door when the thin one spoke for the first time.

'Your accent, Countess . . . Your German is excellent, but you are not from East Prussia, are you?'

'I travelled a great deal in my childhood. My father was a businessman. We lived in many different places.'

'I see.'

'I was so pleased to be able to settle down after my marriage.

344

And in such a beautiful part of Germany.' She wondered whether she had overdone it, but the fat one beamed.

'Yes, yes, Countess. Your situation is indeed enviable!'

Then they made their salutations and Georg showed them out. When she was alone, Miranda pressed her fingers against her mouth. Her head was aching — she disliked drinking wine at midday but had felt obliged to share a glass with her visitors. She heard the front door close and went to one of the rooms at the front of the house, where she stood in the shadow of the curtain, watching until the car had turned in the courtyard and headed up the long, tree-lined avenue, away from the house. After the car was out of sight, the house seemed altered, as if the two men's presence had left behind it some chemical change — a little more darkness gathering in the corners, a colder edge in the air, perhaps.

She hurried upstairs to the Countess's room. The maid rose as she came in. Miranda asked after the Countess, and the maid whispered that she seemed a little better today and had taken some lunch. Miranda sent the girl away for her own lunch and sat down beside the Countess's bed, taking her mother-in-law's thin, blue-veined hand in hers.

Her mother-in-law's eyes flickered open. 'Will you take a little more soup?' Miranda pleaded.

'I'll try.'

Miranda helped the Countess to sit up. Three weeks ago, the Countess had fallen ill with a chest infection. Dr Kornblum had at first feared for her life, but she was slowly beginning to recover.

The Countess drank some soup. Then she put the spoon down. 'Is there any news?'

'Of Friedrich? No, I'm afraid not.'

345

'I thought I heard a motor car.'

'It was no one, no one important. Only some people who had lost their way.'

The Countess nodded slowly. Then she said, 'I must write to Susanne.'

'I'll write for you, if you like.'

Miranda fetched pen and paper. Her mother-in-law dictated a letter to her niece in Switzerland. When she had finished, the Countess signed the letter and Miranda folded it and put it in an envelope.

The Countess smiled at Miranda. 'Thank you, my dear. You're a good girl.'

Miranda stooped and kissed the Countess's translucent, papery cheek. Leaving the room, she went through the morning's encounter in her mind, recalling their questions, her answers. She thought it had gone all right. She wondered whether the Gestapo officers had truly lost their way or whether they had intended from the outset to come to Sommerfeld. She couldn't tell.

She went downstairs to Herr Bernard's office.

'Franz, I must speak to you.'

They had become allies, she and Franz Bernard. He was in his mid-forties, tall, thin, bespectacled and cultured. He had been wounded in the First World War and walked with a limp. Franz had been Friedrich's tutor; after Friedrich had reached adulthood, Franz had remained at Sommerfeld as his secretary.

He rose from his seat as Miranda came into the room, and closed the door behind her. 'Georg told me that we had visitors,' he said.

'They asked about you, I'm afraid. I had to explain that you'd been excused army service to look after the farms. I couldn't risk them searching the house. They might take our food or our last remaining horses. And it would have upset the Countess.'

'How is she?'

'Feeling better, I think.'

'I'm pleased to hear that.' Franz glanced out of the window. He said, 'They may have other things to think about just now.'

'How was your trip to Rastenberg?'

Franz took off his glasses and rubbed his eyes. 'They're saying we've lost Stalingrad. That General Paulus has surrendered.'

Miranda had heard rumours, yet still it came as a shock. Stalingrad had been under siege for five months. The city was being fought for hand-to-hand. Every house, every ruined factory and shop had become a battlefield.

'Do you think it's true?' she said.

'It's always hard to be sure, Countess. People are afraid to speak openly. But yes, this time I'm afraid it is. Rastenberg is full of injured troops, and they talk, of course. The hospitals are overflowing and there are trains full of wounded returning from the front all the time. The children have been sent home from school so that the buildings can be used as makeshift hospitals.' Franz was polishing his glasses. He said steadily, 'They're saying that the entire Sixth Army, General Paulus included, has been killed or taken into captivity and that we're retreating along the whole of the Eastern front.'

Miranda stared at him in disbelief. She thought of Friedrich and Klaus. Of the four male cousins, they were the only two still serving in Russia. Max had died and Katrin's brother, Oskar, had been badly wounded the previous autumn. His right leg had been amputated and he was slowly recuperating at the family home in Königsberg.

She said, 'What will it mean for us?'

'We're safe,' Franz Bernard said, 'for now.'

She thought about that for now. Then they talked of other matters, estate matters. There were bills to be paid, and there was the continual struggle to find the materials with which to repair broken machinery and buildings, as well as manpower to carry out the daily tasks necessary to maintain a large estate such as Sommerfeld. Afterwards, she signed her name to the dozen letters that Franz had prepared for her. When she had finished, as she was about to leave the room, he said, in a tired voice, 'We're being beaten back on two fronts now. I wonder where it will end.'

'I find it best not to think about that, Franz,' she said. 'I try to get through each day and not worry too much about the future.'

'Very wise, Countess.' He gave her a crooked smile.

'I want to go back to Paris,' she had said.

It had been five months after the baby had died. Friedrich had at last been able to return to Sommerfeld on leave. By then, Miranda had begun to emerge from the black cloud of grief and depression that had accompanied her loss. The process first of physical recovery from the birth, and then of learning to live again, of forcing herself to eat, to sleep, to leave the house and to converse with people once more, had been slow. She had emerged changed, tempered by grief. She saw her situation with stark clarity. She did not belong at Sommerfeld, would never belong at Sommerfeld. Since she had married Friedrich, she had been living a lie.

She did not love Friedrich as he loved her. The Miranda who pretended to be the Countess von Kahlberg was a sham. In her darkest moments she wondered whether this was why her baby had died, whether God was punishing her for marrying a man she did not love, for marrying one man when she was in love with another.

She had pretended for a long time, but the loss of her baby had left her scoured, torn apart, unable to pretend any longer, even to herself. She spoke the truth as she saw it, she no longer bothered to dress it up or tried to make the best of things. The hopes she had once treasured had died with her child. Her old dream of becoming an actress seemed to her ridiculous now. She had lost Olivier for ever.

Friedrich, too, had changed. His features were scarred by the frostbite he had suffered the previous winter and he had lost weight. In the first few days after his return to Sommerfeld, he was exhausted and slept a great deal. Later, when he tried to talk to her about the baby, she always cut him off. She did not want to talk about the baby; the baby was gone, so there was nothing to say. At night, in bed, they slept with a careful distance between them. If he insisted, she let him hold her for a while, but then she moved away. When he tried to kiss her, she was unresponsive. Though these days she always woke early in the mornings, often, when she woke, his side of the bed was already empty. She wondered whether he was angry with her, whether he blamed her for falling on the ice, for not looking after his son better.

I want to go back to Paris, she said. They were in the drawing room, listening to Grieg.

Friedrich looked up at her. 'That's not possible. If you feel you need a holiday then I'll ask Franz to book you into a hotel on the Baltic coast.'

'I don't want a holiday. I want to live there again.'

'I don't understand.' He frowned. 'What are you saying?'

'I can't stay here, Friedrich.'

She had had, for so long, a persistent feeling of being in the wrong place. She had often reflected, these past months, that she should have listened to Olivier. She should have gone to England, to Kay, as Olivier had told her to. She seemed to have arrived here, in East Prussia, by chance, and by her own poor choices. She felt disorientated; she remembered that she had sometimes felt like this as a child, when, arriving in a new city, she had listened to the unfamiliar sounds from the streets outside and breathed in the new scents that wafted through the open window – roses, a bonfire, drains. At night, when she could not sleep, all the places she had lived in flickered through her memory. The house in Paris, a flat in Rome, the London house in Charles Street – she supposed it was still there, if it had survived the bombing. Yet she found it hard to remember the Denisov houses with any clarity. She remembered pieces – yellow curtains, a Persian rug – but they did not add up to a whole. She needed familiarity. Paris had always been the city she liked best. She imagined arriving at her father's apartment, knocking at the door, then put aside the thought almost immediately. No, foolish of her even to consider it; she would be unable to live under her father's thumb again. She must think of something else.

'I want to leave Sommerfeld,' she said. 'I don't belong here.'

She heard him sigh. He put his brandy glass down on the table. 'Miranda, I understand that you have suffered a great loss. And I regret very much that I could not be here with you. I won't tell you that you'll get over it – I wouldn't say anything so facile or untrue. But you will grow stronger, and in time we can try again. There's no reason why another child should not live. I spoke to Dr Kornblum and he told me that what

350

happened was simply bad luck. It's very hard, I know, but one day we'll be able to put this behind us.'

'I don't want another baby,' she said.

'Not now, perhaps, but later, when you're fully recovered.'

'No, I don't think so.'

He was sitting on the sofa; she had taken a seat by the fire. He took a cigarette from the silver case on the table beside him and struck his lighter.

He said, 'You're saying that because you're still grieving.'

'No. I'm asking you to let me go, Friedrich.'

'No.'

Just that, *no*. 'Please, Friedrich.'

He drew on the cigarette. 'As soon as the war's over we'll make a new start.'

'Do you really believe that?'

He shrugged. 'It doesn't matter what I believe. We may as well continue to assume there will be a future, because if we were to consider the opposite, then what would be the point of doing anything?'

'I was talking about our marriage, not the war. I think you know, as I do, that it was a mistake.'

'A mistake?' He laughed. 'What? Like breaking a glass or finding oneself staying in an unsatisfactory hotel? Hardly. I think we both knew exactly what we were doing.' His eyes, which had gone hard, held hers.

'I married you for the wrong reasons,' she said steadily. 'I know that now. I thought they were good enough reasons at the time, but now I know that I was wrong.'

'I never thought you were marrying me for undying love, Miranda.' His tone was cynical. 'I was never under that illusion.'

'Then let me go.'

'No.'

'But I've betrayed you, Friedrich.'

If her words hurt him, he gave no indication of it, and instead looked away, tapping ash from the end of his cigarette. 'You're speaking of that spring before the war,' he said. 'You're speaking of Paris?'

'Yes.'

'Who was he?'

'Someone I knew before I met you. When I married you I didn't think I'd ever see him again. And then, that spring, it happened.'

'Did you love him?'

'Yes.' She looked down at her hands. 'I'm sorry. I'm not asking for forgiveness, I know I don't deserve it. I'm asking you to let me go.'

He gave a small smile. 'I knew what I was doing when I married you, Miranda. I went into it with my eyes open. If you like, I made a bargain with myself. I decided that I'd take what some might consider second best because it seemed to me far better than nothing at all. Of course, I hoped you might grow to love me. But if that's not possible, then so be it.'

'But I can't go on like this.' She could hear the desperation in her voice.

'Of course you can.' His tone was pitiless. 'So many people endure so much worse than you. You are free from want, and you are at liberty. In that, you have so much more than the vast majority of people in Europe.'

'But I'm living a lie!'

He laughed. 'Aren't we all?'

His laughter angered her. 'I want a divorce, Friedrich.'

'No, that's not possible. There has never been a divorce in my family.'

'So you choose to remain married to an adulteress?'

Anger flared in his eyes. 'I have little choice, it seems,' he said. 'But I will not tolerate divorce in my family. You will not speak of this matter again. Consider this, too, Miranda – as you yourself have pointed out, you have nowhere else to go. You talk of Paris, but do you imagine that Paris is as you remember it? The occupied countries are not, shall we say, comfortable places in which to live. Few Frenchmen welcome our presence. The Resistance groups grow ever more active and the only way of dealing with them is through terror. You do understand what I mean by terror? I mean that if, say, one German soldier or Gestapo officer is shot on the Paris Métro, then ten political prisoners will be taken out and shot in retaliation. Or a hundred, perhaps. It shows them who's in charge, you see.'

'I understand that, but—'

'No, you don't.' His voice, as hard as ice, cut into hers. 'No one who hasn't lived through terror understands the choices you're forced to make and the way it eats away at your soul. Shall I tell you the truth, Miranda, about our little venture in Russia? Shall I tell you the truth – or would you prefer to hear only the version we keep for our family and friends?'

She remembered what Anna and Klaus had told her. The endless winter, the battles with partisans, the atrocities.

She looked up at him. 'Tell me the truth, Friedrich.'

'Are you sure that's what you want? Very well. I've always believed myself to be a civilized man. Civility has been, if you like, my guiding light. But in Russia, every aspect of civilization is stripped away. We live like animals and we kill like animals. Warmth and food and shelter are the only matters of importance. When I'm there, none of this,' he looked round the room, 'seems real. This house becomes a fantasy. And the thought persists even now that I'm home, that all this is a dream, and that I'll open my eyes and my house will be ruined and the crops in the fields will have been burned, and you and my mother will be dead – or perhaps you never existed.' The passion drained from his voice; he said softly, 'When I was told my leave had come through at last and I knew that I would see you again, I wept. I wept for joy, Miranda.'

Now, she could not meet his eyes. 'I'm sorry,' she whispered. 'I'm so sorry.'

'So, you see, I can't let you go. It would make a mockery of everything I've endured. And besides, your feelings, your wishes, are no longer of any importance. You must stay at Sommerfeld because you're needed here. The estate needs you. You must ensure that the farms are still productive and the food is fairly distributed, because otherwise people will starve. If Franz is sent away, you must look after Sommerfeld, Miranda. People depend on you. In the future they may depend on you for their lives. There was a time when I would have hesitated in asking this of you. When we first met, I imagined you fragile and in need of protection. But since then I've realized that there is a remoteness about you – a coldness, perhaps. I find that I can have confidence in you. I may not be able to trust you as my wife, but I would trust you to look after my home.'

She stared at him. 'Run the estate? Me? Friedrich, I couldn't!'

'We all have to adapt these days – in these difficult times, as our Führer would say.' His lip curled.

'Friedrich, please.' She pressed her hands together. 'Please let me go.'

'No.'

She half rose from her seat. 'Then I'll just leave. I don't know where I'll go – anywhere.' She could hear her voice rising, shrill and hysterical. 'I can't bear to be here any more, not without – without . . .'

He gripped her shoulders. 'Listen to me. Any travel permit you apply for will be refused. I'll see to that. I still have influence.'

Her defiance dissolved and she covered her face with her hands. As he let her go, he said, 'You once told me that I saved you, Miranda. You owe me this.'

And she did. She saw that. Without Friedrich, what would have happened to her? She might have starved herself to death. Her father might have forced her into marriage with a man she hated.

The Grieg had come to an end. Friedrich took the record off the turntable and slipped it back into its sleeve. She heard him say, his tone cooler now, 'You must be sensible. You must keep your head. If you draw attention to yourself, or if you fail to cooperate with the authorities, you may find yourself interned, or worse. Factories all over Germany are staffed by labourers from the occupied territories. The Slavs fare particularly badly. Girls much younger than you work in factories for twelve hours a day. They are not well fed and they are not kindly treated. There will be nothing to be afraid of so long as you're careful. My name still provides some protection. We're fortunate – here, in Sommerfeld, we can live as we choose. You see, my dear, though you may have found marriage to me disappointing, it still gives you some advantage. I can protect you. You'll be safe here.'

She looked at him and read the lies in his eyes. She shook her head slowly. 'I don't think you believe that, Friedrich.

I don't think you believe it at all. People are talking, you know. They're wondering what would happen if the Russians were to win the war. What would happen *here*.'

He took a record from its sleeve. 'That's defeatist talk,' he said. 'You can be punished for that.'

'If we were to retreat — if the Russians were to drive our armies back over the border — if it were to be their turn to invade us — what would happen to us then?'

He put the record on the gramophone. Tchaikovsky, this time. 'Russian music,' he said softly. 'I've always admired it. So passionate. I wonder if I could be imprisoned for saying that, too? If the Russians come here, then it will be even worse than the last time. They will take their revenge, you see. What we have visited on them, they'll visit on us. We've sown the wind so we can expect to reap the whirlwind. If the Russians come here, then God help us all. But they won't. We won't let them. That's what I'm fighting for. It's the only thing I'm fighting for.'

There was a time when she had thought of escape. There was a time when she had thought of getting on a train and going away, leaving Sommerfeld, leaving her marriage and going, well, anywhere. Sheer folly — she had been a little mad then, perhaps. Travel permits were not given out freely, and besides, she had nowhere to go.

Even if escape had been possible, she could not have left the Countess. It had been the Countess who had coaxed her to eat when she would have preferred to starve herself, the Countess who had comforted her as she had cried, and the Countess who had listened to her when, eventually, she had been able to talk of her baby, the blueish scrap the nurse had placed in her arms to greet and say goodbye to. She had wondered at the perfection of his features and his limbs and she had wept that no one would know him but her. She had known even then that one day she would no longer clearly recall his face, that his features would blur and become indistinct, taking on the aspect of every newborn baby's face.

It had been the Countess who had coaxed her out into the garden when spring had come, and who had had the groomsman take her on short rides across the fields and around the lakes. She might be remote, as Friedrich had told her, her cold little heart might have shrivelled to a nut, but she wouldn't leave the Countess because she loved her.

Over the past year, the Countess had become increasingly frail. When she walked around the garden, she leaned on Miranda's arm. These days, Miranda rode to the village on the Countess's behalf, to give a soft white loaf and a bottle of blackcurrant cordial to an old woman with no teeth, or to offer words of condolence to a mother whose son had been lost at sea. Friedrich had been right. There were people who needed her. An odd thing, that – no one had ever needed her before.

A year had passed since her baby had died. There remained a hollow inside her, dark and frozen like the lakes in winter, but she covered it over well, she thought.

The day the Gestapo came to the house, Miranda had a number of worries. One of the kitchen maids had found maggots on a side of ham. Margret, the housekeeper, was unwell, had been bent double that morning with the pain in her back, and Miranda had sent her to bed. And the cook had told her that they were running short of firewood – unprecedented, that, someone must have made a mistake: they never ran out of firewood at Sommerfeld. And then, of course, there was the news that Franz had given her. *They're saying we've lost Stalingrad. The entire army, General Paulus included, has been killed or taken into captivity.*

After she had eaten her lunch, she went back to the pantry. She told the maid to trim off the tainted meat and to hang the damaged hams in the adjacent room. They had been stored too close together, perhaps.

Firewood, she thought. Returning downstairs, she put on her fur coat, hat and boots, called Gisela and found one of the lads, Margret's twelve-year-old grandson, a sweet-faced boy called Erik, to accompany her to the barn where they kept the firewood. There had been a thaw the previous night and the banked snow at the sides of the paths was dirty and pocked with hollows. To the east, the sky was a heavy iron-grey.

She unlocked the barn door and swung her torch across the stacks of wood. It was hard to estimate how many logs and how much kindling would be needed to keep Sommerfeld warm during the remaining months of winter. A rat scurried out from beneath the stores of logs, and Erik hurled a stone at it.

Miranda told Erik to fetch Herr Bernard, and the boy ran back to the house. After a short while, she heard their footsteps crunching across the snow.

'I can't help thinking,' said Miranda to Franz, as they surveyed the wood stacked in the barn, 'how much more use I would have been if I'd been taught mathematics instead of ballet, or housekeeping instead of the piano.'

He smiled. 'Philosophy was my subject at university, Countess.' He ran his gaze over the woodpile. 'We do seem rather short.'

'Perhaps we should order some coal.'

'Coal's in very short supply these days. Most of it goes to

the trains and hospitals and factories. I'll get together a party of men and we'll see what we can find in the forest.' Franz went to the door and looked up at the sky. 'It looks as if we're in for more snow.'

Shortly afterwards, the men left for the pine forest: Franz, the prisoners of war, the old groomsman, Tomas, who was small and wiry and curled up like a fern frond, and the boy Erik. By the time they returned to the castle with the horse-drawn cart loaded with logs and branches, it was snowing again.

Many weeks after Stalingrad had fallen, they received a letter from Friedrich, telling them that he was safe. Of Klaus's fate, they discovered nothing.

Kay met Rowland Latimer at Josephine's engagement party. It was June, a day of sunshine and showers. The celebrations took place at Josephine's parents' house in Wiltshire. In the evening, very old servants handed around glasses of sherry and canapés in a big square room with royal blue walls. At midsummer, it was still light, and the room was perfumed by the cut-glass bowls of roses and sweet peas on the mantelpiece and side tables.

Kay, who had forty-eight hours' leave, had travelled down to Covington Hall that afternoon with a friend and fellow AT, hitching lifts and catching buses. She had missed lunch and tea, and so, discovering an abandoned plate of food, was sitting on a window seat, eating canapés. Looking out of the window, down to the garden below, she saw that someone was walking along the narrow paths between the flower beds. The evening sun painted the man's long shadow across the grass. Every now and then he would stoop and look more carefully at a rose.

She watched him for a while. He was young and he was in army uniform. He had black hair and his stride was confident and graceful.

Plate in hand, she left the room and went downstairs, then made her way through corridors that were at first hung with oil paintings of dead pheasants and overflowing fruit bowls, and then contained more mundane things – hooks bearing huge iron keys, mackintoshes and a stand of rusty umbrellas. A little, low door spat her outside. It had rained, and there was a sheen on the golden flagstones of the terrace.

The black-haired man looked up and smiled at her. 'Hello.'

'Hello. Would you like one?' She offered him the canapés. 'I think it's fishpaste inside them.'

'Splendid.' He took one. 'The first time I came to stay with Freddie, I thought the food would be terribly grand – caviar and grouse, that sort of thing. But it was almost as bad as at school.' He held out his hand to her. 'I'm Rowland Latimer.'

'Kay Garland.'

'I'm very pleased to meet you, Miss Garland.'

He had nice eyes, dark brown, almost black, large and expressive. His face was well-shaped, but rather thin and bony.

She said, 'Weren't you enjoying the party?'

'I was, enormously, but I thought I'd nip out while it was still light and find my mother's rose.' He smiled at her again. 'I mean the rose that's named after my mother. Would you like to see it?'

'Very much.'

She followed him down one of the narrow grassy paths. The names of the roses were impressed on little metal tags attached to their stems – *Empereur du Maroc*, *Gloire de Dijon* and *Fantin-Latour*. They gave a perfect impression, Kay pointed out and Rowland agreed, of scented opulence, of grand, lazy personages wearing rich, beautiful clothes.

'My mother was an actress,' Rowland explained. 'People were always falling in love with her. One of her admirers was a rose-grower and he created a new rose for her.' He stopped by a rose with petals of a deep purplish-pink. The name on the metal tag was 'Madeleine Latimer'.

'It's rather a good name for a rose, don't you think?'

'Perfect. Madeleine Latimer . . .' Kay frowned, then stared at him. 'So your father is—'

'Was, actually. But yes, Peter Latimer, the playwright.'

'Oh. How extraordinary! I saw two of his plays before the war — Brighter Skies and The Manufacture of Hearts. I was teaching at a school in Hampstead. My boyfriend at the time was very keen on your father's work.'

'My father had rather a revival just before the war. The political situation being what it was, one or two directors dug out his plays and put them on.'

'I remember weeping buckets when Sally died in Brighter Skies.'

'It's a tear-jerker, isn't it? I've always thought that was his best work. My father wasn't all that successful until he met my mother. It was the combination of the two of them that worked so well. After they met, my father always wrote for her — and they were marvellous roles for an actress, full of passion and drama.' Breaking off a bloom, he handed it to her. 'Here, this should go with your dress.'

'This colour's called feuille morte, apparently. Josephine calls it dead mouse.'

'Whatever it's called, it suits you.'

Kay found a hairpin.

'Let me,' he said. As he pinned the rose to the strap of her dress, she felt his fingers brush against the bare skin of her shoulder. She breathed in the scent of the rose, which was rich and heady and delicious.

He asked, 'You're one of Josephine's ATS friends, aren't you?'

'Yes, we've known each other for years. We were at Camberley together, learning to drive lorries.'

'Are you still driving lorries?'

'No, thank goodness, I have a very nice brigadier to drive around now. And you?'

Rowland explained that he was in an infantry division and that he was currently stationed on Salisbury Plain. He had known Josephine's brother, Freddie, for years. 'We were at school together,' he told her. 'The Covingtons were very decent to me. After my parents died, they always invited me to stay here in the school holidays. Covington Hall's been like a second home to me.'

'What happened to your parents?'

'They were killed in a car crash when they were on holiday in the south of France. They were driving along a cliff road and they must have misjudged a bend and their car went over the edge.'

'How awful! How old were you?'

'I was eleven. I can't remember them all that well. Just odd images, almost like snapshots. What about you, Miss Garland? Have you any family?'

Kay explained about losing her parents and about Aunt Dot and the house in Pimlico.

'I've a flat in Tufnell Park,' he said.

'Lucky you. I'd love to have my own flat.' She was twenty-seven years old, she thought, and she had never had a place of her own.

'Have you stayed here before?'

'Never.'

'Covington Hall's supposed to have one of the largest collections of old roses in England. They're trying hard to hang on to it – just about every other flower border has been dug up and planted with vegetables. Come and see the view from the terrace. It's marvellous.'

At the end of the terrace was a low brick wall, grown over with ivy. They went to stand at it, resting their elbows on top of the wall as they looked out across the countryside. On the far side of the wall, the hill sloped down to a green valley. As Rowland pointed out landmarks to her, Kay found herself looking not at stream and river, but at his face. His long, thin nose had a small bump on it and his dark eyes were deeply lidded. They had a slightly mournful look in repose, she had noticed, but now they were lively and animated.

Suddenly, he said, 'Listen to me, boring you like this. I'm sorry, I'm not usually so verbose. I expect you're longing to get back to the party.'

She shook her head. 'No, not at all. You love it here, don't you?'

'Yes, I do. Still, we should be sociable. There's going to be dancing in the ballroom later.'

She sighed. 'How extraordinary, to have your own ballroom.'

'Isn't it? You will dance with me, won't you, Miss Garland?'

In the time they had been in the garden, the sun had dipped in the sky and the blue-black shadows of the tall trees standing to one side of the house stretched across the terrace. She felt his gaze on her, felt the blood rise to her skin. Something in the tone of his voice told her that the answer to his question mattered to him, and she heard herself say, 'Yes, of course, I'd love to.' And as they walked back to the house, she felt a thrill of anticipation and wonder, as if she was standing on some great height altogether more vertiginous than the terrace, looking down to the rich and unexpected landscape that had opened out in front of her.

At first, dancing, and then at supper they talked. He had come into the money his parents had left him ten years ago, when he was twenty-one, and had bought the flat in Tufnell Park. Before the war he had worked for Wolseley Motors and then in a shipping office. He laughed, a little apologetically. Not an ounce of his parents' theatrical blood seemed to have been passed on to him. He couldn't have written – or acted in – a play to save his life. The shipping office had been OK, a bit dull sometimes, but he wouldn't have said he had been unhappy. He'd always had an idea there was something else he meant to do with his life but hadn't been able to pinpoint what it was. Then the war had broken out and he'd joined the army.

Dancing with him, she felt the beat of his heart against hers and the pressure of his hand on her back. One wall of the ballroom, which was at the rear of the house, was made up of windows and French doors and looked out over a lawn. As dusk fell, shadows pooled in the corners of the high-ceilinged room. Only when the darkness was absolute did they draw the blackout curtains and light the chandeliers. The candlelight cast over the room a magical, enchanted air, disguising the cracks in the plasterwork and the worn upholstery and muting the girls' dresses to subtle shades of grey and silver and tawny brown.

The music, his nearness and the glitter of lights hypnotized her and they fell silent, lost in each other's arms. The sharp awareness of the passing of time that more than three years in the ATS had drilled into her drifted away. At length, looking round, Kay saw that the couples on the dance floor had thinned out and the more elderly Covingtons had retired to bed.

'What time is it?' It seemed hours since she had spoken; she felt as if she was trying to wake from a dream.

'Almost three.'

She blinked. 'So late? I'd no idea.'

'Are you tired?'

'No, not at all.' Her energy seemed limitless, she could not have slept if she had wanted to.

'Nor me. Funny that – I've spent the last two weeks charging round Salisbury Plain on a training exercise and I'd have said I was whacked.'

'I expect it's the champagne.'

'Maybe. Or perhaps it's you, perhaps it's being with you, Kay. Shall we go outside for a breath of fresh air?'

She followed him out of the French windows. He found a half-bottle of champagne and put a couple of glasses in his pocket; they chinked against each other as they walked across the lawn. He asked her when she had to return to Aldershot. She must be back by nine on Monday morning, she said. He told her that he had to leave Covington Hall at six – he had been given only twenty-four hours' leave. *Six o'clock*, she thought. Only three more hours.

She must not assume anything, she told herself, she must not hope for anything. They had spent an evening together, that was all, and how many such evenings had there been over the years of the war, dancing with men whose names she could not now remember? But all her instincts told her that some-thing *had* happened, that something *had* changed. Yet surely she had felt so before, with Johnny, and it had taken her such a long time to realize that Johnny Gilfoyle had never felt the same about her as she had about him. She became involved too quickly, perhaps. She had a sudden horrible vision of herself as an emotionally clingy person, seizing gratefully on any attention or affection that came her way.

She said, 'Perhaps you should get some rest, then.'

He glanced at her, frowning. 'I don't know about you, but I don't want to miss a minute of this.'

'This?' she echoed.

'I meant being with you.' He stopped, turning to face her. 'Do you think it's possible to fall in love at first sight?'

Her heart hammered. 'I don't know – I'm not sure. Do you?'

As he spoke, she recognized a different side to him, uncertain, more vulnerable. 'You probably think I'm trying it on,' he said, 'but it's not that, I promise. I suppose if things were different, I'd be more cautious – not because I'm not sure what I feel but because you may not feel the same. But we may not see each other again for months, Kay, so I might as well come clean. You rather took my breath away when I saw you in the garden earlier on.' He gave a short, embarrassed laugh. 'But you must tell me if you think I'm talking utter nonsense and then I'll change the subject and we'll talk about the weather or about how nice Josephine looked instead.'

She whispered, 'I don't think you're talking nonsense.'

He drew her to him, his lips brushing against hers. They kissed for a while, small, tentative meetings of skin against skin, learning to know each other. And then his kisses became deep and consuming and the world in all its clamour and confusion narrowed down to the two of them, on a lawn bathed in moonlight. As they kissed, she knew that something extraordinary was happening, something transformatory and so wonderful she was almost afraid to consider it, in case it slipped through her fingers like thistledown.

Drawing away from her, he said, 'Poor girl, you're freezing. Here, have this.'

He took off his tunic and wrapped it round her shoulders as they crossed the lawn. Inside a summerhouse, he poured out the champagne. They sat side by side on a bench, her head resting on his shoulder. Through a window, she could see the crescent moon.

'I remember,' she said, 'my first summer in the south of France, thinking how wonderful it was that it was still warm at midnight.'

'Have you travelled much?' he asked her.

She told him about Miranda and the nomadic eighteen months she had spent wandering around Europe with the Denisovs. She explained where Miranda was living and how worried she was for her.

'They so often have the worst of it,' he said, 'these Central European countries.'

'Better to be on the edge of Europe, like us.'

'Yes, I think so.' His hand stroked her hair.

'It's so lovely to be here. This feels so *civilized*, don't you think, after barracks.'

'Almost unreal. A sort of oasis.'

She sighed. 'The house, the music – and no one barking orders at you. Whenever I go home on leave, it's such a relief to be *me* again. Sometimes I'm afraid that if the war goes on much longer, I won't be able to remember how to be me. I'll be Lance-Corporal Garland all the time and poor old Kay Garland will be some vague acquaintance I've almost forgotten.'

'What will you do when it's over?'

'I hadn't thought. It's going to take an awfully long time to put everything back together afterwards, isn't it? But I suppose I'll go back to teaching. What about you?'

'I want to be a farmer.'

'A farmer?' She looked up at him.

'Yes. Are you surprised?'

'A little, yes,' she said honestly.

'What, don't you see me as a sturdy man of the soil?'

'You have rather an intellectual look, I'd say.'

'I'm flattered. But yes, I think that's what I'd like to do. It just came into my head and I can't seem to get it out again. I don't think I could go back to the life I had before the war. I think I'm going to want something different.'

'So what will you do? Buy a farm?'

He laughed. 'Not straight away, I wouldn't know what to do with it. I'd have to go to agricultural college first and then maybe spend a couple of years working for someone so that I had some practical experience. Then I'd look for somewhere of my own. I wouldn't mind finding a place round here – I love the countryside.'

Her eyes closed. She imagined white ducks walking through long grass in an orchard. The image shimmered, solidified: for a moment she was asleep. But the caress of his mouth on the back of her neck woke her, and she sat up and they kissed again.

Dawn came early, a streak of light across the grass, a lifting of the darkness. At half past five they walked back to the house. Dew pearled the grass, the sunlight casting up jewelled colours. She had taken off her high-heeled shoes and walked barefoot across the lawn, holding his hand. Her senses seemed heightened that morning and she heard the birdsong and saw the bright colours of the new day with great clarity.

As they reached the house, he said, 'You speak French, don't you? There's a French phrase for it, isn't there, when you just look at someone and know?'

'*Coup de foudre*,' she said. 'A thunderbolt. That's what it means – a thunderbolt.'

During the week that followed, Kay had to drive the brigadier first to North Wales, then to Norfolk and then back to London. As the car wound through narrow country lanes, she thought about Rowland Latimer. She remembered how he had looked up at her as she had stepped out on to the terrace and how he had pinned the rose to the strap of her dress. She remembered dancing with him and she remembered sitting in the summerhouse, watching the night come and go. She remembered everything they had said to each other and how they had seemed so perfectly in tune. She remembered kissing him, the press of his body against hers and the urgency of his embrace.

Ridiculous, she tried to tell herself, to feel so attracted to someone she hardly knew. Yet she, who prided herself on being practical, and who knew what forces romances were like, all partings and absences and disappointments and tears in the small moments of privacy that were all that the army allowed you, felt herself slipping, sliding, could not stop herself, did not want to stop herself.

And it had its advantages, being in love. She hardly noticed the boredom and discomfort of army life. The war news – the landings in Sicily, and then, at the beginning of September, the embarkation of troops drawn from General Montgomery's

Eighth Army across the Straits of Messina to Reggio di Calabria on the Italian mainland — all this touched her less now.

In the ensuing weeks, they wrote to each other. Driving the brigadier through the chalk hills of southern England or the flatlands of East Anglia, where the great expanse of sky dominated field and copse, she thought of what she would write to him. She wrote amusing descriptions of her day — the herd of cows that had blocked the road, making the brigadier late for a meeting, or the afternoon they had become lost in deepest, darkest Somerset. She and the brigadier had pored over the map, trying to make sense of the warren of narrow country lanes. She wrote to Rowland about a week so long and relentless that, arriving at her final destination and too tired to search for a free bed, she had fallen asleep on the floor of the Nissen hut. *The floor, darling! All the other girls were very kind and stepped over me.*

His letters were taken out of her pocket and read over and over again, whenever she had a minute to herself. His letters she learned by heart. *I always thought that the idea of there being someone perfect out there, waiting just for me, was romantic guff until I met you, Kay. Now I know that I was wrong and they were right, and it seems a miracle.*

Towards the end of September, Rowland wrote to her that he had a week's leave, which he planned to spend at his flat in Tufnell Park. Their leaves coincided at last and on Friday afternoon Kay drove the brigadier down from Yorkshire, arriving in London late that evening. After spending the night in Pimlico, she set out for Tufnell Park. On the tube, the first chink of doubt. Perhaps this time it wouldn't be the same. Perhaps they had been beguiled by the magic of that summer's night, perhaps they had imagined a connection between them. Perhaps it had been the house, the garden, the party, a hunger for glamour and romance; now, with the coming of autumn, the air would have grown colder. Or perhaps, in the weeks that had passed since their meeting, she had invested him with an aura of romance that had simply not been there. Perhaps she had rewritten him, moulding him into something she longed for. Perhaps this time he would not be attracted to her. Perhaps this time she would not be attracted to him.

Rowland's flat was in a tall, eighteenth-century building, faced in stone. There was rubble in the small front garden and one side of the steps that led up to the front door had sheered away. There were three doorbells. Kay pressed the one that said 'Latimer'.

He greeted her with a kiss on the cheek and let her into the house. A pram stood in the hallway and from one of the ground-floor rooms she could hear a baby crying. As she followed him up two flights of stairs, talking of her journey from Pimlico and her drive down from Catterick the previous day, she found herself glancing at him, comparing the real Rowland to her memory of him.

He let them into the flat. 'Here we are. Home sweet home.'

'It's lovely. So bright and airy.'

'Can I get you a tea or coffee?'

'No thanks.'

The triteness of their conversation depressed her. She found herself wondering how she would bear the disappointment if the day were to peter out in silences and witless phrases.

He said, 'Let me show you why I bought the flat.'

At the far end of the sitting room was a glass-panelled door that led out on to a balcony. There was room for a couple of deckchairs and a small wrought-iron table. The balcony looked out over the roofs of the surrounding houses.

'How marvellous,' she said.

'Best view in London, I think.' He announced, in the ponderous language of estate agents, 'The dwelling benefits from a delightful balcony with views across London.'

The tiles and slates seemed to have been washed clean by the previous night's rain. Pigeons cooed on the chimney pots. Looking down, Kay could see where bombs had fallen, leaving areas of waste ground, rubble and roofless jagged walls.

'When I was living here, before the war,' he said, 'I had pots of geraniums out here.'

'Your garden in the sky.'

'Yes, that's it exactly.' Then he smiled and said, 'Kay, I'm so happy you're here, I can hardly find the words to speak. I feel as if I'm seventeen again, on a first date.'

'I'm glad you're not seventeen. I'd feel like a cradle-snatcher.'

His hands rested on her waist, and as his lips brushed against her forehead, all her doubts fell away. She said, 'I was so sure something was going to go wrong. I was afraid the car would have a puncture and I'd get stuck in Stamford or the brigadier would suddenly get a message telling him he had to go to Scotland.'

'Before I left Covington Hall, I tried to memorize you. I said to myself, she's tall and slim and she has shoulder-length blonde hair and greeny-hazel eyes. But you're far more beautiful than I remembered.'

She was wearing a floral print cotton dress and she had parted her hair to one side and let it fall loose to her shoulders. When he ran his hand up and down her spine, for a moment the roofs that surrounded them seemed to shimmer and tilt.

He said, 'Would you like to see the rest of the flat?'

'I'd love to.'

Indoors, the sitting room was high-ceilinged and the plaster covings and ceiling rose were ornamented with sculpted curling leaves. There were sofas, bookshelves, a gramophone and a stack of records. The dining room was furnished with a large mahogany table and chairs. In a display cabinet were half a dozen wine glasses, rose-pink, decorated in gold, and a Lalique bowl. Mermaids with long, flowing hair swam through its clouded glass.

'They were my mother's,' explained Rowland. 'My father bought the glasses for her when they were on honeymoon in Venice. Every time I come back to the flat, I expect to find them in little pieces, because of the bombs, but somehow they've survived. I suppose I should have packed them away, but I like to see them.' He ran his eye over the furniture. 'The table and chairs belonged to my parents too. I feel I ought to give grand dinners here.'

On the walls of the room there were framed photographs and theatre programmes. Rowland showed her a photograph of his mother, Madeleine Latimer. She had large brown-black eyes, like her son.

In the afternoon, they took a bus to Green Park. The sun had come out and there was a warmth in the air. Couples were lying on the lawn or strolling arm in arm along the paths. Three GIs were sitting on a bench, watching the girls go by, and some boys were playing with balsa wood aeroplanes, making ack-ack noises and blowing air through their cheeks to make the sounds of explosions as the planes swooped and dived.

Rowland bought ices and they lay on the grass and listened to the band. He told Kay that there had once been an ice-house and two temples in Green Park. He remembered as a child visiting with his parents a very grand house in the north of England that had had an ice-house. While his parents were at lunch, he had gone off by himself to explore. Dug into the sloping ground beside a lake, the ice-house had been a narrow tunnel gouged out of the earth. Ice was hacked off from the lake in winter and stored inside the tunnel for the summer. It had been dark and cold inside the tunnel and the rich smell of soil had been overlaid by something less pleasant.

'All of a sudden,' he said, 'I was terrified. I was overcome by this black, awful fear. I couldn't move at first and then I ran out. When I got outside, I was shaking. I've never felt so afraid in my life. I've often wondered what it was that frightened me so much, whether I thought I might become trapped, or whether I was thinking, perhaps without quite knowing it, of tombs, dead bodies, ghosts, that sort of thing. Or perhaps it was just the loneliness, the darkness.'

'Poor Rowland.'

He nuzzled her neck. 'I wouldn't have felt lonely if you'd been with me.'

They kissed, then she said, 'Did you travel a lot when you were little?'

'All the time, before I went to school. My parents took me round the country with them whenever they were touring a play. We went to Le Touquet a few times. It's funny to think that probably the next time I'll be in France will be when it all happens. When they open the second front, I mean.'

Looking up, she could see through the dappled sunlight a fretwork of leaves, black against the sky. She could smell the sweet, leafy scent of the horse-chestnut tree.

She heard him say, 'I wonder if I'll feel afraid. That's what people say about the army, isn't it, that it's a mixture of boredom and fear. Well, I've certainly had my share of boredom. Which is worse, do you think, the boredom or the fear?'

'Boredom,' she said. 'At least you feel alive when you're afraid.'

'You're right.' He smiled. 'I'll remember that if I ever get the wind up.'

There was an inevitability, she thought, to the rest of the day. They both knew where it would end, and there was a languorous pleasure in its anticipation. After they left the park, they went to a restaurant in Piccadilly, where their fingertips touched across the table top, resisting even that small separation. And then, the journey back to the flat, where they would make love, had known that they would perhaps since the moment they had stood side by side on the balcony, looking out over the roofs.

His body was long, brown and muscled because he had spent August and September training in Devon. She shivered as he ran his fingers over the curves of breast and waist and hip. There was a fire inside her; their bodies locked together and she felt the hardness of bone and sinew. Afterwards, they lay face to face. She discovered the curve of cheekbone and jaw, the scent and texture of his skin, the slight knobbliness to his right collarbone, which he had broken during his first year in the army, the white scar on his shin from where he had fallen off a bicycle when he was a child. Kissing the hollow of her throat, he drew her to him, the flat of his hand between her shoulder blades, then she closed her eyes and let him make love to her again.

Theirs became a winter love affair. In a nightclub, a girl sang 'The Way You Look Tonight' to the silky melody of a piano and the low thrum of a double bass. Dancing with Rowland, Kay felt the slight roughness of his cheek. When his lips brushed against hers, it seemed to her a gesture of such intimacy that she caught her breath.

Once, they went to the theatre together, to see *This Happy Breed* in the West End. Afterwards, they headed on to the French Pub in Soho – it was really called the York Minster, but had been nicknamed the French Pub because General de Gaulle and the Free French soldiers liked to drink there. After they left the pub, Rowland bought fish and chips and they ate them as they walked back to the tube station.

A workman's café in the early hours of the morning. The flimsy hut, erected on a bomb site, was tacked together out of packing cases and metal advertising placards, Bovril and Lyons Maid Ices. Inside, the wind rattled through the gaps in the structure. The clientèle were in factory overalls or in uniform, and on the rough wooden tables there were plastic salt and pepper pots and ashtrays made out of sardine cans. Posters on the walls exhorted them to eat more carrots and to save bones to make fertilizer. After they had drunk their tea, they walked down a narrow alleyway, the haunt of tomcats and spivs, Rowland's arm round her shoulders, both of them dazed with fatigue and desire.

At home on a weekend's leave, waking early one morning, Kay opened the curtains, looked down, and saw him sitting on the low wall that bordered Aunt Dot's front garden. Pulling on her clothes, she hurried outside. He had an hour, he told her, before he must entrain for the north of England. She touched his cold face with her fingers and heard the clink of a milkman's dray and the drone of an aeroplane, high in the sky. Then there was only the two of them, alone in the grey dawn light, and she became lost in the taste of him, the feel of him.

But mostly that winter her life – the best part of her life – was metered out at railway stations. At Liverpool Street Station, the waiting room was crowded with soldiers and their kitbags and a dozen WAAFs, chattering like goldfinches. Rowland's train was delayed: it might arrive in five minutes, the guard told them, with a pessimistic sucking of the teeth, or it might be an hour. She had never in the past, she thought, felt so joyful at a train's delay. They walked along the platform to keep warm, her hand tucked in his arm, her head resting against his shoulder as they threaded between knapsacks and suitcases. Naval officers with gold braid on their sleeves walked up and down, every now and then glancing at their watches. Soldiers played dice and sailors with their hats tipped over their faces dozed on benches. A girl in a violet coat slept with her back propped against a door, her mouth open. There was the smell of smoke and coal dust and every now and then a hiss of steam as a train made ready to pull out of the station. The guard's whistle blared and the pistons of the engines cranked and smoke billowed up towards the glass roof.

In January 1944, Rowland wrote to her that he had been posted to Scotland for three months for training in the Cairngorms. He should have half an hour in London changing trains en route to Scotland.

The brigadier was in London that day; Kay ferried him between government offices. At six o'clock he told her to go off duty, by seven she was at Euston Station. She was early, so she checked her face in the ladies' room. Then she went back outside to the station concourse.

Time ticked past. A quarter past seven, he had written — but now it was twenty past, and, in a moment it seemed, another five minutes had gone by. People in uniform milled around her, every now and then she stood on tiptoe, trying to make him out from the crowd of khaki, navy and air force blue. Had she muddled it up? Had he arranged to meet her on the platform and not on the concourse? She was sure she had not but as the minutes ticked by and as the incoming train drew into the platform, she felt a sudden doubt and hurried to the gates to speak to the ticket inspector. Then she walked quickly along the platform, her gaze darting here and there, looking at benches and walls and into waiting rooms and among the clumps of people waiting to get on the train and those pouring out of the carriages on to the platform, their voices diminishing as they walked away, smothered by the dark and the cold.

He was not there, and she shivered and dug her hands into her pockets and turned back towards the gates. The waiting passengers filed on to the train, and there was a screech of steam.

Then, above all the clamour, she heard his voice, calling out to her and saw him, running towards her from the metal gates. And he was there at last and his arms were round her and he was kissing her and saying her name.

'Your train—' she said.

'Yes. Listen. There's something I have to ask you first.'

The guard was walking along the platform, slamming carriage doors shut. And Rowland was telling her how much he loved her and how much he would miss her and how much he wanted her. As the guard raised his flag and blew his whistle, Rowland asked her whether she would marry him. And she considered him: the shape of his mouth and the utter seriousness in his eyes and she said, 'Oh Rowland, I love you, I adore you, of course I'll marry you.' And then he pressed into her hand a small box and climbed on to the train and she waved to him as he leaned his head out of the carriage window while the train got up steam and pulled out of the station.

When she could see him no longer, she opened the box. Inside it was a ring, an emerald set between diamonds. She put it on; it fitted perfectly. She pressed her hands to her face as she watched the train shrink into the blackness of the evening.

Chapter Thirteen

After Franz was called up for military service, Miranda and the Countess became responsible for the running of the house and the estate. Before Franz left Sommerfeld, he ran through the account books and files with Miranda, showing her where to note a payment by a tenant and where to file a letter from a lawyer or official. She wondered, glancing at his narrow, intelligent face as he emphasized to her the importance of not running foul of government regulations, whether he was afraid. And whether he would ever return to Sommerfeld.

She had also taught herself how to ride a bicycle. It was not something she had ever tried before. Konstantin Denisov's daughter had been chauffeured in a Rolls-Royce or had travelled in a first-class carriage of the Golden Arrow. But with Franz gone she must be able to travel under her own steam. They no longer had petrol for the tractors and many of Sommerfeld's horses had been requisitioned by the army, leaving the estate with scarcely enough animals to pull the old-fashioned farm implements that had been unearthed from the barns.

In January, she cycled to Angerberg on estate business. There had been a thaw and meltwater gathered in the ditches and in the ruts on the road. Herr Dr Steltzer, the von Kahlberg lawyer, had come out of retirement to keep the family firm going while his sons were in the army. Miranda spent an hour at his office discussing a disputed boundary.

At the end of her visit, she emerged on to the street. Recently, Angerberg had changed. Before the war it had been a pleasant country town, quiet and sleepy – a backwater, you might say. But Angerberg had the feeling now of a frontier town. In the course of a year, since the disaster of Stalingrad, the Red Army had fought fiercely, regaining lost ground and pushing relentlessly westwards. For Germany, the last year had been one of reversal and retreat. Kharkov, Kursk and Kiev were in Soviet hands once more. The Red Army was now only twenty-seven miles from the old Polish border.

Everywhere in the town there were troops, in vehicles, speeding along the tarmac or sitting in the taverns or limping along the pavements on crutches. A Mercedes headed down the main street, its black paint spattered with mud, and Miranda caught a glimpse of SS men inside. Three soldiers, standing beside a coal brazier, eating chestnuts, watched her as she passed them. She felt their gaze on her as she fetched the bicycle from where she had left it, propped against a wall. *You have a Russian father and an English mother*: she didn't leave Sommerfeld often these days, and when she did, she was careful.

As she cycled out of the town, the houses fell away and the countryside opened up into field and copse. Snow lingered in the valleys and on the north-facing slopes. The puddles on the road reflected the blue of the sky, and the browned remains of reeds and rushes fringed the overflowing ditches.

She must have been cycling for a mile when she came to a

halt. A column of prisoners of war filled the narrow road. Their uniforms were ragged and dirty, their boots muddy. Some had bound lengths of cloth round their hands and shins in an attempt to keep warm. Catching a muttered phrase of French, Miranda searched, as she always did, from face to face. Her gaze, skimming from young faces to old, handsome to plain, would pause fractionally, and then move on. He was not there, he for whom she searched constantly.

As the column passed her, she caught sight, in its heart, of a head of wavy chestnut-brown hair. She dropped the bicycle and clambered up on to the verge. She looked again. It *could* be him, it *could* be Olivier. Struggling through the thick snow on the verge, she tried to get a better look at the prisoner. Her heart pounded. His height, the way walked – yes, perhaps it really was him! Sliding off the verge, she began to fight her way through the column of prisoners. One of the guards called out to her but she took no notice. Fleetingly, she caught a glimpse of the prisoner's profile. It *was* him, she was sure of it. His hair had been just that colour, his cheekbone at just that angle. Her heart seemed about to burst with joy. 'Olivier!' she called out. 'Olivier!' The column of prisoners parted; she had almost reached him.

And then, as he turned to look at her, she saw that it wasn't him at all, that it was someone quite different – much younger, a boy merely. The prisoners were staring at her and one of the guards had cocked his rifle. She saw how it must look – a woman in fur coat and boots shouting and waving her arms about like a madwoman. Somehow, she made herself smile to the guard, apologize, and tell him that she had made a mistake.

The prisoners went on their way. She watched them turn

out of sight round a bend in the road and then she pressed her hands against her face and wept. It hadn't been him, and there it was, the emptiness, to be faced all over again. Her sobs racked her.

Eventually, shivering and drained, she picked up her bicycle. Her belief that she had found Olivier had been born of her own need, her own loneliness, she saw that now. Would she even recognize him, after a parting of four years? Might they both have changed so much they would no longer know each other? And if, one day, he were to pass by her in one of the innumerable columns of prisoners that tramped over Germany, would he hate her for living with the enemy? Even if he were by some miracle to survive the war, and even if they were, by another miracle, to meet again, he might no longer love her. Too many terrible events stood between them, too much horror and enmity and oppression. You couldn't expect to pick up the pieces. You couldn't assume that friendship, love or affection would survive the cruelties of war. They had both been swept up in a whirlwind; they might be flung down anywhere.

Yet he might still be alive. It was possible. She must not give up hope. And it came to her, as she began slowly to pedal along the road, that there was something she could do for him. There were POW camps all over Germany, housing tens of thousands of men, French, English, Belgian, Dutch and Russian, and many other nationalities besides. Many of the men would have already been separated for years from their homes and their families. Who knew how much longer their separation might last? For each of these men, someone waited — a mother, a wife, a sister, a child, a lover. There must be countless women who, like her, knew little or nothing of the fate of those they loved. A prisoner's existence was precarious, dependent on fate and on the whim of his captors. He might die of the wounds he had received in battle or of illness or neglect. He might become a chance victim of the Allied bombing campaign. If he tried to escape, he could be shot.

There was one last thing she could do for Olivier. There were so many nameless dead in this war, but while there was still breath in her body she would ensure that he was not one of them. She had vowed to wait for him, and that was what she would do. Whether he was alive or dead, she would discover what had happened to him. She would be his memorial. While she lived, he would not be forgotten.

The military hospital was on Salisbury Plain. Leaving the bus, whose cargo of women was leavened by a handful of soldiers, Kay found herself confronted by a series of brick-built, tin-roofed huts.

A nurse directed her to Ward 4. There, she spoke to the sister, asking for Captain Blacklock. The sister said, 'Just fifteen minutes, then. He gets easily tired.'

Kay looked along the rows of beds and saw him. She took a breath, suddenly afraid of what she might find, and crossed the room to him.

There was a large, square bandage on the side of Tom's head, where they had shaved off his hair, and his left arm was encased in plaster. One of his legs was in traction, suspended by a complicated pulley and wire arrangement from the ceiling.

'Tom,' she said softly.

He opened his eyes. 'Kay. What a lovely surprise.'

'I didn't wake you, did I?'

'No, I was only dozing.' He shuffled into a more upright position. 'Could you – the pillows . . .'

She plumped them up so that they supported him better and sat down beside the bed. 'I brought you these,' she said, showing him a bunch of violets, wrapped in ivy and moss.

'They're pretty. Makes me think of spring. Kind of you.'

'How are you, Tom?'

'Oh, better today.' He glanced round the ward. 'Starting to get sick and tired of this place. That must be a good sign, don't you think?'

'I'm sure it is. I'm sorry you've such had a rotten time. Does it hurt a lot?'

'It's not too bad.'

'What happened to you?'

'I was at Anzio.' He screwed up his face.

'I'm sorry.' She had heard about the ferocity of the German opposition to the Allied beachhead at Anzio, between Monte Cassino and Rome, and the consequent loss of Allied life. 'If you don't want to talk about it . . .'

'It's not that. It's just that I can't remember what happened clearly.'

She squeezed his hand. 'It was kind of Minnie to write to me.'

'I asked her to. My family can't get down here too often because of the distance and I thought, who else did I want to see? Kay, of course.'

She caught a glimpse of his old, quick smile. 'It's good to see you, Tom. And at least you're back home now.'

'Are you and Rowland married yet?' he said. 'You must have written to me the date but I've forgotten, I'm afraid.'

'The wedding's on Saturday.'

'Congratulations. I wish I could be there.'

'I wish you could too, Tom. I'll be thinking of you.'

'Oh, I shouldn't waste your time doing that. Have some fun, won't you, Kay. Are you going on honeymoon?'

'Yes, to a little place in the Cotswolds. We've got forty-eight hours' leave.'

'When the war's over, you can go somewhere exciting.'

'Yes, I suppose we can.' She thought for a moment, then said, 'Though to be honest, I don't seem to want to travel any more. All I want is to be peaceful, for everything to be ordinary and run-of-the-mill again. I want us to be living in Rowland's flat in Tufnell Park and doing everyday things, shopping and going to work and listening to the wireless in the evenings. All the things I used to think so dull and middle-aged.'

'What's he like, this chap of yours?'

'We never seem to run out of things to say to each other.' She smiled. 'And when I'm with him, even the most ordinary things seem wonderful.'

A ward orderly pushing a tea trolley stopped at the end of Tom's bed. 'Tea, Captain Blacklock?'

'Please.'

Tom said, when the trolley had moved on, 'They used to make me drink using a bloody straw. I feel I've been promoted now I'm allowed a cup and saucer.'

She saw how his hand shook as he reached out for the cup, and said, 'Perhaps you should let it cool down a little.'

'Yes.'

'I love him, Tom. And the even more amazing thing is, Rowland loves me.'

'He should do. He's a lucky man.'

As they talked, she thought he looked tired and rather sad. There was a feverish glitter in his eyes. She handed the teacup to him and put it back on the locker after he had taken a few sips. 'Is there anything I can get you, Tom?' she asked. 'Is there anything I can do for you?'

'I wouldn't mind a book or two, if you could find something light. Or some crosswords – nothing too demanding. I don't think I'd make much sense of The Times crossword just now.'

'I'll bring them with me next time,' she promised. She hesitated. 'I wondered . . .'

'What?'

'Whether you'd like me to contact Edie.'

For a few moments he said nothing. Then, 'No, I don't think so. Kind of you to offer, but no.'

He drank some more tea, and then she told him she had to go because she must be back in camp that night. As she was buttoning up her coat, she said, 'Oh – that house where you were working, when we met in Berlin . . .'

'Cold Christmas?'

'Yes. Only I was driving the brigadier through Suffolk the other day and I recognized the name. It's been requisitioned by the USAAF.'

'Good grief,' he said. 'I wonder what Miles Culbone thinks of that?'

'Anyway, I thought you might be interested.' She squeezed his hand. 'I must head off. Look after yourself, Tom.'

He gave her a smile. 'I hope everything goes marvellously on Saturday. I'm sure you and Rowland will be very happy, Kay.'

Before she left the ward, Kay tapped on the door of the sister's office.

'I wondered whether you could tell me how Captain

Blacklock is. I mean, how he *really* is. He didn't want to talk about it.'

The sister slid a letter into an envelope. 'Paperwork,' she said. 'There's always far too much paperwork. Don't you find that, Lance-Corporal?' She was young and pretty and had a rather debby drawl.

'I just drive cars.'

'Lucky you. I sometimes wish I'd gone in for something like that.' She gave a brisk smile. 'Captain Blacklock has been very unwell. The surgeon took four bullets and half a dozen fragments of shell out of his legs and abdomen. One of the bullets was half an inch from his heart. He developed a high fever on the hospital ship and was in a pretty bad way by the time he ended up here. However, there's been a steady improvement and he's young and strong so with any luck he should pull through.'

'How long will he be in hospital?'

'Six to eight weeks, at a guess. He should be able to leave as soon as his leg has healed enough for him to manage on crutches. His mother's a doctor, so we may be able to send him home a little earlier than we otherwise would.'

'Thank you, Sister.'

As Kay turned to leave, the sister spoke again. 'Did Captain Blacklock tell you how he came to be wounded? The lorry struck a mine, you see. Captain Blacklock was thrown clear by the explosion but some of the men were trapped in the burning lorry. He tried to pull them out. That was when they shot him. Your friend's a brave man, Lance-Corporal.'

'No, he didn't tell me that,' said Kay. 'Thank you, Sister.'

Walking out of the building, Kay found that she couldn't see properly because her eyes had blurred with tears. She couldn't work out what she was crying about – Tom was going to recover, and at least he wasn't in Italy any more, and she and Rowland were going to be married on Saturday. But the tears brimmed and fell and, outside in the cold, fresh air, she had to stand still for several moments and make herself think of wedding plans, of florists and cakes, before blowing her nose and heading for the bus stop.

Tom's head was hurting rather badly. He pondered for a while on why pains in the head always seem so much worse than pains anywhere else. The orderly asked him whether he wanted any more of his tea and Tom said no thanks, and then they sorted out his pillows for him and he lay back, his eyes closed. The least little thing made him tired and getting tired so easily made him fed up with himself. There was something he needed to work out, something important, that remained just out of his grasp because he was too tired to focus.

He'd have liked to have talked to Kay for longer. He thought how happiness seemed to shine out from her. Good for her, she deserved it. She had always had a great capacity for happiness, had been delighted by such small things – a slice of *apfelkuchen* in a café in Berlin, a comfortable seat on the night ferry. And at least Rowland Latimer sounded a better bet than that snake Johnny Gilfoyle.

Footsteps: Tom opened his eyes. The nurse put a thermometer in his mouth and took his pulse. 'Your temp's up again, Captain Blacklock, I'm afraid,' she said, tutting. 'Perhaps it's too soon for you to have visitors quite yet. Are you in a lot of pain?'

'A bit,' he admitted.

'I'll get you something to help.'

'No,' he said. The word came out sharper than he had

intended; the nurse looked startled. 'I'm sorry,' he said quickly. 'It's just that the pills make me dopey and I want to stay awake for a while.'

'I'll leave it half an hour, then,' she said. 'Don't tire yourself out.' She patted his hand and walked away.

When she had gone, Tom sifted through his memory. He did this several times a day because of the gaps. In September of the previous year, he had been among the Allied troops who had crossed the Straits of Messina from Sicily to mainland Italy. Six days later, the US Fifth Army had landed at Salerno, south of Naples. The landings had been fiercely opposed and it had taken several days of bitter fighting before, with the arrival of the Eighth Army from the south, the bridgehead had been secured. Naples had fallen to the Allies at the end of September. As they had retreated from southern Italy, German troops had mined the roads. Clearing them was a slow, painstaking, dangerous business.

The things he had seen, travelling northward that winter from the toe of Italy. The storm-lashed Tyrrhenian Sea, glimpsed when the clouds parted. A wide path of broken paving stones, slicked by driving rain, leading up a hillside. Olive trees in fractured terracotta pots, their roots exposed, the grey-green leaves trembling as the raindrops struck them.

Once, driving around bomb craters and potholes to transport an attaché case of documents to the HQ of another division, he had stopped outside a villa on the Sorrento coast. The villa stood alone, surrounded by a mixture of forest and scrubland. Dark, slender evergreens stood like sentinels beside the paths and parterres. Part of the garden wall, of stone so old it might have stood there since Roman times, had collapsed.

It must have been pleasant, once, to escape the heat of an

Italian summer on the villa's verandah, but now one side of the building was shorn away and a heap of stones and tiles lay beside what was left. Not so long ago, Tom would have thought that no one could live in such ruins. But he had learned that human beings could endure the most adverse circumstances, that they would cling on to what had been their homes for as long as possible, and he saw, looking through the rain, indications that the villa was still inhabited – a pile of logs, stored in an empty fireplace, tea towels hanging on a makeshift washing line beneath a jagged portion of the roof. In rooms that were open to the elements, shards of glass littered the floor, mingling with brown and scarlet vine leaves that smeared the marble like blood and bruises. The accoutrements of what must once have been a gracious salon remained – a heavy sofa with sodden upholstery, a grand piano whose wooden frame was swollen and blistered by damp.

He heard light footsteps, running away. He called out in Italian to whoever still lived at the villa, reassuring them that he meant them no harm. He had seen, on his travels, children who lived among the ruins, scratching among the debris like foxes. He left a bar of chocolate on the arm of the sofa and went back to the jeep.

He could recall very little of the incident in which he had been wounded. He remembered fractured images, like film stills – sitting in the cab of the lorry, looking out through the windscreen at the countryside south of Anzio, all browns and greys in the depths of winter. It was freezing cold but the men in the back were joking and laughing. Another image: he was lying in the scrubland at the side of the road and the lorry was on fire. After that, nothing. He had no memory at all of the casualty clearing station but recalled a little of the hospital ship and the long voyage home. Mixed into his memories were fever dreams, vividly coloured and frightening. The doctor had told him that he had pulled one or two of the men out of the lorry, but he had no memory of that. He wondered whether it counted, doing something that other people thought brave, if you could not remember it. It bothered him that he had forgotten so much – at university, swotting for his exams, he had been able to recall an entire page of a book just by visualizing it; and now here he was, vast passages of memory lost to him.

His greatest fear, since he had emerged confused and exhausted out of semi-consciousness, had been that his brain would never be quite up to things any more. The surgeon had reassured him that his head wound had not been deep and that the concussion would in time repair itself, but the fear haunted him. The medics were also optimistic that his leg would heal, though he would probably always walk with a limp. All the various injuries to his abdomen would knit themselves together eventually, he assumed. But it frightened him to think that his mind would never quite be clear again. 'It's because of who we are,' Minnie had said to him, when she had visited at the weekend. 'The Blacklocks. We rather pride ourselves on our brains, don't we? Do you remember how, when we were little, Pa would give us spelling tests while we were eating our dinner? Words like archimandrite and onomatopoeia and parallelogram. Even nowadays, whenever I eat treacle pudding, part of me thinks I'm going to have to spell some complicated word. The trouble is, we're afraid we'll be nothing if we're not brainy. And I don't think that's true.'

Think. There was something he needed to work out. What was it? He had asked Minnie to write to Kay. It had seemed to him of the utmost importance that he remember to ask Minnie to write to Kay – he had had a nurse scribble down a note for him and leave it on the bedside table to remind him. Then, today. Opening his eyes, he had seen her. It had been the first time in more than two years. He had felt a flood of relief and well-being. He had forgotten the pain of his injured body. Kay was with him and she was just the same, untouched by the war and as beautiful as ever, and everything was all right.

Kay's offer to write to Edie had taken him by surprise. Who had he thought of, who had he longed for, as he had travelled through the broken landscape of Italy? Not Edie, not any more.

It didn't take a genius to work it out. It seemed to him that somewhere along the line he had fallen in love with Kay. Could one fall in love *in absentia*, as it were? Perhaps it had always been there, like a seam of gold through a rock, and he had been too stupid to see it. His timing, never good, had become astonishingly poor. Kay was to be married in three days' time. He groaned out loud and the nurse, who was checking another patient's chart, turned, shaking her head. 'You need to rest, Captain Blacklock,' she said. 'I'll get you those painkillers now.'

Miranda went to the forest almost every day to collect firewood. Some days she took the boy, Erik; on other days she went alone, with only Gisela for company. Though the winter had passed, they must have firewood, for the kitchen stove and to heat water. She saw that their survival might depend on their having firewood. She had the remaining men, the older servants and the POWs, store the wood in different parts of the house and grounds, in case the Gestapo should come to the house and commandeer their fuel for the war effort.

Sometimes she went to the birch wood and sometimes to the pine forest. That afternoon, she chose the pine forest. She walked along pine-needle paths, gathering up fallen twigs and branches. Gisela ran ahead. Though the sun shone outside, inside the forest it was cold and dark. The air smelled of resin and rotten wood. She walked deeper and deeper into the forest, searching for a spot she had not foraged in before. She wore a mackintosh and leather gloves, because the pine sticks and twigs that she gathered were rough and sharp.

Gisela trotted back to her side and whined. 'What is it, my darling?' Miranda asked. In the cold enclosure of the trees, her voice lacked timbre.

She heard a rustle in the undergrowth and stood still, looking ahead. A deer, perhaps, or a wild boar. But then, another sound.

A voice. She bent, looped the lead round Gisela's collar, and put a finger to her lips. 'Quiet, Gisela,' she whispered.

The pine forest was on Sommerfeld land. Only the von Kahlbergs and their servants and tenants were permitted to hunt or collect firewood here. She walked a short distance ahead to where the trees thinned. She could smell woodsmoke. Through the narrow black columns of the tree trunks she saw figures – men, some sitting on fallen logs or beneath makeshift shelters, others standing, walking or smoking. She counted more than two dozen of them. They wore torn, filthy shirts, coats and jackets, peppered with an army tunic, a sailor's cap. A coil of smoke rose up from a fire with a cooking pot suspended above it. Water bottles hung from the branch of a tree. Occasionally someone spoke, but the distance muffled their voices and she could not distinguish their language.

Gisela gave a low growl. One of the forest men looked up and then took something from inside a shelter. He walked forward, away from the others, closer to where Miranda was standing. As he came towards her, she saw him more clearly.

His hair and beard were wild and unkempt and his eyes were hard and narrowed. His rifle moved in a slow arc. She stepped backwards, careful to tread only on the pine needles, never on a dry branch, and walked quickly away.

All the time, heading back along the narrow path between the trees, Gisela at her side, the bundle of twigs clutched in her arms, she felt their presence behind her and saw the black, circular mouth of the gun. She listened for the soft thump of running footsteps on pine needles, the hiss and thwack of a branch roughly pushed aside. Who were they, these men who lived in Sommerfeld's forest? Were they deserters or criminals? Or were they escaped prisoners of war, or perhaps Poles or Jews who had fled slave labour and transportation? She had heard that there were partisan camps inside the deep, dark forests of Eastern Europe, places of refuge for those who fled from terror, bases for those who were fighting back.

Out in the open, she still felt the prickle of danger. The spring sunshine fell on her but she was cold inside. She would go back to the house and warn the servants not to go deep into the forest any more. They were coming, the trespassers, the invaders. Sommerfeld was no longer safe.

After five weeks in hospital they sent Tom home to Cambridge. His mother looked after him, left him his lunch on a covered plate in the larder on the days she was working at Addenbrooke's, and reminded him to take his medicine. His father popped home between tutorials to say hello and spend a companionable half-hour continuing their chess game. When he was alone – and he was often alone – Tom made himself limp around Midsummer Common on crutches, throwing a stick for the dog. An icy east wind blew; Cambridge people always said it came straight from the Urals. Once or twice a friend called to see him, but most of his friends were away, in Italy or in Burma or ploughing the North Atlantic on a ship carrying supplies to Archangel or Murmansk. Others were holed up in army camps in southern England, waiting. They were waiting for the day they would cross the Channel and the battle to liberate Europe would begin.

Tom felt curiously separate from all the war news. Neighbours looked in and chatted to him and inquired after his health or talked about the war and asked him when he thought it would happen – it being the second front, of course. Soon, he always said, because they seemed to expect some sort of answer. One evening, his mother gave him a sharp look, and said, 'Not feeling miserable, are you, Tom?' and he was able to answer honestly that he wasn't, not at all. He didn't feel miserable and he didn't feel happy – in fact, he didn't feel anything much. It was as if the explosion of the mine had turned some switch in his head, wiping away his capacity for feeling. He could not see, in any way, what he would do next. He supposed that when his convalescent period was over – the MO had told him that it would probably be another three months before he was up to scratch – they would assign him to some sort of desk job. Translating, perhaps, because he had languages. But then, after the war ended . . . The future seemed dark and shapeless and utterly unenticing. He could think of nothing he wanted, he had no sense of purpose.

The east wind eased and was replaced by soft breezes and sunlight glimpsed through skittering clouds. On the horse-chestnuts on the common, great white candles bloomed. Tom was able to abandon the crutches and walk with the aid of a stick. He made himself walk a little further each day. Along the river, round the Backs, and then through the town. He thought he was limping less. What struck him was how kind strangers could be. Once, when he was pausing for breath, an older chap in civvies offered him a cigarette. Another time, when his leg hurt too much to stand and he had to sit down on the steps of a house in Bateman Street, a smartly dressed woman came out of the front door. He made to rise, but she patted his shoulder and told him not to get up, that he could sit there as long as he liked.

Slowly, he felt himself recovering. He was able, if he was not walking too far, to leave the stick at home. One day, he jogged along the towpath. His leg muscles were screaming by the time he reached Bridge Street, but he was in one piece and he felt so pleased with himself he celebrated with a pint in the Pickerel.

He began to travel further. He knew that he needed to get his confidence back, knew that only by pushing himself would he be able to believe that he was wholly well again. The posters at railway stations asked him whether his journey was really necessary, but he disregarded them – he had done his bit, he thought, and was due the odd train ride. He didn't plan, but bought a ticket and alighted at whichever little branchline station in the middle of nowhere took his fancy. Then he walked around fields, through woodland, alongside rivers. It seemed to him that the act of walking healed. He didn't mind waiting for trains that were cancelled or delayed or the hours spent in draughty waiting rooms.

One day he went to Lavenham. From the station, he made his way to the centre of the town. It was a beautiful day and the May blossom on the hedgerows made his heart lift. The sun was softly warm, so different to the desert sun.

Lavenham was as he remembered it, quaintly charming, but

like the rest of England, rather down-at-heel. Some of the medieval buildings, with their cantilevered frontages and oriel windows, were tumbledown, the thatch grey and mossy, the decorative plaster designs on the walls falling away from the clunch beneath.

A man sweeping the pavement outside a shop recommended a café for lunch. The Black Cat café was opposite the Guildhall. There were chequered curtains in the windows and a sign saying 'Open' on the door. A bell rang as Tom went into the café, where very old ladies sat at the tables, drinking tea and eating lunch. The floor was uneven and the tables were small and close together and the chairs spindly. Tom felt conspicuously large and clumsy; he was afraid of putting a foot wrong and tumbling tables, chairs and ladies to the floor.

A waitress in a pink chequered apron came and asked him for his order. After he had chosen something from the menu, he asked the waitress about Cold Christmas. The waitress knew Mrs Bowles, who had been Miles Culbone's housekeeper. Mrs Bowles, Tom discovered, had left Mr Culbone's employ when the house had been requisitioned. She was now staying in Shropshire with her sister. Mr Culbone had been permitted to remain at Cold Christmas, where he was living in the flat over the garage – the chauffeur's flat, it had been called while Tom was working there, though Miles Culbone had employed no chauffeur.

After he had finished his lunch, Tom made his way to a bus stop. Reading the timetable, he discovered that the bus passed Cold Christmas only twice a week, so he began to walk. Leaving the town behind him, he found himself heading along the familiar road, branched over with tall trees. When he had worked for Miles Culbone, he had driven this road twice a day, morning and night. In the beech woods, bluebells gleamed and sunlight glittered on the streams and ponds. Beyond the hedgerow, crops grew on every inch of fertile land.

He had walked for an hour and was tiring when a jeep drew up beside him. A voice called out, 'Want a lift?'

There were two American officers in the jeep. Tom told them he was making for Cold Christmas.

'Then you're in luck, pal. That's where we're heading. Hop in.'

As they headed down the road, the driver, steering the jeep one-handed, offered Tom a packet of Lucky Strikes. 'Help yourself. Cold Christmas – what a place. Plumbing's out of the Ark and I whack my head on a lintel every time I go into a room.'

They talked, of course, of the second front. *Any moment*, said the driver. Ike's waiting for fine weather, isn't he, but do you ever get fine weather for more than a day in this country of yours?

The jeep slowed as they reached the wrought-iron gates that barred the entrance to Cold Christmas's winding driveway. The driver spoke to the sentry and the jeep swung on to the gravel drive. For a moment it seemed to Tom that nothing had changed, but then, as they emerged from the woodland and saw the house, he knew that everything had changed. The courtyard was parked up with jeeps, cars and motorcycles. Half a dozen men were throwing a ball around the lawn. Through an open window, he could hear someone talking on the telephone. 'Whitehall three six seven. That's three, six, seven – thanks, honey, I'll hang on.' A *phone*, thought Tom, at Cold Christmas.

Leaving the jeep, thanking the officers for the lift, Tom was about to make for the grounds when a figure emerged from the house. Miles Culbone seemed to have shrunk in the six years since Tom had seen him. Always slight, he looked older

400

and thinner than Tom remembered, and he moved slowly, a stick in one hand, his other arm curled protectively round half a dozen books. Culbone's grey hair was sparse, his face hollow and lined, and his tweed jacket and trousers flapped loosely on his bent, fragile frame.

Tom crossed the gravel to him. 'Good afternoon, Mr Culbone. May I help you with those books?'

'Who's that?' Startled, Culbone froze, the books clasped to his chest. 'What do you want?'

'It's Tom Blacklock, Mr Culbone. Don't you remember me?'

'Of course I remember you,' Culbone snapped. 'Do you think I'm a fool?'

Culbone's eyes, behind the thick lenses of the glasses, turned towards Tom. But they did not focus, and Tom wondered whether Miles Culbone's eyesight, poor when he had worked at Cold Christmas, had deteriorated further.

Culbone said sharply, 'Why are you here, Mr Blacklock?'

'I thought I'd like to see the house again. I always admired it. I wanted to see whether it was still the same.'

Culbone made a disparaging sound. 'You can see what has become of it . . . Those young men have no conception of the value of my library. It is outrageous that such people should have been foisted on a house like Cold Christmas. Somewhere less precious could have been found for them, surely.'

'I doubt if they'll inconvenience you much longer,' said Tom coldly. 'I daresay they'll be clearing out of your way quite soon.'

'I hope you're right.'

As Culbone turned, the topmost book slipped from his grasp. Tom caught it, and said, 'Let me,' and took the stack of books from Miles Culbone.

'Yes, yes,' said Culbone irritably. He began to limp towards the chauffeur's flat. Then, to Tom's amazement, he added grudgingly, 'Thank you.'

Tom followed him, books in hand. What a pair they must make, he thought with wry humour, the old man and the young, limping across the gravel.

The garage and the chauffeur's flat above it was a small, square structure built of brick and weatherboarding, which stood at the far side of the house. Culbone opened the front door to the flat and went inside. Tom followed him up the steep, narrow stairs. Culbone climbed slowly, holding the banister, feeling his way in the gloomy light. It came to Tom that Culbone was now almost blind.

The stairs gave into a small, low-ceilinged sitting room with a sofa, an armchair and a great many books, stacked on shelves and piled on the floor.

Culbone fussed around, making sure Tom put the books in exactly the right place. Then, surprising Tom for the second time, he said, 'I suppose you want tea.'

'Tea would be terrific. Thank you.'

Culbone shuffled slowly into an adjacent room. Through the open doorway, Tom could see a tiny kitchenette. It was sparsely, and to Tom's mind, depressingly furnished, with table and chair and a single ring gas burner, over which Culbone placed a kettle. Beneath a net cover Tom could see the end of a loaf of bread and a glass jar with a few scrapings of something – jam, perhaps – inside it. Half a dozen tins stood on a shelf and there was a milk bottle on the window sill. Crockery was stacked in the scummy water in the sink. The room looked grubby, as did the room in which Tom was sitting. These were bachelor's rooms, the rooms of a man who has kept servants all his life and does not know how to manage without them.

The tea, when it came, was greyish and lukewarm. Tea leaves floated on the surface. They spoke for a while, Culbone complaining of the weather, the progress of his researches, the rowdiness of the American servicemen.

Then, suddenly, he coughed and said, 'Since you are here, perhaps you would do something for me, Mr Blacklock.'

Tom glanced quickly at him. 'Yes, if I can.'

Culbone had taken off his glasses and was polishing them. Without their covering of lenses, his eyes, a blurred dun grey, looked vulnerable.

'I need someone to write a letter to my solicitor. My eyesight . . .' Culbone paused. 'I am not well, you see.'

'I'm sorry to hear that.'

'Cancer.' Culbone made a quick gesture, silencing Tom. 'They say they cannot cure it. A relief, in some ways, I've always disliked hospitals. But there is the house. I have to make provision for the house.' Culbone reached out, in a gesture surely instilled by habit, for a book from the side table. His fingertips ran over the binding but he did not look down at the pages. 'It would be intolerable if Cold Christmas were to fall into the wrong hands. I have heard of old houses that have been broken up into flats.' Culbone said the word with loathing. He twisted his hands together. 'The house should stay in the family. The thought of Cold Christmas going to a stranger is intolerable.'

'Mrs Fielding has three daughters. Why not leave the house to one of them?'

Culbone's expression was contemptuous. 'Women. If my cousin had managed to produce a son . . .'

'Mrs Edith Dangerfield has a son. And she's always loved the house. You could leave Cold Christmas to her. I've met

Mrs Dangerfield's husband once or twice, and he's a cultured man, interested in history and the arts. And he's well-off – whoever inherits Cold Christmas would need to be able to afford its upkeep. I believe that Edie and her husband would look after the house.' Tom shrugged. 'It's only a suggestion. If you'll tell me where you keep pen and paper, I'll write your letter for you.'

After the fusty gloom of Miles Culbone's flat, it was a relief to be out in the open air again. There was a screech of car brakes as a jeep roared into the courtyard, sending up a skirl of gravel. 'Lavallo, you jerk!' someone shouted. Doors slammed and a flight of rooks rose up from the tall trees.

Tom walked through the grounds. In his pocket was the letter he had written to Miles Culbone's solicitor, asking him to call on Mr Culbone. He had promised to deliver the letter by hand to the solicitor's office in Lavenham.

In the herb garden, greyish buds had formed on the lavender, and bees hummed among the leaves of sage and thyme. A ginger cat dozed on a stone bench, one paw stretched out languorously. Tom looked up to the house. The oriel windows were dark and unrevealing; the face of a Green Man, rotund and haloed with leaves, gazed out from the high ochre walls.

Cold Christmas, which had so captivated him when he had first come to work here, captivated him still with its history and grace. The ball players had gone in, and, as Tom crossed the grass, heading for the trees that bound the perimeter of the grounds, Cold Christmas was quiet again. Near the slender white trunks of the birch trees the marble child still slept, protected by his columned catafalque. Tom circled the tomb, reading the inscription. *Erected in the year of his grief 1880 – CC.*

To lose a beloved wife and child within a few months of each other – now, that was grief indeed.

Old loves, long gone, long forgotten. Only the house, Cold Christmas, would endure. Why had he asked Miles Culbone to will Cold Christmas to Edie? Some sort of settling up, he thought. A full stop, a line drawn.

And as for himself – he stood for a moment, his eyes closed. His leg hurt, and so did his heart. Love, he had discovered, sometimes involved renunciation. Sometimes standing back and letting the one you loved live their own life was the best you could do for them. Kay was not his, and he had no claim on her. Friendship would be his only gift to her. There would be nothing more.

Tom crossed the lawn, walked back down the driveway and set off down the road to Lavenham.

Chapter Fourteen

And now it was almost over, the waiting. All leave had been cancelled and the troops that were to take part in the invasion of occupied France had been moved from the concentration areas to the marshalling areas, where they were encamped behind barbed wire and patrolled by sentries. The phone lines had been disconnected, the postboxes sealed, the men forbidden to communicate with the outside world. Southern England, which had during the first half of 1944 been turned into a vast military camp, was quiet now. Stores of ammunition had been moved on from the corrugated-iron dumps in which they had been secreted in Hampshire woods, vehicles had been stripped of their coverings of camouflage netting and tree branches and moved into place. The ships were massed at anchor in the mouth of the Solent, moored six and seven abreast, making ready to cross the Channel. In London, and in countless towns and villages across Surrey, Hampshire, Wiltshire, Dorset and Devon, the streets were empty. The GIs, with their endless supplies of sweets and chewing gum, had gone, along with the American bands that the local girls had loved to dance to. The dashing Polish officers, the charming Free French, the tall Canadians and smiling Australians – all had gone. The great railway stations of London were unpopulated, travel permitted now only for troops, and in streets that had been, until the end of May, clogged with military vehicles, the quiet was broken only by the whirr of a bicycle wheel or the clip-clop of a pony pulling a governess cart. Only a crushed hedgerow or the chipped corner of a house bore silent witness to the convoys of tanks, half-tracks and lorries that had rumbled through town centres and country lanes alike, heading for the army camps.

As soon as you woke in the morning, you put on the wireless to listen to the news. None of the rest of it – Italy, Russia, the Far East, the Pacific – seemed to matter so much now. Whenever you left your house or your office, your gaze flicked to the newsvendors' placards. There was an electricity in the air. You read the faces of your fellow passengers in the tube and the people you passed on the pavement. You waited.

Scorching heat at the end of May gave way to thunderstorms. Grey skies, choppy seas in the Channel. It couldn't happen, they said, in bad weather. Always, everywhere, a sense of expectation and fear.

Which is worse, Rowland had asked her, *the boredom or the fear? Boredom*, she had answered. *At least you feel alive when you're afraid.*

She was staying overnight at a camp in East Anglia. Woken at dawn, she climbed out of bed and went to the window. Pushing the blackout aside, Kay looked up. The girl who had come to stand beside her said, 'Gawd, there's bloody thousands of them.'

Red, green and yellow aircraft lights flickered across a sky the colour of steel. As their numbers increased, the black bodies of the aeroplanes almost blotted out the backdrop of sky. They were uncountable, wave after wave, the roar of their engines swelling, their vibration seeming to pass through the flimsy hut, through brain and bone, deafening, pulsating. She couldn't think, couldn't speak. She felt as if she was standing on a seashore and the storm waves were crashing around her.

The girl beside her said, 'You got someone going over there?'

'Yes, my husband. What about you?'

'Bloke I've been out with a few times.' The girl made a disparaging sound. 'He's a bastard – I know he sees other girls. He's cute, though.'

They had had such a short time together. They had married in a register office, neither of them being in the least religious. Rowland wore his uniform and Kay had worn a wedding dress of cream-coloured lace, altered by Aunt Dot from one of her own evening gowns. Freddie Covington had been their best man, Josephine her matron of honour. Kay had carried a posy of primroses and ivy. After the ceremony, they had gone back to Aunt Dot's house for the reception. Neither of them had much in the way of relations, but oh, so many friends. Rowland's army friends and friends from his civilian days, Kay's ATS friends and the brigadier and Brian from the bookshop and old friends from Oaklands, and neighbours and colleagues of Aunt Dot's from the magazine. The party, Aunt Dot had later written to her, had lasted into the night.

They had spent their honeymoon in Castle Combe in the Cotswolds. Narrow, winding streets, cottages of golden stone, RAF officers billeted in the boarding house, and a bed that creaked. In the day, they had borrowed bikes and cycled out into the countryside. At night, they had made love in the creaky bed.

Then, after forty-eight hours, they had returned to their separate barracks. You might almost think that nothing had changed. She had a wedding ring on her finger and she was called Lance-Corporal Latimer, but she still slept alone at night and still lived for his letters. A couple of times they managed to meet — a rendezvous on a railway station platform, lunch in a funny little pub near Aldershot one Sunday.

And then, embarkation leave. They spent it at the flat. It was the first time she felt properly married. They did ordinary things, slept in late, had breakfast in bed, then she unwrapped wedding presents and unpacked the suitcases she had brought from Aunt Dot's house. She hung her clothes in the wardrobe and put her toothbrush in the bathroom. She put a pot of geraniums on the balcony and covered the sofa with a length of blue and yellow cloth, bought years ago in Provence. Her photos stood next to his on the mantelpiece. A wedding portrait, taken on the steps outside the register office, and a photograph of herself and Miranda, in Antibes. They were wearing shorts, halter-necked tops and picture hats. They looked, Rowland said, like film stars. In the afternoon, they went out for a walk. Then they mooched around the shops and Rowland bought her a gold locket in a shop in Hatton Garden. Later, back at the flat, she cut a piece of his hair and enclosed it in the locket.

That was when the fear began: a fast beat of the heart, a squeeze of the belly. What if, she thought, this is all I have left of him? She damped it down, made herself be a proper soldier's wife, bright and cheerful and calm. She cooked dinner, which they ate at the mahogany table in the dining room of the flat. Rowland found some candles; the flame reflected in the satiny crimson-brown of the table top.

After dinner, they dragged the sofa out on to the roof garden, where they sat side by side, watching the sun go down, finishing a bottle of wine that Freddie Covington had given them as a wedding present. A pigeon cooed on a nearby roof and, in the distance, the last rays of sunlight caught the silver of the barrage balloons. Their conversation became fragile and intermittent, as tenuous as the wispy white clouds high in the sky.

Later, making love to him, his heart beat against hers and his breath was warm on her cheek. Afterwards, lying in his arms, she felt the rise and fall of his chest slow as he drifted off to sleep.

In the middle of the night, she woke and looked up to find him sitting on the edge of the bed. She knelt behind him, wrapping her arms round him. 'I keep thinking about it,' he said. 'I keep thinking about crossing the Channel and what it's going to be like on the other side. I haven't had to shoot anyone yet, you see. Only on training exercises and you don't really shoot people then, do you, unless you make some terrible mistake. What if, in spite of everything that's happened and everything I know, the bombs and what they've done to the Jews, what if I can't actually pull the trigger?' He shook his head. 'It's thinking that's the problem, isn't it? If we didn't think, we wouldn't be afraid. It would all be so much easier not to have an imagination, or if one could just put it aside until all this is over. I'm not sure I'm particularly made for times like these.'

She kissed and stroked him until desire flared again, erasing fear and doubt, so that there was only the two of them, alone in the darkness, and he pulled her back down on to the bed and she closed her eyes in the certain expectation of bliss.

In the morning, he went back to his barracks. She hadn't heard from him since.

Which is worse, the boredom or the fear? And how wrong she had been in her reply to Rowland's question, because the fear was far, far worse.

Because the brigadier was to go abroad to serve with the invasion force, Kay was now stationed at Camberley, training raw recruits to drive lorries. Fear – mixed with excitement – gnawed at her as she listened to the 8 a.m. bulletin on the wireless. *Paratroopers have been landed in northern France.* The invasion had begun. Fear was at the back of her mind as she went to the garage and was saluted by her recruits and began to explain to them how to service the lorries. They looked so *young*, all of them, schoolgirls almost, tugging at their scratchy khaki uniforms or putting up a hand to check their hair was neat. Had she ever looked like that, so young and raw and ignorant? Fear made her belly squirm as she lined up in the canteen for lunch, and made her jump whenever one of her trainees dropped a spanner. At night, lying awake in the darkness, she thought of Rowland. She thought of him at the marshalling camp, and then travelling to the docks. Then, boarding the ship and the long wait for the weather to fair up. He was a good sailor, he had told her, so at least he wouldn't have been seasick. Had he been cold, had he felt lonely, had he felt frightened as the ship weighed anchor and pulled out of the Solent?

Where was he now? Queueing for her supper that night, she had overheard someone say that hundreds of wounded men were already being shipped back to the Channel ports. Had Rowland crossed the Channel with the first wave of troops, or was his moment of taking the plunge, of diving into the unknown, still to come? Had his landing been easy, unopposed, or had they had to fight for the beach, inch by inch?

The next day she took her recruits outside to practise starting up the lorries and changing gear. Better to be outside, she told herself. More distracting. You always felt better in the sunshine.

In the afternoon, one of the other instructors, a small, dark woman called Valerie, came and chatted to her.

'How are your lot?'

'Not too bad, when they concentrate.'

'One of mine's an absolute sloven. Stood there polishing her nails while I was trying to explain about the carburettor.' Valerie looked at Kay. 'Are you feeling jumpy?'

'Rather.'

'Me too. I've smoked so many cigarettes my mouth tastes like an ashtray. Rowland's in infantry, isn't he? Ed's in the paras – someone told me that half of them didn't even make it to the landing ground.'

She didn't bother with supper that night. She lay on her stomach on her bed, and wrote a letter to Rowland, and when she had finished, she dug out *Rebecca* and read. She was half dozing, and she was at Manderley, wandering up the misty path, when the door opened.

Kay opened her eyes. A voice said, 'I say, Latimer, is that you? I've been looking everywhere for you.'

'Sorry, Corp.' She shuffled to her feet.

'The CO wants to see you.'

Kay tugged at her uniform, ran her fingers through her hair. The corporal retrieved her cap from where it had fallen beneath the bed. She dusted it off and handed it to her.

'Here, better not forget this.'

'Thanks, Corp.' And with that small act of kindness, and the expression in the corporal's eyes, the fear returned, flooding into her, chilling her, making her knees weak and her hands shake as she put on her cap.

Outside the Nissen hut, she told herself that she was being silly. The corporal was a decent sort, she mustn't read so much into every little word and action. It's OK, she said to herself, they're only going to tell me off about something. Or they'll have found me another officer and are taking me off training again.

Her footsteps pounded out a drumbeat. A pulse throbbed in her ears as she neared the CO's office. *If it is him, please let him be wounded. If it is him, please, please let him be wounded.*

For some time now, the refugees had been coming. They came from the cities in the west, escaping homes that had been reduced to embers and ash by Allied bombing, and, increasingly, in the spring and summer of '44, from the east, as the Red Army drew ever closer to East Prussia. First the Lithuanians arrived, hauling wagons loaded with their belongings, their livestock – a cow or a goat – roped to the back of the wagon. Then the people from Memel, on the Baltic coast. Miranda passed them on the road as she cycled back from the village. Herds of cattle flowed like brown and black waves over the roads and fields. She saw babies carried in cloth slings, bound to their exhausted mothers' bodies, and tiny grandmothers wrapped in shawls and blankets, perched among the cooking pots and bundles of linen on the wagons. So many of them. Sometimes there were refugees billeted at Sommerfeld. Sometimes, waking in the morning, they discovered that there were no eggs in the henhouse or that the cows had been milked dry, or bundles of firewood had gone from the barn. Tomas, the groomsman, took to prowling the fields, a shotgun in his hands. In the village, they muttered angrily about the foreigners.

The Gestapo came to Sommerfeld again. This time, there were four of them. They were searching for escaped prisoners, they told Miranda. They were polite, but they refused her offer of refreshment and no longer listened to her stories of hats being mistaken for game birds. As they searched the outbuildings and house, Miranda sat in the morning room, outwardly calm, inwardly calculating. Had they sent away that morning the correct amounts of butter and milk to be distributed by rationing? Would the Gestapo discover the side of bacon, hidden in the laundry, from the pig they had slaughtered against regulations last autumn? And, most importantly, had she remembered to turn off the radio? She was certain she had, certain that the BBC announcer, whose smooth tones she liked to listen to, could not still be relating German military defeats to an empty room.

One of the officers asked to see Sommerfeld's account books and records. Asked or demanded – his tone teetered on a fulcrum between the two. The heavy tread of his boots followed her as she led him to what had formerly been Franz's office. The officer sat at the desk, thumbing through the books, while Miranda took a chair, her face blank, her hands folded in her lap, as her heart raced.

No prisoners were found; the policemen went away. A few days later they heard the news that Allied troops had landed on the French coast, near Cherbourg. By 13 June, Rouen was in English hands. Miranda's spirits rose – surely the war would soon be over. Then a setback for the Allies: a wedge had been driven into the invasion forces and south-east England was being bombarded by a new weapon. The radio spoke of mass flight from London, of retribution for the terrible bombing raids that Germany endured.

At the end of June, cousin Katrin called at Sommerfeld to see the Countess. Since spring, the Countess had been confined to her bed. She had suffered a minor seizure which had left the right side of her body weakened. Katrin had married at the beginning of the year. She was now Frau Schäfer and was expecting her first baby. Beneath the yellow and white silk of her frock, her belly swelled. Gunter was delighted about the child, Katrin told Miranda, as they drank coffee in the drawing room. They both hoped for a boy.

Had Miranda heard from Friedrich? Katrin inquired. She hadn't seen him since he had come home for a few days the previous summer, Miranda explained, to recover from a minor wound. Since then, she had received only the occasional note, the last one arriving at Sommerfeld over three months ago. It was possible, Miranda thought but did not say to Katrin, that Friedrich was dead.

'I'm sure that, once the Russians are defeated, you'll be able to see a great deal more of Friedrich,' said Katrin. 'And then you must have another child, Miranda. It's a woman's duty to provide her husband with children.' With the self-satisfied smile of one who confides a wonderful secret, Katrin added that she had had the privilege of being invited to sit in Gauleiter Koch's box at the theatre the other night. Herr Koch – such an inspirational and gracious man – had told her that these wonder weapons, these explosive rockets that were devastating London, would soon have the English begging for mercy. Katrin patted her blond curls into place. People must have faith, she said. East Prussia must set an example to the rest of Germany; they must ensure that not one Russian set foot on German soil.

Miranda's disbelief must have showed on her face because Katrin gave her a sharp look. 'I suppose you don't feel quite the same as we do,' she said.

'What do you mean?'

'After all, you're not German, are you?'

'I'm not anything, really. I'm a hopeless mixture. A mongrel.'

Not the right thing to say. Katrin made an expression of distaste. As she gathered up her bag and gloves, she asked, 'Wasn't your father Russian? What was your name before you married, Miranda?'

'Denisov,' she said. She gave a light laugh. 'Miranda von Kahlberg sounds much more distinguished, don't you think?'

After Katrin had gone, Miranda went upstairs to her bedroom. She stood at the window, watching the car disappear along the linden-lined driveway. Katrin had a car. Katrin had petrol and a driver because Katrin was married to a high-ranking party official.

Miranda's gaze moved away from the window to where her dolls, the only two she had kept from the collection she had had before she had married, sat on a small wicker chair. There was the large, blue-eyed china doll her mother had given her for her sixth birthday, and the Little Red Riding Hood doll. She picked up the Little Red Riding Hood doll and twisted the head beneath the scarlet hood. Maiden, crone and wolf: the three faces stared back at her in succession. Cycling back from Angerberg to Sommerfeld the other day, a boy had thrown stones at her. *Foreigner*, he had called after her.

Dirty foreigner. The stones had landed in a puddle, splashing mud on to her stockings.

Now the air raids came as far east as Sommerfeld. Each night, Miranda toured the house, checking the blackout. Sometimes she heard the distant wail of the air-raid sirens and the thrum of the bombers overhead. Now, when they were among those whom they could trust, people spoke of escape. But where would they go – and *when* would they go? At what moment did you abandon your home, your farm, your livelihood, and take to the road, another refugee among thousands of refugees?

Now, the tenants and the staff came to her with their problems. If they were short of food or if they were struggling to clothe their children on a widow's pension, they asked her for help. Often, these days, Miranda ate her meals in the kitchen with Margret and the maids. When they were busy, she helped out in the kitchen. Darkness pooled in the corners of Sommerfeld's grand, high-ceilinged rooms.

Still, the refugees came. She fed those who were hungry and found clothing for those who were ragged. Shoe leather gaped open and their coats were inadequate for the thunderstorms that blew up at this time of year. There was always fear in their eyes, like the dart of a rat behind a barn door.

Storks nested on the chimneys and sunlight glittered on the lake. She was returning to the house early one morning after taking Gisela for a walk, a bundle of kindling tucked under her arm, when she looked up the linden avenue and saw a man heading towards the house. Another refugee, she thought. Another poor soul tramping through East Prussia in search of safety that didn't exist anywhere any more.

Then she looked at him a second time. Though his clothing

was dirty and dishevelled and his hair was overlong, there was a familiarity about his stride.

'Friedrich,' she whispered.

He could stay only an hour, he told her, and then he must return to his unit. He washed and shaved and then went to sit with his mother while Margret made him something to eat. Afterwards, Friedrich and Miranda sat in the orangery at the back of the house. Sunlight streamed through the windows and the trunks of the birch trees in the distant copse shimmered, white threads against a blue sky.

Russian troops, Friedrich said, were now little over a hundred miles from Rastenberg.

Miranda felt a flicker of dread. 'Cousin Katrin still seems to think that Germany will win the war.'

'Katrin always was a fool.'

'She's a great friend of the Gauleiter. She believes everything he says.'

A sideways glance to check that the door was closed, then Friedrich said, 'Koch is a fanatic and a criminal. He's already been responsible for the deaths of innumerable people in the Ukraine. I don't doubt that when it comes to it he'll save his own skin and he won't give a damn about anyone else, Katrin included. We'll hold off the Russians for as long as we can, but in the end they'll win. As for us, our troops are exhausted and depleted. Just now, the only rational course would be for us to admit defeat.'

'To surrender?'

'Yes. But I'm afraid that won't happen. Our leaders have never acted rationally, and the longer the tyrants and madmen continue to be in power, more innocent people will die.'

Friedrich gave a bitter smile. 'Soon, I daresay, they'll draft old men and schoolboys into the army.' A silence, then his voice dropped. 'I've longed for this. I've longed to come home just one last time. You are to leave Sommerfeld, Miranda. The Russians will destroy it. You must leave before they reach here. That's why I came here today, to tell you this.'

'Friedrich, I can't.'

'You have no choice. You should go to Anna, in Berlin. And then, as soon as you can, head west.'

'I can't leave Sommerfeld, Friedrich. I can't leave your mother.'

'My mother's dying,' he said roughly. 'We both know that. She knows it too. You can't sacrifice your own life for a dying woman. My mother wouldn't expect that of you. Listen to me, Miranda. I know what will happen to Sommerfeld when the Russians arrive. I beg you to do as I say.'

'I can't just walk away.' And yet, so often these past two years, she had imagined doing just that. Walking away, fleeing from a marriage that had died long ago.

He sighed, ran a hand through his hair. 'Try to understand. Before the invasion in nineteen forty-one, the officers of the Wehrmacht were told that certain "special orders" applied to Russia. In effect, the Russian people were deprived of any protection under the law. Our soldiers could do as they liked – they could rape, murder and loot, and they wouldn't be punished. I can assure you that those orders were carried out to the letter. Indeed, I've helped to carry them out.'

She stared at him. 'You, Friedrich?'

'What, not quite what you expected from your noble husband?' He gave a raw laugh. 'Then let me tell you how it happens. At first, you refuse. Then certain threats are made. Eventually, you say to yourself that you've no choice but to carry out your orders because, if you don't, your family will suffer. You say to yourself that, if you continue to refuse to do as you are ordered, they'll shoot you, and then you'll be no help to those who depend on you. I've even told myself that what I did, I did for you, Miranda.' He pressed his lips into a thin, hard line. 'I used to believe that I could stand aside from the war. That it wouldn't touch *me*. What a fool I was. I regret that I didn't stand up for what was right, whatever the consequences. I regret that bitterly. Then I could have died with honour, at least.'

'Friedrich,' she said. Her voice trembled. 'Please don't talk like this.'

'Others of my rank have had the courage to look for ways to rid us of Hitler and his cohorts, but I refused to have any part in their schemes. I told myself it was because I could see that they were hopeless, doomed to failure. My God, how I've lied to myself. Now, when I look back, all I can see is cowardice – and pride and arrogance and a mistaken belief that I can see clearly while others can't.' His fist thumped his palm; he shook his head slowly. 'I'll pay for what I've done. I'll pay a hundred times over. And I wouldn't dispute there's justice in that. Why should the Russians spare us when we didn't spare them? But you don't have to pay, Miranda. You must leave Sommerfeld.'

He took a map from the inside of his tunic and spread it out on the table. 'Come here,' he said.

She went to stand at his side. 'If, for any reason, you can't get to Anna in Berlin, there are others who'll help you. There's cousin Marta, in Allenstein, and the Lindners, in Braunsberg – you remember Hanna Lindner, we visited her that first summer. And the Kahns and the Sussmans – they're good people. I understand that you don't wish to leave my mother, and it does you credit, but . . .' His finger stabbed the map. 'If they overrun us, they'll come from the east, and perhaps the south as well. There is a danger that East Prussia will be cut off from the rest of Germany. From Pillau or Danzig you should be able to sail west, to Stettin perhaps. From Stettin you'll be able to travel to Berlin.' He threw her a sharp glance. 'You'll do as I say?'

'Yes, Friedrich.'

'Poor Miranda. I meant to give you something better than this. I should have let you go to Paris. I should have let you leave me in thirty-nine.'

Then he said, 'Tell me about him. Tell me about your lover. I won't be angry with you. I only want to know the truth.'

So long since she had said his name. It was hard to break the silence with it. Then, 'He was called Olivier,' she said.

She recalled with perfect clarity the day she and Kay had gone to the park. The spring sunshine, the scent of lilacs, a feeling of promise in the air. And a man sitting on a bench, reading a newspaper.

'Go on,' he said.

'I met him when my father and I were staying in Paris. We didn't know each other long. When my father found out, he wouldn't let me see Olivier any more. He sent Kay away and took me with him to Switzerland. I wasn't allowed to speak to anyone or to write to anyone.' She loosened her fists, then said, 'And then, a few months later, I met you, Friedrich.'

'The party in Grünewald,' he said. 'The polonaise.'

'Yes. You were so kind to me. At that time, I didn't think I'd ever see Olivier again. I didn't even know whether he loved me. When I agreed to marry you, it was in good faith.'

He had gone to the window. 'I think I knew even then,' he said softly, 'that you weren't mine to keep.'

The years had ravaged him. His once handsome face was gaunt and scarred by frostbite. His hair, which had been a pale reddish-gold when they had first met, had turned to silver.

She took a step towards him but he turned away from her.

'After we married . . .' he said. 'When you went to Paris to see your father . . .'

'We met by chance, in the street.'

'And you still loved him?'

'Please, Friedrich.' Another silence, then she said, 'I still loved him. And he loved me. And now – I believe he's dead. I've thought so for a long time. Olivier loved his country. He wouldn't have just stood by when France fell. He would have fought, and he would have gone on fighting.'

Friedrich rolled up the map and put it back inside his tunic. 'We can be loyal to the dead, Miranda.'

The expression in his eyes made her flinch. She murmured, 'I'm sorry I haven't been the wife you wanted. I'm sorry I've hurt you.'

'But then, you were always a dream,' he said softly. 'An intoxicating dream, and one that made me forget everything else for a while. But a dream, nevertheless.' He gave a short laugh. 'It makes no difference now. I have no future. None of us who remain here have a future.'

'What will you do, Friedrich?'

'What I have to do. I'll fight to the end.'

'On the wireless they said—'

'Everything you hear is lies, Miranda. We can't win. We are retreating on every front. We're short of fuel and men and we're abandoning trucks and tanks and weapons as we retreat. The most we can hope for is to try to stave off the Russians until our people can reach safety.'

'If the British and Americans reach here first—'

'Stalin won't allow that to happen. Stalin will want Berlin. He'll want to take his revenge. And to reach Berlin, he must take East Prussia first.'

She saw how vulnerable they were. He said, 'No matter what anyone says, and no matter how hard it is, you must leave Sommerfeld before the Russians get here. You must go west. You must *walk* to safety, if necessary, Miranda.'

Shortly afterwards, Friedrich left. Miranda saw him to the front door of the house.

'I've known for a long time that one day I would lose you,' he said. 'But this,' he gazed out over the front garden, towards the avenue of limes, 'to lose this, too – this is unbearable.'

Then he bowed, and walked away.

To begin with, what Kay felt most of all was anger.

Anger that she had been left alone. Anger that they had had, when you added it up, only a few days of married life. Anger that other women's husbands still lived when hers had died. Anger that Rowland, who had been loving and kind and brave, should have died in such a way, shot through the heart on a Normandy beach only minutes after he had left the landing craft.

After a week's compassionate leave, she went back to work. The anger had gone by then. She was always tired and, when she was alone, she cried. She couldn't sleep, couldn't eat, felt nauseous much of the time, and instructed her pupils with utter lack of heart, thinking all the time how *bland* they were, how young and blank-faced and unprepared. Sometimes, while she was speaking to them, she forgot what she was saying. Her mind drifted off and she was in the rose garden again, and

Rowland was breaking off a bloom and handing it to her. Or it was the night before he had had to travel to the marshalling area and he was sitting on the edge of the bed, talking to her of his fears for the days ahead. She'd blink, the memories would retreat, and she'd look up to find her recruits staring at her. Then she'd try to gather up her thoughts and carry on.

In the evenings, she tried to read, couldn't, but sat in an armchair in the mess anyway, a book open in front of her so that no one would talk to her. One night, she let Valerie persuade her into having a drink and ended up crying, couldn't stop herself, tears and snot pouring down her face, her hands wet, her hair wet, unable to get out a word, appalled at the void that yawned in front of her, unable to bear the thought of what he must have endured, leaving the landing craft, sliding into the sea, running through the waves to the beach. Dying.

In the flat, ghosts whispered as she sorted through his things. Socks and pants and hankies for the WVS. Old clothes – a school rugby shirt that can't have fitted him for years, a mackintosh with a tear in it – went into the bag as well. She found the letters she had sent to him in a chest of drawers, tied up with a piece of string. Her wedding photograph stood on the mantelpiece. I, Rowland James Latimer . . . with this ring I thee wed, with this body I thee worship.

She found tins of soup in a cupboard in the kitchen; she ate the soup cold out of the tin. She wore one of his old sweaters; though it was summer, she felt cold. At night, she curled up in the bed with the sweater, which smelled of him.

Tom came to the flat. She made an effort, tidied up a bit, cooked a pie out of an oddment of cheese, half an onion and a tin of peas. He still limped; she heard his uneven step, heading up the stairs. They'd given him a desk job, he told her. Once

425

more, he was being bored for England. 'To be honest, though,' he added, 'I don't mind. I seem to have had enough of adventure.' He was thin and tired-looking and looked as wrung-out, she thought, as she herself felt. Together they went through the paperwork, the bills and bank statements, the legal business involved with the inheritance of the flat, which Rowland had left to her.

At Camberley, she wasn't the only one, of course. There was the girl whose fiancé had been shot down during the Battle of Britain, the officer who'd lost her husband of six months at El Alamein. There was Valerie, whose husband had survived the landings and was now part of the Allied forces that were fighting their way towards Paris. There was the woman who worked in stores, whose son was in a Japanese prisoner-of-war camp in the Far East – though she smiled and was always pleasant, there was a dead look in her eyes. A whole community of women who waited or mourned. There was no consolation in that – if she was honest, she found no consolation in anything – but at least there were those whose company did not jar.

Sometimes, in the street, or when she was at Camberley, she thought she saw him. A man in army uniform, a long, gangling stride, a way of turning his head, a flash of a smile. A song they had loved – 'The Way You Look Tonight' – and she could almost see him, almost touch him. And then he was gone again, and each time her loss was unbearable.

She had lost him and with him she had lost her future. All the might-have-beens had been crushed to a powder and buried. What had she left? A lock of hair, a rose with dry, brittle petals, a wedding ring, a flat. His presence, which she still felt in the flat, would ebb away. The lock of hair would fade.

She was sick of the army and sick of the war. Now, she went

426

about her duties with only passable competence, doing just enough to avoid a reprimand. She wondered whether to apply for a transfer: she was starting to hate Camberley. She hated the food, the clothes, the conversation, the dreary familiarity of it all, and the new recruits, who, conscripts rather than volunteers, as she had once been, were so often, it seemed to her, lazy or stupid. Once, faced with a particularly trying half-dozen, she found herself shouting at them. Her voice, hard and sarcastic, reminded her of something. She sounded like Sergeant Preston, she realized, the harridan from her own days of basic training. Soon, she thought, she'd be cutting her hair in a lesbian crop. Soon, she'd have forgotten there was a world outside the army.

In the end, though, she didn't apply for the transfer. That was because by then she had realized why she couldn't do up her skirt, and why she felt sick and tired all the time, and why she hadn't had her period since May. The MO confirmed it on the day that Paris was liberated. She was pregnant.

At Sommerfeld, the Countess dreamed.

She dreamed it was harvest time. The music was playing and, as was the custom, she was to open the harvest dance with Sommerfeld's foreman. There was the smell of newly mown hay and she could see, in her partner's hair, a powdering of golden dust, from the wheat. She was wearing a long, full skirt of lilac silk, which whispered as it brushed the floor, and a spray of cream-coloured roses at her breast. She breathed in the scent of the roses. She had always loved to dance, but Paul had never cared to. The foreman, a tall, handsome man, was the best dancer at Sommerfeld, they said. When he took her hand and led her out on to the dance floor, her heart seemed about to burst with joy.

The Countess opened her eyes. The music had faded, but she still thought she could hear it. It sounded faint, as if the pipes and strings were far away in the distance. It was as if the music was calling her. Sunlight fell through the window in great golden squares. She yearned to see out, to see the roses growing against the walls of her garden and the scythed fields with their acres of golden stubble. The maid, who was sitting on a chair to one side of the room, had fallen asleep. The Countess clawed at the sheets. If she could only sit up . . . Her fingers gripped the pillow, fighting for purchase. The music was louder now. She could smell roses.

Then a tearing pain in her chest made her fall back on the pillows. Pain gripped her like a vice and she gasped. Her gaze fixed on the light from the window. Gleaming and gold, she watched it intensify. Then the darkness smothered it.

Kay was eighteen weeks pregnant the day she left the army. It was the one surefire way of getting your discharge, they always said: get yourself up the duff. The baby must have been conceived on Rowland's embarkation leave. His last gift to her, she sometimes thought.

At other times, she couldn't see how she'd manage, on her own, with a baby. She didn't know anything about babies. She had never been the sort of girl who played with dolls or knocked on neighbours' doors to ask if she could take their baby out in the pram. What if, looking at her child for the first time, she felt nothing? And how could she love it, this unexpected legacy, when she didn't feel capable of ever loving again?

And then there was money. She had the flat, her widow's pension, a small sum that Rowland had had in savings, and she would inherit the income from the copyright of Peter Latimer's plays. Would it be enough to feed herself and a child? And if not, how would she work and look after an infant at the same time?

The sickness had gone; her appetite, when it returned, was unpredictable. She craved the unobtainable and the rationed – oranges, bananas, a steak, a bacon sandwich. Once, she dreamed of a pomegranate and woke almost able to taste the burst of juice from the jewelled ruby seeds. The greengrocer, a kindly man, who told her that her smile made his day, saved treats for her – a bag of plums, some hazelnuts and, once, a quince. She held it to her nose, breathing in the peppery scent as she walked home from the shops.

Autumn came. The first of the V-2 rocket bombs struck Chiswick on 8 September. One night, Kay was woken by an explosion so immense it seemed to pass through her like an electric shock. The flat shivered, the earth vibrated. In the morning she saw that several of the windows in the flat were broken. From the balcony, she looked down on the crater that the rocket bomb had made. A row of tall houses had once stood there: there was no trace of them now.

That afternoon, she wrote to Virginia Lancaster. Oaklands School had been evacuated to Devon at the beginning of the war and was sharing the premises of a boys' prep school. Virginia wrote back by return of post. Kay must come and stay for as long as she liked, she said. If Kay wished to do a little part-time teaching then that would be marvellous, but she was under no obligation, none at all.

Kay packed her suitcase, locked up the flat, and caught the train to Devon. She knew, as soon as she arrived at the school, that she had found a sanctuary. Perched on the edge of Exmoor, the old house and outbuildings nestled in a deeply wooded combe. To the east was the high moorland and to the west lay the coast of the Bristol Channel. In the mornings she taught, and in the afternoons she walked through the woods. Coppery leaves drifted on to the paths. Streams rushed beneath narrow bridges and, as the weeks passed, the air became tinged with the cold of the coming winter. That autumn, she walked out her grief, pressing it step by step into the red Devon soil.

She didn't read the newspaper any more and she didn't listen to the radio. The war, which had taken from her the man she loved, would roll on, crushing the innocent and the guilty, the defeated and the victorious alike, but she would have no further part in it. Her old conviction, that war was destructive and immoral, and that it must be avoided at all costs, reasserted itself, stronger than ever. I'm not sure I'm particularly made for times like these, Rowland had said to her. Neither am I, thought Kay. Neither am I.

Chapter Fifteen

In October, Russian soldiers crossed the East Prussian border. Newspapers and cinema newsreels reported the atrocities at Nemmersdorf and other border villages. Hardly any of the inhabitants had survived. Children had been murdered, women raped and then butchered. When German troops retook the area shortly afterwards, they discovered bodies strewn on compost heaps and nailed to barn doors.

Now, when they were working in the kitchens at Sommerfeld, the women discussed not the state of their children's health, nor the letter they had received from their husband, but how to acquire poison. How much strychnine a woman must take to kill herself. Where to find the fungi that killed quickly and cleanly. Though Miranda missed the Countess, who had died at the end of September, she was at the same time thankful that the Countess, who had loved Sommerfeld, had not survived to see such times.

Though the Countess had gone, Miranda herself was not yet able to leave. Posters had gone up in the towns and villages, printed on the orders of Gauleiter Koch. Any civilian who tried to flee their home, or was found to be preparing to flee their home, could be shot on the spot. Miranda put through a call to the government office, asking for a permit to travel to Berlin. Her request was refused.

You were forbidden even to speak of leaving East Prussia, because to do so was to acknowledge that defeat was possible. The wireless still proclaimed German victories and hinted at wonder weapons that would change the course of the war. Yet when, after she had closed the drawing-room door and turned the sound down, Miranda tuned the radio to the BBC, she heard a different story. In the west, France had been liberated, and so had Brussels. In the east, Hitler's armies had withdrawn from Estonia, Romania had signed an armistice with the Allies, and Soviet troops were drawing close to Budapest.

Thousands of Hitler Youth had been sent to East Prussia to dig defensive trenches, on the orders of Gauleiter Koch. In the towns and villages, the horror of war was written in the limping gait of the amputees on crutches and on the disfigured faces of the soldiers in the streets. *You are to leave Sommerfeld and you are to travel west as fast as you can*, Friedrich had told her. She understood. She planned.

They were a strange company at Sommerfeld, these days. There was Great-Aunt Elsa who, alarmed by the increasing proximity of the front, had left her home in Goldap to the east and moved, with her suitcases, her black astrakhan coat that reached to her ankles, and her canary in its cage, to Sommerfeld. Great-Aunt Elsa was short and plump and her gentle grey eyes and snub nose were set into the soft, pouchy folds of her face. She had been widowed for more than twenty years, after her husband, Friedrich's father's uncle, had died of pneumonia, leaving her with a small annuity to live on. She always remembered family Christmas and birthdays, marking them with a letter and a thoughtful gift. Arriving at Sommerfeld, she had asked Miranda for news of Friedrich. She had heard nothing, Miranda said, and the old lady had pressed her hand, tears in her eyes.

Then there were the Misses Kestners. The Misses Kestners were acquaintances of Katrin's, three unmarried sisters in their late thirties from Königsberg, whose home had been destroyed in the RAF bombing raid in August that had obliterated almost half the city. They wore calf-length dresses made of some stiff woollen material, coloured bottle-green, navy or maroon. Pearl brooches were pinned to their flat bosoms. They complained of the cold as they sniffed into their embroidered, lavender-scented handkerchieves. Fervent Nazis the three of them, devoted admirers of Hitler and Gauleiter Koch, they discussed complacently over their morning coffee how any Russian daring to set foot on German soil would be sent packing, as they had been after the border incursions of October.

And there were the refugees, of course, the continuing river of the dispossessed that poured along the roads and byways. At first, Miranda housed them in the barns and stables. Then, as the winter became colder and the snow deepened, they took shelter inside the house. Rooms that had once known only the muted whisper of a silk frock or the tap of a high-heeled shoe now resounded to the howls of hungry children and the snores of adults worn out by their long journeys. Black-shawled grand-mothers jostled with the maids in the kitchens. Arguments erupted over a missing jar of pickles, a trail of muddy foot-prints across an Aubusson rug.

Wrapped up in the fur coat her father had given her for her sixteenth birthday, Miranda toured the house, walking from room to room, peering into cabinets and chests. The barley sugar stem of a glass goblet, a blue butterfly perched on a porcelain cream jug, a silver mermaid. These were the treasures that Friedrich's ancestors had collected over the centuries. She ran the back of her hand over the cool satin covering of a sofa. What should she take with her on her flight? The Dürer engravings in Friedrich's study? The Meissen figurines?

Nothing. These things had never been hers and she would take none of them. Konstantin Denisov had left Russia with a pebble and a shell in his pocket. Well, then, she was, in the end, her father's daughter. In her bedroom, she took a small rucksack and put inside it a torch, matches, soap, handkerchiefs, warm gloves and socks, bandages and salve and a flask of brandy. Then her most precious possessions: her passport, the title deeds of the London house and the papers her father had given her, on which he had listed the numbers of his bank accounts. And a ceramic bluebird, a plump ceramic bluebird that had once bobbed in the window of an apartment in Paris. Remembering her White Russian friends in the Rue Daru, and how the women had hidden their jewellery in their clothing when they had fled Moscow and St Petersburg, she unpicked the hem of a warm woollen skirt and sewed into it her most valuable pieces: her emerald bangle, a sapphire pendant that had once belonged to her mother, the string of black pearls Friedrich had given to her.

In the stables were the flat, open hay carts that they used to take the women to the woods to pick wild strawberries or mushrooms. Only four horses now remained at Sommerfeld:

434

all the others had been commandeered for use at the front. Miranda carried wicker baskets to the stables and packed inside them food that would not perish: cheese and dried sausages and bottles of pickles and fruit. Inside the house, she spread out a map on the desk in Friedrich's study. *They will come from the east and perhaps the south as well.* Allenstein, Elbing, Braunsberg, and the ports of Danzig and Pillau – she traced the routes to each of them with her fingertip. The location of the river crossings, the railway stations, the homes of friends and family: she must remember where they were. Which road would be best for winter travel? Which would not become blocked by snow or flooded by a sudden thaw? Because she must leave in the winter. She must leave soon.

She had almost finished her preparations, and was at breakfast one morning when Margret came to tell her that an official had called at the house.

Miranda went to speak to him in the hall. He was wearing steel-rimmed spectacles and his dark hair was sleeked back like an otter's. He introduced himself as a representative of the Gauleiter.

'I have received information, Gräfin,' he said, 'that you are making preparations to leave the area.'

She felt a rush of fury, which she crushed down. 'Who told you this?'

'I regret I can't say.'

'You were misinformed,' she said coldly. 'It isn't true.'

'You are to show me the stables, Gräfin.'

His footsteps sounded behind her as she crossed the path the French POWs had swept through the snow in the courtyard to the rear of the house. She thought of the boxes of food and the blankets and tarpaulins she had stored inside the cart.

Her mind seemed as frozen as the icicles hanging from the gutters. She pushed open the stable door. *Think.*

In the stables, he strode ahead of her, peering inside the buggy and the coach. Then the hay wagons. One of the horses in the stalls whinnied, and Miranda's breath caught in her throat. He frowned, looked again, and made a triumphant sound as he flung open the lid of one of the wicker baskets and drew out a jar of pickled cauliflower.

Miranda shrugged. 'I'm afraid we've had to store some of our food in here because of the refugees. They steal things from the pantry, you see. They can't be trusted.' Her voice authoritative, perhaps a little bored.

As he put the jar back in the basket and let the lid fall, she glanced quickly into the cart. The blankets and tarpaulin had gone.

She injected a little more boredom into her voice. 'Is that all?'

'For now, yes, Gräfin.' He had the look, she thought, of a fox who has been kept from the chickens. He gave her a curt nod. 'Be sure to remember that you can be punished severely for making preparations to evacuate.'

'Yes,' she said. 'So I've heard.'

After Margret had seen the official off the premises, Miranda returned to the dining room. The Misses Kestner, she noticed, evaded her gaze and applied themselves with great concentration to their breakfast eggs.

As soon as she had breakfasted, she went to find Margret. The blankets, the tarpaulin, she murmured. Erik has hidden them, Margret explained. She had sent him to the stables while the gentleman was speaking to the Gräfin in the hallway.

'Thank you.' Miranda squeezed Margret's hand.

Shortly afterwards, she told the Misses Kestner that they would no longer be able to have their jug of fresh coffee in the drawing room at mid-morning. They had run out, she lied; the sisters would have to drink ersatz. There was a pleasure in seeing the outrage on the Misses Kestners' faces, and a pleasure, later that day, in sitting in the kitchen with Margret and Great-Aunt Elsa, drinking delicious coffee made from their shrinking supply of beans.

You are to leave Sommerfeld. Friedrich's words haunted her as she went about her duties. But how? And when?

Christmas. The Misses Kestner had left the house two days earlier, triumphantly clutching their train tickets to Berlin, allocated to them as party members.

This year, no Christmas tree stood beside Sommerfeld's great staircase, decorated with wooden ornaments and candles. Miranda, Great-Aunt Elsa, the POWs, the servants and some of the refugees dined together. Miranda had scavenged gifts from cupboards and chests – gloves, mufflers, a coat, a pair of boots. They slaughtered and roasted three fowl and opened the best bottles of wine from the cellar – no point, someone said, in leaving them for the Russians.

After dinner, they sang carols in the drawing room, in front of a log fire. Later, Miranda put on a record, something contemporary and light, from a musical, perhaps, not Friedrich's usual taste.

One of the POWs, a quiet, cultivated man called Henri, who had worked for a Parisian publishing house before the war, drew Miranda aside.

'Some of my friends,' he said, 'are talking of leaving before the Russians reach here. They're afraid of leaving it too late, of being caught up in a retreat.' He ran a hand over the bald dome of his head. 'Armies in retreat are never orderly, madame. I remember France in nineteen forty. The retreating soldiers, the refugees fleeing their homes – and the Boche pursuing us, of course.'

'You should be safer than most, surely,' she said. 'You're French – and you're prisoners of war.'

'I doubt if that will make much difference. We're talking of men who've fought their way from Moscow to the German border. They've been at war – a particularly cruel and destructive war – for three and a half years without respite. They've endured every horror it's possible for human beings to endure.' Henri gave a small smile. 'I don't think they'll stop to ask me my nationality.' He added pointedly, 'Or yours, madame.'

There was a day, not long after, when she woke to find that the POWs had gone. That morning, she once more phoned the office that issued travel permits; again, her request was turned down. Now, the refugees heading west through the deep snow were German civilians evacuated from the border towns. The Red Army was massing along the border, the refugees told her. Cold and exhausted, they took shelter in the stables, and then, after a night's rest, moved on, always heading west.

Old men and young boys were pressed into the Volkssturm, armed with cumbersome fowling pieces and revolvers from the previous century. Margret wept as her seventy-year-old father, who worked in the dairy, and her grandson, Erik, who was only fourteen years old, were marched out of the estate along with other lads and old men.

That evening, Miranda toured the barns and stables, ensuring that the doors were locked. In the bitterly cold weather, her feet crunched on the snow and her breath and Gisela's made clouds in the icy air. The darkness was absolute except for the dimmed light from her lantern, which gleamed palely on the snow flurries. The silence was broken by the low rumble of planes overhead and, from somewhere in the distance, the clatter of military vehicles.

She opened the door to the henhouse and looked inside, and her heart leapt to her mouth as her gaze locked with that of the man sitting in the straw. He was young, his face was unshaven and his eyes were wild. He was wearing the uniform of the German army. A deserter, she thought. As he scrambled to his feet, his hand went to his overcoat pocket and he drew out a knife. The hens clucked, disturbed in their roosts.

The blade flickered in the darkness. Miranda held up her hands, palms out, and said quickly, 'It's all right, you can stay here, I won't tell anyone.' She saw him glance over her shoulder, out into whirling snow. 'I promise you.'

As she turned to go, he spoke to her. 'You should leave here,' he said. 'They're coming. We can't stop them. No one can stop them now. They're coming.'

The next morning, the deserter was gone. After breakfast, Miranda walked to the road that lay at the far end of the alley of limes. What she saw made her shiver and grip the lapels of her coat tightly to her throat. The river of humanity had swelled; now it had become a sea, tumbling and pouring over the country-side of East Prussia. There were hay carts and wagons, loaded high with family belongings. Black-shawled peasant women pushed prams and wheelbarrows. Children perched on pony traps, their faces pinched with cold, and horses' hooves skit-tered on the icy ground. And above it all were the sounds of

439

the exodus, the lowing of the cows, the grinding of cartwheels on snow, and the thin, high wail of a baby.

Miranda's gaze darted, noting the grey uniforms of soldiers dotted among the mass of people. One of the soldiers was carrying a machine gun, others had small arms.

She stopped one, and asked him where he was heading. Fleetingly, his eyes fixed on her. 'Haven't you heard?' he said. 'The Russians have broken through.'

'Are we to be evacuated? Are we free to go now?' But he did not answer; he had already walked on.

Miranda hurried back to the house. The food, blankets and tarpaulins were packed into the carts. Their route was decided. They would leave Sommerfeld that morning.

And then, to her frustration and anger, the servants refused to leave. An entire morning wasted in fruitless argument and coercion. The delay infuriated her, frightened her.

'You must make them see reason,' she told Margret impatiently, as she drew her aside in the kitchen. 'We can't wait any longer.'

'They won't go, Gräfin,' said Margret gently. 'They were born here. They've never lived anywhere else. And how will their fathers and husbands and sons ever find them again if they were to go away?'

'They may never see their menfolk again anyway. They may as well save themselves.' Miranda's fists were clenched. 'Very well, I shall order them to leave.'

Margret's hand on her sleeve stopped her from leaving the room. 'No, Gräfin. Let them be. It'll be hard enough, taking the old lady with you.'

Miranda stared at the housekeeper, registering her words. 'But you, Margret, you'll come with me, won't you?'

Margret shook her head. 'I'll wait here for my father and Erik.'

It was on the tip of Miranda's tongue to point out that old Helmut and Erik might already be dead, but she swallowed the words down.

So there were, in the end, just the two of them, herself and Great-Aunt Elsa. In the stables, Miranda unloaded some of the blankets and food from the hay cart into the two-seater buggy. In the icy air, her fingers fumbled with the stiff leather buckles of the harness. Gisela, crouching in the straw, whined.

Kneeling down, she wrapped her arms round the dog's neck. 'I can't take you with me, my darling,' she murmured. 'I won't be able to take enough food for you, you see.'

Great-Aunt Elsa, dressed in tweeds and her black astrakhan coat, was waiting for her in the hall. Miranda helped her on to the seat of the buggy. She said goodbye to Margret and the other servants, and then, for the last time, headed out of the courtyard and along the alley of limes.

She looked back only once, as they reached the top of the incline. Sommerfeld lay behind her, pale and graceful, its snow-covered roof glittering in the fading afternoon light, its pillars and porticoes the frosted white of a wedding cake, looking, in that final moment, as magical and untouched as the very first time she had seen it.

She made for Rastenberg. They would catch a train from Rastenberg to Elbing, she explained to Great-Aunt Elsa, and from there they would continue on to Danzig or Berlin, whichever was possible. It should take them an hour, maybe two, she estimated, to reach Rastenberg, which was about eighteen miles away.

It took six hours. The roads, clogged with traffic and people on foot, reduced their speed to a snail's pace. Every so often they would come to a halt as something – a broken-down cart, a car that had run out of petrol – impeded the procession. The verges and fields were strewn with possessions – a set of dinner plates, a chest of drawers, a sewing machine – cast out of a handcart or bundle when it became too heavy to bear. Families sat in the snow, the children gathered on to their mothers' laps, feeding on scraps of bread, resting from their journeys.

So many women. Women drove the carts, women led the horses, women carried their children on their backs and drove the livestock. Toothless old women lay in handcarts, pushed by their sturdier daughters, and small girls, their noses pink and their blond plaits peeking from beneath their woollen hats, walked hand in hand beside them. Among them were a leavening of men, soldiers in retreat, an old man limping, pausing to rest every step or two on a stick, and half a dozen young boys wearing the black armbands of the Volkssturm militia. Their faces, wrapped in scarves and caps, were children's faces, smooth and soft. One carried a *Panzerfaust* – a bazooka. Others wore school satchels.

Darkness fell. The moon was at first a dull silver sickle in a charcoal sky, and was then masked by the thin mist that crept over the low-lying land. Miranda's hands, clutching the reins, were frozen into curls, like the crescent moon. Steering the pony and trap between the pedestrians, she noticed that now hardly anyone spoke. All effort, every scrap of energy, was concentrated on putting one foot in front of the other. The sounds of the exodus were reduced to a child's whimper, the bark of a dog, the soft pad of footsteps on snow, the creak of a cartwheel.

With the night came the aeroplanes. Lanterns were extinguished and torches switched off. Miranda had to strain her eyes, struggling to find in the dark the turn-offs to Rastenberg. She was afraid of being swept along in this sea of people, of being caught up in their flight, of becoming lost. The planes flew on. A flicker of lamplight, the rasp of a match. They were heading up a long, shallow hill. As they neared the summit, the driver of the cart in front glanced over her shoulder, looking back. A whisper. Another woman looked back, gave a darting glance.

She couldn't make out the whispers. At the top of the hill she too looked down. Orange lights, bursts of colour against the black silk of the night, burned on the horizon. She pressed her hands against her mouth. Now she knew what the women were saying.

They are burning our farms. They are burning our villages.

Rastenberg, and no prospect of driving even the narrow buggy through the crowded, chaotic roads. Every inch of every street was packed, private cars jostling nose to tail with military vehicles — a truck, an armoured car, a gun carriage. Horns hooted, a man in SS uniform fired a gun into the air, and vehicles shoved their way on to the pavements, careless of pedestrians. The low, dispersed light from the headlamps carved shadows into faces, as if the skull had begun to show through the skin.

Miranda helped Great-Aunt Elsa out of the buggy, shouldered her kitbag, and picked up the wicker basket containing food and blankets.

'The station?' asked Elsa.

Miranda nodded. 'Can you walk?'

'Most certainly.' Elsa gave a brave smile, linked her arm through Miranda's, and they set off.

It was a struggle to make their way through the churning people. Soldiers pushed past them; she felt the older woman flinch as they barged against her. A little girl, wrapped up in a shawl and headscarf, stood beneath a street lamp, weeping. An official wearing a swastika armband and blowing a whistle held out an imperious hand, halting the crowds to allow the progress of a huge black Daimler. The women inside the car wore lipstick and smart little hats.

As they neared the station, the crowds thickened. Ambulances painted with a red cross forced a path through the throng. As each ambulance made its way through the entrance into the station, people swarmed into the gap left by its wake. Miranda felt as if she had become caught up in a current, swept in a wave towards rocks. Great-Aunt Elsa stumbled and it took all Miranda's strength to haul the old lady upright so that she was not crushed beneath the crowd. She took the wicker basket in her right hand and tucked her left arm round Elsa's waist as the force of the crowd carried them towards the entrance to the station. Elsa was shorter than she was; the weight of the basket made her shoulders ache.

They were inside the station. She tried to push towards the ticket office, then saw how pointless that would be and let the movement of the crowd take her in the direction of the platforms. *You must go west*, Friedrich had told her. Well then, she would catch the first train west, to Braunsberg or Elbing or Marienberg. Anywhere.

On the platform, people were crushed forty or fifty deep, and the crowd had become a living entity, gathering itself up, rushing out to the edge of the platform, then surging back, crushing those contained inside it so that it was hard to breathe. Mothers wept, separated from their children; on the fringe of the mob, a girl jumped up and down, calling out and waving her arms.

Standing on tiptoe, Miranda made out, at the far end of the platform, a gap in the crowd. Again, she and Elsa forced a path through the milling people as, with a shriek and a grinding of pistons, a train pulled into the platform. The crowd swelled forward. Something was announced over the tannoy – Miranda could not make out the words. There was the sharp report of pistol shots and the crowd swayed back.

She headed for the gap, Aunt Elsa's hand in hers. A final shove, and then she was standing at the edge of the mass of the crowd, and she saw them for the first time, the men lined up on stretchers or lying uncovered on the concrete floor of the platform. Young men and old men and boys, their uniforms bloodied, torn and filthy, hundreds of them, a terrible, uncountable number, their wounds hideous, their suffering palpable. Her gaze ran, mesmerized, from man to man. She saw faces that had been shot away, mutilated limbs, gaping holes in abdomens. She saw a motionless figure whose head was a mass of reddish-brown bandages; she heard the keening of another, like the howl of a wolf. There was the warm, sickly smell of blood. Her stomach rose, and she turned her face away, biting her teeth sharply into her lip. As the train drew to a halt, doors were flung open and medical attendants began to load the wounded men into the carriages.

After a while, the train pulled out of the station. Great-Aunt Elsa, at her side, was swaying like a leaf. To one side of the platform Miranda spotted a small waiting room. She told Elsa to hold on to the back of her coat as she began, once more,

445

to force a passage through the crowds. There was no space in the waiting room but she found a scrap of outside wall, put the wicker basket against it and helped the old lady sit down on the basket.

'I'm going to fetch the buggy,' she said. 'Will you be all right?'

'You mustn't worry, dear.' Elsa managed a smile. 'I'll just have a little rest.'

'We'll ride on and catch a train from a station further west.'

'An excellent idea. I'm sure it'll be less crowded if we travel west.'

Again, that seemingly endless, exhausting journey through the crowds, this time back into the town. Outside the railway station, she clung to the trunk of a sapling while she tried to remember where she had left the horse and buggy. Yes — she had tied it to a railing outside the draper's shop. She pushed her way through the throng that was still pouring into the station. It was hard now because her direction lay against the flow of the crowd, yet her progress was eased by the absence of the old lady and the wicker basket.

A party of men in grey overcoats, carrying suitcases, stood outside the draper's shop. She peered round them, trying to see the spot where she had left the horse and buggy.

It wasn't there. She looked again, back and forth, along the road. The railings were empty. Wildly, she elbowed her way towards the street, trying to pick out the Sommerfeld horse and trap from all the other vehicles.

She couldn't see it. She sank back against the railings. Her heart was pounding and she felt close to tears. Someone had taken the buggy. Of course someone had taken it. How could she have been so stupid as to leave it there? She was shaking, with exhaustion, with anger at her own foolishness, and most of all with fear. What should she do? Should she walk back to Sommerfeld and take one of the hay carts instead? Every instinct told her to press on, to travel west as quickly as possible. She wiped her eyes on her sleeve and began to make her way back to the station.

She had decided they would take the train after all, she said to Great-Aunt Elsa when, at last, she reached the platform. A train must come soon. Elsa took a flask of coffee out of the wicker basket and poured a cup and gave it to Miranda. She was sure that Miranda had made the right decision. She told Miranda of a similar flight she and her husband had undertaken, during the first war – they had travelled through the night in their coach and four, she said, to escape the army of the Tsar. Rather exciting, though it had been frightening at the time. As Elsa spoke, and as they drank their coffee, crouched by the wall of the waiting room, Miranda's panic receded.

Hours passed. Trains came and went. Sometimes they took only the wounded; at other times they went east, carrying supplies to the front. In the early hours of the morning, a train full of soldiers drew into the station. Word ran along the platform that the train would take no civilians; a collective moan of despair rose up from the waiting people.

Miranda found herself looking up into the face of the soldier standing at the carriage door. Her eyes met his; she felt herself mouth the word: *Please*. And then, a miracle: he reached out a hand to her and pulled her on to the running-board. Another hand, and Great-Aunt Elsa and the wicker basket were on the train beside her.

Where were they going? she asked the soldier, as the train pulled out of the station. Elbing, he said, and she gave a great sigh of relief. She found a few inches of space in the corridor for Elsa to sit down on the basket and then, kept upright by the men she stood between, swaying with the gathering rhythm of the carriage, she closed her eyes and slept.

When she opened her eyes, the train had stopped. Dazed and disorientated, she looked round. Outside, she could see only blackness. Her soldier, the soldier who had helped her on to the train, was leaning out of the window and looking down the track.

'What is it?' she said.

'I don't know. I can't see.'

A long wait. She found herself concentrating hard, as if she could force the train to move again by the strength of her will, so that they could reach Elbing and safety. It was warm in the crowded carriage and there was the smell of bodies and the damp wool of the soldiers' overcoats. Aunt Elsa, crouched on the wicker basket, dozed.

The soldier looked out of the train once more. He rubbed his eyes. 'Something's burning,' he said. Following his gaze, Miranda saw against the black of the night the unnatural haze of reddish light she had glimpsed earlier, when she had looked back on her journey to Rastenberg.

They waited. At last there was a shudder as the train shook itself and began to move. But her initial relief was replaced by alarm: they were heading the wrong way, east, back along the track they had just taken. She stared at the soldier in horror; he shrugged, leaned against the door, and closed his eyes.

Not long afterwards, the train juddered to a halt again. She heard the sound of doors being flung open and raised voices. The Russians had reached Elbing, someone called out. All civilians were to leave the train.

The carriage door was opened, letting in a blast of icy air. A rough voice ordered them to climb out. And then she was standing on a railway platform once more, Great-Aunt Elsa and the wicker basket at her side, and the train was drawing away and disappearing into the distance.

The shock of being out in the freezing air again. The sense that she was miles from civilization, and that she was almost alone, and lost. At first, only opaque blackness spread away from the platform. Then, as her eyes began to accustom themselves to the darkness, she was able to pick out the straggle of refugees, ejected, like herself and Elsa, from the train. Then the flat fields to either side of them, covered in snow.

She did not know where she was. She did not know where she should go. Panic rose in her throat; it was hard, this time, to choke it down. Great-Aunt Elsa, sensing her despair, pointed out to her that they had travelled west for some hours, and so must be safer than if they had remained at Sommerfeld or Rastenberg. Miranda was too cold and too frightened to smile, but managed to say, 'Yes, yes, of course you're right.' Yet the thought gave her little comfort. If the Russians had reached Elbing . . . Elbing lay on the Vistula delta, less than ten miles from the western end of the Frisches Haff, the lagoon that was separated from the Baltic Sea by only a thin spit of land. She struggled to remember clearly what Friedrich had told her. *They will come from the east and perhaps the south as well.* The Red Army must have advanced, at great speed, from the south, up towards the Vistula River, cutting off Königsberg and the bulk of East Prussia from the rest of Germany. The realization, and its implications, almost paralysed her.

She made herself look around. Solve this problem, don't

449

think of the next. One thing at a time. The handful of other civilians who had been on the train had left the platform. Miranda made out their footprints in the snow. She held out her hand to Elsa.

'You go on, my dear,' said Elsa. 'I think I'll stay here.'

When Miranda protested, Elsa shook her head. 'I'm too tired to walk.' The old woman's face was white with pain and fatigue. 'Another train will come. I don't want to hold you up. You'll be able to travel much faster without me.'

Miranda walked to the edge of the platform. It was little more than a narrow concrete block in the middle of the wilderness. There were no station buildings and no railway staff.

She went back to Elsa. 'This must be a branch line – or it may be just a halt for military traffic. There may not be another train for hours. You can't possibly wait here, you'll die of cold. And anyway,' she glowered at the older woman, 'I won't leave here without you. If you insist on staying here then I shall stay here with you.'

After a few moments, Elsa rose unsteadily and shuffled along the platform towards the track. The narrow pathway was bordered by poplars. In the ditches the water was frozen solid, grey and opaque. The snow lay deep on the ground, uncompacted as yet by feet or wheels, slowing their progress and making every step a burden. Miranda wound her scarf round her face to keep the frozen air from her nose and mouth and helped Elsa to do likewise. She could see no sign of the others who had left the train at the same time as them. A fitful moonlight, glimpsed whenever the mist thinned, intermittently lit the surrounding fields. There were no houses, only the occasional barn or stable. Remembering the ominous red light she had glimpsed from the train, she shuddered.

At last the track gave on to a road, and she saw, with an odd mixture of horror and relief, that once again they were part of a long column of refugees. Yet the column had altered in composition. Now, military vehicles forced a route between the farm wagons and carts. Every so often an army lorry would head along the road and the fleeing people would hurry out of its way to seek the safety of the verges. Another difference: this time, she and Elsa were on foot; this time, she hauled along her burdens like the old peasant women garbed in black. Where were they heading? she asked someone. Braunsberg, came the reply, near the coast of the Vistula lagoon. And after Braunsberg? No one knew.

A grey light on the horizon announced the coming of dawn. She took bread and cheese from the basket and offered it to Elsa. The old lady's hands were too cold to grip the food. Elsa's fingers, beneath her fur-lined leather gloves, were white, numb and peculiarly hard. Searching through the kitbag, Miranda found a pair of warm woollen socks and wrapped them round Elsa's hands before helping her back on with her gloves. Tiny flakes of snow drifted through the frozen air. Miranda noticed that the children she saw did not cry any more, but sat motionless on the seats of the carts or in their mothers' arms, their eyes closed. Every now and then they passed parties of refugees sitting by the road, regardless of the snow, or crouched beneath the inadequate shelter of a cluster of willow trees. A woman had lit a small fire and was heating a billycan over it. Another woman, heavily pregnant, lay in a cart with a broken wheel, moaning.

The road wove beside a river. The sky was growing lighter and the clouds were clearing. Now, scattered among the fields, she glimpsed farmsteads and barns. The sun, burning off the mist, touched her face and Miranda felt her spirits rise. They would go to Hanna Lindner in Braunsberg. Hanna, an old friend of Friedrich's, a wonderful pianist and a gracious hostess, would have a car, or at least a pony and trap. They would be able to rest and eat in the Lindners' comfortable home. Then they would continue west, to Danzig or Stettin, after Elsa had got her strength back. They would be safe soon, by the end of this day, perhaps. Yet when she tried to match the pattern of road and river to the lines on Friedrich's map, it seemed to her that they were still a long way from Braunsberg.

And their progress had become painfully slow. They constantly fell back – the hay carts, and even those on foot, with whom they had once been level, were soon far ahead of them. Miranda was worried about Elsa, who seemed to be nearing the end of her resources and needed to stop to rest at increasingly frequent intervals. Though Elsa never complained, Miranda could see how much each step cost her. She had helped Elsa put on almost every spare item of clothing they had brought with them, to try to keep her warm, yet the small area of face that showed between Elsa's scarf and hood looked pinched with cold. In the afternoon, Miranda was able to beg a lift on a cart for Elsa. There was no room on the cart for her, so she walked beside it.

As they travelled on, more people added themselves to the procession of the dispossessed. They came from every track and byway, from field and marsh and hill and hamlet. There were high wagons, heaped with gaudily embroidered blankets, and there were motor cars and women on horseback, sometimes with a child sitting on the front of the saddle, and motor-cyclists and pedal cyclists struggling to make their tyres find purchase on the ice. With them were all the signs of an army in full retreat – soldiers, in small groups or ones and twos, their uniforms dirty and their faces grim, and lorries, trucks, gun carriages and, once, a tank. The cart on which Elsa was riding pulled off the road to fetch relatives from a nearby village: Elsa must leave it. Once more, Miranda and Elsa walked together.

Not long afterwards, hearing a noise in the sky above, Miranda looked up and saw an aeroplane. A black smudge against the white sky, she found herself, in the moments before she understood what was about to happen, hypnotized by the beauty of its downward sweeping arc. Then screams, and the drumbeat of bullets as the plane fired on the column of refugees. People ran for cover, dropping their bags and their bundles. The horses neighed and reared, pulling at the traces, toppling the carts and scattering blankets, chests and passengers into the road.

And then, as quickly as it had appeared, it was gone. She was in a ditch, kneeling on the ice, curled up in a ball, her hands over her head. Shuddering, she looked up. Along the length of the road lay the aftermath of the incident: the splintered wood of the hay carts, the motor car with a neat row of bullets across its bonnet, the discarded bundles, split open like overripe fruit. And the dead and the wounded. A woman clutched her belly, screaming. A tiny old lady lay motionless beside the ditch, her meagre bulk hardly distinguishable from the blankets and clothing that were scattered over the crimson snow. A child's body dangled from the rear of a cart, as limp as a puppet.

Miranda crept out of the ditch to Great-Aunt Elsa's side. Neither woman spoke as they clutched each other. Miranda felt the older woman's body shake against her own, and was thankful for the comfort of another human being. After a while they travelled on. An inch at a time now. Don't look at the horrors lying at the roadside, don't listen to the screams and the moans. Don't dare to think about what might lie ahead.

They spent the night in a deserted farmhouse, two of several dozen refugees crowded into a small building that had been stripped of food and furnishings. Cows, their udders swollen with milk, clustered in the farmyard, lowing. In the morning, a woman milked a cow and fed the milk to her children.

Waking, Miranda was stiff with fatigue and cold. Standing in the doorway, she watched the snow fall. When she went back inside the house, she saw that Elsa was awake.

'We have to go,' she said.

'I can't.' The words were a whisper.

Miranda felt a sudden rush of fury. How could she have come to this — lost in the wilderness, trying to drag a slow old woman countless miles through the appalling East Prussian winter? She couldn't do it, she wasn't up to it, it was too hard for her — she would fail.

'Elsa, please,' she said. Impossible to keep from her voice a bossy, hectoring tone. 'You must get up. We have to get on to Braunsberg. You'll feel better once you've had something to eat.'

'I can't, my dear. I'm so sorry to be a nuisance. But it's my feet, you see.'

Elsa was wearing short, black boots. Struggling to suppress her rage, Miranda knelt down beside her. 'What's wrong? Are you cold?'

'They hurt.'

'You probably have a blister or two. I've some salve in my bag. Let's have a look.'

454

She began to unthread the old lady's bootlaces. Then she peeled off a sock and then the black woollen stocking beneath. As she rolled the stocking down over Elsa's ankle, the old woman gasped in pain and Miranda failed to stifle her own exclamation of horror.

Much of Elsa's foot was red and swollen. Both the sole and top were covered with large, weeping blisters. And yet her toes were pale and waxy, and when Miranda touched them they felt frozen and lifeless. She knew the symptoms of frostbite. Margret had treated a number of the refugees at Sommerfeld for it. Now, she felt ashamed of her impatience.

There were aspirins in the kitbag; she gave several to Elsa while she salved and bandaged the old woman's feet. As she worked, her mind darted, searching for a solution to this new problem. Elsa could not possibly walk – perhaps she might find an abandoned handcart or pram – or perhaps she might once again persuade someone to give Elsa a lift . . .

Elsa's voice cut into her thoughts. 'I've decided that I'll stay here. I'm perfectly comfortable here. You must go on, of course, Miranda.'

'I can't possibly leave you here. The Russians—'

'Why should the Russians pay any attention to an old woman like me? I'm sure they'll have better things to do. I shall be quite all right.' Elsa's voice was calm. 'I've made up my mind. I'm staying here.'

So they ate a breakfast of sausage and bread, and then Miranda divided the remaining food and water between them, packing her portion into the kitbag. Catching sight of the ceramic bluebird that Olivier had given her, which she had wrapped in a handkerchief, she tucked it into her coat pocket. Company, of a sort. Then she helped Elsa into the most sheltered part of the house and tucked both the blankets she had brought around her.

Then they said their farewells and Miranda walked back to the road.

She was once more a part of the great column of refugees. The weather had worsened overnight, the temperature dropping sharply, puffy flakes of snow falling from a clotted grey sky. Snow whitened the furrows in the road and blanketed the trees and hedgerows. It settled on the guns and vehicles of the soldiers and on the knitted hats of the children and the babies carried on their mothers' backs. The cold seemed to sap the oxygen from the air, making it painful to breathe, gnawing into the extremities – hands, feet, face. It became impossible with numb hands to tuck the scarf back round your face after you had stopped to swallow a mouthful of water, agony to undo the metal buckles of a bag or a horse's harness, and misery to feel step after step the ice through layers of sock, stocking and boot. She had once thought the snow beautiful, but now it had become a bitter enemy, a greater enemy even, perhaps, than the Russians.

One step, then another. As she walked, she recited verses in her head, forcing herself to put one foot in front of the other in time with the rhythm. Shakespeare, Keats, and a verse of Swinburne's, over and over again, like the pounding of her heart:

> Sister, my sister, O fleet sweet swallow,
> Thy way is long to the sun and the south;
> But I, fulfilled of my heart's desire,
> Shedding my song upon height, upon hollow,

From tawny body and sweet small mouth
Feed the heart of the night with fire.

As the day wore on, Miranda found herself walking through a grey and white landscape that seemed to her without limit. The snow whirled, masking the horizon, imprisoning those who marched in this endless trek through ice and snow. It came to her that this was the world's punishment for the war – the erasure of the sun, the coming of deep, dark winter, and this unending journey. She was caught up in a great whirlwind of destruction, whose epicentre had come to rest, in this last, perhaps most dreadful stage of the war, in East Prussia.

And yet, what she was enduring now, countless others had already known. During the six years of war, millions had been torn from their homes and families and forced to journey to unfamiliar and cruel places. She passed some of them as she walked, grey wraiths driven on some fruitless, hellish odyssey, marching seemingly without destination, a futile progression that would end only with death. She passed prisoners of war, the snow like white epaulettes on their uniforms, being moved from one prison camp to another in advance of the Russians. She saw the inmates of a concentration camp – true ghosts, these, men who had been diminished to shadows by cold and hunger and maltreatment. Their gaunt faces and wild eyes and stick-thin limbs protruded from thin, ragged clothing as they struggled to march on, goaded and beaten constantly by their guards, shot or left to freeze to death at the roadside if they stumbled.

Horror upon horror, as her journey went on. An old couple, sitting beneath a tree, motionless, a layer of snow settling over their bodies. Women and children, sprawled on the snow, the victims of another air raid. A small bundle at the side of the road: Miranda stooped to move aside the fold of a knitted shawl. The baby's face had frozen, still and white and perfect.

Taking shelter in a stable that night, closing her eyes and trying to sleep, she saw the face of her own stillborn son. She could see, just then, no point in carrying on. She would remain here and accept her fate, as Great-Aunt Elsa had done. She had lost everyone she had once held dear – her child, Olivier, the Countess, Kay. Friedrich might have already died in the defence of Königsberg. As for her, she did not deserve to survive. *Perhaps I thought I could stand apart from it*, Friedrich had said to her – well then, of that arrogance, that self-deception, she, too, was surely guilty. Like her father, she had carved out her own journey through life, had believed that she could drift from place to place, belonging nowhere, taking what would nourish and keep her, and giving so little back. She had never been much of a wife to Friedrich, she had not even been able to give him a healthy son. There was something rotten inside her, something cold and selfish and ungenerous. Her heart was frozen as solid as that of the dead infant.

And yet something made her rise in the morning, choke down a few mouthfuls of food, and begin to walk again.

That afternoon, she reached Braunsberg. But the Lindners had already gone, and though she hammered for a long time on the door of the house, there was no reply.

It surprised her, in a way, that she did not despair. She seemed now to see herself from the outside, a little machine, of no significance at all in the greater scheme of things, joining once again the endless trek of the dispossessed as they headed towards the Frisches Haff, her movements mechanical, all emotion gone. Feeling had been reduced to the crude sensations of cold, hunger and exhaustion. The stories of the other refugees she encountered, as they walked through the snow towards the lagoon, had no power to move her now. Stories of fifteen-year-old girls spreadeagled on a floor and raped by a dozen soldiers in turn, of women raped until they begged to be shot, of great houses that had stood for hundreds of years looted and torched, and of farmsteads and villages razed to the ground: she murmured horror but felt nothing.

She found herself standing that night at the edge of the ice-covered lagoon that divided the sandbar on the coast of the Baltic from the mainland. Soldiers helped to guide the carts and wagons across the ice. Walking across the five-mile-wide expanse of the frozen lagoon, she felt as though she had entered another element. There was a stillness on the ice and the sounds of the exodus, which had been with her since she had left Sommerfeld, had altered. The ice creaked and strained beneath the weight of the people who walked across it. Their voices were muted, robbed of reverberation by the open expanse. It was perfectly possible, Miranda knew, that she would die out here, poised between water and sky. She had long ago lost all sensation in her hands and feet and when she reached into her pocket she could no longer feel the comforting presence of Olivier's bluebird. She was too nauseated by fatigue to swallow anything more than the occasional mouthful of water. Death might come from the sky at any moment, or, if she were to step on to a less solid stretch of ice, she might plunge into the cold, dark water beneath.

Halfway across the lagoon, between the mainland and the sandbar, all was silent. Not a creak of a cartwheel, nor the thrum of a plane. Above her, the sky had cleared, and the stars, sharp and vivid, burned as fiercely as a scattering of diamonds. *Feed the heart of the night with fire*, she thought. She stood still, looking up, and felt the blessing of the stars.

Two days later, she reached Pillau, the seaport at the entrance to the Vistula lagoon. She had walked along the sandbar. To one side of her lay the frozen lagoon, to the other the Baltic. The grey sea surged, crashing on the sandy beach, casting up shells and driftwood. As she had travelled along the beach, she had remembered the summer days that she and Friedrich had spent here, hunting for golden pieces of amber.

Now, she was the hunted. By day, Russian planes strafed refugees and soldiers alike, forcing them to take what cover they could find in the narrow fringe of pine trees that grew on the highest part of the ridge of sand. Because of the planes, they travelled mostly by night, heading east, towards Königsberg and its port of Pillau. At Pillau, thousands of soldiers and refugees crowded on to the harbour, hoping for a passage on a ship sailing west.

After the quiet of the lagoon and the sandbar, the noise of the port shocked her. She drew her coat around her as she tried to work out what to do next. Mothers wept as they searched among the crowds for their lost children. Soldiers hooted the horns of their lorries, pushing through the throng to unload supplies from the steamers and freighters in the harbour.

But it was easier now that she was alone. Unlike the mothers and children, she could slip through the smallest gap in the crowd. Unlike the old women in their widow's black, leaning on sticks, she was young and lithe enough to squeeze on to a gangplank, to cling to a guardrail, to refuse to let go after she had fought her way towards a freighter bound west, for the Pomeranian port of Stettin.

An aeroplane plunged from the sky, jetting out bullets. The people crushed on to the gangplank screamed and swayed. Miranda was at the edge of the narrow walkway; thrown suddenly sideways, she felt the kitbag slide from her shoulder.

She looked down towards the sea. Her kitbag bobbed for a moment on the waves, then gave a sideways movement and was swallowed up. Food, clothing, papers and passport slid into the Baltic.

It would be so easy, she thought, to go with it. All she had to do was to let go.

Then a voice said in guttural German, 'I've got you, lovey.' A strong hand gripped her upper arm and hauled her upright. A push on the small of her back, and she was on board the ship.

Kay's son had dark blue eyes and a sparse headful of feathery black hair and tiny starfish hands which he held up, palms open, in a gesture almost of disbelief, when he cried. At other times, his expression was quizzical, a little perturbed, as if he couldn't quite decide what to make of his new surroundings. His toes were a row of pale pink beads, his nails like tiny fragments of seashell. There was a web of blue veins on his eyelids, and his mouth moved as he slept, his little pink tongue working, almost as though he was gathering up the words, about to speak. He had creases on his forearms and his face, as if he had been wrapped up too tightly in the womb. After the first few days, the creases disappeared and a pearly white milk blister formed on his upper lip.

When she fed him, his expression was at first fierce and intent. As he sucked, he relaxed into blissfulness, satiated with milk. She could lose hours just looking at him. How had she filled her time before Jamie had been born? She would try to do something – write a letter, say, or read a book – and then her attention would drift away, distracted by his broad, gummy smile or his plump little hands, making their slow, waving, undersea motion.

Born at the end of February, her baby had been two weeks late coming into the world. She had always, she now saw, had a certain impatience with life, had leapt hastily, without much of a look around her, into the next stage – her journey abroad with Miranda, her first love affair, the ATS. But now she must learn patience. Her baby would come when he was ready and not before. During those last, long weeks of her pregnancy, she had plodded slowly through the woodland she had come to love, careful of her footing on the slippery wet earth, or rested in her room at the school, leafing through a library book. She gave birth to her son in a state-run maternity home that had once been a hotel, on the north coast of Devon, a long, painful labour that left her bruised and bleeding. From her room, lying on the pillows, she could see the sea. As, slowly, she began to get her strength back, she liked to glance out of the window as she was feeding her child and see the ships sailing down the Bristol Channel.

After she left the maternity home, she and Jamie returned to their room at the school. She had bought a second-hand pram from a woman in a nearby village, and Roger Lancaster made her a wooden cradle. She had spent her special allowance of fifty clothing coupons for the baby's layette carefully. Virginia had made bibs and nappies from some old towels and had cut up a sheet and blanket and sewed bedlinen for the pram and cradle. There was little coal to be had, so Roger and some of the older schoolboys went to the woods each day to forage branches that had been blown down by the spring storms. The kitchen, with its large cast-iron wood-burning stove, was the warmest room in the house. They dried the baby's nappies on the stove and Kay spent much of the first six weeks of her son's life in the kitchen, sitting in an old wicker chair, feeding Jamie under the cook's benevolent eye.

As soon as she was well enough, Kay pushed the pram round the school grounds. As she walked, she planned. When the V-2 attacks were over, she would go back to the flat in London. She would make the second bedroom, which had been Rowland's study, into a nursery. She would find work. She would give her son the best possible start in life, to try to make up for him not having a father. Most of all, she would give him every scrap of love she possessed.

Spring came early in Devon. Aconites gleamed in the shady spots beneath the beech trees and, on the hedgerows, the buds were tightly furled. A thrush sang, perched on a blackthorn bush. Sometimes, pushing the pram along the narrow Devon lanes, she sensed that something was starting to repair inside her.

In April, not long after British troops in the Far East had completed the recapture of Burma, Allied soldiers crossed the Rhine into Germany. Tom saw the newsreel of the liberation of Belsen concentration camp in a cinema in Leicester Square. There was complete silence in the auditorium as Richard Dimbleby's commentary described what the British had found.

Inside the camp, an acre of ground had been littered with the dead and the dying. Staring at the black and white footage on the screen, Tom found it hard to distinguish what lay beneath the fir trees as human. The living were as skeletal as the dead, jumbled together, so many of them, thousands of people cast aside like rubbish, skin, rag, bone, hair. There was no food at the camp, and no water. The inhabitants fed off disease and pestilence and they breathed in the stench of death.

His leg ached from sitting but he made himself watch the entire programme twice. After he had, for the second time, heard Dimbleby finish his report with the words, 'This day at Belsen was the most horrible of my life,' he left the cinema. Outside, he screwed up his eyes against the light. The ordinary images of wartime London – the traffic on the road, the people on the pavement, the ruined buildings – took time to settle into shape, to reassure rather than jar. That's what you were fighting for, he told himself. That's what this was all about. Then he found a pub and drank until the images in his head blurred and the alcohol breathed warmth into his veins.

The ship Miranda had embarked on at Pillau had taken her to Danzig; from there she had been able to sail to Stettin, on the mouth of the Oder. With hundreds of other refugees, she had taken a train to Berlin. As they pulled into the outskirts of Berlin, she had stared out of the window at the ruined city. Such desolation the Allied bombing had brought: churches without spires, tenement blocks where a side wall had been ripped away to reveal the honeycomb of small, shabby rooms behind, and acres of rubble, over which Berliners, wrapped up in shabby coats and hats against the bitter February weather, picked their way.

Not all Berliners were welcoming of the people who had taken refuge in their city – the East Prussians, they pointed out, had lived without rationing or bombardment for most of the war. *Do them good to have a taste of it*: Miranda sensed the thought, mostly unvoiced, that flickered through the Berliners' heads. But Anna welcomed her. Anna, who was nursing at the Charité hospital, took her in, fed her, found her clothes to replace the filthy, ruined ones in which she had travelled, and dressed the cuts and blisters on her feet.

Three weeks after her arrival, Miranda left the city. The Russians were by then only forty miles to the east of Berlin. Knowing what the Russians would do to German women when they entered the city, she tried to persuade Anna to come with her, but Anna refused. Her place was at the hospital, Anna pointed out, which received hundreds of new casualties each day from the air raids.

So once more, Miranda was travelling alone, this time heading south. To begin with, her journey was complicated by bureaucracy: the need for food coupons, for entitlement permits, for travel permits. In fleeing East Prussia, in losing her passport and ration book, she had lost her identity. As she completed and signed the necessary papers that would enable her to eat, to take a train, and to reside for a night or two in a town or village, she became Miranda Kahlberg, dropping the aristocratic 'von'. Arriving at the home of friends of Anna's in a small town ten miles from Leipzig, she fell ill. When, after a week, she began to recover, she looked in the mirror and saw in her black hair a broad streak of white, an inch thick.

As soon as she was well enough, she took her leave of Anna's friends and continued her journey. Travelling, she slept in station waiting rooms, on park benches and in woodland, with her old fur coat drawn over her, surrounded by the whisperings and murmurings of the forest. When she had finished the food that Anna's friends had given her, she queued in soup kitchens or begged for bread from shopkeepers and tavern keepers. She was always hungry; sometimes she did not eat all day. She drank water from village wells and from forest streams. She took trains when she could, but the trains were erratic and infrequent because rails, stations and sidings had been destroyed by Allied bombs. She might wait hours for a train and then travel only a few miles, then stop for another hour on some dreary plain dotted with pines. Then the train would start up again, so slowly she felt she could have walked faster. A rumble of a low-flying plane overhead, and engine and carriages would reverse into the cover of woodland.

When there were no trains, she hitched rides. A horse and cart carried her from one village to another. A military vehicle stopped for her and took her five miles along the road. Once, she let one of the soldiers make love to her – he was a sweet boy, very young and very disillusioned, and there was something about his smile that reminded her of Olivier. And besides, she was cold, she was always cold now, and the cold was worse to her than the hunger and the tiredness, and it was good to curl up in a man's warm arms at night. When they parted, she kissed him before he drove on.

Hundreds of others travelled alongside her, military vehicles heading for the front, which came closer each day, bands of Hitler Youth, teenage boys all but out of control, taking potshots at the birds in the trees or anything that moved, as well as exhausted families, seeking refuge from bombed cities.

She avoided officialdom as far as possible, turned the other way when she caught a glimpse of a Gestapo or SS uniform. Her destination became clearer to her as she travelled. She listened to the radio when she could – now, dials were turned from Goebbels' ranting speeches, still proclaiming imminent victory, to the BBC. The Allies were in Cologne, they were in Frankfurt am Main. The Red Army was in the suburbs of Berlin. Munich had fallen. There were rumours that Hitler had shot himself.

Tom's friend, Willi Becker, who had once talked of love in a café in Berlin, had slipped outside to queue for water. The queue was in the Hermannplatz, close to the cellar dressing station in which Willi was operating. Most of those in the queue were women. Whenever a piece of shell struck one of the women, the others would shuffle forward, filling her place.

There was a moment when the noise of the Russian bombardment died away and Willi heard birdsong and saw across the square a laburnum tree, its brilliant yellow blossom vivid against the grey of the dust and rubble. Then the battle began again, a shell exploded overhead, and, just before the fragments struck him, he looked up and saw the sky. Its blue, before the darkness fell, seemed extraordinary.

Anna von Kahlberg was hiding in a cellar along with half a dozen women and children. One of the women had recently given birth; Anna had delivered the baby, which mewled feebly at its mother's breast.

In the day, the younger women had taken it in turns to brave the bombardment, running outside to fetch water or scraps of food. Now, at night, they waited. The noise of the shelling had died down and had been replaced by the rumble of military vehicles. No one spoke.

Footsteps, and Anna hugged the child sitting on her lap tightly. The door opened, a torch shone into the cellar. A Russian soldier, holding a machine gun, stood at the top of the steps. He was heavily built, with a shaven head and a scarred face. At his barked order, the women hastily removed their jewellery and watches and handed them to him.

The light of the torch ran over the women and came to rest on Anna. When he beckoned to her, Anna whispered to the child to go to her mother. Then, trembling, she rose and followed him out of the cellar.

Olivier was marching. He was part of a long column of forced labourers who had been ordered by their guards from their prison camp and had taken to the roads. He did not know where they were going and he had lost track of how many days he had been marching – two or three, perhaps. Every now and then a prisoner collapsed, from hunger, thirst, exhaustion or sickness. Then one of the guards yelled at him. If the prisoner didn't get to his feet in time, the guard shot him.

Olivier had been ill since the winter. He had contracted a cough that wouldn't go away and had woken in the nights in his narrow bunk bed in the camp, his body greasy with sweat in spite of the cold. Now, as he walked, an iron band closed round his chest, constricting his breathing. He had an idea that the war must be all but over – whispers and rumours as well as their hasty exit from the camp and the crowds of German refugees they encountered on the roads – so all he had to do was to just keep going until, with luck, they met up with one of the Allied armies.

The trouble was, he wasn't sure that he could *just keep going*. And his luck had run out a while ago. At first, when their journey had begun, it had cheered him to see the green verges and fields to the side of the road, and to have left the cramped, squalid camp. But during the march his world had shrunk, first to the men on either side of him, and then, in another closing-in, to the road itself. The act of putting one foot in front of the other became as holy as a sacrament, demanding from him every shred of concentration, will and strength. The memories that flickered through his head – of the first prison camp, where they had taken him in 1940, of the second, harsher, prison that had followed his attempt at escape, and of the factory in which he had worked long, long hours as he listened to the sounds of the Allied bombard-ment of some town not far away – crystallized momentarily and then disappeared. He had endured so much. He wanted to go home. He wanted to live.

So when, stumbling in a rut, he fell to his knees, as much as anything he wanted to rage at the cruelty of it all. Struggling to stand up, he buckled to the ground, as if his bones were made of rubber.

The guard aimed his rifle.

The shot struck Olivier in the chest. He heard himself sigh, a small sound like a lament. Blood streamed from the hole in his chest, mingling with the mud on the road. It wasn't what he would have chosen, he thought, to die in a strange land, so far from home. His eyes closed, but he could still feel the blood pumping, draining the life from his body. At least he'd be able to rest now. He was so tired. Then, second by second, a disintegration of feeling and thought until he was a husk, bleeding to death on a roadside in Germany.

And then, blackness.

One night, Miranda slept in the back room of a tavern. In the morning, the innkeeper's wife let her wash out her blouse at the sink and press her crumpled skirt. It was a warm, sunny day, and her blouse dried quickly, hanging on the line.

The Americans, the innkeeper's wife told her, were six miles down the road. She wished they would hurry; she was afraid that some fool – she had lowered her voice because SS officers had requisitioned one of the rooms upstairs – would start a battle and get them all killed. She wanted it to be over. She wanted life to be normal again.

Miranda washed her face and hands and brushed out her hair. Then, while the innkeeper's wife was taking coffee to the SS officers, she took her papers, the identity card, food coupons and travel permits, out of the small suitcase that Anna had given her and put them in the stove. The flimsy paper crackled and burned. She was twenty-six years old, she had lost a lover, a husband and a child, she had endured war and destruction, but there would be, perhaps, a chance to start again, somewhere. She dressed in her clean clothes, picked up her suitcase and began to walk again, in the direction of the front.

Sporadic gunfire and the song of a blackbird. She walked for a long time. Overhead, the sun shone, making her feel warm for the first time in months. Soldiers in khaki, not the grey of the Wehrmacht, crashed through the woodland to one side of her. She took a narrow path through a meadow, where small white flowers starred the lush grass, which brushed cool against her ankles. The meadow gave on to woodland and she walked beneath the trees, a moment of peace before she reached the road again. When she looked to both sides of her, she saw that, in the direction from which she had just come, army vehicles were parked at the roadside. Soldiers, tall men, both white and black, dressed in the grey-green of the American army, were leaning against the trucks, smoking cigarettes. She heard their voices and their loud laughter. She had passed through the front without realizing it. It had flowed around her, taking her in, absorbing her.

The soldiers threw away their cigarette stubs and climbed back inside the cabs of the trucks. Engines started up and the convoy set off along the road towards her. She stood still at the side of the road, watching as it passed her.

Then, one of the trucks to the rear of the convoy braked. A skirl of wheels and it reversed, coming to a halt beside her. A man, sitting in the open back of the truck, leaned out and called to her.

'Where are you heading, honey?'

He was young, with close-cropped black hair, and beneath his open khaki jacket she glimpsed the camera slung round his neck.

'There.' She pointed in the direction that the convoy was going.

'You're in luck, then. Hop in.'

She passed her suitcase to him and he put it in the truck. Then he gave her his hand and pulled her up into the open back. She sat down opposite him.

'What's your name, honey?'

'Agnès,' she said. She remembered Olivier's Agnès, small and dark and chic. 'Agnès Leblanc.'

'My name's Jake Brennan.'

'I'm pleased to meet you, Mr Brennan. Thank you for giving me a lift — it's very kind of you.'

He laughed. 'Any time, Agnes.' He pronounced the name the English way. 'What are you, French?'

'Yes.'

His eyes, which were blue, studied her, watchful and curious. 'Your English is good.'

'I travelled a lot when I was a girl.'

'Are you hungry, Agnes?'

'Very.'

He tossed her a bar of chocolate. 'Eat that.'

She unwrapped the bar carefully and broke off a piece. It burst with an explosion of flavour in her mouth. As she ate, he rested an elbow on the side of the truck and leaned out of the vehicle, taking photographs. She heard the click of the shutter and the whirr as the reel was wound on.

After she had finished the chocolate, she curled up in a corner of the truck and closed her eyes. She was very tired, and the sun, the chocolate, and the rhythm of the vehicle on the rutted road had made her feel sleepy.

When she opened her eyes, she saw that he had opened her suitcase and was going through its contents. She thought of her pearls, her emerald bangle and sapphire necklace, sewn into the hem of her old woollen skirt.

She must have made a sound, because he looked up.

'Sorry.' There was charm rather than apology in his smile. 'I'm a reporter, so it's my profession to be nosy. I was interested to see who you were.'

'I told you. My name's Agnès Leblanc and I'm French.'

'French. Yeah, French, of course.'

472

He let the lid of the suitcase fall shut. She pulled it towards her, wrapped her arms round it.

He pointed the lens of the camera at her. 'French, English, German, whatever you really are, Agnes Leblanc, you have a very pretty face.' The shutter clicked.

The truck drove on. The sun burned down, her eyelids were heavy, she could not keep them open.

Miranda slept.

Part Three

The Lilacs in the Park

May 1947–April 1948

Chapter Sixteen

London in the aftermath of the war was like a grand old lady who had lost her looks and fallen into impoverishment, and hadn't yet recovered the energy, money or sparkle to renew herself. Though rebuilding had begun, progress was slow, and there remained great stretches of derelict ground grown over with saplings and weeds, wastelands that were the haunts of small boys playing war games and spivs selling black-market goods.

A part of Kay had fantasized that as soon as the war ended, the shops would be full of wonderful things. But Kay now ate less well than she had during the war. In the ATS, she had been protected from the worst impact of rationing, which was still in force. Bread, which had been freely available during the war, had been rationed the previous year. Britain had been bankrupted by the cost of war, and would pay for it, the gloomier newspaper pundits pointed out, for decades to come. As if to compound the dreariness, the winter of 1947/48 had been the harshest in living memory. Ice floes had been sighted off the Norfolk coast, the Thames had frozen and food had had to be

dug from the frozen farmland with pneumatic drills. Fuel short-
ages had meant that everyone was permanently cold. All Kay's
energies had been concentrated on keeping herself and Jamie
warm and well. The coming of spring seemed like a release
from imprisonment.

Kay knew that in many ways she was lucky. At a time of
great housing shortage, she owned a bright, spacious flat.
Soldiers returning from Europe or the Far East were fortunate
to find a single room to rent. Many newlyweds had no choice
but to start married life by sharing the homes of their in-laws.

After work on Friday, Kay collected Jamie from Liz's house.
Liz was a war widow, like Kay; she supported herself and her
daughters by looking after other women's children. Jamie adored
her and as Liz lived only half a mile from the flat in Tufnell
Park, it was a convenient arrangement. At two years old, Jamie
was a sturdy little boy, tall for his age, with Rowland's black
hair and dark, melting eyes. It had been Kay's heart that had
broken the first day she had left him with Liz, not Jamie's.
Jamie had an adventurous spirit. She, too, had once had an
adventurous spirit, Kay sometimes reflected. Not any more.
Something – the war, Rowland's death – had knocked it out
of her.

Kay had been employed by a translation agency in Golden
Square for the last eighteen months. The agency translated business and legal documents and some full-length non-fiction,
farmed out by publishers and literary agencies. The agency was
owned by Nigel Peagram. He was smoothly patronizing towards
the few women who worked for him. His headmasterly style
spilled over into the offices, where his male employees tended
to call each other by their surnames, as if they were at public
school. Kay had been lucky to get the job: some of the social

constraints that wartime had released had returned. Women were no longer essential to the war effort, and most were back in the kitchen. What Kay had now – her work, her independence, her income – she had had to fight for.

That evening, she was to go to the theatre with Tom. He arrived at the flat at half past six, shortly after the babysitter, and then they headed on to the theatre in Islington. The play was Noël Coward's *Hay Fever*. The auditorium was half-empty, the production undistinguished, the sets and costumes tired-looking and the acting wooden. Kay's mind wandered. The electricity bill: she must remember to pay the electricity bill, which had been sitting behind the clock on the mantelpiece for a week. Jamie's shoes needed to be taken to the cobbler's. She and Rowland had once seen a Noël Coward play together – which had it been? *This Happy Breed*. Yes.

Something made her sit up and take notice of the play. A new character had come on stage, the flapper, Jackie. A ripple of laughter ran through the audience. The actress – small and pretty, with platinum-blond hair – could, unlike the rest of the cast, act. She seemed to inhabit the character, to make her, all at the same time, ridiculous and sympathetic and charming. The audience were responding, engaging with the performance at last.

But it wasn't only the sudden lifting of a mediocre performance that sent a shiver down Kay's spine. A bright glimmer of memory – extraordinary how one could recall after so many years the timbre of a voice – and Kay leaned forward in her seat, transfixed, staring at the actress, trying to make out her face more clearly.

Tom whispered, 'What is it?'

She shook her head. 'I don't know. I'm not sure.'

Someone in the row in front shushed them. Kay fell silent. She was trembling. Such a shock. She must have seen *Hay Fever* half a dozen times before, but it wasn't the *play* that seemed so jarringly, unexpectedly, familiar to her, it was the actress on stage.

In the interval, while Tom was getting the drinks, she thumbed through the programme. Her gaze ran down the cast list; finding the name she was looking for, her heart hammered.

Tom came back with the drinks. 'What is it? You look as if you've seen a ghost.'

'I think I have.' She showed him the programme. 'The actress who's playing Jackie—'

'She's the best thing in it.'

'Isn't she? I think it's Miranda.'

'Miranda . . .' He frowned.

'My Miranda. You remember, Tom.'

The autumn of 1937. Berlin, the day at the zoo, Herr Reimann, and that last, disastrous dinner in the Denisovs' apartment. She could almost smell the flat, watery scent of the aquarium, almost hear the patter of rain on the windows.

'It says Miranda Marshall in the programme and my Miranda's surname was Denisov, but Miranda's an uncommon name, isn't it? It *can't* be a coincidence. Marshall could be a stage name.'

'Are you sure it's her?'

'Almost.'

He gave her a close look. 'Almost?'

'She looks different. For one thing, there's her hair. Miranda had black hair.' She frowned. 'I lost touch with her in the war. Afterwards, I tried to trace her, but I didn't have any luck.'

They went back into the auditorium. During the second half of the play, Kay watched attentively. Whenever she closed her

480

eyes and listened to that voice – low, husky, tinged with laughter – she was certain.

After the performance came to an end, they went out to the foyer. Tom said, 'Well?'

'It's her, I know it's her.'

'I'll have a word with one of the usherettes, if you like. Ask her to take a note backstage.'

'No.' The word came out before she could stop it.

'Why not?'

'I haven't time,' she said. 'I have to get back for the babysitter.'

She knew she was being evasive. Why, suddenly, did she find herself wanting to hold back? Because it was ten years since she and Miranda had seen each other? Because they might have nothing to say to each other – they might no longer have anything in common? No, none of those things.

'You might not get another chance,' said Tom. 'What are you afraid of, Kay?'

'Nothing,' she said sharply. Then she sighed and said, 'I'm not sure whether I want to get involved again. Miranda was always . . . complicated. I haven't room in my life for all that these days.'

'Ah,' he said. 'I see.'

'You don't, Tom. You don't know Miranda.'

'You can't go through the rest of your life trying to avoid involvement, Kay.'

'I don't!' She glared at him. 'That's not true!'

'Isn't it? Looks like it to me.'

She gave him a furious look and then stalked across the foyer. Would the usherette take a message to Miss Marshall? If she remembered Kay Garland, perhaps Miss Marshall might be so kind as to come out to the foyer.

481

The usherette disappeared through a door. Kay tapped her foot, waiting. She saw that Tom was leaning against a pillar, and she felt suddenly ashamed of herself. She had forgotten his leg – he never talked about it. She went to stand beside him, gave him an apologetic smile and tucked her hand through his arm.

And then the door opened again and a young woman came out, and Kay heard her own gasp of recognition.

In Miranda's eyes, there were tears.

'Oh *Kay*!' she cried. 'I *knew* I'd find you again one day!'

Tom caught the train back to Cambridge that evening. It was a stopper, halting at every godforsaken station on the King's Cross line, and because the previous train had been cancelled, all the carriages were crowded. Tom gave up his seat to a lady burdened with shopping bags. Someone was smoking a pipe; pungent blue smoke curled round the carriage, mixing with the tang of soot from the engine. Standing, Tom's leg ached. He took out the book he had slipped into his coat pocket before he had left Cambridge, opened it, and began to read.

After he had been discharged from the army, he had gone back to university to study law. He had also, with his army severance pay and an opportune legacy from an uncle, bought himself a house in Priory Road in Cambridge. It had been a relief, at the age of thirty-four, to find himself free at last of lodgings and army camps. The house was terraced and Victorian and close to the river. Tom loved the liveliness of the river, its constant state of flux.

Tonight, though, letting himself into his home, the rooms seemed cold, empty and unwelcoming. He put on the light, poured himself a Scotch and sat down in an armchair. The entire house needed renovating, a project that filled his spare hours. But he knew he couldn't blame his depression on the gloomy décor. Whenever he saw Kay, his frame of mind invariably went through the same cycle. There was the pleasurable anticipation of seeing her, the utter delight of being with her, and then, as if in payment, afterwards a kind of descent, a sliding into regret and loneliness.

After Kay had returned to London with Jamie, Tom had tried to give her practical help. Widowed, and with a baby son, the last thing she had needed was him bleating of love. But as the months and years had passed, he had begun to feel a flatness of spirit, a deadening of expectation. It was always very plain to him that she thought of him as nothing more than a friend. Good old Tom, who sorted out any repair to the flat that needed extra muscle, who took her out every now and then, and who played with Jamie the sort of rough and tumble games his father would have done, had he survived. Most weeks, they wrote or talked on the phone. Every month or two he took her out. This was his ration.

He thought through the events of the evening. Kay had looked beautiful in her leaf-green dress. During their journey from her flat to the theatre, the discomfort of the ride in a crowded tube train had been negated by the fact that she was with him. The play – he had had to stop himself looking at her rather than the stage. And then, the unexpected discovery of her friend, Miranda. *You can't go through the rest of your life trying to avoid involvement, Kay.* Something had altered, he thought, to make him point that out to her. Something was breaking, perhaps.

When would he see her again? Weeks – maybe months. The thought depressed him. Tom poured himself another whisky.

But it wasn't weeks; he saw her again just five days later.

He had spent the day working on an essay, something knotty

to do with property law. By five o'clock, he was stiff with sitting. He yawned and stretched, looked out of the window, and saw a rusty Hudson draw up by the pavement in front of his house. Then Kay stepped out of it.

He went out to meet her. 'This is a surprise.' He kissed her. 'A very nice surprise.'

'You're not in the middle of something, are you, Tom?'

'No, not at all. Only too delighted to have an excuse to stop, to tell the truth.'

'I've spent the day in Peterborough, with a client, and Cambridge wasn't much out of my way.' She patted the bonnet of the car. 'It's not mine, unfortunately. It belongs to a colleague.'

'Where's Jamie?'

'He should be at Aunt Dot's by now. She said she'd pick him up from Liz's for me. Actually, Tom, I wanted to talk to you about Miranda.'

Miranda: a beauty, no two ways about it, Tom thought, remembering the encounter in the theatre. Petite, and with that piquant combination of pale hair and chocolate-brown eyes. A restlessness about her, along with intensity, but the obvious sincerity of her pleasure in seeing Kay had made him like her.

He squinted up at the sky, which was the colour of forget-me-nots. 'If you're hungry, I could make you a cup of tea and a sandwich. Or, if you'd rather stretch your legs, we could go for a walk by the river.'

She beamed at him. 'The river, please.'

They headed down Priory Road. Reaching the river, Kay rested her arms on the railings and watched a rowing boat with a crew of eight speed by. Then they walked on, past the gasworks and the old Victorian waterworks.

'I saw Miranda yesterday,' she said. 'She came to tea.'

'How long has she been in London?'

'About six months. She told me that she'd tried to find me. My name's changed, and I've moved house as well, so she didn't get anywhere.'

Tom dodged out of the way of a speeding bicycle. 'Does she plan to stay here?'

'I think so.'

'And she's working as an actress?'

'It was what she always wanted. She's had a few parts in semi-professional productions, and then the role in Hay Fever. She told me that she's auditioning for something else next week. She was very excited about it – I've forgotten what it was called.'

They walked by a row of small, terraced cottages. In the tiny front garden of the end cottage, a woman in a red silk evening dress was sitting in a deckchair, listening to The Marriage of Figaro, played on an old-fashioned wind-up gramophone. The music followed them as they passed through a gate to Stourbridge Common. Cows grazed on the rough grass and the hawthorns were pink and white with blossom. Brightly coloured barges were moored to the riverbank, and cyclists and dog-walkers and mothers with prams headed along the towpath.

'Miranda's lost everything,' said Kay. 'After the war, she went to Paris. She discovered that her father died of a stroke a few months before the end of the war. She contacted the Red Cross and asked them whether they could find out what had happened to Friedrich, her husband, and to Olivier.'

'Olivier was her lover?'

'That's right. We both knew him in Paris. Anyway, Friedrich died during the siege of Königsberg. And – it's so sad – Olivier is dead too.'

'What happened to him?'

'He was in a prisoner-of-war camp for most of the war. In nineteen forty-four, he was transferred to a factory making machine parts. When the Russians advanced, the prisoners were made to march west. It was winter, and Oliver had been unwell for some time. They had to march day and night and he couldn't keep up. He collapsed, and one of the guards shot him.' Turning to Tom, she said, 'So he almost made it. That's what's so terrible. Only a few more weeks, and the camp might have been liberated and he and Miranda could have been together again. All those years she was waiting for him – she told me that she never quite gave up hope. And he was such a lovely person, Tom, talented and handsome and funny.'

'Poor Miranda.'

'She's had to start again from scratch. She told me that she lost her passport and papers when she was travelling from Sommerfeld to Berlin. All her father's fortune, it's all gone. So she's penniless.'

They were heading along the towpath. Swallows soared in the warm air and there was a flash of blue as a kingfisher dived into the river. A railway bridge spanned the water; as they passed beneath it, a train roared overhead. They emerged from beneath the bridge into a meadow. A creamy-white froth of cow parsley grew along the riverbank. Beyond the far end of the meadow, the spire of the church at Fen Ditton showed above the tree-tops. Here, there were fewer walkers and cyclists; here, the sound of the city receded and was replaced by birdsong and the buzzing of bees.

'This is one of my favourite places,' he said. 'I often come here.'

'Lucky you, having all this on your doorstep.'

'So Miranda's making a new life for herself here, then?'

Kay gave a rather wry laugh. 'You could say that. A brand new life.' She went to stand on the riverbank, looking down at the minnows that darted in the clear water. 'Miranda hasn't just *changed*, Tom. She's reinvented herself. She's become another person.'

'What do you mean?'

'Well, for a start, there's her appearance. Her hair began to turn grey a couple of years ago, she told me, so she decided to bleach it blond. Casting directors don't give grey-haired girls starring roles, she said. And she's knocked a few years off her age. She tells people she's twenty-five, but she's actually twenty-eight.'

'There probably isn't an actress in the land who doesn't do that.'

'And there's another thing. Miranda Marshall isn't just a stage name. Her passport's in that name.'

He gave her a quick glance. 'So she remarried?'

'No. She made up the name before she came to England. She thought it had a ring to it.'

'So the passport's a fake?'

'Some crook made it for her in Paris. I suppose her ration book must be a fake as well.'

'She told you this?'

'She doesn't want anyone to know who she really is. She asked me not to tell anyone. You already know, of course, so that's partly why I came here today, to tell you all this.'

Partly, he thought. He said, 'What nationality is Miranda?'

'French, I think. Or does a woman take her husband's nationality? I can never remember. That would make her German. But then, her mother was English, so Miranda's half English, so in a way it's not unreasonable that she should say she's English now.'

'Illegal, though.'

'Yes.'

They passed between a row of hawthorns and brambles. Tom said, 'When we were kids we used to come blackberrying here, Minnie and I, in the autumn.'

'So perfectly lovely.' The long grass was starred with butter-cups. She gave a sigh of pleasure. 'How's your leg, Tom?'

'Not so bad.'

'We could sit down, if you like.' She took off her jacket and spread it out on the grass. He sat down beside her. She said, 'What you said to me the other day—'

'When?'

'At the theatre. When I couldn't make up my mind whether to find out if it was really Miranda. You told me that I avoided involvement. And I told you it wasn't true. But I've been thinking about it. Perhaps you were right.'

'Perhaps,' he said, 'I should shut up sometimes.'

'No. When Miranda was telling me these things, a part of me wished she wouldn't. A part of me didn't want to know. A part of me almost wished we hadn't found each other.'

'Why?'

She wrapped her arms round her knees. 'Because I don't want Jamie and me to become caught up in complications. Not now, not after I've worked so hard to make us settled.'

'There's being settled,' he suggested, 'and there's being in a rut.'

'Am I in a rut?' She turned to look at him. 'Do you think I'm in a rut, Tom? No — don't answer. Perhaps I'd rather not know.'

She took out the clips that were holding back her hair, and gave her head a shake, so that it tumbled over her shoulders.

She lay down, resting an arm over her face to shade her eyes from the sun. For a long time they did not speak. There was the warmth of the sun and the song of a thrush and the plash of oars as a lone rower headed downriver. Move his hand an inch or two and he would touch her hand. Reach out, and he could have stroked her hair.

Time passed; she sat up. 'Goodness, I must have drifted off.' She blinked. 'I suppose we'd better get back.'

They spoke little as they walked back through the meadow and across Stourbridge Common to Riverside. He was content with the proximity of her, the friendship and understanding that lay between them, and his gratitude for the unexpected gift of these hours.

And she must have felt the same, because, as they reached his house, she turned to him and said, 'What a lovely afternoon, Tom! I feel so refreshed. It's been a real breathing space. I'm so glad I thought of coming to see you.'

'You said—'

'What?'

'That you came here partly to talk about Miranda. Why else?'

She looked surprised. 'To see you, of course.' She kissed his cheek. 'Dear Tom.' Then she climbed in the car and drove away.

Driving back to London, the sense of peace Kay had discovered in the meadow remained with her. The glitter of the river, the gleam of buttercups in the grass and the soft, warm breeze seemed to have seeped into her consciousness, so that even as she returned to the city, even as she stopped for traffic lights and pedestrian crossings or edged down narrow lanes and crawled behind bicycles, she did not, as she usually did, glance at her watch and tap a finger impatiently on the steering wheel, but was content to let herself be part of the flow of everything, sure that she would, in the end, reach her destination.

It made Miranda very excited to think that here she was, stepping on to the stage of a West End theatre. She was auditioning for a role in a review called *Sun and Sand*, which was to tour the provinces in July and August. Two whole months' work.

A moment of dazzlement as she walked on stage – the lights and the vast empty blackness of the auditorium – and then the director, a man called Sammy Lewin, said in a bored voice, 'When you're ready, Miss Marshall.'

After she had sung her song and danced, she recited Orsino's speech from *Twelfth Night*, 'If music be the food of love, play on.' When she had finished, there was a silence, and then Mr Lewin said, 'What do you think, Piers?' and Miranda saw for the first time that there was someone else in the auditorium besides herself, Mr Lewin and the pianist.

He was sitting to one side of the stalls. Because of the lights, she could see only his silhouette. He was leaning forward in his seat, his arms resting on the back of the seat in front.

'No,' he said.

'Thank you, Miss Marshall,' said Mr Lewin.

Miranda left the stage and went back to the green room. The room was crowded with actresses and dancers auditioning for the revue; it stank of nervous sweat and cheap perfume. 'Any luck?' one of the girls asked Miranda and she shook her head. Then she found her coat and hat and left the room.

She was crossing the foyer of the theatre when someone said, 'Miss Marshall?'

She recognized his voice from the auditorium. It was the man who had destroyed her chances with that single, damning no. She could see him clearly now. He was perhaps half a dozen or so years older than her, and he had curly dark brown hair and a fleshy, handsome face.

She said coldly, 'Yes?'

'Do you have a moment?'

She had dozens of moments, endless moments, but she glanced at her watch and said, 'I'm afraid I'm in rather a hurry.'

'That's a shame, because I was going to ask you to lunch.'

She gave him a withering look. 'I don't think so.' Then she swung out of the theatre's revolving doors.

As she headed up Shaftesbury Avenue, he fell into step beside her. 'Are you angry with me because I told Sammy you wouldn't do?'

'It didn't exactly help me, did it?' She didn't try to keep the fury out of her voice. Two months' work. Two whole months, the theatres the revue was to tour already booked, so no chance of the show coming off after a few weeks, like *Hay Fever*.

She said, 'I might have got it if it hadn't been for you.'

'Yes, you might. You weren't right for it, though. You can't sing. You were in tune, but they'd never have heard you in the back of the stalls.'

She came to a halt, the crowds on the pavement flowing round her. 'I needed the work,' she said. 'I don't know who you are or why you're bothering me, but please leave me alone.'

'You don't know who I am?' He looked startled.

'I've no idea.'

'I'm Piers Hennessy.' She must have looked blank, because he gave a surprised laugh and said, 'Good Lord, where have you been these past few years? You've never heard of me, have you? Come on, let me take you to lunch and I'll tell you all about myself.'

'And why on earth,' her voice was like ice, 'should I want to do that?'

'Because I'm absolutely right, you can't sing, and the role wouldn't have done for you. But you can act, I suspect. And I have a nice little theatre company all of my own.' He offered her his arm. 'Now, will you come to lunch with me?'

He took her to the Savoy Grill. She had been there before, a long time ago, with her father. Now, she was aware of the darns in her gloves and the ladder in her stocking. She ordered scallops followed by fillet of beef, because she was ravenous.

He said, 'The show's rubbish, anyway. Poor old Sammy doesn't seem to have noticed that the revue died in the nineteen thirties.'

'I enjoy them,' she said stiffly.

'Do you? I'm not sure I believe you. I think you're saying that to annoy me. You look more of a tragedienne to me.'

She gave him a cool look. He laughed and said, 'Your Orsino wasn't all that bad, actually. Why did you choose a man's speech?'

'I like the words. And perhaps I'm a little tired of heroines who end up dead – or tamed, which is almost worse.'

'Pity. I can imagine you playing Juliet.' He added patiently, 'If you'd joined Sammy's lot, it would have given you a couple of months' work but it wouldn't have led anywhere. And the next step down would have been dire little seaside theatres run by the local am dram society and a diet of murder mysteries and *Charley's Aunt*. So you see, you should be grateful to me.'

'Should I, Mr Hennessy?'

He chuckled. 'Piers, you should call me Piers.'

The waiter arrived with Mr Hennessy's whitebait and

492

Miranda's scallops. She hadn't eaten yet that day, and it was all she could do to stop herself devouring them immediately, and say instead, 'You told me that you had your own theatre company.'

'That's right. It's my new project, the Piers Hennessy Players. I'll direct as well as act. I'm tired of directors who don't know what they're talking about. I see it as a return to the purity and verve of the Elizabethan theatre. Cut out the money men and the talentless clods who've been in the business so long they haven't a spark of life left in them, and you'll discover something spontaneous and magical. We're going to start by touring to get the company working together and then, in the autumn, we'll transfer to the West End. I've chosen most of my actors, but I've been looking for some new faces. Keeps up the interest, especially with the press. Who wants to see the same dreary old crones year after year?' He picked up a whitebait with his fingers. 'What do you think?'

'Of what?'

'Of joining us, of course.'

She stared at him. 'Do you mean it?'

'Yes. You'd have to audition. I'd need to see a bit more of what you can do – I'm not interested in watching you simper your way through some corny song. If you get through the audition, there'd be a trial period of six weeks to see how you get on. The money's not great for junior members of the company, but it would be enough to live on. I'm trying to find actors on their way up – you know, that pool of talent that's simmering just below the surface – rather than paying out vast sums of money to stoke the inflated egos of stars.' He grinned. 'I'm the only star – and the only ego.'

His gaze returned to her; she saw that his slightly slanting, almond-shaped eyes were a warm toffee brown – fleetingly, she was reminded of Olivier.

He said, 'What do you say, then? Is it a deal?'

She agreed that it was. He said, 'I think this calls for champagne, don't you, Miranda?'

He signalled to the waiter. After the bottle had been uncorked and the glasses poured, he said, 'Come on now, eat up, like a good girl.'

As she ate, he told her about himself. He described his childhood – 'Rather raw and northern,' he said, 'and my family was terribly poor.' His father was a miner, his mother cleaned other women's houses. He had no idea where his talent came from. Neither of his parents had the smallest interest in the arts. He had been noticed at grammar school by a sympathetic teacher, who had encouraged him to apply for drama school. 'My dad didn't like that,' he said. 'He hit me when I told him what I was going to do. He thought drama school was only for nancy boys and poofs.'

'Your father hit you?'

'Oh yes. Rather often, actually. Are you shocked?'

'No.' She had finished the scallops and the waiter had set the plate of steak in front of her. 'My father used to hit me, too.'

She wasn't sure why she had told him that. To puncture his vanity, perhaps, by showing him that he wasn't uniquely scarred.

He sat back in his seat, looking at her. 'Funny, I imagined you the spoiled princess type.' Then he told her about his struggle for work after he had left RADA, and his first big break with a role in *Journey's End*. The film roles that had followed. Then the war years, and ENSA, and a series of patriotic dramas in which he had played fighter pilots or Arthurian heroes. After the war had ended, he had had a huge success with his *Macbeth* in the West End. 'The first night,' he said, 'I was so frightened about what the critics might say that I couldn't face the after-show party. I went for a walk instead – God knows where, just tramping about, trying to take my mind off things. I was afraid they'd destroy me. When I got back to the theatre, the early editions had come out and everyone was opening bottles of champagne. They cheered me when I came into the room. I don't think I've ever felt so happy. MGM offered me the role in *The Lion's Mouth* as soon as the run was over. The money I made with the film meant I could buy my house, Foxhall.'

'Where is it?'

'On the Suffolk coast, between Aldeborough and Orford Ness. The garden goes right down to the water. Do you know that part of England?'

'Not at all.'

'I love it. I go there as often as I can. I often drive up after the Saturday night performance. We have the most marvellous parties at Foxhall.' He topped up her champagne glass. Then he smiled at her. 'Perhaps I'll invite you one day, Miranda.'

She was neither foolish nor conceited enough to think that he was only interested in her acting ability but, catching a bus back to her lodgings in Finsbury Park, she felt elated. Piers Hennessy was not unattractive, and if she ended up going to bed with him because he reminded her a little of Olivier, well then, there were a lot of reasons why one might end up sharing a man's bed. Hunger and cold and loneliness and the need for human company when the nightmares returned, for example.

She reached her stop and walked to her lodgings. She let herself into the house and went upstairs. There were ten other lodgers; they shared a bathroom on the second floor. Miranda's room was at the back of the house, overlooking the garden. The nicer rooms were at the front. They had a view of Finsbury Park, but were more expensive.

In her room, she took off her best clothes and put on an old skirt and blouse. She hung the frock she had worn for the audition on a hanger on the back of the door after she had inspected it for loose buttons or a fallen hem. A certain Bohemian abandon in one's dress at auditions might be acceptable, but to be down-at-heel was not. Her few nice pieces, bought on the black market in Paris, must be kept in good condition.

She made herself a cup of tea and sat down on the bed. She was tired – the couple next door had a newborn baby who screamed all night, and there was only a thin partition between the rooms – but she was more hopeful than she had been for a long time. Perhaps today had been a turning point. Perhaps at last her luck had changed.

Luck, she thought, had tossed her all the way from Sommerfeld to this room in London. If the soldier had not helped her on to the train at Rastenberg . . . If she had not squeezed herself on to a ship at Pillau . . . If Anna had not helped her leave Berlin . . . and if she had not met the American war correspondent Jake Brennan, then she would not be here now.

She and Brennan had been together for three months. They had become lovers the same day that he had made the truck halt for her, as she had stood at the side of the road. They had travelled together through the chaos of a ruined, defeated Germany. She had left him because she had discovered beneath his breezy, easygoing exterior a darker side to his nature. Jake Brennan liked to control, he liked to own. She was his possession, no one else's, to be rewarded with food and cigarettes when it suited him. To him, she was one of the vanquished. A spoil of war.

She had left him because she needed to get to Paris, so that she could find Olivier. Some American airmen had smuggled her from Germany to Belgium on their transport plane – they smuggled arms, jewellery and crates of wine, so why not women as well? From Brussels, one of the displaced millions cast up by the war, she had been able to make her way to Paris.

If the discovery of her father's death had been a blow, her visits to the Parc Monceau had almost destroyed her. She had waited for Olivier for so long. Her fragment of hope, that he had survived the war, had been slowly ground to dust. Day after day, after the remains of the summer had died, and after autumn had turned to winter, she returned to the park. When, eventually, a Red Cross worker had shown her the letter from Olivier's fellow prisoner in which he described how Olivier had died, then she, too, had wanted to die. She had starved herself – always that compulsion to pare herself down to the bone whenever she was forced to endure the unendurable, as if she loathed her own flesh.

Yet somehow, in spite of her despair, by the time spring came she was still there, still breathing, still living in a little room in Montmartre and paying her rent with the sale of the jewellery she had smuggled out of Germany. She began to eat again, to regain the weight she had lost. Another chance meeting – she had been sitting in a café when a stranger had offered to buy her coffee. Arnaud had been twice her age, unhappily married, the owner of half a dozen pharmacies, a kind and generous friend to her in a bruised, traumatized city where a great many people had nothing. They had become lovers. She had wondered whether Arnaud had installed other mistresses in the apartment in which he housed her – it was rather a cliché, had red velvet curtains, fussy little tables and chairs – but when, eventually, they parted (Arnaud's wife had become suspicious and had attacked him with a pair of sewing scissors), he had paid the rent for the next three months.

By then, she had begun to earn a living for herself. She couldn't work in an office because she didn't know how to type, and she couldn't take a job in a shop because the shops weren't taking on new staff because they had nothing much to sell. Instead, she worked a few evenings a week in a bar. She poured out drinks and sold cigarettes and chatted to the customers. The *patron* offered her an extra evening when he saw how much the gentlemen customers enjoyed chatting to her. One evening, the girl who sang with the pianist had a sore throat, so Miranda offered to sing instead. She knew she wasn't much of a singer – Piers Hennessy had been right about that – but she sang jaunty little café songs and put in jaunty little gestures and danced and the café's clientele seemed to like it. In fact, they loved it. They stamped their feet and hammered their fists on the table and roared their approval. After that, she sang in the café every night.

Other work followed. A theatre in the Pigalle and a chorus of half a dozen girls, kicking their legs in the air so that they showed their frilly knickers. A role in an existentialist play that folded after a couple of weeks. A solo in a cabaret: she wore shorts and a sailor top and sang about the boy she loved. Nothing much, but after a while they began to add up to something.

She was sometimes hungry and the room in which she lived was the size of a cupboard. Often, she had a friend. Her friends were American army officers, or they were musicians, or they were intellectuals or nightclub owners. Or they were moody, dark little men from Marseilles, who specialized in the black market – gangsters, you might say.

It had been through her lover from Marseilles that she had met Toto. Toto's speciality had been forgery. Ex-Resistance, with a lame leg and a horribly scarred face, he had made her the British passport and ration book. Paris, she had realized by then, would never give her a career, not a proper career. And she intended to have a proper career. On stage, she felt alive. The collective gaze of an audience gave her an identity she lacked in real life. She liked to bring the audience with her, to make them laugh and weep and moan. Hold up a finger and they would fall silent. Sweep up her hands in a great arc and they'd howl out a roar of applause. After a performance she felt exhilarated, effervescent. Odd that only when she was pretending did she feel most true to herself.

But she knew that Paris wasn't safe for her. There were too many people in Paris who might recognize Miranda Denisov or Miranda von Kahlberg or even Agnès Leblanc. She couldn't risk that. In the tired, sour aftermath of the war, old hatreds lingered and there were debts to be paid. She needed to break free from the past.

So she gave up dyeing her hair black and became a blonde instead. She liked being blonde, it had a perky feel to it, and the men seemed to appreciate it. She dressed differently, spoke differently, walked differently. She avoided the sort of people who asked questions, and her fear of authority, born during the war years in Germany, remained with her.

Packing up her belongings to leave Paris for England, she had pressed the ceramic bluebird against her cheek and closed her eyes. She had wondered how it was possible to act when your heart had been turned to stone. How you could walk and talk and laugh and smile when your soul was dead. She made friends but never disclosed to them the secrets of her heart. She took lovers, but never loved.

Nigel Peagram always closed up the agency for the whole of August. Aunt Dot had rented a cottage on the Isle of Wight and Kay and Jamie travelled down to join her. They turned nut-brown in the sun, paddling and building sandcastles and fishing for crabs in rock pools. When, at the end of the month, they went back to the flat, a fine trickle of sand ran out of the corner of Kay's suitcase.

Miranda returned from her tour of the provinces with Piers Hennessy's theatre company. She was wearing a full white skirt that reached her calves and a black and white spotted blouse, and a little black straw hat with a ridiculous frill of a veil. 'I spend all my money on clothes,' she told Kay as they walked together to the shops. 'Almost every penny. I spend this much,' she held her finger and thumb only a very short distance apart, 'on food. It's for when I'm in films, you see. If you are even a pound overweight, the camera makes you look fat.'

At the shops, as Kay paid for her purchases and handed over ration cards, Miranda told her about her summer. The theatres, the Sunday train journeys from one town to another. The theatrical lodging houses in dingy backstreets, with signed photos of actors and actresses on the walls, and their scribbled signatures: 'To darling Bee with love and gratitude, Kenny', 'Ella, who cooks the best breakfast in Manchester, Pansy Bryant'. And the rehearsals – Piers Hennessy's crystal-clear vision and Piers Hennessy's temper. In a baker's shop in Green Lanes, Miranda mimicked the time Piers had made her rehearse the same line twenty times. 'Only seven words, Kay!' The other customers stared and laughed as Miranda alternately growled and squeaked.

Rehearsals all morning, performances every evening except Sundays, plus two afternoon matineés. 'Most of the time,' Miranda added, 'I was a maid or a spear-carrier or an understudy. But one night, the actress who was playing Jane Bennet in *Pride and Prejudice* was ill and Piers told me I was to take her place. I was so frightened I was sick before I went on stage.'

'How did it go?'

Miranda shrugged. 'Not too bad, I think. The newspaper said I had brought fizz and sparkle to the play. As if I was a glass of champagne.' She giggled, and Kay glimpsed the old Miranda, who had found the world so absurd.

There were things she hadn't told Kay. That, after Piers had made her say her line over and over again, his sarcasm deepening at her every unsatisfactory attempt, she had slipped away as soon as she had been able to leave the stage, and had found a quiet corner of the theatre. Alone in the wardrobe department, she had not cried, exactly – she hadn't cried since the day she had found out how Olivier had died – but she had felt frightened. Perhaps she wasn't good enough. Perhaps she would never be good enough.

Then, hearing a sound behind her, she looked round and saw Piers.

'I've been looking for you, Miranda,' he said. 'I was a bit rough with you back there. I haven't upset you, have I?' He came into the room, which had the stale, old-clothes smell of all wardrobe departments. 'I only find fault with the ones I think might be good one day. I don't bother with the others.' He took her hand, a gesture which might have been meant to offer comfort and might have meant something else. 'I wouldn't try to get the best out of you if I didn't think you had some talent.'

'It's hard to show talent when my longest speech is seven words long.'

'Not true. You have to make every word count, whether you have seven words or seven hundred. In any decent play, every word will have been put there for a purpose. This word chosen rather than another. You owe it to the dramatist to make the most of whatever he gives you. Do you understand, Miranda?'

'Yes,' she said. And she did, and was grateful to him for pointing it out to her.

Then he raised her hand and pressed it to his lips and gave her his smile — his special Piers-Hennessy-at-his-most-fascinating smile, one of the other girls in the cast called it, rather bitterly.

The Piers Hennessy Players ran two plays in repertory for a month, then another two plays for another month, and so on, throughout the winter season. 'Uh-oh, nervous break-down time,' someone in the cast had muttered, when Piers had explained the schedule. The play that Saturday night was *Henry V*, which meant that Miranda was alternately a lady-in-waiting and a messenger boy in a tabard and tights. Piers made a brilliant Henry, heroic and inspiring, with a tender, thoughtful side. Columns had been written in newspapers comparing the differing merits of Piers's Henry and Laurence Olivier's.

After the performance, Miranda had changed and was leaving the dressing room when she passed Piers in the corridor. He was heading away from the green room, where the cast were giving a party.

She said, 'Aren't you coming to the party, Piers?'

He blinked, and seemed to see her for the first time. In his eyes, there was a blank, ecstatic look. 'Actually,' he said, 'I was thinking of driving to Foxhall. Would you like to come with me, Miranda?'

She considered his offer, with all its implications. 'Yes,' she said. 'I'd love to.'

'You'd better fetch your coat, then. Wrap up warm. I like to drive with the top down.'

Miranda knotted a silk scarf over her hair as they headed out of London. Piers drove his sports car very fast. They had entered the deep, mysterious countryside of Suffolk, a landscape of wood and field and soft, rolling hills, when he said, 'Sorry, I'm not talking much, am I?'

'I don't mind.'

'It takes me a while to come down from a performance. I promise I'll be more civilized once we get to Foxhall.'

A half-moon showed above a clump of trees on a hilltop; a deer ran across the road. Every now and then Miranda almost dozed off, lulled by the motion of the car.

She became aware of the proximity of the sea — a tang in the air, a ribbon of silver moonlight slung across the water. Fewer houses, now, and narrow creeks that Piers had to navigate by driving inland. 'This isn't the quickest route,' he explained, 'but I enjoy it.' As the car slowed, Miranda heard the whispering of reeds in the marshland — she had heard that same soft sussuration by the lake at Sommerfeld.

Reaching a low, wooden gate, Piers stopped to open it and then drove down a grass track. Lamplight illuminated the house at the end of the track. Foxhall was substantial, its upper storey clad in timber, a row of shuttered windows along its front.

To one side of the building, a tall willow was silhouetted by moonlight.

Inside the house, Miranda took off her mackintosh. Piers's housekeeper, Mrs Hutchinson, came to greet them. A supper had been prepared for them in a room warmed by a log fire. As they drank their soup and ate thick, delicious baked ham and mustard sandwiches, Piers explained, 'When I bought Foxhall, it was rather down-at-heel. I'm having it done up, but it takes time. I had the London flat, of course, but I needed an escape. Do you ever need to escape, Miranda?'

'Often,' she said.

'There's something irresistible about the way the house is poised between two elements, earth and sea, as if it can't quite make up its mind. I've sometimes wondered whether, if there was a really bad storm, Foxhall would survive. Or whether the sea would just consume it.'

After supper, Piers showed her round the house. The rooms were spacious and comfortable, coloured in a palette of blue-green, cream and grey, and decorated with pieces reminiscent of the sea – a cormorant sculpted out of driftwood, a huge pink and cream conch shell, and a magical painting of a boat by Christopher Wood. Foxhall's layout was unconventional, with sitting rooms on two floors at the back of the house, to make the most of the sea view. In these rooms, the rear wall was almost entirely made of glass.

In the ground-floor sitting room, Miranda went to the window and placed her hand against a pane, looking out.

'Shall we walk down to the sea?' Piers asked her, and she smiled at him and said, 'Yes, I'd love to.'

He opened the door and stepped out into the garden. Flower beds and lawn, bordered by a white picket fence, gave out on to a garden of pebbles and strange, thick-leaved plants. The low, globular bushes were outlined with white stones. In an upturned rowing boat, filled with earth, tall plants grew, topped with feathery heads. Then they clambered up the ridge of pebbles that divided Foxhall from the shore, Miranda laughing as her high-heeled shoes sank into the stones, and Piers taking her hand to haul her up.

On the top of the ridge he turned to her. 'You look cold, poor girl. Come here, let me warm you up.' He stroked her cheek. 'You're so beautiful, Miranda,' he said softly. 'You look as though you're made of moonlight. I've longed to bring you here. I've wanted you ever since I saw you at that crummy audition.'

His lips brushed her forehead, then her mouth. As they kissed, she tasted the salt on his skin, and heard, not far away, the crash of the waves on the shore.

When she woke in the morning, Piers was still deeply asleep, his strong, naked body partly covered by the sheet. Miranda dressed and went downstairs. She glanced at the clock; it was almost half past six. She went outside.

A fierce wind blew and, in the grey dawn light, Miranda saw that the waves had cast up flotsam – tin cans, a length of rope, a child's rubber ball, scarred by the sea. Tiny parachutes burst from the seedcases of the thistles in the rowing boat and then were blown away by the wind. Grains of sand stung her face as she climbed to the top of the pebble ridge. The sea was patched with light where the sun showed between the clouds. She walked along the shoreline. Some distance from the house, she took off her boots and dabbled her toes in the waves. The water was numbingly cold.

Returning to the house, she chatted to Piers's housekeeper, Mrs Hutchinson, in the kitchen while she ate toast and drank tea. She wondered how many of Piers's other lovers Mrs Hutchinson had fed and talked to of storms and shipwrecks.

Over breakfast, Piers told her that he had decided to take a chance on her. 'I've been thinking about it for some time,' he said. 'I want to play Romeo again before the critics can sink their teeth into me and tell me I'm too old. And I'd like you to be my Juliet, Miranda.' Reaching across the table, he took her hand. 'Do you think you can do it?'

Sometimes, as they walked through the park that autumn, kicking up fallen leaves, Miranda held Jamie's hand as she declaimed at the top of her voice, 'Gallop apace, you fiery-footed steeds, towards Phoebus's lodgings.' Passers-by turned to stare at them; Jamie threw himself on to a heap of leaves and laughed uproariously.

And then there were the nights when Miranda was too tired to eat, too tired to talk, and sat curled up in a ball on the corner of Kay's sofa, white-faced, fragile, frightened. *What if it's a disaster, Kay? What if I forget my lines? Or what if it just doesn't work? What if I let Piers down? What if this is my big chance and I destroy it?*

And then, in a sudden change of mood, Miranda would stand up and smooth down her frock, and smile, saying lightly, 'What nonsense I'm talking. You must be so tired of me, Kay. Don't take any notice. It's stage fright, that's all. It'll be fine. And if it isn't,' she flicked her fingers, 'then, pouf, no matter.'

Tom accompanied Kay to Miranda's first night. In the theatre bar, people screamed at each other over the hubbub. Wedged up against Tom on a corner seat, Kay drank her gin and tonic rather fast and then waited while he fetched more drinks. After the second G and T, she felt herself become magically more conversational, more amusing, the dowdiness of office and domesticity falling away from her. *Tell me about your job, Tom. Tell me what you do all day.*

He had gained his post-graduate qualification that summer and was now working for a firm of solicitors in Cambridge. 'It's all right,' he said, when she paused for breath. 'You don't have to pretend. I always assume that what I do seems as dull as ditchwater to other people.'

Her glass was empty. 'Was I gabbling?'

'A bit.'

'Oh Lord. Drunk on two gins. How depressing to be so out of practice. Sorry, Tom.'

'I don't mind.' He grinned. 'You're quite funny when you're drunk, you know.'

They finished their drinks and went into the auditorium. Good seats, about halfway back in the stalls. There was a knot of tension in Kay's stomach. She had helped Miranda learn her lines, had tried to soothe her nervousness, had sent her flowers to wish her luck. There was nothing more she could do.

The lights darkened, the curtain raised, the play began.

> *Two households, both alike in dignity,*
> *In fair Verona, where we lay our scene . . .*

And then it was over, and the applause, which had been tumultuous, rang in Kay's ears as they shuffled along the row of seats to leave the auditorium. She caught fragments of conversation from the crowds funnelling out into the foyer. *That girl who played Juliet, marvellous I thought . . . something of the young Gertrude Lawrence . . . stunning performance.*

In the foyer, there was a solid mass of people. Tom forced a way through the crowd, Kay following in his wake. Outside, the fog had thickened, a yellowish-grey curtain that masked the far side of the road.

She glanced at her watch. 'It's twenty to eleven. I promised Cheryl I'd be back by eleven.'

'Better get a taxi.' Orange moons of headlamps showed through the fog; Tom stepped forward, his arm raised.

As the cab slowed, someone shoved between Kay and Tom, rushing across the road to speak to the driver.

Tom said, reasonably politely, 'Excuse me, we were here first.'

'I don't think so, old chap.' The door was wrenched open. The man, followed by several women in evening dress and velvet capes, climbed into the cab. It drew away, disappearing into the fog.

Tom swore under his breath.

'It doesn't matter,' said Kay.

'I *detest* people like that,' he said furiously. 'Thick-skinned as elephants, and with that ineradicable bloody sense of entitlement. You'd have hoped the war might have made them think twice, but no, they don't change.'

'Tom, it doesn't matter.'

'Are you all right? That confounded idiot, barging into you like that.'

'I'm fine. Let's not let it spoil a lovely evening. Please, Tom.'

No more taxis arrived, so they began to walk to the tube station. But progress was slow, and the fog, where it was thickest, appeared like a solid wall.

She said, 'Tom, you don't have to see me home, honestly. It's going to take ages in this. You should go straight to King's Cross.'

'No.'

Just that, no. She thought of arguing, then didn't. Instead, they walked arm in arm to the tube station, where he bought tickets before they headed down the escalator into the tunnel. On the train, they stood by the doors of the carriage, Tom holding a ceiling strap, his other hand reaching out to steady her whenever the train jolted into motion or swayed round a corner. They talked of the play, of how good Miranda had been, how touching and believable. Their conversation came in fragments of phrases, each finishing the other's sentences, confident that together they would find the right word, interspersed with laughter or disputing sometimes, a slight, pleasurable disagreement, pleasurable because they had always loved talking to each other.

At Tufnell Park, the fog was thicker. They walked slowly, cautiously, blind in the murky darkness, sometimes using a metal railing or a low wall to guide them. The air smelled of cold and soot and they spoke little now, concentrating on making their way over obstacles of kerb and pothole, hand in hand.

Outside her house, a moment of relieved laughter.

'Made it.'

'I was afraid we'd end up in Shepherd's Bush or somewhere.'

'What about Cheryl?'

'She can stay the night. I'll ring Liz. We're not a bad team, are we?' And she linked her arms round his neck and kissed him. 'Thank you, Tom. Won't you come in?'

'Better not. Train to catch.' He hugged her. She watched him disappear into the fog.

With the success of *Romeo and Juliet*, Miranda's life changed. She was able to rent a small flat in Chelsea. The flat had a sitting room and a bedroom and a tiny kitchen and bathroom. Piers had found the flat for her, which belonged to a friend of a friend, who was working abroad. In the flat, she gave parties, small, late-night, intimate affairs where people crushed into the rooms, eating, drinking, talking, dancing. It amused her to discover that there had become a cachet in being invited to one of Miranda Marshall's parties.

There were the parties at Foxhall, too, grander occasions, written about in the press with a salacious fascination. All sorts of people attended the Foxhall parties – actors and film stars, writers, musicians, socialites and the more unconventional kind of politician. The parties went on into the next morning, becoming more outrageous as the hours passed. By the time dawn came, some of the guests would have dozed off in armchairs or on beds, but others would still be playing poker or dancing or wandering into the kitchen to raid something to eat from the larder. Empty wine glasses lay scattered on the floors and cigarette ends overflowed from the ashtrays. As the needle swung to the end of the last song on the gramophone record, it remained there, wearing itself out in the groove.

Since her relationship with Piers had become public know-ledge, photographers took pictures of them leaving restaurants – 'Theatre's golden couple, Piers Hennessy and Miranda Marshall' – and gossip columns followed their every move. Captions blared, 'Has hellraiser Piers found love at last with his Juliet?' But Miranda knew that whatever it was that attracted them to each other was not love. Their affair was stormy, made of quarrels and reconciliations, of sulks and rages on his part and coaxing or disdain on hers. She knew that he was shallow, vain and egotistical, and that he had had many other lovers before her. She knew that he wanted her because she was beautiful, and because he would have wanted anything that was glittering and lovely and desired by other men. Beneath his vanity ran a deep vein of insecurity and a need for constant reaffirmation. An older actress in the company had told Miranda that the Piers Hennessy Players had been a gamble to revive a career that had seemed, even if only to Piers, to be flagging a little. Miranda's success, which augmented his own, had helped Piers claw back the attention of the press. 'Such bores, aren't they, working-class boys made good,' added the actress, with a yawn. 'Always so bloody unsure of themselves.'

As for her, she was attracted to him – after all, he was tall, handsome, well-made. In bed, he was experienced and imaginative and completely without shame. He liked the finer things of life, good food, champagne, expensively tailored clothes, as did she. His passion for the theatre was genuine; they could talk about it for hours. And, self-obsessed and incurious, he never asked her about her past, and that suited her.

Kay had heard of actors and actresses becoming stars overnight, but had never expected to see it at such close quarters. The newspaper reviews of *Romeo and Juliet* were unanimous in their praise of Miranda's performance. 'Miranda Marshall brings a touching vulnerability to the role,' wrote one, and, 'Miranda Marshall portrays the ecstasy and tragedy of young love with complete conviction,' wrote another. A third, rather wildly, splashed a headline above an article at the foot of the front page: 'A Star Is Born!'

There were photographs of Miranda in the newspapers and gossip magazines – Miranda coming out of the theatre, smiling at the cameras, and Miranda walking down the red carpet at a film premiere. She was wearing a shimmering rose-pink dress and her arm was in Piers Hennessy's. And it was good to share in Miranda's excitement, and to have her darting into the flat every now and then and talking of interviews and photo shoots and parties.

Kay needed to be distracted because something was troubling her. Something rather ridiculous and embarrassing had happened. She would have liked to have forgotten it but couldn't get it out of her head. She kept thinking about her journey home with Tom after Miranda's first night. Their conversation on the tube train, and his hand, warm in hers as they stumbled blindly through the fog. When they had reached the front door of the house, they had said goodbye. She had kissed him and he had hugged her.

And she had wanted him.

And though she tried to brush it off, to tell herself that she must be mistaken, to say to herself, oh for heaven's sake, you can't possibly be attracted to Tom, not Tom, and though she pointed out to herself that since it was more than three years since she had been to bed with a man she would probably have had the hots for the *postman* had he hugged her, nothing really worked. Desire was treacherous. It forced her to acknowledge feelings she might otherwise have chosen to ignore. It lingered, colouring her day with a mixture of elation and longing, seeping into her ordinary life, transforming her routine. It made her — and here was the thing — *happier*.

It's just physical, she told herself, and rather inconvenient. It didn't *mean* anything. It would pass, this distraction, this longing, this *thing*.

At Christmas, Piers gave Miranda an amethyst necklace and earrings, set in gold. She gave him a cat, a black witch's cat with slanting, almond-shaped eyes, just like Piers's own. She thought Piers needed a cat, something he might learn to love, and she trusted Mrs Hutchinson to look after it during the week.

In January, she played the ingénue's role in an Agatha Christie thriller and had a small part in a children's play that Piers had commissioned, The Winter Princess. Rehearsals had begun for Webster's The White Devil, which was to open at the beginning of February. Miranda was to play Vittoria Corombona. Methought I walked about the mid of night/Into a churchyard . . .

As she took her curtain call one night after the Agatha Christie, red roses were thrown on to the stage. She gathered them up and blew kisses and the audience roared their appreciation. Other bouquets awaited her in her dressing room. As always, after a performance, she felt exhilarated. She thought how extraordinary it was how life could turn out. Little more than a year ago, she had been dancing in a grimy little theatre in the Pigalle, darning her stockings and wondering how she was going to afford her next meal.

Miranda took off her stage make-up and then carefully made up her face again, this time more lightly. She put on the sapphire-blue satin cocktail dress and coat that were hanging on the back of the dressing-room door. She had been invited to a party in Mayfair after the show. The house was only a short distance away from her father's old house in Charles Street. Once, she had tried to peer through the windows, but the curtains had been drawn. She imagined the rooms inside, their furniture shrouded in dust sheets, festooned with cobwebs.

Satisfied with her reflection in the mirror, she drew on her gloves, gathered up her handbag and half a dozen roses and left the dressing room. The stage hands wished her goodnight as she left the theatre by a side door, which led into a narrow, cobbled alleyway. There was the click of camera shutters and the blinding white light of flashbulbs as she stepped outside. She posed, smiling over her shoulder at the reporters and photographers. 'Where's Piers?' one of them called out to her. 'When are we going to hear wedding bells, Miranda?' called another. She blinked to clear her gaze of the after-image of the flashbulbs, called out a goodnight, and made to walk on.

And saw, standing on the edge of the group of men, Jake Brennan.

Chapter Seventeen

'I met Jim Reynolds when I was in North Africa in forty-two,' explained Tom. 'Nothing out of the ordinary, but decent, utterly decent, like a lot of them were. Cheerful, practical, never complained. There'd been a skirmish and we'd both lost our units, so we stuck together, trying to find our way back to where we thought the rest of the army was. We walked for two days across the desert, dodging German tanks and eking out our water. We told each other our life stories. Reynolds had left school at fourteen and gone to work on a farm. He'd never been out of England, had hardly ever left Hampshire. And then the war came and he ended up in North Africa, this Hampshire farm boy. Anyway, there we were, in the desert. Every now and then, we'd stop for a rest and one of us would walk up to the high ground to see if he could make out any landmarks. Reynolds was unlucky. While I was looking at the map, he wandered off and stepped on a mine. Fortunately, we'd almost reached the front line and I found a first aid station over the next ridge or he wouldn't have made it. As it was, the poor devil lost both his legs.' Tom ran a hand across his face. 'Christ knows how he puts up with it. I couldn't.'

It was a clear, cold, frosty day in January. They were in a pub in a village outside Hungerford. A week ago, Tom had telephoned Kay. Each year, he told her, around this time of year, he visited a few old army friends who'd fallen on hard times. He took them a small gift to wish them a happy New Year. Chatted, reminisced, if they wanted to. Would she come with him? It would make all the difference if she would. He had no doubt the men would prefer to look at her rather than at him, and she might help to keep the conversation going.

Kay had not felt able to refuse. She had taken Jamie to Aunt Dot's house the previous evening, which meant that she was ready when Tom rang the doorbell at nine that morning. They had called on two of Tom's friends before midday, the first in Reading, and then Mr Reynolds, who lived with his mother in a village between Hungerford and Marlborough. After leaving the Reynolds' house, they stopped at a country pub for sandwiches and beer.

'I suppose,' said Kay, 'poor Mr Reynolds hasn't much choice but to put up with it.'

'Yes. But *that's* bravery, isn't it, enduring something like that.'

Glancing at him, she said curiously, 'Do you ever miss it?'

'The war? No. Some men do, I think. I remember someone once saying to me that he thought there was something in war that men found exciting. Perhaps there was to begin with, but for me, at least, it stopped being so after North Africa. I suppose there have been times when I've missed the camaraderie, but to tell the truth, I'd had enough long before I was wounded. I'd seen too many of my friends die.' He ripped open a crisp packet and put it on the table between them. 'What about you, Kay?'

'I made some good friends,' she said. 'We're still in touch

with each other, so I suppose I've the war to thank for that. But the war took Rowland from me.'

'You must miss him a lot. Especially at this time of year.'

'We never had a Christmas or New Year together. Our only Christmas, Rowland was in Scotland and I was at Aldershot. I remember I tried to phone him, but the lines were awful and in the end all we had was a minute or two. But it was wonderful to hear his voice.' She ran a fingertip through a splash of spilled beer on the table. 'Most of the time it was like that. Letters and phone calls – mostly letters. We had about a dozen evenings and a handful of weekends. All the rest of the time we were apart. Even once we were married, if you add up the days, we lived together for less than a week. I'll always treasure my memories of Rowland, and I'll never forget him. But I won't have him turned into some sort of *saint*. I won't have him someone we only talk about in hushed voices, or someone who stops us doing the things we want to do. I don't want Jamie's life to have this, this *shadow* over it, or to feel that something wonderful he should have had was taken away from him, and he can never recover from it. I don't want his life to be founded on loss.'

'And you, Kay? What about you?'

There was a directness in his gaze that she found herself almost shying away from. What would happen if she were to reveal herself?

She said, 'I don't want that either.' She struggled to crystal-lize her thoughts. 'What you said to me that night at the theatre – about avoiding involvement—'

'Oh, that.'

'If it hadn't been for you, I might not have contacted Miranda. I might have told myself I hadn't time, I might have walked

517

away and never spoken to her. And all because I couldn't face all that − that . . .'

'Emotional expenditure?'

'Yes. All that anxiety and fear and concern that's a part of loving someone. And I'd have regretted it, Tom. I'd have missed out on a lot. It's been wonderful getting to know her again.' She smiled. 'Of course, it's different now.'

'It's bound to be. Relationships change.'

There was a warmth in his eyes as he looked at her that made her heart race.

'Miranda was always secretive,' she said. 'I suspect the only person who knew her completely was Olivier. She's so different to me. Perhaps that's why we've always got on so well, because we're so very different. I've never been the least bit mysterious.'

'You are to me.' His expression was serious.

She laughed. 'Oh Tom. Not me. We've often irritated each other, and we've sometimes annoyed each other, but we've never—'

She broke off. She had started to say, we've never *fascinated* each other. What nonsense. Of course he fascinated her. What he thought, what he said − the way he moved − all these things fascinated her. It had been his long absence, first in North Africa and then in Italy, that had made her see him more clearly. She remembered visiting him in hospital, after he had been wounded. She remembered how, leaving the hospital, she had wept for him.

And she heard him say, almost as if he echoed her own thoughts, 'But we've never bored each other either, have we, Kay?'

And then half a dozen people, shedding coats and chafing cold hands together, slid into the seats beside them, and Tom said, 'We'd better head off. The next chap, Bob Parry, lives in the middle of nowhere. It'll be easier to get there while there's still light.'

They left the pub and drove on. The road narrowed, threading through woodland. In the car, his words seemed to burn into her consciousness. *Relationships change*, he had said; was it possible that he had been talking not of Miranda, but of the two of them? She hardly dared think so.

The Parrys' house was in a clump of woodland on the far side of a field. Tom parked the car on the verge. The ploughed earth in the fields had been whitened by frost; ice had formed between the ruts on the track.

'You'll like Bob Parry,' Tom said, as they walked up to the house. 'He's rather a one-off. I should warn you, there are a lot of Parrys. Have a good look before you sit down or you might end up in someone's lap. Bob's put the family's name down for a council house but he thinks it'll take years.'

There seemed to Kay to be dozens of Parrys, their ages ranging from a few weeks old to a great-grandmother, who hobbled round the cottage living room clearing small children, cats and dogs from her path with a stick. Kay was introduced to Bob, a spare, dark, wiry man with bright, black eyes, his wife and three children, his parents, grandparents, sister and brother-in-law, and their children. There was the slight awkwardness, which she had encountered twice already that day, of explaining that she and Tom were just friends – and then, from various outspoken Parrys, a chorus of *Snap her up, that's what I'd do* and, *About time you settled for someone, Captain Blacklock, don't know what you're waiting for*. Then they were plied with tea and currant cake, the children were banished outside to play in the remains of the light, the great-grandmother fell asleep in a chair, and Tom and Bob were left to talk in peace.

And, watching him, a revelation. That this was no short-lived physical attraction, though attraction was there, warm and molten inside her. But it was more than that. She loved him. She loved everything about him. She loved his kindness and his generosity and his protectiveness towards her. She loved to talk to him, to dispute with him, and to be quiet with him. She loved to lie in a sunlit meadow beside a river with him, to cross seas with him, to drive through a winter's evening with him. She would not rather have been anywhere than where she was now, sitting on a lumpy sofa in a room that smelled of pipe tobacco, baby sick and dog, because he was here.

After they said their goodbyes to the Parrys, they left the house and started down the track as the sun set behind the lacy black outlines of the trees in a sky ablaze with coral and gold.

Then Tom said, 'It always reminds me of Cold Christmas, this place. Those tall trees, and the silence, and the way you have to keep an eye out for the track, or you'd miss it. Have I told you that Cold Christmas is Edie's now?'

'Edie?' she echoed.

'Miles Culbone died a year ago. He left his house to Edie.'

Edie, she thought. How did Tom know that Edie had inherited Cold Christmas? Was he still in touch with her? Was he still in love with her? Now the cold seemed to reach inside her; now she told herself that she was glad that she hadn't given her feelings away, glad she hadn't made the same mistake twice, exposing herself to his anger and rejection as she had in 1939.

'Kay,' he began, but as she moved away from him, her foot slipped on the ice and he caught her arm, steadying her. She pulled away, hastening her footsteps, half running until the space between them widened and she knew he would not be able to see the tears in her eyes.

He had almost said it, had begun to form the words — *Kay, we have to talk; Kay, you have to understand what I feel about you* — and then, in a moment, in a gesture, all the pleasure he had taken in the day had been destroyed. He had taken her arm when she had slipped on the ice, and she had pulled away from him as violently as if his touch had burned her.

Only an hour or two ago, they had talked in the pub, and he had allowed himself to hope. And this day, a carefully manoeuvred attempt on his part to find out if they could ever be anything more than friends, had seemed to contain a possibility.

They drove back to London. Kay sat in silence, her face turned away from him, looking out of the window as they passed through villages and towns. Darkness had fallen and lights glittered and the words and phrases they exchanged were brief and meaningless. Tom knew that he had been a fool to hope. She could hardly, he thought grimly, have made it more clear.

It couldn't have been Jake. Once Miranda had recovered from the shock, she was sure she must have been mistaken. Even if it had been him, he had not recognized her. She had changed herself completely from the exhausted vagabond he had discovered in the funeral pyre that Hitler had made of Germany.

Still, she tried to take her mind off things. There was always a party somewhere in London, and she, the fashionable crowd's newest darling, was always invited. Piers's thirty-fifth birthday party, at the end of January, outdid all the others at Foxhall. More than a hundred people came. The music and the dancing went on long into the night. Couples wandered off, closing the bedroom door behind them. At dawn the next morning, those guests who were still standing ran down the pebble ridge into the sea, tearing off their clothes before plunging into the waves. The cold took Miranda's breath away and made her scream with shock and laughter. Swimming, she felt the waves seize her, lifting her up and throwing her down until she was as limp and weak as a puppet. She was still laughing when Piers hauled her bodily out of the sea, and told her that she was a fool and no use to him at all if she drowned herself.

At the beginning of February, The White Devil opened. Making herself up, Miranda's hands shook as she painted on shadow and liner. She had been sick from nerves at the flat, was sick again at the theatre. Made up, dressed in her costume of scarlet taffeta, she waited, shivering. She couldn't remember any of her lines. She couldn't remember her first cue. She couldn't go on, Piers would have to put the understudy on instead.

And then, it seemed to her, in the blink of an eye, it was over and there was her reward: the curtain calls, the applause and the sense of having passed through something trans- formative and liberating. As she left the theatre, she looked for Jake Brennan among the crowd of photographers, but he was not there.

The days passed. She slept better, buoyed by the success of the play. She began to feel safe again.

One morning, after a late-night party, she slept in late. As sunlight seeped through the curtains, she dozed, half aware of the distant sounds of her daily, who had let herself into the flat and was vacuuming the hall.

The telephone rang. Miranda reached for the receiver. 'Hello?'

'Is that Miranda Marshall?'

She was suddenly wide awake. 'Who is it?'

'Aw,' he said. 'And here was I, thinking you'd know my voice as soon as I said your name. Though it isn't really your name, is it? And Agnès Leblanc wasn't either. I think it's about time you and I met up for a chat, Miranda.'

She met him in the park. He was sitting on a bench, reading a newspaper; he folded it and rose as she neared him. She was wearing her old fur coat and dark glasses, and had knotted a silk scarf over her head.

'Look at the pair of us,' he said. 'We look like two Soviet spies.'

She didn't smile. 'Hello, Jake.'

'Hello — what should I call you?'

'Miranda. Miranda's my real name.'

'I know.'

There was, in his blue eyes, that self-satisfied, watchful look she remembered from Germany. She said, 'It's too cold to sit. We'd better walk.'

They headed down a pathway between a tennis court and a children's play park. 'Running off like that,' he said, 'without saying goodbye to me. That was unkind of you, Miranda. You hurt my feelings. And after all I'd done for you.'

'I had things to do.'

'Where did you go?'

'Here and there.'

'Paris. You went to Paris, didn't you?'

She glanced at him sharply. 'If you know, why do you ask?'

'I wanted to hear it from you. We were friends, weren't we? Friends always tell the truth to each other.' He took out a packet of cigarettes and offered it to her.

She shook her head. 'No thanks.'

'When we first met, you'd have done a lot for a cigarette.'

She looked away. 'That was then and this is now. People change.'

'Do they? I'm not so sure.' She heard the rasp of a match. He said, 'After you left me, you went to Belgium. I traced the guys who gave you a lift on their plane, and they told me. *Belgium*, I thought, no one goes to *Belgium*, no one *stays* in Belgium. I said to myself, I bet she's gone to Paris. That's where my little Agnes will have gone. So I got myself there and had a look round. Dead end. You'd disappeared. Gone up in a puff of smoke. And there I was, heartbroken.'

'I'm sure you were, Jake,' she said coolly.

'Then the paper sent me back to Germany. I showed your picture to everyone I met. I was curious, I guess. I knew you'd been lying to me. I wanted to know your true story. You told me a lot of stories, Miranda, but never the true one. But still,' he shook his head, 'nothing. I began to think I'd never find you.'

'I wish you hadn't, Jake.'

'Don't be like that, honey. Anyway, then I had a stroke of luck. I was in Berlin – Jesus, what a mess. A city of ghosts, picking through the rubble. Must have been hell in the air raids – and then, when the Russians came.'

Miranda said nothing. She remembered sheltering in a bunker in an air raid during the weeks in which she had been staying with Anna. Along with thousands of other people, she had been trapped in the bunker for two days by the fierceness of the bombardment. She remembered the terror, the darkness, the crush, and the stench as people were forced to relieve themselves where they sat. And the thirst. She would have sold her soul for a glass of water.

He said, 'I was almost on the point of giving up. I thought I'd never find out who you really were. Only then, as I said, I had a stroke of luck. I was writing an article on Nazi women. I asked around and someone introduced me to this girl. She was blue-eyed, a strawberry-blonde. Taller than you, Miranda, nice figure. She must have been pretty once, but none of the women in Berlin were pretty then. Her family were East Prussians, from Königsberg. They'd once been wealthy. Her name . . .' he screwed up his eyes but she knew he was only pretending to have forgotten, 'Schäfer. Yeah, that's it, Frau Schäfer.'

Schäfer. It took her a moment to place the name. Then she remembered Katrin, Friedrich's cousin. Her married name had been Schäfer.

'The interesting thing is, she knew you, Miranda. Frau Schäfer was the widow of a Nazi Party official. No one important, but when I showed her your photo she recognized you straight away. She didn't want to talk to me at first, but then we had a chat and I explained to her what I could do for her, and she came round. She told me everything about you.' He smiled, showing white, even teeth. 'Miranda von Kahlberg. My, my. Who'd have guessed it? My little Agnes, a *countess*.'

They were at the park gate. She reached out for the latch, but he gripped her hand, digging his fingers hard into her flesh.

'I thought of publishing my story there and then,' he said. 'From countess to whore – not bad.'

Never a whore, she thought. For all her lovers, she had felt, at least to begin with, liking or attraction or the need for human warmth. But she knew how he would make her look.

He was still talking. 'My story hadn't got an *ending*, you see. I needed my ending. I took another look round Paris, but still, zilch.

And then, a couple of weeks ago, I was sitting in my hotel, thumbing through a copy of *Paris Match*, and there you were, Miranda Marshall, London's newest starlet. What a turn-up for the books. But I still wasn't a hundred per cent sure it was you. You were looking more polished, shall we say, than when I'd known you. And the hair – it suits you, by the way. So I hopped on a ferry and came over to have a look. And it was you. I'd found you at last.'

She pulled away from him, cradling her bruised hand. 'What will you do now, Jake? It'll make a good story, won't it?'

'It would make a fantastic story. One of the best. I expect it would make my reputation. London's sweetheart turns out to have been married to an officer in the Wehrmacht. Wow, what a scoop. But I wouldn't want to do that to you.' He smiled at her again, but his eyes were cold. 'Unless you make me, Miranda.'

'Do what you have to, Jake. I don't care.'

'Nonsense. Of course you do. You don't want to lose everything you've got, do you? Because that's what would happen, make no mistake. All those people telling you how wonderful you are, all those reporters toadying to you, they'd crucify you once they found out who you really were. They'd think you'd cheated them. They wouldn't applaud you in the theatres any more, they'd be baying for your blood. Your career would go,' he clicked his fingers, 'like that. And I don't imagine the boyfriend will hang around for long once he found out you'd lied to him.'

She said coldly, 'What do you want, Jake?'

'Only to pick up from where we left off.' He smiled. 'My editor wants me back in New York for a few weeks. You think about what I've said. I'll give you a ring when I get back.'

Minnie said, 'Giles didn't like Ma's parrot. I hadn't realized he was afraid of birds – it hadn't come up. And then Pa came down to lunch wearing his pyjama jacket. Even Ma noticed that. She made him go and change. Poor old Giles made a run for it as soon as we'd finished pudding. He said he had work to do but I think the parents scared him off.'

Tom and Minnie were walking back along the river after attending a concert at Trinity College. It was dark and cold; a full moon wavered on the water like a silver coin cast on a length of black silk.

'I sometimes wonder,' added Minnie, 'whether the house will one day somehow sink into the ground. Too many books, too much dust and dogs and cats and parrots. Or perhaps it'll slither across the meadow and just slide into the river with a very large glug. It's always my test, you know, of a new boyfriend. Whether he can cope with the parents.'

'And poor old Giles flunked it.'

'Looks like it. That's him off the list.'

Tom couldn't help mentally applying Minnie's test to Kay. Kay, he knew, would see through the chaos of his parents' house to their essential kindness and generosity. She would notice their unending thirst for knowledge and respect them for it. She would welcome the dinner-table discussions and would not be alarmed by them. She would join in.

Minnie said, 'So . . .'

'So what?'

'Who is she?'

'Who's who?'

'Tom.' Minnie sighed loudly. 'You're only ever this morose when you're in a stew over some girl.'

Because he and Minnie had always been close, he said, 'She's not "some girl". She's the girl.'

'Oh.' She took a look at him. 'You mean it, don't you?'

527

'Unfortunately, yes.'

'Why unfortunately? It's about time you found someone. We can't both stay crabbed old bachelors our entire lives.'

He said, 'It's Kay.'

'At last. You've been mooning on about her for ages.' She touched his hand. 'I'm sorry. I shouldn't be flippant. I take it she doesn't—'

'She thinks of me only as a friend. Good old Tom, who takes her out for a drink from time to time. It's bloody frustrating. Every now and then I think I'm getting somewhere, and then the next moment I'm back at square one. Or worse.'

Briefly, as they walked along Riverside and then up Priory Road to his house, Tom told Minnie about the day he and Kay had spent together visiting his old army friends. About his hopes, and how, leaving the Parrys' house, they had been dashed.

He let them into his house. Inside, Minnie peeled off her scarf and gloves. 'Perhaps you said something to annoy her, Tom.'

'Me? I don't think so.'

She gave him a look. 'What were you talking about?'

'I've no idea – about the Parrys, perhaps.' He went into the kitchen and put the kettle on. 'Oh, and Cold Christmas.'

'Cold Christmas?'

'I told her that Edie had inherited it.'

Minnie perched on the edge of the kitchen table, swinging her legs. 'Kay knows about Edie, doesn't she?'

'The lot. Pretty much the unexpurgated, unedited version.'

'Oh Tom.'

He was spooning coffee into mugs. He turned to her. 'What?'

'You were talking to Kay about an old girlfriend. An old lover.'

He stared at her blankly, then he said, 'Do you think she

might have got the wrong end of the stick? But I haven't thought of Edie in that way for years.'

'Does Kay know that?'

He ran the scene through in his head. *Miles Culbone died a year ago*, he had told Kay. *He left his house to Edie.* And then Kay had slipped on the ice, he had caught her, and she had pulled away from him. And had hardly looked at him for the remainder of their journey home.

'For heaven's sake, Tom,' said Minnie, as she searched through his cupboards for biscuits, 'talk to her.'

My editor wants me back in New York for a few weeks. I'll give you a ring when I get back. And he would, Miranda knew that. Whatever his motives – desire or control or the need to pay her back for having escaped from him two years ago – he wouldn't let go. Jake Brennan would pursue her until he had got what he wanted.

Which made things difficult for her. She didn't intend to go to bed with Jake Brennan again. The thought revolted her – which was odd, because she hadn't minded before, had she? It made her realize that she had changed. The dullness of feeling that she had experienced since those last, terrible months of the war – perhaps it was lifting at last.

Yet if she didn't take Jake Brennan as her lover she would lose this life that she had made for herself, this fiction of her own creation, Miranda Marshall. Sitting on the pebble spit on the beach at Foxhall in the early hours of one morning, looking out to the sea, she tried to work out what to do. From the house behind her she heard the distant sounds of music and laughter. Who would she miss, if she were to start again once more? Not Piers, who would soon find someone else. Nor the other members of the company, or the people she had met at

Piers's parties. She would miss only Kay, but she knew that whatever happened, their friendship would endure, like a gold thread through a piece of cloth.

She would regret little else. Miranda Marshall would vanish, but some time, somewhere, another actress would take her place. She would dye her hair black again, or perhaps auburn – the thought made her smile. She would become someone else. After all, she had played a great many parts in her twenty-eight years. The dutiful daughter, the chatelaine of the country estate, the refugee, the starlet. She had always acted, and always would. She would not miss fame: she had found it to be a false friend, always demanding more of her, needing a bigger piece of her. Something in her longed for yet loathed the public gaze. The applause at the end of a performance barely outweighed the agonies of doubt she endured before she went on stage. The girl whose face smiled out from the newspaper photographs was no more her true self than the daughter of the glovemaker she had pretended to be on her first meeting with Olivier.

Only with Olivier had she been her true self. She knew, in her heart, that she would never love anyone else. Men had used her and she had used them, and sometimes she regretted that. She had hurt Friedrich, and yet in the end he had tried to save her. Now, she thought of him with tenderness. Only with Olivier had she been honest, only to him had she laid bare the secrets of her heart. She had been able to do that because, of all her lovers, he had not tried to possess her. He had loved her enough to let her fly free.

It was cold. She rose and walked down the ridge of pebbles to the shore. She had kicked off her high-heeled shoes and peeled off her stockings; the sea, breathtakingly cold, licked her feet. It wouldn't be so bad, starting again from scratch. After all, she was used to it.

She found herself remembering her journey from Sommerfeld. She hoped to God she would never have to undertake such a journey again – she hoped that no one in the whole world would. She had survived, and sometimes that shamed her. She had done whatever she must to save herself. In some ways, she thought, she took after her father. If something didn't work out, then she went on to the next thing. Yet there were some things, she had discovered, that remained with you for a lifetime, that she had never spoken about, not even to Kay. Standing on the beach, she recalled her stillborn baby, whose tiny, perfect body she had cradled in her arms. She smiled, but there were tears in her eyes. Then she picked up her shoes and stockings and walked back to the house.

She returned to the flat on Monday morning. She had had her bath and was putting her hair in rollers when the post fell through the letter box. She sorted through it as she went back into the bedroom. Bills, fan letters and a small package. There were French stamps on the package. She found her scissors, cut the string, peeled back the brown paper. There was no letter to accompany whatever it was that was wrapped up so tightly in tissue paper. More string to cut, layers and layers of tissue to unfold. Whoever had sent her this present had wanted it to arrive in one piece.

As she reached the final layers of tissue paper, recognizing the shape of what was enclosed inside it, her heart began to pound. Sweat slicked her hands as she cut the last length of string and the gift revealed itself. She sat down and pressed a shaking hand to her mouth.

In her other hand lay a small, ceramic bluebird, the twin of the one that she kept on her bedside table, the twin of the one Olivier had given her all those years ago.

It was proving infuriatingly impossible to talk to Kay. She had been out – or she had not answered the phone – or he had been too busy. His colleagues had gone down with the flu, leaving Tom to hold the fort alone. For the last week, he had not left the office before nine o'clock in the evening, and he had had to work through the weekend as well.

Nipping out for some fresh air and to post some letters in the late afternoon, Tom noticed the headlines on the news-vendors' placards. *Actress Feared Drowned*. As he passed the stand, he glanced absently at the heap of papers.

And recognized the face that stared out at him from the front page. It was the sort of face that, once seen, you never forgot. He was captured for a moment by her remarkable, unearthly beauty, her fragile smile and haunted eyes. Fumbling in his pocket for change, he bought a newspaper and read it as he walked back to the office.

Then he sent the typist home, put on his coat, locked up the office and walked fast to the railway station.

'I tried to phone you,' Kay said, as she opened the door to him. And then, 'Oh Tom,' she flung her arms round him, 'I'm so glad you're here!'

'I came as soon as I saw the paper. Kay, I'm so sorry. I know what this must mean to you.'

He followed her up the stairs to the flat. Jamie was in his playpen, playing with his Dinky cars. He shouted out Tom's name when they came into the room, and jumped up and down, gripping the bars of the playpen.

Tom picked him up. 'I tried to phone a few times, Kay, but you weren't in.'

'I was busy,' she said. Then she gave an exasperated sigh. 'No, that's not true. I didn't answer the phone because I was afraid it might be you. But there's no one else I can talk to about Miranda, so it had to be you, Tom, whatever I think about Edie.'

Jamie delved into Tom's jacket pocket and took out his fountain pen. Rescuing it, Tom said, 'Edie?'

'I think it's a real mistake, Tom.' Kay was pacing back and forth; she sounded angry. 'You'll only make yourself miserable again. I suppose you're going to tell me that it's no business of mine, but that simply isn't true!'

He said calmly, 'I haven't seen or heard from Edie for over six years. I met the solicitor who was handling Miles Culbone's estate at a Law Society dinner. He told me that Culbone had left the house to Edie. I'm pleased for her, because she always loved it. That's all, Kay.'

'Oh.' She sat down on the sofa. Suddenly, she was smiling. 'Oh, Tom. Really?'

'Really.' He sat down beside her. 'Now tell me about Miranda.'

Most of what she knew had been in the newspaper article he had read. There had been a party at Piers Hennessy's house, Foxhall, on Saturday night. In the morning, the occupants of the house had discovered that Miranda was missing. At first it had been assumed that she had gone out for a walk, but then the housekeeper had pointed out that her coat was still hanging in the porch. It had been the housekeeper who had found first Miranda's shoes, and then her clothes, neatly folded and weighted down with a stone, on the beach. The alarm had been raised, the coastguard and police had been alerted. Piers Hennessy had confirmed to the police that Miranda liked to swim in the sea. Though the coastline had been searched, no sign of her had been found.

Tom noticed, as Kay spoke, that she seemed not grief-stricken, but preoccupied, or perhaps puzzled. When she had finished, he said, 'Why don't you make some coffee while I put this little chap to bed? Then we can talk properly.'

Jamie fell asleep during Tom's second reading of *The Three Billy Goats Gruff*. Tom tucked him in and went downstairs.

He said, 'Tell me.'

Kay poured out the coffee. 'I first heard the news on the wireless this morning, when I was getting ready for work. I was so upset – you can imagine. At the office, everyone was talking about it. None of my colleagues know that I know Miranda. I was her secret, if you like – and I held some of *her* secrets. Anyway, they were talking about what might have happened. Someone suggested Miranda and Piers might have quarrelled and Piers might have lost his temper and drowned her, but most people thought that was crazy. So it came down to an accident or suicide. I know Miranda, Tom. She's not a fool, and I don't believe she'd decide to go bathing naked on a freezing April night. When you think of how much she's survived, why would she risk her life doing that? Which leaves suicide.'

'Have you any reason to think she was suicidal?'

Kay pursed her lips, shaking her head slowly. 'I'm sure she has some terrible memories. I'm sure there are lots of things she's never told me. And I'm equally sure that she's never recovered from losing Olivier. You don't *recover* from something like that – if you're lucky, you find something else that makes life worth living, but you don't *forget*.' She looked at him. 'I was lucky. I had Jamie. And – other things.'

He found himself taking her hand as naturally as if they had been lovers for years. 'Other things?' he repeated.

'Other people.' He felt the pressure of her fingers. 'You, for instance, Tom.'

'Kay—'

'Not yet. Don't say anything yet. I need to think about Miranda. I need to work it out.'

But he drew her to him, his arm round her, and she rested her head against his shoulder, closing her eyes for a moment, and he found himself remembering their voyage across the Channel in the night ferry, all those years ago, the warmth and weight of her, and how, as she had slept, he had put up a hand and touched her hair, felt beneath his fingertips its fineness and softness.

She said, 'I don't think Miranda was suicidal. She's always had such a capacity for life. She's never lost it. It was always the best thing about her.'

'You think she's faked it, don't you, Kay?'

'I've tried to imagine what happened that night. Listen, Tom. You're distraught. You wander out on to the beach in the middle of the night and you decide to end it all. Would you neatly fold your clothes and put a stone on them so that they didn't blow away, if you didn't mean to come back? Would you even bother to get undressed? Would you really, Tom? If you meant to drown yourself, wouldn't you just hurl yourself into the waves?'

'Rather dramatic, don't you think, the midnight disappearance, the pile of clothes on the beach?'

'Miranda always was dramatic. It's as if she *wanted* people to think that she was dead. I keep thinking she'll just turn up. That the doorbell will ring, and there she'll be, laughing about

535

all the fuss, telling me some extraordinary story about what happened to her.'

'But,' he said, 'why now? Why now, when she seemed to have everything going for her?'

'I don't know.' A silence, then Kay said slowly, 'When I knew her in Paris, Miranda had this doll. It had three faces – Red Riding Hood's, the grandmother, and the wolf. Nothing's ever as it appears to be with Miranda, Tom. Even back then, she had secrets. She had to, it was how she survived. Her father was a tyrant. He could be perfectly charming when he wanted to be, but he never forgave anyone who crossed him. That was why he sacked me, because he found out I'd lied to him. Poor Miranda, she's had so many changes in her life. Different lives, you could say. Different lives, different names, different countries. And such huge changes of fortune. Perhaps you get into the habit of it. Perhaps, if you've lived like that, you never really settle anywhere. Or perhaps something happened – I've no idea what – that made her think she couldn't stay here any longer, and so she ran away.'

'Where would she have gone?'

'Paris,' she said. 'It's the closest she had to a home.' She straightened. 'I want to go and look for her, Tom. She might need me.'

'I'll come with you.'

'Dearest Tom, that's very sweet, but it may be a complete wild-goose chase. Miranda could have gone anywhere. Even if she is in Paris, I don't know if I'll be able to find her. I like to think she'll be sitting in one of the cafés we used to go to, drinking coffee, but it doesn't seem very likely, does it? I'm going to Paris on a whim. I'll probably lose my job because of a whim. There's no reason for you to disrupt your life as well.'

'Isn't there?' Gently, he brushed his fingertips from her cheek-bone to her chin. 'I think there is. Two heads are better than one. We can split up, if you like, then we'll cover more ground. I'll carry your suitcase for you. I'll cheer you up if we can't find her. I'll buy you a kir *royale* in Les Deux Magots – it'll blow most of the currency we're allowed to take out of the country, but what the hell. I'll even buy you a ticket home if you lose your money this time. And there's another reason. I love you, Kay. I've loved you for years. I don't want to let you out of my sight. I love you.'

She whispered, 'As a friend?'

'Yes, as a friend. But not only as a friend. I love you in every possible way. I love you and I want you and actually I'd like to spend the rest of my life with you.'

A moment in which they seemed poised on the edge of a chasm. Such an extraordinary turn of events. And then they kissed, and she said, 'Oh, Tom,' and they kissed again.

He didn't stay the night. They both agreed that they should take it slowly – for Jamie's sake, for one thing. Though, goodness knows, she pointed out to him, no one could accuse them of being fast: they had known each other for more than ten years.

Love transformed. Hope had returned; she had a future again. Every so often, the following morning, as she walked with Jamie to Liz's house and sat in her office at work, she glimpsed it flicker, bright and redeeming. They'd live in Cambridge, perhaps, in Tom's house on the edge of the city, near the river. She'd show Jamie the canal boats and the rowing boats and the cows on the common. Perhaps one day they'd hire a boat and sail downriver to Ely. Perhaps one day they'd have a sister for Jamie.

And then, leaving the office at the end of the day, the

bombshell. The headline was chalked on the newsvendors' placards. *Miranda*, it screamed. *The Truth.*

Perhaps something happened, she had said to Tom. *I've no idea what. Perhaps something happened that made Miranda think she couldn't stay here any more.*

Now she understood. *An exclusive by our reporter, Jake Brennan.* Kay read it standing on a crowded bus, heading home to Tufnell Park. Jake Brennan had first met Miranda three years ago, in Germany. There was a photograph of Miranda, thin-faced and hollow-eyed, sitting in an army truck. *Even then, this woman of many disguises did not tell me, her rescuer, her true identity. At the time I knew her, she had assumed the name of Agnès Leblanc.*

Brennan went on to write that, during the war, Miranda had been married to a high-ranking German officer, Friedrich von Kahlberg. From some archive, a picture of Sommerfeld had been unearthed. Atrocities were described that had taken place not far from the region of East Prussia in which Miranda had lived. The slaughter of civilians in German-occupied Poland, the concentration camp at Stutthof, by the Baltic, where tens of thousands of Poles and Jews had been murdered. By the third paragraph of Jake Brennan's article, Friedrich had mutated into a 'powerful Nazi official'.

All the layers of Miranda's complex identity were being peeled away, leaving the core of her for public display. By tomorrow, Kay thought, admiration and adulation would have turned to hatred. Miranda, who had once been London's darling, would become an abomination. It was possible, Jake Brennan suggested in his closing paragraph, that Miranda had not drowned, but had left England to begin a new life elsewhere. The British people, who had taken her into their hearts, had been duped.

Quickly, she and Tom made their arrangements. Tom's colleagues had recovered from flu, so he was able to take a few days off work. Aunt Dot agreed to look after Jamie for a long weekend. Nigel Peagram refused to allow Kay any extra time off, but then Nigel Peagram could go hang.

On the Channel crossing, they reminisced.

'I thought,' she said, 'the first time I met you, in Berlin, that you were such a dreadful know-all.'

'Me, a know-all?' Tom smiled. 'I expect I was. I thought you were wonderful. The first time I saw you, in the café in Berlin, you were wearing a green jersey and you were reading a book.'

'*Dusty Answer*,' she said. 'We argued about it.'

'Did we? I don't remember.'

'We did. And we argued on the train as well. About pacifism.'

'I remember that,' he said. 'We won't argue any more, will we?'

'Never.'

It was a fine day, and they were sitting on deck, on a slatted wooden bench. He said, 'Do you still want to go to the Aegean Sea?'

'Of course. Why?'

'That was what you told me, on the night ferry. That you'd like to sail round the Greek islands. I thought we could go in the summer, you and me and Jamie. For a month. We could hire a boat.'

She thought of it – a boat, a turquoise sea, a pale pink sandy cove. 'I'd like that very much,' she said.

And they sat, arm in arm, waiting for the coast of France to emerge from the mist.

In Paris, it was springtime.

They booked into a hotel on the Left Bank, decorously, in

separate rooms. Next morning, after a breakfast of rolls and coffee, they went first to the Denisovs' old house in the Eighth Arrondissement. Walking from the Métro station, the sun shone, and Kay found herself peeling off her mackintosh and then rolling up the sleeves of her cardigan. They walked hand in hand, as lovers do in Paris, stopping every now and then to look at some glorious sight and to kiss. Over the walls of the gardens, pink and white blossom tumbled. A ginger cat sat on a doorstep, sleeping in the warmth.

The windows of the Denisovs' old house were shuttered, and when Kay knocked on the door, there was no reply. When she looked up at the house, she was transported back over the years. She had been eighteen years old, and it had been her first trip abroad. She remembered the excitement she had felt, when she had looked out of her bedroom window, and how she had longed to explore the city. In one day, in her journey from London to Paris on the Golden Arrow, she had grown up, had left her childhood behind, had fallen in love with adventure and travel. She had learned the taste, the smell, the colour and texture of another country, and had played her part in lives utterly different to her own. Her year and a half with Miranda had moulded her. Without it, she would not have become the person she was. Something had entered her soul that day she had stood with Miranda on the deck of the ferry, watching the coast of France emerge from the haze. It was still there, bright and optimistic, waiting to be set free, like a bird.

'Madame Baranova used to serve us tea with jam in it,' Kay told Tom. 'That was how the Russian émigrés used to drink their tea. Miranda's father always had his tea with milk and sugar. He preferred to think of himself as European.'

They were in a café in the Rue Daru, drinking coffee. They had walked past the Cathedral of St Alexander Nevsky, with its mosaic saint and golden onion domes. Strangers now lived in Alexandra Baranova's old apartment with the tall windows and shabby crimson curtains. Kay wondered where the photographs had gone: the little boys in sailor suits and the wistful girls in white dresses with high, pie-crust collars.

'Do you realize,' he said, 'that this is only our second whole day together? Our first was the day we left Germany, in nineteen thirty-seven. Since then, we've only had parts of days.'

She threaded her fingers through his. 'We should celebrate.'

'We will do.'

His thumb stroked her palm; she felt herself blush like a girl, and she looked away, out of the window. She found herself willing Miranda to walk past. Yet she realized after a few moments that it was the old Miranda she was imagining, the girl Miranda had once been, with her glossy fall of black hair and the laughter in her eyes. And as the day passed, as they walked by the *bouquinistes'* stalls on the Seine, or crossed the Pont Neuf to the Left Bank, or, in the afternoon, explored the Marais, where Olivier had once lived among the high walls and cobbled streets and enclosed courtyards, she found the mood of the city seeping into her, changing her. Less often now did she scan the faces in the crowds. The photograph of Miranda, which she had brought with her to show to shopkeepers and café *patrons*, remained in her handbag.

He came to her room that night. No nonsense any more about taking it slowly. They wanted each other, needed each other. Buttons were torn from cloth, zips jammed and then were yanked open. Their lovemaking was no fragile thing of poetry, but hurried, desperate, desiring, almost painful in its intensity. Afterwards, lying back on the pillows, catching her breath, she glimpsed a piece of the moon between the shutters. She thought of Jamie, at Aunt Dot's house, and of Miranda, wherever she was. And then Tom began to kiss her again, and she took him in her arms, welcoming him, enfolding him, taking him inside her body, loving him.

In the morning when she woke, she lay still – was there anything more wonderful than waking in the morning beside your lover? She thought of the Parc Monceau, remembered the day they had met Olivier there, and how he had risen from a bench and walked towards them. Yet she did not wake Tom with a kiss, did not rise and walk to the park. Let Miranda decide, she thought. Let her choose. If Miranda wished to, then she would reveal herself eventually. A letter would arrive one day, speaking of great adventures and extraordinary happenings. Or she would glimpse a familiar face on an escalator or in a crowded shop, and they would look at each other, and smile. And perhaps, old friends, they would stop to speak.

Inside the house, you could still see signs of its occupation during the war. Walking from room to room, Edie found a khaki water bottle, hanging on a peg, and graffiti scribbled beside a window, and, in the bathroom cabinet, a jar of American shaving soap. During the last six months of his life, Miles Culbone had been confined to his bedroom, cared for by a succession of nurses. The last time Edie's mother had seen him, he had been fading rapidly, blind, his pain controlled by morphine. The first thing Edie had done, arriving at the house that morning, had been to strip the bed and pour the remaining medicines down the lavatory. Then she had flung open the windows and let the sun into the house.

It still seemed extraordinary to her that Uncle Miles had willed Cold Christmas to her. He had never shown her any affection, never seemed to favour her over her sisters. Walking into a sunlit room at the back of the house, she found herself looking it over with a new eye, imagining what she might do to it, the exact shade of paint to use on the walls, the furnishing fabrics that would bring out the beauty of the room.

The oriel window looked out over the garden. Edie could see to the lawn, where Charles was with the children. He had brought a small bat and ball and was playing French cricket with five-year-old Henry. Rosalind, who would be nine at her next birthday, was exploring the garden. Every now and then she'd run to Charles to show him something – a leaf or a flower, perhaps. Edie smiled and laid the flat of her hand on her belly. She was four months pregnant – over the worst of it, she said to herself. She had had to coax Charles rather to try for another baby, because she was always so ill. It would be easier this time, she had pointed out to him, because he would be here to look after her, and besides, how lovely it would be to have a peacetime baby.

She went downstairs to the library. Uncle Miles's desk was still heaped with books and papers. She picked up a stack of papers and blew off the dust. Idly, her gaze wandered over them. Their content was dull, a catalogue of the books in Cold Christmas's library.

Then, turning a page, her heart missed a beat. She recognized Tom's writing; she had seen it often enough in the letters he had written to her when they had first dated and on the notes he had sent her during their affair. And she had a sharp, sudden memory of the year of 1941, and its strange mixture of terror, guilt and elation.

Would this be enough for her? Would Cold Christmas and a baby every four or five years for as long as she was able compensate for a marriage which, though not without love, was devoid of passion?

Yes. Edie rolled up the papers and stuffed them into the wastepaper basket. It *must* be enough. She had so much, a rich life full of love and interest, and now this house, as well as a lasting and powerful awareness of the great good fortune that all her family – mother, sisters, brothers-in-law, nieces – had survived the war. No one had everything. It would have been wrong of her to wish for everything.

Leaving the library, she went outside. As she walked through the herb garden, Charles came to meet her.

'What do you think?'

She smiled at him. 'I'm afraid I still adore it.'

'It'll be a lot of work – and expense.' He looked worried. 'Until I manage to sell Taynings, we'll have two crumbling old houses to look after.'

She said mischievously, 'But tell me honestly, Charles, if you were forced to choose between Cold Christmas and Taynings . . .'

'No contest.' He looked back at the house. 'It's a fascinating old place, Edie.'

'And it wouldn't be just for ourselves. I'd think of it as belonging to the whole family. Nicky and Laura could come here with the girls and just think how Mummy would enjoy sorting out the garden.'

He nodded. 'If you're sure . . .'

'Absolutely sure.'

'Then we'll keep it.'

She felt a surge of happiness. 'Dear Charles.' She flung her arms round him and kissed him and his expression was a mixture of surprise and pleasure.

After Miranda had left her clothes on the beach and tiptoed back into the house, she had taken an old pair of slacks and a jersey from the laundry room – guests were always leaving odds and ends at Foxhall – along with a pair of wellington boots from the porch. Her passport, a headscarf and the French and English money she always put aside for emergencies were in her handbag. She took the money, the headscarf and the passport, but left the handbag and purse in the house. Then she walked the route she had earlier worked out on a map, that took her to a branch-line station. It was a longish walk, and by the time she arrived at the station the sun was up. A train took her to Ipswich. From there she caught a train to Colchester and then another to London. She had crossed the Channel wearing shabby corduroy trousers, a khaki-coloured jersey with leather patches on the elbows, and wellingtons. She hid her hair beneath the headscarf. She hunched her shoulders, took the spring out of her step, made herself look gawky and unattractive. No one looked twice at her.

In Paris, she booked into a cheap rooming house. The next day, rising early, she bought herself a few things from the shops – a dress, a handbag, sandals, stockings. After she had changed into her new clothes, she walked to the Parc Monceau.

Sometimes, in the months after the war, she had almost felt his presence there, had felt as if the strength of her longing might conjure him out of the ether. She remembered the promise they had made to each other, that if they were ever parted she would wait for him in the park, where they had first met. She remembered how, after the war was over, she had gone there each day even after she had known that there was no hope, even after she

545

had known that he was dead and that she had lost him for ever, because she had felt close to him there.

And then, only a week ago, hope had returned. She had put the two bluebirds, her own and the one from the mysterious package, side by side on the table. They matched: the blues and golds were the same blues and golds. When she closed her eyes, she saw them, spinning in circles in Olivier's flat in the Marais.

Was it possible . . . ? Hope transformed her, but it also frightened her. She did not think she could bear to lose it again. Feverishly, she went through what little she knew of the circumstances of Olivier's death. The prison camp, the forced march, away from the approaching Red Army. *I saw the guard shoot him,* Olivier's fellow prisoner had written. *I was sorry that he died; Olivier was a good sort.* There were gaps in that, she thought, there were possibilities. There was space for a miracle.

In the park, the lilacs were in bloom. She walked to the bench, sat down, waited. Smartly dressed women walked ridiculous little dogs, nursemaids pushed prams. The sun shone.

And then, looking up, she saw him, walking towards her. Olivier. His chestnut-brown hair was greying a little at the temples, his smile flowered as he caught sight of her.

Rising, weeping, she pressed her hands against her mouth, waiting for him.

They liked to walk in the park in the early mornings. Walking, they told each other their stories over and over again, filling in the missing parts of their lives, making up for the years of separation.

Olivier had been left for dead at the side of the road. He had lain motionless, his eyes closed, after the guard had shot him, praying that he would not be thought worth the expenditure of another bullet. Bleeding from the wound in his chest, he had crawled to the shelter of a barn. That evening, a woman had come to the barn to milk the cows, and had found him there. She had patched up his wound and fed him soup. Two days later, the American army had arrived, and had taken him to a military hospital.

And then, for a long time, he had been very ill. The wound had become infected and he had been suffering from tuberculosis, which he had contracted in the prison camp. For weeks, his life had hung by a thread. By the time the fever had abated, his brother, Marc, had arrived at the hospital. As soon as he was judged to be no longer infectious, Marc had taken him home with him to Brazil. Olivier had been too ill to argue, and besides, he was weary of Europe.

It had been the sun that had healed him, he told her. He had sat in the sun in a garden in Brazil, and he had thought. At first his thoughts had been bitter. The waste of his life, incarcerated in a foreign country. The wreckage of his health, the death of everything that had been important to him – youth, career, art. He had even hated her. She had forgotten him. She had betrayed him. He could not love her because she had been married to the enemy, one of his captors. But as the months passed and his health returned, he had begun to think differently. You did the best you could with the choices you were given. You took your chances, if you were lucky enough to find them. It was perfectly possible, he thought, that he, a soldier, had killed, and she, in her castle, had not. Who was to say which of them was the more guilty?

He had remained in Brazil for a year and a half. He had returned to France in the early months of 1947, shortly after Miranda herself had left for England. Like her, he had gone to the park every day. Though he had made inquiries, he had been able to find out little of her fate. Sommerfeld had been burned to the ground; it was all too likely, it seemed to him, that she had died inside it.

He had begun to pick up the threads of his old life. He had some money – dear old Marc had made himself a rich man in Brazil, and rather fancied the idea of investing in a French film company. He rented an office, found some of the old crew – Agnès, who had married and had had twins, and was bored to death in a Parisian suburb, and Benoît, who had spent the war in Vichy France, fighting with the Maquis after 1942. He read some scripts, an idea began to form, small and unclear as yet, but it had that itch that all good ideas had.

Then he had seen her photograph in *Paris Match*. Miranda, as lovely as she had always been, living in England, and making her name as an actress. A moment of jealousy as he read about her lover – but it passed, and then he thought of sending her the bluebird. He kissed it before he wrapped it in tissue paper. He thought of it winging its way to her, a message of love and hope.

This, then, was what she would one day write to Kay: that they had just missed each other so many times. That she had travelled to England only weeks before Olivier had returned from Brazil. That he had gone to the park every day, as she had done. That he, too, had despaired. That together they could endure anything. That one day, with him to give her strength, she would join together all the pieces of herself into a whole and step out of the shadows. Then the world could judge her.

This, then, she would tell Kay. The rest she would keep in her heart. The joy of their reunion, the bliss of their rediscovery of each other. These things could not, she knew, be put into words.

JUDITH LENNOX

Before the Storm

A wild autumn day in 1909: Richard Finborough catches sight of twenty-year-old Isabel Zeale at the harbour at Lynmouth and is captivated by her beauty. Scarred by her past, Isabel has no intention of letting anyone get close. But Richard pursues her, and his persistence and ardour win her heart.

The couple marry and have three children, Philip, Theo and Sara. A fourth is added when Ruby, the daughter of Richard's old friend, comes to stay with them after her father mysteriously disappears. The Finboroughs' lives seem enviably perfect.

Then, in the 1930s, the reappearance of an old acquaintance turns Isabel's world upside down, while Ruby uncovers a series of dark truths about her father that lead her to a terrible conclusion. As conflicts simmer in Europe, it seems that love, war and secrets are set to tear the family apart . . .

Judith's Lennox's novels have been highly acclaimed:

'A beautifully turned, compassionate novel. Judith Lennox's writing is so keenly honest it could sever heartstrings' *Daily Mail*

'Great, old-fashioned storytelling in the best sense' *Daily Express*

978 0 7553 3134 5

headline
review

JUDITH LENNOX

A Step In the Dark

Simla, India, 1914.

Married at eighteen to the dashing Jack, beautiful Elizabeth Ravenhart is devastated when her marriage is cut tragically short.

Left penniless, Bess is persuaded by her domineering mother-in-law Cora to return to England, leaving her infant son Frazer behind until she can afford to send for him. But Cora has no intention of parting with the child, and Bess's desperate attempts to track him down come to a shattering conclusion.

Twenty years later, a knock on Bess's Edinburgh door sets in motion a chain of events that no one could have foreseen. For Frazer has come to claim his family – and his birthright, the majestic Ravenhart House. None of their lives will ever be the same again . . .

A breathtaking journey from colonial India through wartime London to the remote wilds of Scotland, Judith Lennox's stunning new novel is an unforgettable story of love and loss, greed and desire, and the secrets that can bind a family – or ultimately destroy one . . .

Judith Lennox's novels have been highly acclaimed:

'A fast-moving, complex story' *The Times*

978 0 7553 3132 1

headline
review

ANDREA LEVY

Small Island

It is 1948, and England is recovering from a war. But at 21 Nevern Street, London, the conflict has only just begun.

Queenie Bligh's neighbours do not approve when she agrees to take in Jamaican lodgers, but with her husband, Bernard, not back from the war, what else can she do?

Gilbert Joseph was one of the several thousand Jamaican men who joined the RAF to fight against Hitler. Returning to England as a civilian he finds himself treated very differently. Gilbert's wife Hortense, too, had longed to leave Jamaica and start a better life in England. But when she joins him she is shocked to find London shabby, decrepit, and far from the city of her dreams. Even Gilbert is not the man she thought he was.

Small Island explores a point in England's past when the country began to change. In this delicately wrought and profoundly moving novel, Andrea Levy handles the weighty themes of empire, prejudice, war and love, with a superb lightness of touch and generosity of spirit.

'Wonderful . . . seamless . . . a magnificent achievement' Linda Grant

'A great read . . . honest, skilful, thoughtful and important' *Guardian*

'A cracking good read' Margaret Forster

'Never less than finely written, delicately and often comically observed, and impressively rich in detail and little nuggets of stories' *Evening Standard*

'Is as full of warmth and jokes and humanity as you could wish' *Time Out*

'Gives us a new urgent take on our past' *Vogue*

978 0 7553 0750 0

headline
review

Now you can buy any of these other bestselling
books from your bookshop
or *direct from the publisher.*

FREE P&P AND UK DELIVERY
(Overseas and Ireland £3.50 per book)

Before the Storm	Judith Lennox	£6.99
A Step In The Dark	Judith Lennox	£6.99
Small Island	Andrea Levy	£7.99
The Return	Victoria Hislop	£7.99
Rumour Has It	Jill Mansell	£7.99
Someone Special	Sheila O'Flanagan	£6.99
The Message	Julie Highmore	£6.99
All You Need Is Love	Carole Matthews	£6.99
Dance With Wings	Amelia Carr	£7.99
Backpack	Emily Barr	£7.99
The Saffron Gate	Linda Holeman	£6.99
Good Things I Wish You	Manette Ansay	£7.99
The Vanishing Act of Esme Lennox	Maggie O'Farrell	£7.99

TO ORDER SIMPLY CALL THIS NUMBER

01235 400 414

or visit our website: www.headline.co.uk

Prices and availability subject to change without notice.